WAKEFIELD

ALSO BY ANDREI CODRESCU

it was today: new poems (2003)

Casanova in Bohemia (2002)

Messiah (1999)

A Bar in Brooklyn (1999)

Hail, Babylon! In Search of the American City at the End of the Millennium (1997)

Valley of Christmas (CD: 1997)

Alien Candor: Selected Poems (1970–1995) (1996)

The Dog with the Chip in His Neck: Essays from NPR and Elsewhere (1996)

The Blood Countess (1995)

Zombification: Essays from NPR (1994)

Road Scholar: Coast to Coast Late in the Century (1993)

The Muse Is Always Half-Dressed in New Orleans (1993)

The Hole in the Flag: An Exile's Story of Return and Revolution (1992)

The Disappearance of the Outside (1991)

Belligerence (1991)

Raised by the Puppets Only to Be Killed by Research (1989)

The Stiffest of the Corpse: An Exquisite Corpse Reader (1988)

At the Court of Yearning: The Poems of Lucian Blaga (1989)

Monsieur Teste in America (1987)

A Craving for Swan (1987)

Comrade Past and Mr. Present (1987)

In America's Shoes (1983)

The Life and Times of an Involuntary Genius (1975)

The History of the Growth of Heaven (1973)

License to Carry a Gun (1973)

Andrei Codrescu
WAKEFIELD

ALGONQUIN BOOKS
OF CHAPEL HILL
2004

Published by
Algonquin Books of Chapel Hill
Post Office Box 2225
Chapel Hill, North Carolina 27515-2225

a division of
Workman Publishing
708 Broadway
New York, New York 10003

Library of Congress Cataloging-in-Publication Data
Codrescu, Andrei, 1946–
    Wakefield / by Andrei Codrescu.—1st ed.
        p. cm.
    ISBN 1-56512-372-7
    1. Motivational speakers—Fiction.   2. Conduct of life—Fiction.
3. Architecture—Fiction.   4. Devil—Fiction.   I. Title.
PS3553.O3W34 2004
813'.54—dc22   2004041052

10 9 8 7 6 5 4 3 2 1
First Edition

Imagination, in the proper meaning of the term,
made no part of Wakefield's gifts.

—NATHANIEL HAWTHORNE, "Wakefield," 1835

WAKEFIELD

PROLOGUE

Late in the Twentieth Century

ONE DAY THE DEVIL shows up. "I've come to take you."

"I'm not ready," says Wakefield.

"Why not? You don't have any reason to live."

Wakefield is scandalized. "Are you crazy? What kind of a thing is that to say to a man in the prime of life?"

"You're a failure. Time to die." The Devil is bored. He has this argument what, six, seven times a day? Nobody welcomes death. They are ready for it, they need it, but when it comes right down to it, they won't go.

"What do you mean, a failure? I'm quite well respected."

"Awright," sighs Satanik, "I'll play the game. Why do you want to stay? Worried about the people you'd leave behind?"

"I have no interest in people," Wakefield pronounces haughtily, drawing himself up and looking down on the thinning fur between the horns of the Unholy One, who's actually fairly short. "I just want to be left alone." He tries to slam the door in the Devil's face, but the Devil's got a hoof in it.

"Okay, so you're a loner. No loved ones, no next of kin, no pets. Nothing to live for but a few bad habits."

"That's not what I said. I've got lots of friends." Wakefield sounds doubtful. "My daughter Margot would probably be very upset. . . ."

The Devil sees an easy shot and takes it. "Don't kid yourself, buddy. You haven't seen your daughter in years, we both know that. Tell the truth, what's the real reason you want to stick around?" The bit about the daughter is unfair. He talks to Margot on the phone every two weeks. He's not a model father, but he's no deadbeat.

"Well, actually, there's some reading I'd like to do," Wakefield improvises, gesturing to the crammed bookshelves that line the walls of his garret.

That's a real thigh-slapper. "You can read when you're disembodied, nothing to stop you, but I haven't got all day. You've read enough already to know how it works."

Wakefield does know how it works, in books. You keep the conversation going. Keep the Devil talking until you find a way out.

"It's like this. I honestly wasn't expecting to see you. Couldn't you give me another chance?" Wakefield puts on his most sincere expression. "I've had this feeling for a while, you know, like I went wrong somewhere, like maybe I should have lived a different life."

"*O sole mio!* I hate the bookish ones. It ain't like reincarnation, friend. I don't know anyone who thinks they've lived the right life, they all think it's been some kind of dream. I have only one question: do you believe in me?"

This is important to the Diablo. He's obligated by an ancient professional code to give believers another chance. Unbelievers he just scoops up and closes the book. If you don't like it, contest it in court. The afterlife is one long hearing.

"Oh, I believe in you, don't get me wrong. I read somewhere that there is a black hole at the center of the universe, some kind of supermassive gravity not even light can escape from. That's you, right?"

"Sure, that's me. There are a lot of us, actually."

"So don't you have to give me another chance, if I believe?"

El Malefico rolls his eyes at the stars, where his dark-bearded masters sit around the fire eating the souls he's brought them.

"Don't tell me, you got that from a book, too."

"Yeah, well. What do you say? Can't we make some special arrangement? I'm not the most demanding of men, to quote Frank O'Hara."

The Devil's lower back is beginning to bother him, standing in a drafty doorway like this. "You think I could sit down for a minute, pal? I'm under no obligation, you understand, but we could, perhaps, discuss your request."

That's more like it, thinks Wakefield, ushering in his guest. "Maybe I could get you a drink? I know I could use one. What'll it be?"

"Scotch," grunts the Devil, easing himself into a plump leather armchair.

The cell phone in Wakefield's pocket has been vibrating at intervals throughout this unusual encounter. While he prepares the drinks, he listens to his messages. There's one from his lecture agent, urging him to take a gig for half his usual fee; his friend Ivan (his only friend), inviting him to a poker game; his broker, trying to sell him shares in a new IPO; and his ex-wife, Marianna, who wants to talk about their daughter. Wakefield pours his own drink extra deep.

The Devil, meanwhile, is checking out Wakefield's digs. The guy's got good taste for a schmo, he thinks, admiring the Murano chandelier, the faded kilims, the three fake netsuke in pornographic poses on the mantelpiece, next to a few family photos: a woman with bouffant, a man in Sunday suit, a boy with baseball bat. Bought at the flea market, like most families these days. He's got a soft spot for fakes. The Devil himself has a collection of family photos from the offices of middle-aged men he's collected at their desks. He had taken the men first; then, for his own pleasure, their family pictures. Invariably, these turned out to be fakes, props, simulacra of real families, which is what made them desirable in his world, where value is based entirely on the differential between the fake and the genuine. The bigger the lie, the greater the value. The phony photos left no doubt he'd scooped up the right souls.

"I think you'll enjoy this whiskey," says Wakefield, returning with their drinks. "It's a single malt, a gift from one of my fans." He takes a seat opposite the Dark One, who sips the scotch and nods his approval.

"I haven't been the best host, have I," Wakefield goes on, "just talking about myself, what I want, and so on. What about you? It can't be easy, wandering the earth, always on call—" Wakefield's phone vibrates again, and the buzz is audible in the quiet room.

"Turn that damned thing off, will you? Noise drives me crazy," the Devil growls, swallowing the rest of his whiskey in one gulp.

"You're the one with supernatural powers, you turn it off," blurts Wakefield, forgetting his manners.

"I'm sorry to disappoint you," the Devil says apologetically, "but I have no power over cell phones, computers, cable TV, satellite communications, or microwaves. No, it's true, really. Things used to be more simple, more fun. I enjoyed a frivolous and pleasant existence as a beloved, comic, quasifictional character. It was great—classic literature, opera, ballet . . ." He sighs deeply, then leans closer to Wakefield.

"Then one year I went from being revived at the Bolshoi to being deified by Khomeini and Falwell. Since then it's been a mess. A bunch of religious freaks spouting tacky rhetoric, demanding apocalypse-size work. I don't want to play World Ender for these lunatics. I was looking forward to a lighter quota, maybe some R & R in the arms of a kinkishly altered soprano. And now you're giving me shit?"

Wakefield is astonished by this outpouring. Who knew the Devil had such middle-age problems? Poor old Pan, weeping in his mossy cave as the blinding light of a neon cross invades his darkness and his joy. Wakefield, too, regrets the passing of the pagan era, and could almost hug the Old Goat, but he's got a deal to make.

"How would you like an opportunity to cut down your workload and postpone some of that heavy eschatological lifting? Give me a chance to find my true life. If I succeed—and you'll be the judge of that, of course—I get to go on living. If I fail . . . well, you do what you have to do. It would be a hell of a lot more relaxing than smiting and scourging on a massive scale."

The Devil is tempted. In his profession, gambling is the only way to pass eternity, which just doesn't pass and is subject to multiple interpretations and migraines.

"How long do you figure this business will take?" the Dark One asks, putting his hooves up on the low table.

"Oh, I don't know. . . ." Wakefield pretends to calculate. "A year, maybe. Two years, max."

The Devil is toying with his empty whiskey glass. Wakefield fetches the bottle from the kitchen and pours them another stiff one.

"It would have to involve some travel, you know. You can't just stay in this apartment and luxuriate. Nice place, by the way."

"No problem," Wakefield hastily agrees, "I travel a lot in any case." The sucker's going for it, he congratulates himself.

The Devil falls silent, savoring the second whiskey. He closes his tired yellow eyes, and for a moment Wakefield imagines he's asleep, until he grunts and his eyes flutter open.

"And you'd have to bring me something from every place you go."

"Bring you something? Like what, a souvenir, something valuable, some kind of sacrifice?" He's trying to be cooperative.

"Can't say, really. Something you think I'd like. Could be anything."

"Are you sure you don't want something more abstract? Isn't it customary to take my soul in this kind of exchange? That's how it works in *Faust, The Master and Margarita,* all the classic texts."

"Give me a break!" the Devil groans. "I'm drowning in souls. It's a buyer's market. Look out that window and see for yourself."

A line of young women stretches out of sight down the sidewalk. Wakefield knows what they're waiting for. A famous director is shooting a movie in his neighborhood, and the girls are there to audition. The director has already cast the role; the audition is just a way for the old guy to get some nookie. Wakefield sees the Devil's point.

"So you really don't want my soul?"

"You're assuming, dear sir, that you have one, but whether you do or you don't, I don't want it. I want a *thing,* pure thingness, something that proves you found this so-called true life. Beyond that, the vortex of terror and self-doubt my simple request has created in you is adequate compensation. We have a deal, Mr. Wakefield, if you agree to these terms. I'll give you one year. It's an outlandish opportunity, but now that my existence has been proved by the discovery of black holes, I can afford to be a little generous."

Wakefield considers the practical aspects of his journey. "What about all the people who depend on me? My ex-wife, our daughter, the credit card companies, the people listed in my cell phone?"

"They won't even notice that you're gone."

"So when would this spiritual scavenger hunt begin?" Wakefield asks, sounding more relaxed than he feels.

"You must listen for the sound of the starter pistol," says the Devil supermysteriously, holding up his empty glass, "but for now, you can pour me another drink."

PART ONE

OLD QUARTER

WAKEFIELD LIVES ALONE in the old quarter of an indulgent port city known for its vigorous nightlife. It is in fact nighttime now, a rainy night about ten o'clock, and Wakefield has just concluded his deal with the Devil. Energized by that encounter, he grabs an umbrella and, as is his habit, heads for the corner bar, his home away from home. He bumps into a mob of tourists obstructing the sidewalk. They are clustered around a caped guide, leader of a ghost tour. They look sad, wet, lost, and a little scared. Adhesive badges identify them as members of the group so that nonpaying customers can't attach themselves to the tour for free.

All the tour guides in the city have their own stories, and ghosts to go with them, and they are fiercely, even combatively, competitive. Rumbles can break out between the costumed guides, and often do: silk-caped vampires attack other silk-caped vampires, and tourists sometimes get hurt in the process. Ordinarily, Wakefield avoids these groups like the plague that they are. This guide seems to be pointing directly at him, but Wakefield knows that the gesture is meant for the building behind him, the city's first icehouse, now a hotel where the ghosts of Confederate soldiers make frequent appearances. Some of the tourists have rooms in the hotel and yelp with delight at the guide's revelations. Others stare at Wakefield as if he is a ghost. He evades the gawkers and quickly arrives at his destination.

Ivan Zamyatin, Russian émigré cabdriver and unknown American philosopher, is sitting at his usual post in the bar, at a window open to the street yet shielded from the rain. He can be found in this place most evenings after five; the bar is his living room, just as his taxicab is his office.

Wakefield closes his dripping umbrella and takes the stool next to Zamyatin's. "Have you ever read any Hawthorne?" Wakefield asks his friend by way of greeting.

"I know *The House of the Seven Gables,* and the story 'Young Goodman Brown,' about this poor young man who meets the Devil in the forest and there is a witches' sabbath and everyone in town is involved. . . ."

"No, not that one. There's this other story, about a guy who leaves his wife and home and everyone thinks he's dead but he shows up again after twenty years, no explanation, no questions asked."

Zamyatin scratches one of the luxuriant sideburns that descend from his bald pate.

"In Russia, if someone disappears, everyone knows what happened. KGB picks him up and ships him to Siberia, if they don't kill him on the spot."

Wakefield gives his friend a sideways look. "That's not the point. This guy was living in England, a democratic country, where they respect privacy and the rights of individuals. He wanted to split, and he did it, and then he came back. Period, end of story."

Ivan is not impressed by people who disappear voluntarily, having himself been disappeared by the State, first for six months in a mental institute. After that experience, he had worked for five years below the Arctic Circle, but he didn't regard that quasisolitary episode as a "disappearance." It was more like a gradual reentry into the world. In America, he had purposefully shed his taste for solitude.

"You know," he says, looking deeply into his vodka, "I smoke in restaurants, park my taxi by fire hydrants, talk to everyone I meet. I leave many clues, so people can say, 'Ivan was just here a minute ago, I gave him a parking ticket, I talked to him at the bar, he's alive, he's okay!' Not like Russia, where it's poof! Gone in a New York minute."

Wakefield is silenced for a few minutes by this undeniable wisdom, typical of Zamyatin.

"The Devil showed up today," he finally says, knowing he can trust Ivan with anything, no matter how absurd.

"What you talking about, the devil!" Ivan looks disgusted. "Don't be stupid. We Russians are sick of the devil, he did enough for us already. I come here to get away from devils. You a rich American, not too ugly, you have money to eat out, go to a show, anything you want. What you need the devil for, or God, or any of that stuff?"

Zamyatin has no time for devils. He's too busy leaving his mark on everything, filling space with smoke, noise, lewdness, strangers. If a witch tries to eat him, all the people he met (maybe just once, but marked real good) will come to his defense.

Wakefield is quite a busy man himself. He is a travel writer and a lecturer on almost any topic, including travel. He often lectures in places he's already written about, giving the natives a quaint "outsider" perspective on their familiar world. Maintaining a trademark naïveté, he will discourse on anything: life, money, art, or architecture.

His subjects are not at all academic to Wakefield. He has lived what he considers an interesting life, and his observations are based on experience. He feels that his insights make people better human beings somehow and that he's contributing to the common good, and his casual air of knowing whereof he speaks gives him authority, so people trust that under the skin of the studious traveler there lies a beating heart. He's even developed a reputation as a "motivational speaker," though not a typical one, far from it. He's not the type who helps people find their inner selves through juggling, for instance. There is something about Wakefield's point of view that is quite dark, even dispiriting, making it hard sometimes for his audiences to finish the salad, to say nothing of the infamous "convention chicken."

The lecture business pays well: employers shell out a fortune to "motivate" workers, with the result that most employees are over-motivated and radiate so much positive energy that their companies are forced to grow to provide new (sometimes fictitious) outlets to contain this boundless enthusiasm. Some shrewd CEOs quietly seek out realists, even pessimists, to temper the aggressive good cheer. Wakefield's brand of motivation uniquely fits this latter need, and his schedule has become very busy.

"How is the lecture biz?" Zamyatin asks, dismissing the devil from the conversation.

"Terrific, actually. There is a shortage of nonpositive points of view," Wakefield explains, "so it's a seller's market. I've heard that corporations are even importing speakers from ex-communist countries where a nonpositive perspective is the norm, correct me if I'm wrong. Unfortunately, you imports don't speak English too good and that makes it difficult for you to convey your bleak beliefs to a large audience. You could make a mint, Ivan, if only you were more intelligible."

Ivan is used to Wakefield's provocations, but still he bristles. "What's wrong with my English? Anyway, no fat cats want to hear what I think: everything is shit. That's 'nonpositive,' okay, but you should also be happy anyway, and that's optimism." He turns away from Wakefield and shouts, "Beautiful bartenderess, two vodkas, if you wouldn't mind!"

"Optimism," Zamyatin continues, "was the official product of communism, but the people couldn't eat optimism, so they became pessimists. God forbid such a thing should happen in America! We produce enough to feed everyone and we need pessimists to make us feel okay about not being hungry. Here are the vodkas!"

Zamyatin's English is evidently good enough to charm the bartendress, who has poured two huge shots. She sets one on a napkin in front of Zamyatin and sloshes the other carelessly on Wakefield's shirt. As she walks away she wiggles her tiny blue-jeaned butt for the Russian and glares at Wakefield.

"It's hell in here," Wakefield remarks to her sympathetically, gesturing toward the crowd at the bar waving money to get her attention. He wants her to like him.

"Hell's okay if you can keep up with it," she shouts back, pouring with both hands.

Ivan resumes the conversation. "I met a man in my taxi today. He said he was a money manager, so I asked him where I should invest. He said buy a place in the country with chickens and goats. Fill the basement with soup cans and toilet paper. I said that's just like Russia, I don't live there anymore. In America everybody's making money on the stocks. This country believes in the future. He said it's all a scam. A bubble."

"It's easy to make money in the market," interjects a grungy person who's been studying the jukebox. "All you do is buy IPOs. I'm a musician and with the money I've made I've been buying instruments I only dreamed about back in Ohio. I have two e-trade accounts and I'm rolling in it."

"Playing any music?" the vixen on the next bar stool asks, joining the discussion. She has a nose ring, a tongue stud, floral tattoos up and down her bare arms, and a bursting sun on the back of her neck. "I'm making like six hundred bucks a day on e-trades, but all I do now is sit at the bar and drink."

"Me, too," admits the musician, sitting next to her, "but at least I've got the instruments. When I stop trading, I'll play some gigs." They begin comparing tattoos and their conversation becomes inaudible.

"No pessimists here," Wakefield whispers to Ivan, "they've got a future: drinking at the bar and planning which body part to pierce next."

"Meanwhile, they may fall in love, like me. I'm in love with the Beautiful Bartenderess!" Ivan bellows, kissing his fingers and throwing the kiss her way.

"People of the world, drop your schmaltziness." Wakefield suspects that "love" is dangerous. It makes people euphoric and delusional. Herman Melville wrote something to the effect that the universe was formed in fright by an invisible sphere of dread. Then Walt Whitman came along preaching brotherly love and New World optimism. They proposed these different visions of the universe, and ever since, he thinks with some annoyance, we have believed one or the other. He imagines Melville and Whitman bent over a crystal ball, watching at the moment of creation. "Evil," pronounces Melville. "Love," effuses Whitman.

Wakefield takes out his pen and scribbles this idea on a napkin. He'll work it into his speech on "money and poetry (with a detour in art)," a speech he hasn't written yet, though he'll deliver it in less than thirty hours. Ideas always come to him randomly, from books, items in the newspaper, conversations overheard. "I belong to the Ted Berrigan school of 'I can't wait to hear what I'm going to say next,'" he tells the people who hire him to lecture. Ted Berrigan was a New York poet and a genius talker who lived by a maxim attributed to another poet, Tristan Tzara: "All thinking is formed in the mouth."

Zamyatin, meanwhile, is absorbed in watching two attractive women on the sidewalk studying a map. The street is atmospherically lit by the old-fashioned gaslights the city has recently installed in the historic district.

"Can I help you?" he calls to them. "I'm a taximetrist!"

The women lay their map on the windowsill in front of Ivan. The rain has stopped.

"We want to know exactly where we are," one of them says. "I think we may be lost."

You're tourists, thinks Wakefield, of course you're lost. It's your destiny. You're part of a sad fin-de-siècle tribe that wanders the world looking for an excuse to return home as soon as possible. You are a pox, a plague, an obstructive cloud of locusts, a human wall of potbellies and dewlaps! Wakefield despises the actual creatures, though without them he wouldn't have a penny to his name; he'd be an office worker or an alcoholic slacker playing the market. The paradox doesn't bother him, though.

Zamyatin actually enjoys tourists. He likes everybody, except the police. "You are at the best bar in the whole city," Zamyatin tells them. "The martinis are incomparable, the people are very friendly, with the exception of this man here. I'm his only friend, but don't let that scare you. Come in and have a drink and when we are finished I will give you a tour in my taxi. Where are you from?"

They name a large, industrial city in the gray middle of the country. Wakefield knows it well: they make tires there, and plastic, and eat pork sausages and drink beer. The women accept Ivan's invitation. They come in and pull two stools over to the window.

"What are you writing?" one of them asks, picking up the napkin Wakefield's been scribbling on.

Ivan's beautiful bartendress brings the ladies martinis and gives the Russian a dirty look. Wakefield she ignores completely.

"Mel., Whit., looking into cryst. ball," the visitor reads from the napkin. "Who are they? Mel and Whit?"

"They are a couple of guys waiting for chicks!" chuckles Ivan.

The tourists laugh. They aren't lost anymore, they are at home, in Zamyatin's world. One of them folds the map and puts it back in her purse. "Our husbands are at the convention," she explains to the gentlemen.

"Ah, the convention! There are three conventions in town right now. Dentists, geographers, and cardiologists. Which one?" Ivan has been driving dentists, geographers, and heart doctors for three days.

"Dentists," sparkles one woman, showing her perfect teeth. "We are dentists' wives." They look pleased. Being dentists' wives on vacation while their husbands are stuck in workshops discussing the latest advances in the profession makes them happy. They are out at night in a lovely, historic city, the leaves are rustling in the darkly scented sweet-olive trees, a golden statue of Joan of Arc is glowing in the park across the street, and a not unattractive Russian guy is flattering them in a charming accent. Could anything be better?

Ivan shares their delight, but for Wakefield it's not that simple. He imagines row upon row of dazzling white teeth filling a large auditorium. He's lecturing ironically about human evolution and tooth development. In the beginning humanity had strong teeth and ate bark and roots. Then a chosen few grew fangs that pierced flesh. There followed a long, dark period of cavities, infections, death. Medieval dentistry. Wooden teeth. Then the light: anesthetics, fillings, scrimshaw, braces, esthetics. In the future, he tells his audience, teeth will have computer chips in them, analyzing diet, giving advice, e-mailing the dentist at the first sign of decay. He receives a standing ovation.

"What's love got to do, got to do with it," Ivan sings along with the jukebox in his funny accent, and then he answers: "Everything, my friends. I love the bartenderess! She will make me five babies!"

The Midwestern wives high-five him.

"And one of them will be a new Stalin," quips Wakefield.

"In American parlance, you are a bringdown, Comrade Wakefield. When you are in love you know the truth," the Russian says grandly, basking in the adoration of the tourist ladies.

"You mean he's a *downer,*" one of them giggles.

Though Wakefield mostly tells himself everything, he won't admit that lately he has been feeling less skeptical about life. He's been daydreaming about working less and reading more, about regular walks along the river, having the *New York Times* delivered, indulging in a sexual adventure now and then. No wonder the Devil walked right in.

The dentists' wives, warmed by the martinis, are glowing, casting a golden light that gleams off the barfly's nose ring, Zamyatin's bald head, the gin bottle in the bartendress's hand as it hovers over a martini glass. Wakefield struggles not to feel optimistic. Optimism could wreck his career.

The beautiful bartendress, whose name is actually Mitch, cashes out, her shift over. She drapes herself on Zamyatin's lap. On cue, the two tourists down their martinis and stand up to leave.

"What about the tour?" pleads the Russian.

"Maybe some other time." Their teeth gleam.

"Bye-bye, be sure to see everything," mocks Mitch, waving the end of a braided pigtail.

"Mitchka," Zamyatin intones, "don't be jealous. I will tell you a story about Russian men. For ten years before the end of communism, Russian men were becoming impotent. My friend at the Psychology Institute in Moscow studied the problem. He discovered that the future made them so nervous they couldn't perform. Only true love could make them men again."

"The future?" Mitch wiggles herself into a position of greater comfort. "I'm going to go back to school. I'm making good money now, but what about when I'm old? I'm thinking of studying nursing. Or Web design. Ivan, what did you do before you were a taxi driver?"

"I was an Arctic architect. Did you know that buildings in the tundra sink as much as five meters every year, so every year the second floor becomes the first floor? Eventually, the top floor becomes the first floor and everyone lives under the ground."

"Didn't Dostoevsky write something about that?" Wakefield feels the need to say, even though he knows it's lame. He's annoyed by the lovebirds.

"Sad profession, architecture," Zamyatin sighs. "Churches, sad. Big buildings, very sad. Official buildings, sad, sad. Wolves don't need architecture. Nature makes caves for them. Animals don't build anything, except for birds and rodents, and they make nests from whatever they can find."

"Yeah, it's like my apartment," says Mitch. "I find things and I take them home, but I'll have to move soon because there is hardly any room for me anymore." She whips her head around. One of her pigtails smacks Wakefield on the neck, the other gets tangled in the Russian's beard. "Sorry." She yanks her pigtail out of the scraggly salt-and-pepper beard and jumps to her feet.

"I've got to go wash up and get high," she says matter-of-factly. "I'm in hot pursuit of the better person I know I am when I'm high. Be right back."

"Please don't wash," Ivan calls after her.

"That'll be on your tombstone," says Wakefield.

"You're a tombstone," says Zamyatin. "A ten-story one and sinking rapidly."

The ten-story tombstone reminds Wakefield of something from the past, and he laughs. "Do you remember the Swede?"

"Do I? I can still see that red beard up in the air every time I take a leak. Everybody talked to him, you know. They confessed to him, like he was a freaky priest!"

Wakefield had met Zamyatin in the Arctic circle, at the research station at Outpost Mountain, where he'd been sent to write a story for *National Cartographic* about the international team that spent six months there studying the feasibility of living and building on ice. Zamyatin was one of two Russian architects, the fun one. The other one was a tormented teetotaler who never spoke. Happily, Zamyatin made up for it by filling the endless Arctic twilight with extravagant stories. At the onset of winter one of the team members, a Swedish meteorologist, died suddenly of a heart attack. Only a week earlier his body might have been transported by air to Anchorage, but the winter storms had already started and no planes could fly. At first they kept the dead Swede just outside one of the tents, wrapped in plastic, but the wind tore the plastic away and nearly made off with the body. Then they slid the body into a sleeping bag, secured it with nylon ropes, and staked them to the ice. The wind tore the sleeping bag and all the covers thereafter, so the first man to make his way to the latrine every morning had to cover the red-bearded corpse again. After a couple of weeks, they ran out of things to cover him with, so they just scraped away the snow every few days, to keep him from disappearing. Perhaps to reduce his creepiness, the remaining scientists created a playful mythology around the dead meteorologist, who became, among other things, a kind of father confessor. It was not unusual to find one of them carrying on an intimate conversation with the corpse, but then, of course, there was no need to whisper because the wailing winds were loud enough to drown any human voice.

"The shit I told him I never told anyone!" Zamyatin nods. "My roommate in the mental hospital was just about as quiet as the Swede. I told him everything, too, but then the fucker came out his catatonia and ratted on me. No, I really liked the Swede."

Wakefield had also liked him. He'd had his moments with the body, addressing it with rambling monologues about his wife (now ex-wife), Marianna. The Arctic night does funny things. He hadn't found it all that strange to sit there wrapped like a mummy in the swirling snow, telling all to a corpse. In fact, all his conversations during those surreal months had been huge, epic, unequaled since. He and Zamyatin had spent twenty-hour stretches discussing everything. For all that talking, though, what he remembered most was the profound solitude of the

Arctic. All their millions of words fit in a thimble and vanished in the night.

The memory of those days lifts Wakefield's spirits. I swear by the dead Swede's red beard that I'll get the better of you, Beelzebub. The Devil's weary face floats before his eyes and he knows, with a certainty born on the spot, that his Satanic Majesty shares with him an inclination to loneliness.

BY THE TIME he leaves the bar, Wakefield is already feeling freer; the little nubs of vestigial wings are already itching under the skin over his shoulder blades. All he needs to beat the Devil is some imagination. Of course, imagination can be a problem in middle age. When he was a kid the Rimbaud faucet was on full blast; possibilities poured out of it decked in colors like a dragon at Chinese New Year. At fifteen, imagination slunk around like a mermaid in sequins with a sex of fire. But soon enough real bodies and sentiments got pasted onto his fantasies like labels, and imagining began to feel foolish.

And now it's as if he's been given a sabbatical from the life he'd long believed he was living. He is free to consider alternative lives. He decides to make a list of possibilities to exercise his wings.

1. What if . . .
2. Whatever happened to . . .

He tries to think more specifically.

3. What if instead of her was her.
4. What if instead of here was there.
5. What if I wasn't me.
6. What the hell does the Devil mean by that starter pistol?

His listing is interrupted by his cell phone, which, in this story, is never the starter pistol, though it is demonic. He lets the caller leave a message, then takes it out of his pocket and looks at the caller ID. Zelda, his best ex-girlfriend and travel agent. Zelda books the flights for his lecture tours. He calls her back but gets her machine. He's supposed to leave for the Midwest the next afternoon.

Once upon a time Zelda and Wakefield dated, as they say. Sometimes they actually went out, but mostly they stayed indoors because the relationship seemed cursed by unnaturally bad weather. Whenever they planned an outing, a sudden rainstorm or an unusual wind would mess up her hair, tear off his hat, collapse the umbrella. These events were so common that they called them WZ moments, after their initials. After the fiftieth WZ moment, the joke got old.

Zelda was then an associate professor of anthropology, and about the time the joke got old, her studies took her to Siberia. There she met a young shaman, the youngest member of the Shaman Union, formed after the collapse of the Soviet one. He had magical powers, as real shamans do, one of which infused Zelda with an irresistible crush. She decided to stay on in Siberia, where the weather was surprisingly better than it had been on any of Wakefield's dates with her. One day she returned, heartbroken. Her shaman boy-lover had been lost hunting alone. His body was never found, but Zelda received psychic messages from him. One of these instructed her never to resume a romantic relationship with Wakefield.

Zelda wrote an account of her Siberian adventure that was rejected by every academic publication she offered it to, even though she tried her best to keep the "paranormal" references to a minimum. She was denied tenure at the university because of her long absence and failure to publish. Zelda took this not entirely unexpected outcome in stride, and on the counsel of her ghostly lover, she purged the essay of academic jargon and published it as a paperback for popular consumption. The book was a best-seller. With the profits Zelda opened Crossroads Travel, and cultivated a select clientele of people interested in traveling to places where magic is still practiced. Crossroads Travel advertised only in New Age publications, and several cable networks featured programs with Zelda in exotic locales, communing with loin-clothed pygmies or saffron-robed monks.

Wakefield never took her special tours, but Zelda booked all his professional flights, which were mostly to very ordinary places. This service, which could have been performed by any travel agent, came with an educational component, however. For instance, when Wakefield complained that he didn't get enough exercise because he flew too much, Zelda gently lectured him.

"You have to change your perspective on everything, especially flying. Flying is your dharma, your karma, but it can also be your yoga. When it rained and stormed on us all the time, it was because of our inattention. I am normally a very observant person, but something happened when I was with you. I lost my edge; everything looked blurry like I wasn't wearing my glasses. You always were the absentminded type, which was charming for a while, but was annoying as hell when *you* stopped wearing your glasses. You also snore. Anyway, when both of us became inattentive, the universe responded with bad weather."

Wakefield listened to this analysis with growing astonishment until he had to interrupt. "But Zelda, why in God's name would the universe care about us in such an . . . attentive way? Rain and wind drench and smack everybody! Do you mean to say that all the innocent bystanders to our moments were victims of this . . . attention . . . by the universe?" Wakefield rarely invoked God, but it seemed appropriate.

"I can't explain this, Wakefield," she said impatiently, "but I'm convinced that the only way for you to become more focused and more observant is to be confined in a small place with a narrow field of vision, where you can't move very much and have limited opportunities to complain, a place where you can go deeply into yourself and think beyond your usual parameters. If you just learn some simple breathing exercises and some minimal physical ones, you will evolve so fast it will scare you. That airplane seat is your yoga mat, Wakefield. Flying can be your yoga practice. Now let me teach you some breathing exercises."

Wakefield had declined her offer and left her office in irritation. It started raining as soon as he was out the door. He arrived home soaked. After a few drinks and a long phone conversation with Ivan "Reality Check" Zamyatin, he decided to give Zelda another chance. The truth was that she was efficient, she knew his preferences, she had all his frequent flier numbers on file, and she took care of rental cars, hotels, and whatever else he needed. He was too lazy to start over with someone else.

So he invited her over one evening to begin his lessons.

Zelda arrived wearing leotard and tights under her long coat. She sat in the lotus position, and Wakefield sat awkwardly cross-legged. She made him pretend that he was in an airplane seat, though he had never met such a full-bosomed noisily breathing yogin on any airplane. No matter. He closed his eyes and listened. He held his breath and counted, exhaled and pretended to relax, visualized a bright lotus flower on top of his head, slowed his heartbeat (or thought he had), followed the path of his breath through his entire body including his toes, let the light into his belly button, and generally obeyed every syllable of Zelda's instruction, hearing at the same time a familiar sound of sexual excitement that made its (surely) unconscious way between her syllables. He even tried (unsuccessfully) to temper his erection. His penis had never been a very good student.

Surprisingly, Zelda's teaching was not wasted. Wakefield practiced on his next flight and the one after that. Soon he no longer felt embarrassed: he let his breaths in and out, he moved his body in small, often imperceptible ways, and started believing in this flying yoga. It helped, it helped a lot. He did become more attentive, more careful, more responsive to the world around him, and not only when he was flying. He was grateful to Zelda and wouldn't dream of replacing her with an ordinary travel agent. He wouldn't mind sleeping with her, for that matter. That was out of the question, however. Ever evolving, Zelda had become a dedicated "sapphist," as Ivan was wont to call lesbians. Her life partner was a beautiful but icy specialist in infectious diseases at the city's university hospital. Together they traveled to spiritual sites and wretched parts of the world where the rarest infectious diseases rage.

WHEN ZELDA CALLS BACK, he answers the phone.

"Take something warm," Zelda says. "It's twenty degrees and snowing up there. Do you even have a heavy coat?" she nags.

Wakefield waits for her to quiz him about why he is going to a town called Typical, what the job is. When she doesn't ask, he volunteers. "I'm going to Typical to speak about money and poetry and art to the biggest tech corp in the world."

Zelda laughs. "What the hell do you know about money, Wakefield?"

"I know a lot about art and I'm poetry in motion."

"You don't know a thing about anything. But you do know how to fake it. I guess that's your art. Too bad the pay is so mediocre. For such a great gift, I mean."

"Okay, Zelda, you've had your fun. Just give me the flight info, please."

While she brings it up on the computer, he listens to her breathing. He imagines her breath descending down her throat, rounding her breasts, filling her Catholic-flamed heart, hurtling down her flat tummy, funneling to her pubis. He hears the voice of her red-haired assistant answering another line, "Crossroads Travel. How can I help you?" and he feels cozily enveloped by an odd kind of domesticity, achieved by phone.

"Remember to breathe, Wakefield. We have a deal," Zelda reminds him, and the word *deal* evaporates his cozy reverie. Well, yes.

Wakefield has made a lot of deals, and now he's made the Big Deal. Suddenly he feels dizzy.

The Devil is lying at an angle on the roof of the cathedral, playing hooky from an "important" meeting. There's been an annoying increase in demonic meetings lately, and he can't stand the din of loudmouth upstart devils making huge deals out of all kinds of crap. The Internet? Who cares? He's had Internet since the beginning of time and it doesn't bother him in the least that humans use it now. They'll never get up to the speed of thought, no matter how fancy their technology gets. He lazily scans the airwaves and picks up Wakefield and Zelda's phone conversation almost by accident. It worries him. Maybe he's made a deal with a shell, without touching the nut inside. An unshelled chestnut is a favorite symbolic object for the Devil, a lesson, really, about the mistakes even experienced demons can make. You mistake the wrapping for the entire package and then, surprise, the shell falls away and the innocent shiny nut emerges. The whole point of making deals is to harvest souls that are no longer innocent. The payoff is the twisted object the world has made of a person. That's the art he collects. When he hears Zelda tell Wakefield, "Remember to breathe," a drop of cold sweat drips from between his horns and lands on his furry belly. If Wakefield hasn't yet learned to breathe, he may be unborn as well, innocent. The Devil wipes his belly with his triple-jointed fingers and thinks for a moment about turning them into a long-barreled pistol and firing the starting shot. It would be so easy. Wakefield would see a brick fly out of the wall and land with a loud bang at his feet. Or *on* his feet. There would be no mistaking it. In a panic, he'd begin the race against time. No, not yet, thinks the Devil, let him stew a while longer. Let him think he'll get the better of me. There is no way a fresh new creature shiny with the foam of innocence and transcendent irony is going to emerge from a middle-aged motivational speaker. Never happened before. The Devil grabs a passing leaf and puts it to his lips. He whistles through it: "I Did It My Way." A street painter looks up to see who's whistling. The leaf drops on his head.

Crossroads. Wakefield will find the crossroads and then take another direction. If he'd engaged the services of a shaman before Zelda left for Siberia to find her own, he might have improved the weather and saved their relationship. The thought makes him giddy. He could wave a magic wand of amnesia over Zelda and go back in time: He picks up Zelda after her class at the college. They sit outdoors at their favorite restaurant. Not a cloud in the sky. Over rigatoni he hands her a ring. The ring doesn't fall into the noodles. They walk arm in arm to an after-dinner place for an after-dinner drink. Not a breeze. Nothing ruffles Zelda's shoulder-length tresses. His hat and tie stay on. They drink on the terrace. The stars appear, undimmed by city lights or clouds. The sickle moon stays screwed to its velvet pillow. They speak to each other clearly, lazily; no sudden gust of wind snatches syllables away, no cloud bursts on their conversation. They get married and sit on the porch of their little farmhouse, watching their plump baby sleep in his cradle. All is still. A rooster crows in the next village. A dog barks.

He feels himself gag. What schmaltz! It's ridiculous, the road not taken. Corny. And impossible. Whatever happens now will happen for the first time, and whatever choices I make will be the road taken, period. I'll never know if one way is "truer" than another.

The Devil is enjoying himself enormously.

❖ PART TWO ❖

TYPICAL

IN A LARGE AIRPORT half way to Typical, Wakefield is looking to juice up his laptop computer. All around are others like him. There's one now, a little man with a goatee. His eyes roam greedily around the concourse, searching. Then he takes a few determined steps forward, then a leap, and he's there! He crouches, he grins, he opens his shoulder bag, and out come his cords. He plops down on his knees and plugs in his laptop and his cell phone. The devices begin to glow. He closes his eyes. Silence! The vampire is feeding. He's not alone for long. A young woman approaches swiftly. She acknowledges the other curtly, drops down, and pulls out her own vampiric implements.

That's it for this particular feeding station: the outlets are full. Other vampires pass, disappointed. They've come too late. Feeding stations are few and far between. Vampires often must roam the length and breadth of an airport before they find a place to feed.

Wakefield keeps hunting. An inconsiderate lamia is using six outlets for as many devices. She's watching a DVD, oblivious to the world, the juice flowing through her. Wakefield curses her and moves on. At last he spots an outlet under a dangerous-looking sculpture of something vaguely aeronautic. He leaps to it, his cord is out in a flash, he's in. He checks the glow light on his laptop. It's dark. Egads! It's a dead station! He looks around, momentarily disoriented by a sudden drop in his blood sugar level. He sees another vampire grinning at him. That one knew! He tried it and failed and now he is delighting in Wakefield's distress. Wakefield yanks the cord out roughly and resumes roaming, giving his cocreature the evil eye. You'd think our common need would give us compassion, but sympathy does not plague the individualistic, hungry beasts of the computer age. We don't share juice.

Finally, at a deserted gate dangerously far from his connecting flight, he is able to feed. The moment he plugs in, he can feel the lifeblood flowing into his chips. He dials a faraway place and the juice lets him hear the messages in his mailbox. Ex-wife, agent, attorney, Ivan. The icons light up on his desktop, e-mail invites him to grow his penis, enlarge his breasts, refinance his house. All is well in the world. Vampires pass by, hungry, needy, jealous. Let them pass. He has a full hour before boarding.

Suddenly Wakefield remembers a downside of his deal with the Devil. In his year of grace, nobody'll notice that he's gone. How could that ever have seemed attractive to him? If nobody misses you, you might as well be dead. Wasn't that partly why the other Wakefield, the man in Hawthorne's short story, left home? To see if he would be missed? It was vanity; the guy wanted to feel important. Wakefield hugs his laptop, squeezes the cell phone in his pocket, hard. Lord, protect me from what I want. I never want to hear that starter pistol.

At home, Wakefield is master of his universe. Away from home,

he's just a frequent flier, an anonymous drudge, a . . . chronically—
What? Here's an announcement. His flight has been delayed, he's
adrift among the hurrying, inconsiderate, demanding, pushy, self-
absorbed crowd. No one sees him; everyone is talking on cell phones,
blindly pacing. He sends Zelda a bombastic e-mail: "Your familiars
have failed. I'm stuck in the middle of nowhere."

When the flight is finally called, he finds he's in a middle seat,
squeezed between a large woman and a larger man. Their flesh spills
over and under the armrests. By American standards, they aren't all
that fat, but Wakefield prides himself on staying trim and abhors glut-
tons. He trembles as their tentacular flesh adheres to his sweater,
sending unwelcome heat through the knit.

After takeoff the man turns on his laptop and a pie chart appears
on the screen. Wakefield crosses his arms, but the man's elbow reaches
past the armrest and pokes him. The woman shifts her thigh next to
his, absorbing his leg. Americans get larger, the seats get smaller, it's
demonic, seethes Wakefield. Blue-jean manufacturers have figured
out that the average American bottom has grown considerably, so
why can't the airlines?

Wakefield does the deep breathing Zelda taught him, trying to relax, then escapes into his book. He carries Mark Twain's *Innocents
Abroad* on all his trips for precisely this purpose. In the 1860s Twain
went with one of the first organized group tours of Americans to Europe, Egypt, and the Holy Land, traveling by steamship and tele-
graphing his reports back to an American newspaper. Tourists, who
live by guidebooks rather than by their senses, received their first en-
tomological analysis at his hands. He nailed the pathos of tourism in
its early bloom. Travelers' conveyances in Twain's time were at least
more comfortable than your average commercial airplane.

The same grinch that has made it possible to work anytime and
anywhere via electronics has also been quietly shrinking personal
space. Wakefield sinks ever smaller in his middle seat, balancing the

paperback on his knees, but there is no escape from the waves of neighboring flesh. They keep coming, a surf of fat beating against the tender shores of his body. There is an active geometry of evil at work: while airplane seats are miniaturized, airport terminals expand to the size of cathedrals. Walking from the ticket counter to the gate has become a lengthy pilgrimage through soaring atriums and mighty temples of commerce, as if the space taken out of aircraft has been added to the airports themselves, just as nutrients flow at an ever increasing rate from animals and plants into the mouths of greedy humans.

The simultaneous machinery of gluttony and greed works to sacrifice the individual to corporate ego, imprisoning the body in a cell of fat, and every inch stolen from the body's ease ends up in corporate space. Once, there were luxurious staterooms on ships, lovely sleeping cars on trains, and airships with elegant lounges where thin women conversed with handsome men, sipping cocktails from crystal glasses. Travel itself was an enviable adventure, though of course only the wealthy could travel. The ungainly masses stayed home. What happened? When did change come? That's a no-brainer, thinks Wakefield. Two world wars redesigned trains, airplanes, and ships to efficiently transport soldiers, weapons, and prisoners. Efficiency became the ideal of design, and increased profit its overarching peacetime goal.

Wakefield has the creepy feeling that this room hurtling through the sky at thirty-seven thousand feet is zooming toward a reality that will soon make his complaints completely trivial. The future, close as it always is, cannot be known, but Wakefield, listening with one ear cocked for the sound of the Devil's starter pistol, can hear it whispering.

THE LIGHTS OF THE RUNWAY blink feebly on the vast, dark prairie. The plane touches down near a frozen lake. Wakefield has arrived in Typical, headquarters of The Company, the largest purveyor of software on the planet. He is met in the terminal by Maggie, a Company representative and his escort for the next few days. She's blue-eyed and friendly, wrapped in an ankle-length coat, and her hand is warm from being cuddled by a mitten. Wakefield shakes it firmly and follows her to the parking garage. The wind blows fresh snow around, but Wakefield feels warm enough in his sweater, vintage overcoat, and the broad-brimmed felt hat he thinks makes him look like a gangster.

Maggie's ice-encrusted sport utility vehicle pushes dreamily across the white prairie. She hands him his schedule. Tonight is free. Noon tomorrow, lunch with corporate muckety-mucks; 8 P.M., speech: "Money and Poetry (with a detour in Art)." Next day: lunch at restaurant with more muckety-mucks, early afternoon visit to Company headquarters, flight out that evening. He's gripped by déjà vu. How many Maggies have handed him this same schedule over the years?

The hotel looks like a Bavarian castle; there is tinsel on the door-man's cap, shiny red apples in a bowl at the front desk; the phone booths are gothic confessionals strung with little white lights. People with name tags on their jackets mill about the lobby, some wearing Santa Claus hats. Maggie tells Wakefield she'll wait while he goes up to his room, and then they can have a drink "or something."

He drops his bag on the king-size bed, looks out the window at his view: nice parking lot, a solid mass of snow-covered SUVs; then he inspects the bathroom: big bathtub, good. There is nothing like a long bath, hot toddy in hand, while it snows outside; that's his idea of heaven. A hunting dog drags a duck by one wing in the print over the bed. Wakefield splashes some water on his face and goes downstairs to meet Maggie.

Maggie is feeling festive, so they head straight to the hotel bar. Wakefield orders a hot toddy for himself and a German beer for Maggie. She drapes her coat on the back of the chair, revealing a sweater adorned by reindeer that appear to run across her breasts.

Wakefield can't help but look; Maggie looks at him looking. Cheers. At a neighboring table, men wearing plaid shirts and women in bright Maggie-style sweaters are talking about Marilyn Monroe. Her breasts, one of them is saying, were actually augmented with implants. Marilyn was a guinea pig for the emerging bosom-enhancement industry, and also its patron saint. Then there is some technical talk about nipples, artificial and otherwise.

"It's the Breast Pump Convention," Maggie whispers, leaning closer to Wakefield, as if his just looking at her breasts created this synchronicity. For a moment Wakefield panics.

"God, I'm not their speaker, am I?"

"You're not," Maggie reassures him.

His panic subsides. Sometimes he gets confused. So many talks, so many towns. No matter where you go these days, you can't get away from a convention. He makes a living from them, but he's feeling like flotsam atop an ever growing wave. Even small towns are building vast convention centers for professional meetings that get larger and larger. There are more and more professionals, needing bigger and bigger spaces and more and more speakers. Professionals subdivide into more professionals as their fields of expertise grow, specialize, and divide like honeycombs.

"It's not unlike breasts," he mumbles.

"What's not unlike breasts?"

Wakefield can't quite explain. Breasts get larger, domed convention halls inflate in city centers, there is an analogy, albeit tenuous. Eventually, there has to be an end to the inflation. If breasts get too big, their owners topple. If there are too many convention halls, they will one day be empty. There must be an end to the generation of new professionals, and when that end comes, there will have to be new uses for the convention centers. They will become prisons or gladiator arenas or spaceships. Hopeless. Maggie's question still hangs in the air.

"Confusion, never mind. My bad. I just wanted to say 'breasts.' I find that it calms me. I have nightmares where I'm speaking confidently before thousands of people and suddenly I realize that I'm naked, but what's really weird is I have . . . breasts. So I say 'breasts' to myself to dispel my anxiety." He tells Maggie about the time he received a phone call from someone who asked him to speak at the annual meeting of the Fire Sprinkler Association of America. He thought it was a joke at first. "Sure," he said, "I'll do it for twenty-five thousand dollars." There was a pause. "We can't afford that," the fire sprinkler voice said. "We only have fifteen thousand in the budget." Three months later he faced a room full of fire sprinkler salesmen and spoke for an hour on fire *extinguishers*. His audience was deeply offended by the misunderstanding, but that wasn't the worst of it. He had gone on at length about the Shirtwaist fire in New York, where dozens of immigrant girls perished for lack of fire extinguishers, or sprinklers, for that matter, and how the tragedy brought about the formation of the first garment workers' union. There was no applause after his speech, and several tough-looking guys appeared to be waiting for him at the exit. "What did I do wrong?" he whispered to the woman who handed him a check and ushered him quickly out an emergency exit. "There are *two* Fire Sprinkler Associations," she hissed, pushing him out the door. "This one represents the *nonunion* shops!"

Maggie laughs uproariously, then looks at him with amused sympathy, her laughter still echoing through the room.

"Incidentally, what's a *breast pump* convention doing in this Company town? Are all the geeks lactating?"

"Good question. My guess is that our CEO is interested in the subject, we may be designing software. We design software for everything else. We've already redesigned most of the people who work here."

Wakefield shudders. Growing domes and breasts is one thing. A redesigned person is something else. He wonders what's inside Maggie.

After two hot toddies Wakefield feels that he could easily give a great speech to the breast pump conventioneers, no problem. Maggie is radiating motherly warmth, it's still snowing outside, and discreetly piped-in Christmas carols have suffused everything with heavenly peace. Wakefield is hungry. Maggie directs him to a table laden with free happy-hour food and Wakefield comes back with paper plates full of chili-cheese fries, little sausages, and buffalo chicken wings swimming in red barbeque sauce.

"America, land of plenty. My friend Zamyatin always says that if Russians ever found out about America's happy hours, they would invade and eat everything without stopping."

Free food is not prudent, Zamyatin would say, shaking his head. When he first emigrated, Zamyatin had lived by necessity on three American institutions: happy-hour bar food, late-night bar food (things floating in jars behind the bar, pickled eggs, marinated pigs' feet, salted peanuts, that sort of thing), and all-you-can-eat buffets. The institution of the buffet elicited his most lyrical effusions. "Imagine please," he exulted, "the buffet! Hordes of my countrymen hiding in the bushes while one buys a buffet ticket! Soon, the buffet is all gone and the bushes are full of bones and corncobs and everybody is patting their stomachs, singing, snoring, and fucking! Food! Food!"

When Maggie and Wakefield stroll back to her car, full of cheese fries and good feelings, it's still snowing. The darkness is pierced only by the bright signs of the 24-hour supermarket and the fast-food places, which glow through swirling flakes. An interstate highway runs past the hotel to other Midwestern towns, towns that have risen out of the cornfields and become home to corporations looking for a way out of cities. Maggie's talked him into going to a party. Wakefield thinks of his anonymous room with the minibar and the bathtub and maybe soft-core porn on TV, and regrets having accepted. On the other hand, he has a buzz on and he feels very at ease in Maggie's company.

The car radio reports a multiple-vehicle pileup on the interstate, and more snow is predicted. "Do you mind if we stop to check on my daughter before we go to the party?" Maggie asks. "My aunt Greta is babysitting, and she tends to fall asleep early." Wakefield doesn't mind.

Maggie's little house is a friendly jumble of toys, clothes, and books. Disney dialogue from a big TV fills the living room and two shaggy dogs leap on Wakefield. A small girl with a mop of blond hair is sucking her thumb at one end of a couch, absorbed by the cartoon, and an elderly woman is snoring at the other end. Maggie kisses the child, who never takes her eyes off the screen, then drags the dogs off Wakefield. The introductions are brief; Aunt Greta quickly resumes snoring. Wakefield sees stairs leading to a second story or an attic, and though he feels with some certainty that there isn't a husband or boyfriend, he gets ready to shake another hand, just in case.

"There hasn't been a man here in six years. It's quite nice. We are very, very happy." Maggie laughs.

As they drive away, Maggie tells him a little more about Typical. Soon after The Company moved here, the city commissioned a sculpture of the "Typical Family" to be erected in the town square.

"The funny thing is," Maggie tells him, "the divorce rate in Typical was pretty average before The Company came, and the arrival of The Company didn't really change that, but the city council got all disturbed about how we were going to lose our small-town 'family values' if we didn't do something to show them off."

So the city organized a competition, and a sculptor from a nearby university won the commission. She showed the elders sketches of an upright typical family. The sculptor sculpted hidden away in her studio and the marble monument was installed, draped in a heavy canvas sheet, the night before the dedication ceremony. The next day the whole town gathered for a celebratory parade: there was a festive float for guests of honor, a military color guard, the Typical High School marching band, cheerleaders, hot dogs, cotton candy, and lemonade. Even the CEO of The Company was there, though he lives mostly on his corporate jet. The band played, the city manager shook hands with the sculptor, who wore an unusual paper dress made from back issues of the *Typical Ledger*, and the sculpture was unveiled by the town's and the Midwest's oldest veteran, Maggie's one-hundred-and-three-year-old grandfather, who, as it happened, was blind. When the canvas fell away, the citizens gasped. *The Typical Family* consisted of a naked mother nursing a baby with a naked pubescent girl child standing at her side. There was no father figure, no protector, no Man. Maggie's grandfather, thinking that the gasp of horror had something to do with the quality of his work, kept pulling at the cord attached to the fallen sheet until he collapsed. He lay in a coma for three days, then died.

The scandal was complete. The *Ledger* editorialized: "The 'artist' has taken advantage of our trust. A family of naked women with an absent father may be typical in the rest of America, but not in Typical! We should remove this offense immediately, or demand that the sculptress add a man and decently clothe the mother and children." The death of Maggie's grandfather was seen as a judgment: "It is no coincidence that the oldest living veteran in the Midwest was struck dead at the moment of the outrage. This is a world we do not wish to live in."

But other citizens of Typical, including Maggie, thought the sculpture was beautiful and appropriate. She laughed at the newspaper's maudlin connection of the death of her grandfather, who'd had six wives and went to prison for a few years for killing one of them, to the statue, innocent by comparison. There were demonstrations and counterdemonstrations. Maggie, together with a dozen single mothers, protested that the statue stay as it was. Church groups, roused to action, picketed the monument every day, singing hymns and carrying placards that read Daddy Come Home! Someone spray-painted a bra on the mother and a dress on the girl. They even diapered the baby. *The Typical Family* became a cause célèbre that even made the national news. Finally the city sent a bulldozer in one night to destroy the sculpture, in the process killing a teenager who was sitting beneath it drinking a beer.

The sacrifice of the boy sobered everyone. The sculptor, entirely on her own initiative, made a new statue, adding a likeness of the boy, a man in a suit, who looked like a salesman, and clothing the mother and the girl. The baby remained naked, as did the breast she suckled. The controversy might have faded but for the vandalism that followed. Almost every night, the monument was attacked: the father's foot broken off, one of his eyes scooped out, the mother's breasts hammered, the child's nose chiseled.

"I know who was doing it," Maggie tells Wakefield, who by now is fascinated by this uncommonly rich allegory. "Friends of the dead boy, teenagers. They stayed true to the realism. None of them have fathers at home."

The Typical Family was eventually removed by the city fathers, and everyone pretended not to notice. Now only the pediment remains, covered with snow, surrounded by new landscaping. Maggie points it out in the cold blue moonlight.

"I find it extraordinary that nobody checked the sculptor's progress before the unveiling," wonders Wakefield.

"Small-town trust"—Maggie smiles—"or fear of art. Pick one. They either trusted her to do as she said or felt checking up on an 'artist' would be crude. Artists carry a certain aura, folks are superstitious about them . . . they are still sacred beasts, unpredictable. They would have never authorized an abstract sculpture, but figures, well, they've got to be okay."

Wakefield is enjoying himself. He considers, as part of his inventory of alternatives, living here with Maggie in the Midwest: he could work for The Company, go to happy hour at the hotel bar, shovel the snow from the driveway, and play the part of the father figure. It's a soothing vision. But he stops short. What would the Devil think of that? Wakefield hears the Devil laughing. "This is what you got me out of bed for? I'm supposed to give you a reprieve for becoming a frigging cliché? If suburban bliss was the 'authentic life,' I'd never collect anybody. There are millions of normals out there, all of them 'authentic.' I don't even deal with them, we've got cleaning crews for their kind, they scoop them up by the millions. . . . There's even been some discussion about cutting down costs by giving them all a virus at the same time, instead of individual heart attacks. . . . Those cost money!" The Devil's indignation is not lost on Wakefield. Still, this would be his, Wakefield's, idea of "authenticity," a choice he would make deliberately. In any case, it's academic. He hasn't heard the starter pistol yet. The deal didn't include saying, Sorry, I've already found the life I want, I'm staying put.

THE CAR CRUNCHES over ice, glides over snowbanks, and slides into a parking lot behind a windowless brick building shaking with loud music. When they step out, it feels like thirty below zero, the same temperature as Wakefield's anxiety. He's sure that something nasty waits for him inside.

"This is the old high school," Maggie explains. "After the building was abandoned it was taken over by artists." She pushes the door open and they find themselves in a smoky auditorium full of people dancing to a bluegrass band.

It's frigid inside, yet in one corner there is a woman in lingerie posing on a shabby couch, seemingly impervious to the cold. Another woman is sketching her, and drawings of the same woman in lingerie on a shabby couch cover the walls.

Wakefield peers over the shoulder of the sketcher at her sketch. "All these yours?" He nods toward the walls.

"Yup."

"They remind me of the covers of old detective novels."

"Bingo!" The woman stops sketching, offers him a charcoal-covered hand. "Noir. It's my name." She gestures to the model, who shifts lazily and reaches for a cigarette still smoldering in an ashtray on the floor. "Rose, my model."

Wakefield sees Maggie huddled with a tall ballerina in a red tutu and fur slippers. The band gets louder, feedback upchucks through the speakers, and Wakefield's anxiety spikes. This demonstration of artistic life in the middle of nowhere is typical of every small town these days: the need to flaunt a difference has spilled over into something beyond the family. Does the Devil make them do it? The Devil is easily bored, but what could he really have against so-called normality? The "normal" family is, after all, the source of what the Devil enjoys most: anxiety, mental illness, violence, evil thoughts, fear, and social unrest. What the Devil hates are attempts to escape the quotidian horror of ordinariness. These escapes into art, into otherness, must give him headaches because they might, just might, lead to innocence. Neither he nor Wakefield believes that this particular exercise of esthetic difference is going to transcend anything. But before the sneer has time to settle on Wakefield's face, everyone's holding a lantern, a flashlight, or a candle, and Maggie motions him to join her at the front of the line with the ballerina.

Behind the stage a creaky medieval-looking door slides open, and the procession files into a small room. The light of the candles, lanterns, and flashlights illuminates what appears to be an old-fashioned electric chair: the ballerina sits on the chair and snaps a blinding Polaroid of herself. Maggie attaches a collanderlike contraption with dangling wires to the ballerina's head, and in the light of the second Polaroid flash, Wakefield notices that the ballerina is wearing nothing under the tutu and she is shivering, from either the cold or her mock electrocution.

The crowd claps and cheers, and they all move on to another

room, where a long dining table is heaped with platters of eyeballs and guts. A chant begins and the nearly naked ballerina crawls into a coffin. Her friends dump the guts and eyeballs on top of her. More Polaroids. They journey on, crawling sometimes, through other chambers furnished with procrustean beds and iron maidens, through a ghost-filled swamp, through a gallery of life-size statues of serial killers ("Most of them come from the Midwest," Maggie explains). Wakefield trails the flashing Polaroid and rustling red tutu, and knows for certain that the photos will be duly displayed in a soon-to-be-mounted art exhibit at City Hall, the same City Hall from which the Company manager responsible for the sculpture fiasco has retired, making way for a dynamic young politician who has the initiative to, among other things, mount art shows in the halls of government in the hope of stimulating tourism in connection with the famed *Typical Family* debacle. And thus, Wakefield reflects, the Republic moves forward.

If you've lived a long time like the Devil has, or a short but well-read time like Wakefield has, you, too, might be made queasy by such kitsch. If you've seen the, let's say, real Inquisition and had fresh eyeballs full of genuine fear garnishing your plate of brain tartare, or if you've studied Baroque depictions of the suffering of martyrs in the museums of Europe, this kind of display would certainly embarrass you. The genuine item, or the "authentic" if you like, never descends to the level of self-parody and kitsch.

But this is a special time in History. These are the days when the President's penis stars on television every evening, a celebrity in its own right. It takes a lot to make shocking art when everyone, including the political leader of the greatest nation on earth, has become an artist. An artist who uses nothing more or less than his own dick! The philistines declare, of course, that the President is an accidental artist, or perhaps only a medium for the artistic ambitions of others, but be that as it may, there it is! The Presidential penis itself, not in the symbolic form of a scepter, or as the prayed-for virile instrument of a king, but as a dick, pure and simple, has joined a gallery of celebrity dicks caught in the glare of publicity!

At the beginning of the twentieth century, Marcel Duchamp shocked the art world with a urinal, and claimed that bicycles and sewing machines were art because they were simple but one couldn't make them at home. How true. The public is interested in the President's penis, Wakefield speculates, because it is simple, and there is only one President. And yet, there *is* a penis in every home (well, in nearly every home, excepting the norm), but the home penis is sub rosa, not a celebrity. Fashion designers, who invented supermodels, are using musicians and actors in their advertising more and more. Self-starvation, cheaply available heroin, and digital cameras can make anyone look like a supermodel, and the market cries out for something different, for something that, as Duchamp stipulated, cannot be made at home. Musicians and actors possess that something, namely talent. And the President, whatever one might say about him, is a talented man, a unique and powerful personage whose penis is a powerful and instantly comprehensible statement.

The problem with this artlike spasm in Typical is that it's so "artsy," so contrived, so gentle. These people probably don't even believe in the Devil, thinks Wakefield. They think he's just a Halloween costume for the kids. When the procession returns from the tour of grotesque chambers, the lingerie model, who had not joined them, is smoking a cigarette on the stage, chatting up the guitarist, who gazes unabashedly between her legs, proving to Wakefield that the only constant currency is sex. But not even sex, he corrects himself. The *promise* of sex, for the sake of which you will buy something, do something, sacrifice something. Sex is the reward of earning power, of sophistication, of understanding Art.

Now, just when it seems that there might be an end to the evening, there's more. The procession has only been leading up to a campy wedding. The bride is wearing a blood-stained wedding dress, the groom a knife-punctured tuxedo and a top hat with an arrow stuck through it, and both bride and groom are male. An official wearing a prison jumpsuit and holding a staff crowned by a monkey head intones: "I now pronounce you husband and wife, please take turns." Maggie gives away the bride. "Take her. Please," she says.

Wakefield is not amused. It is all so sweetly pop and wholesome, this transgendering in mid-America. He knows that most of the folks fooling around here tonight will be in his audience at The Company tomorrow. The Company encourages "creativity" and tolerance: one can take one's partner to the Christmas party, and same-gender couples can kiss at midnight on New Year's Eve. Wakefield will speak to them about money and poetry (with a detour in art), he will be paid, then he will fly to a big city to make another speech with the same title but, hopefully, different content. After that he is supposed to go west for a rather more mysterious gig. His agent received a request from a Western art collector for Wakefield's *presence*. The agent reported that this collector would pay his fee simply for being at a *party*. He signals Maggie, who's seated on the bride's lap drinking red wine from a bottle, his desire to leave this party. She jumps off, bottle still in hand, and walks toward him.

"Maggie," he asks in the car, pronouncing her name for the first time, "who decorated all those torture chambers?"

Maggie laughs. "The Jaycees. That's their Halloween haunted house. The rest of the year it's a playhouse for the artists who have studio spaces in the building."

Wakefield isn't paying attention to the answer: he's thinking, Will I have sex with Maggie? It's an important question because the answer might determine the shape of things to come. On the one hand, he's attracted and thinks the feeling is mutual. On the other hand, he feels none of the enthusiasm that Ivan Zamyatin would bring to such an encounter. For Zamyatin the opportunity would be accompanied by childlike curiosity and genuine warmth. Without those ingredients, Wakefield feels some disingenuousness. He can imagine very well Maggie's generous body and the comfort he might find in it, the weight of her breasts on his chest and the pulse of her. It's a thought he's sure she must share because she turns on the car radio, as if to banish it, and a song on the oldies station illustrates his dilemma. It's the Clash's "Should I Stay or Should I Go?"

"I didn't find the wedding all that funny," Wakefield finally says.

Maggie looks disappointed. "I thought it was quite sweet. Neal and Bob are both friends of mine."

"Wasn't it just a mock ceremony?"

"No, they're a real couple. We worked on this for months, we discussed the arrow through the hat for days. Neal thought it might look like he was wounded in the head in some way, like he was crazy to get married, but Bob said that it was Cupid's arrow. Bob's mom is a hippie, she said that it was an Indian arrow and it symbolized the fact that all white people carry this guilt-arrow in them. I just thought it looked cool."

Wakefield feels bad that he's let her know that he's read the entire evening as an art event in no way connected to real life. How could he have not understood, after their symbolic little war over the meaning of family, that the community's belief in the power of Art was quite real? Have to show some respect for such quaint beliefs. Especially if you want to get laid. Dufus.

"I thought it was just, like, let's get dressed up and have a party," he says lamely. "You know, an entertainment," he says, digging his hole a little deeper. "Like a happening, maybe . . ."

Maggie does know about happenings, and is very disappointed in Wakefield. She studied art in college! The man has just witnessed the most fabulous wedding ever concluded in the town of Typical, and he can't see past the art to the heart. Her friends had thought long and hard about how to affirm the most basic of life unions in terms that would expose the town's hypocrisy while confirming essential human values. Wakefield is being paid to deliver his insights on money and poetry (with a detour in art), but he's failed to see that art and life can be connected, that it all meant something, especially in a place like Typical.

"I've had too much red wine," she says, suppressing her anger, "but I'm surprised that someone so knowledgeable about art can't see the serious meaning under the costumes."

"Sentiment is not 'serious meaning,' Maggie. Just because they're a real couple . . ." Wakefield's argument trails off. He gave up looking for meaning in art a long time ago. The relationship of art to reality is complex and delicate, depending on whether one spells it with a capital A, or whether one uses it as a noun or an adjective, and myriad other factors that he's given a good deal of thought to but aren't easy to explain now.

The subject of tomorrow's lecture seems suddenly uncertain, even cruel. They won't understand what he's talking about, and he can't re-think his entire view of art and life to fit the profound soul-needs of a company town. Sleeping with Maggie seems out of the question. He has offended her.

"Your friends' wedding was terrific, I'm sure," he stammers. "I'm just so jaded about weddings."

Maggie softens. Familiar territory. "Me, too," she admits. Aha, he's human, after all. Still, she drops him off at the Bavarian castle and says good night with the engine running.

"One more thing," Wakefield says as he exits the car. "Do you believe in the Devil?"

"Don't be ridiculous," Maggie says firmly.

WAKEFIELD DROPPED OUT of college when he was twenty to travel in Europe. The theme of this Grand Tour was ghosts, and he hoped to locate some in their ancient haunts.

In Paris he attended lectures on architecture at the Sorbonne. The lectures were like baroque palaces, elaborate and endless. But with a certain kind of literary Paris firmly in his head, he wandered at night through the streets, communing with the souls of old buildings. The reality (even at night) didn't quite fit his mental map; instead of morphing into the image established by centuries of art and literature, the nocturnal streets and the (rare) citizens of Paris who braved them appeared dull, gray, and postmodernly underwhelmed by the past. It also rained continually and Wakefield could barely afford coffee. After a month, during which he caught both a nasty cold and gonorrhea, he declared Paris exhausted, her secret places inhabited only by tourists and bourgeois spirits. Wakefield sipped his last overpriced espresso at a counter in Gare du Nord, remembering Baudelaire's curse on boredom: "Habitually we cultivate remorse, as beggars entertain and nurse their lice."

Office workers rushed past, hurrying home to their discontented spouses. He overheard an American woman complaining to a friend about her French husband. "I wouldn't even mind him fucking around," she said, "if he were more considerate. But he expects me to iron his shirts, cook his food, and take care of his children. If I complain, he runs to his mother, and she scolds me for upsetting her 'darling baby.' Imagine!"

"Oh, I know," the friend nodded, looking at her watch, "they're all mama's boys!"

Wakefield's study of architecture was not focused on the technical; the mathematics involved in engineering were beyond him, and he was a sloppy draftsman. His true interest lay in architectural aberrations like Ludwig of Bavaria's overwrought castle and Gaudi's bizarre "organic" cathedral in Barcelona. He was attracted to the hybrid, the eclectic, and to structures so deformed by use and time that they were no longer recognizable. He traveled through Europe in search of ghosts and their ghastly habitats.

"Modern architecture," he told a girl named Judith with whom he spent one night in a youth hostel in Padua, "particularly Bauhaus, repels me. It is so transparently, defiantly revealing. I like postmodern ideas, but the buildings themselves are too light for my taste, too 'jocular,' too disrespectful of the history they try to subsume."

"Shut up, you pompous ass!" someone with a British accent shouted from the darkness of the dormitory.

Judith laughed, and Wakefield left Padua the next day.

Before he had left college to travel, he got a failing grade on an essay he'd entitled "Buildings Should Earn Their Postmodernism!" in which he argued that playfully incorporating old styles in new buildings resulted in an "unearned postmodernism" that would eventually drive everyone living in these structures insane. He used as an example the Place of Italy, in New Orleans, an urban park and fountain.

The park itself was a forest of classical columns, some of traditional stone, others of aluminum or glass or cement. "Does anybody like it?" his essay asked rhetorically, Wakefield not having then (or ever) mastered proper academic tone. "The structure will fall apart in less than five years and weeds will start growing through the columns. Even the bums shun it, and bums are true specialists, because their lives are uncomfortable, open to the elements. In effect, bums are the great critics of urban spaces. The Place of Italy," he concluded, "flunks the test. Bums refuse to socialize or sleep here. QED." Wakefield's analysis of the homeless and urban sculpture raised the eyebrows of his professor (while possibly bringing a smile to his lips), and he shared the essay with two colleagues. They all came to the conclusion that this essay was not about architecture, and they told this to Wakefield.

"Well, what is it, then?" asked the outraged young scholar.

"It is sociology, psychology perhaps, colored by artistic considerations," the professors pronounced. Being kindly men, they tried to convince Wakefield to change his major. They had a long conversation with him, after which Wakefield, half-convinced, ventured that he might consider specializing in "psychotecture," which is the effect of structures on their inhabitants, a notion he invented just for the occasion. His professors said there was no such thing; the department produced architects, not psychos. So Wakefield said defiantly that he didn't want to build anything, that he was interested only in what had escaped the architects' intentions, those glitches and mistakes that dwell like small demons in even the most ambitious designs. The professors told him that his sensibility might be better served in a French university, where theory is often valued more than actual construction. Thus began Wakefield's European wanderings.

In Barcelona he found the ghosts more interesting than the ones he had encountered in Paris, but he made a much more important discovery: Love. He met Marianna, a Romanian émigré. She had managed to leave Romania by marrying a Spaniard, but as soon as they arrived in Spain she abandoned him. Now she was a waitress in Barcelona. Wakefield took her to a movie, to a restaurant, and to Gaudi's unfinished cathedral, and then he proposed.

Marianna was interested in Wakefield because he was American. She declared herself bored by Europe and spent most of the time, even when she was waiting tables, encased in a pair of headphones that filled her consciousness with American pop songs. She became animated when Wakefield talked about the U.S., but lapsed into weary inattention when he speculated about architecture, art, and Europe. Wakefield felt safe with Marianna. He could conduct his intellectual life without any fear of her disapproval. She simply didn't care.

Paradoxically, in Europe, thanks to his fiancée, Wakefield realized how American he was. He had expected Old World ghosts to revive him, but only Marianna's restlessness excited him. She was as restless as America. Europe was like an old woman endlessly sweeping her sidewalks and ironing her linens. One afternoon in Cádiz, drinking

Jim Beam on the rocks—Marianna wouldn't have anything else—he was seized by nostalgia for his own, unapologetically unnostalgic country. They took the first available flight.

When we get home, he told himself, as Marianna chewed gum and tossed her hair around to the tune in her head, I will be the cartographer of hidden American spaces, the surveyor of our own *genii loci*. I will show Marianna the real America, not the one she knows from songs and movies.

He returned to school, where he was reluctantly readmitted, but his thesis on "American Buildings: Hiding in the Light" met with a cool reception. He retained from his European journey a fondness for the sharp contrasts of light and shadow near the sea, and the habit of an afternoon siesta, but he experienced none of the elation he had expected to bring to his studies. No one cared about his "unmapped architecture." Eventually he quit school again, and to support himself and his new wife, who spent all her time shopping, he started writing for travel magazines, which paid well.

WAKEFIELD IS STILL in bed when Maggie arrives to take him to The Company's informal luncheon. When she calls from the front desk, he tells her to come right up. Elegantly accoutered in a fashionable business suit, she bursts cheerfully into his room. He is still in T-shirt and boxers.

While he shaves and brushes his teeth, she watches the news on TV and outlines his mission through the half-closed bathroom door. "These guys are supergeeks. All they know is software, that's why we thought it would be a good idea if you talked to them about art, maybe philanthropy. Look at that. Poor Monica. The government is spending six million dollars to force her to describe a blow job!"

"It's not as easy as all that," quips Wakefield. He's feeling something generated by the stimulating expression "blow job." It's dirty, it's shameless, nice work, Maggie.

"They wanted an inspirational speaker. We had a hard time finding someone who didn't juggle balls or do card tricks."

Balls, tricks. Maggie is bad this morning. Wakefield nicks his chin. He watches the trickle of blood in the bathroom mirror, then blots it with toilet paper. Philanthropy, huh? His talk is about money and poetry (with a detour in art), not money *for* poetry (or art).

"So you're the guy," she continues. "How did you get into art?"

"Couldn't juggle. I'm not sure I'm *into* art. I may be more into money."

"By the way, I've gotten over your superficial appraisal of last night's wedding performance. I figured you're one of those art critics."

Wakefield's razor stops midstroke. "I'm sorry, too. I travel so much I don't know where I am sometimes. It was callous of me to say anything before I learned more about this place."

In the other room, Maggie smiles. "Well, don't beat yourself up too much. A gay wedding is a fairly unusual thing here. We didn't even have an Italian restaurant in Typical five years ago. That was considered exotic. We had to drive eight miles to the college town to go to Luigi's for spaghetti and meatballs. There was nothing but the tire plant and farms around here. Stingy German farmers . . . they didn't waste money going out. I know. My folks took me to a restaurant twice: on my thirteenth birthday and when I got accepted to college. Everything changed when The Company came. Now we have Thai, Mexican, Italian, Greek, Indian. There's even a Russian restaurant."

Wakefield finishes his toilet and comes back into the room. He puts on his trousers and a clean shirt and watches Maggie watch him. When he misses a button, she rebuttons him. She stands so close he feels the whole warm animal wash over him. Her perfume is familiar and he fancies he knows what her skin feels like. Then she ties his tie. He's embarrassed.

"That's okay. Lots of men can't really tie a tie."

"What happened to the tire plant? And the farmers?"

She sits back on the bed and crosses her legs. Shapely, notes Wakefield. Well-shaped hips in a nicely tailored skirt. A vooman, as Zamyatin might say.

"The factory closed in the seventies. Then my parents sold the farm and moved to a retirement community in Florida. My brother left for college, and my sisters and I went to New York City. I came back here to oversee the sale of the farm and ended up getting hired for public relations at The Company. Now I run Lectures and Events. That's about everything. You saw my kid last night, my darling, the apple of her mommy's eye. . . . And you? Married?"

"Was." Wakefield doesn't want to get into it. He doesn't like the direction of the conversation; it will only lead to a bunch of platitudes, and he prefers going to bed with someone before this kind of questioning. It's purer that way.

"Florida. Are they happy there?"

"Who? My parents? No, not really. My father was a real farmer, man of few words, churchgoer, all that. Florida's his worst nightmare. He says it's full of Jews."

Wakefield lifts an eyebrow.

Maggie shifts uncomfortably.

"Well, he's just one of those people. When the farm was going under, he joined some kind of church that thinks the end of the world is around the corner and that we all have to fight ZOG—the Zionist Occupation Government. My mother finally put an end to that. Now they're just Baptists. The paranoid right wing has gotten a lot quieter since The Company came. It's practically like Seattle here now." Maggie hesitates, shifts gears. "What do you know about money? Are you some kind of investment counselor, too?"

"Oh, no," Wakefield answers sincerely. "The only thing I know about money is that there seems to be a lot of it around these days. Do you own any stock?"

"Sure, I own Company stock, and I buy every new IPO. I buy and sell quickly, but I mostly buy. I invested my small share of the farm money in stuff that would kill my father if he knew about it."

"Like what?"

"Genetic research. Well, come to think of it, he'd probably like that: better crops, fatter cows. An optic fiber manufacturer, an alternative energy consortium, a company researching youth drugs. Cutting-edge stuff." Maggie's very proud of her foresight. "It's all about the future, right?"

"We will all be rich, rich," Wakefield half-sings. "Doesn't it make you nervous?"

"Why should it? We're far from reaching the top of this market."

"But art is the ultimate investment, trust me."

"I prefer tech stocks," she teases. "And it's time to go."

Maggie takes a backward look at the bed. It's only slightly ruffled. Wakefield sleeps all curled up on one side, keeping the covers smooth. He likes to be invisible.

THE COMPANY'S PRIVATE club is called Finland, and it is not what Wakefield expects. From the outside, it still looks like the tire factory it once was, surrounded by snowy fields. It becomes evident, however, that only the shell of the factory has been preserved.

The entry hall is dominated by a Bengal tiger with bared teeth that looks so alive Wakefield draws back. Maggie laughs. Wakefield likes her laughter; it is musical and abrupt, knowing, not childish.

The lunch with the Company muckety-mucks is being held in the elephant room, so known because an African bull elephant with his trunk in the air dominates a long, low table surrounded by silver-embroidered Indian pillows.

"Is it real?" Wakefield inquires, slightly awed.

"Sure is, and so are the Bengal tiger, the polar bear, and the giant anaconda. If you're wondering how they ended up in Typical, one of these guys will tell you the story in suffocating detail."

The room also houses part of The Company's corporate art

collection. Wakefield is pleasantly surprised to see an early, medium-size Jackson Pollock painting and a Robert Motherwell sketch lurking behind the wildlife, along with a surrealist painting of tiny figures walking toward a vortex of light energy, signed V. Brauner. There are two wiry Giacomettis and a flying cow by Chagall, even a sketch of last night's lingerie model and a small-scale model of the notorious *Typical Family* sculpture sans man mounted on a stand under a glass bell.

The room is almost tropically warm. A few Company men are already there, dressed casually in safari-style khaki. Wakefield feels weirdly overdressed in his jacket and tie. He shakes a few hands and squats on an Indian pillow. Maggie sits next to him, her knee on his calf. As more people arrive, Maggie whispers their abbreviated histories into his ear.

"Mr. Farkash. Born in Hungary, billionaire."

Mr. Farkash is one of several billionaires who work for The Company. The idea of a billionaire working at all doesn't seem right to Wakefield. A billion is enough for several generations to be idle, at least. Mr. Farkash doesn't look like a billionaire. His shirt is too tight, there is a button missing over a slight paunch that looks incongruous on so thin a man. His thick, steel-rimmed glasses are smudged.

A deeply tanned younger man in a very expensive suit makes a noisy entrance. Wakefield doesn't feel so overdressed anymore.

"Paulee," whispers Maggie. "Flies airplanes. Ladies' man."

Paulee notices Wakefield studying Farkash, who is nearsightedly inspecting the engraved menu.

"Farkash!" he shouts across the table. "Mr. Wakefield seems very interested in you. Farkash," he says, turning to Wakefield, "emigrated to the U.S. in 1956. He's got one of those math brains that turn up in the tribe for some reason. Eddy Teller has one. Einstein had one. Farkash may even have two." Farkash looks up from the menu, embarrassed, but his tormentor won't let up.

"I've tried to dress him. I flew him to London in my jet, took him to my tailor on Bond Street, even got him as far as the dressing room. He got away somehow. What happened, Farkash?"

"What happened," Farkash says with a heavy accent, "is that the tailor knows our family from Budapest. He had a shop there and we all made credit. When I finish gymnasium, my father bring me to him for graduation suit, and he says no, first you pay me what you owe, so I never make graduation because he make no suit. That time in London I ordered fifteen suits, Paulee, and I paid for them. Only I don't like to wear them. Thank you very much." Farkash burrows back into the menu and everyone laughs, but Paulee isn't finished.

"Let me tell you another story about Farkash. We were in New York at somebody's house, I won't say who because it would end up in the tabloids, and this beautiful woman comes on to Farkash."

"Not just beautiful," adds another guy. "A famous, rich woman."

Obviously they are all in on it, it's a routine. The famous, rich woman took a fancy to Farkash, as it turned out, and asked him right there and then to have sex with her. Only, according to Paulee, she said, "Do you want to fuck?" and our shy genius nearly dropped his glass of ginger ale. But Farkash had a comeback line he must have gotten from a self-help book. "My place or yours?" he stammered, to which the woman replied, "If it's such a hassle, forget about it!"

Even Farkash laughs with the crowd at this oft-told anecdote.

"The funny thing is," Paulee says seriously, "she called him later and invited him to lunch, and *we don't know what happened!*"

Everyone turns expectantly to Farkash, who, resuming his study of the menu says, "Do you think they have the lamb today?"

Two men arrive whom Wakefield recognizes as last night's bride and groom, now neatly dressed in business suits. He looks for signs of lingering mascara, but they are well scrubbed.

"Hey," intones Paulee, "how is married life?"

"Fuck you," says the bride, perfectly at ease.

The Indian meal is vegetarian, with the exception of the lamb for Farkash, which he eats with the avidity of a starving man. Wakefield drinks a huge bottle of Indian beer to wash down his spicy eggplant Vindaloo.

"We are the world," Maggie whispers in his ear. Wakefield thinks of her farmer folk and ZOG and their fears of Jews. It wasn't that long ago.

"Does he engage in any philanthropy?" Wakefield whispers to Maggie, still fascinated by the Hungarian billionaire. "He could create a foundation, do something for Hungary. . . ."

"Farkash? I don't think he has the time. He's one of those guys who will die at his desk with his paychecks uncashed."

A pity. Wakefield once asked his friend Ivan if he would ever go back to Russia. "No," Zamyatin said. "Never." When Wakefield asked why, Ivan confessed with unusual earnestness that he couldn't forgive his country for treating him so badly.

"It wasn't the country, per se," Wakefield had argued, "it was your countrymen."

"What's the difference? Country, countrymen, it's all the same."

Wakefield suggested that since the fall of communism, many exiles felt that it was important to return, to help rebuild after decades of oppression, but Ivan didn't share that sentiment.

There was little else to say, because Zamyatin ordered another drink and started singing "America the Beautiful." End of discussion.

Wakefield's ex-wife, Marianna, was even worse. During their marriage, if he mentioned Romania she'd turn up the music. If he persisted she cried. Her parents were dead, she was an orphan, she had a brother somewhere in Germany, she didn't want to talk about it. Wakefield even went so far as to buy airline tickets for a short visit, but Marianna tore them up with her hands—and teeth. One night when she was drunk she told him a version of her past that might have been true. She had been arrested as a prostitute, mistakenly, she said, and was sent to a reeducation camp. Her parents disowned her.

Her brother, who was her best friend, had escaped to Germany by hiding on a ship leaving the Black Sea port of Constanta. She didn't know if he was dead or alive. He had never written, and many people who stowed away on ships died.

Sometimes she cried in her sleep, or shouted angrily in Romanian, but she wouldn't talk about her dreams in the morning. Wakefield tried to make friends with other émigrés, but she refused to socialize with them, and she wouldn't go to the Romanian Orthodox church for fear that she might run into someone she knew.

Wakefield is still very interested in the former Communist world and its emergence from total state control, fascinated by the relationship between secrecy and exposure, the crumbling of the walls that kept that world out, and the dramatic revelation of worlds hidden literally behind those walls.

Farkash gives him a sly look. He overheard Maggie saying he would die at his desk.

Wakefield decides to come clean. "I might as well ask you, I'm curious to know if you have any interest in Hungary. Are you helping there?"

Lips glistening with lamb fat, Farkash shrugs.

"I think he's comparing you with George Soros," Maggie explains kindly. "It can't be helped, Farkash. People ask."

This exchange doesn't go unnoticed, and other conversations at the table seem to stop.

"I'm sorry," Wakefield says, "I don't mean to embarrass you."

Farkash snorts. "Embarrass a rich man? Are you joking? I am not Soros. I know George. He is a big dreamer, but he wants to be a messiah, he loves risk and he is a gambler. He makes money, he loses money, some he give away. That's his work. I work in other areas."

Paulee jumps in as devil's advocate. "Sure, Farkash, but even Einstein felt social responsibility, he warned Truman about the bomb. And he fucked Marilyn Monroe. Who have you fucked?"

This guy Paulee is a real asshole, thinks Wakefield. The point is that George Soros does more for his old country than all the governments of the West combined. And he doesn't just help his native Hungary, but the whole former Communist bloc, including Russia. During the Nazi occupation he and his whole family risked their lives arranging false documents for Jews about to be deported to death camps. What makes one person so concerned and another so indifferent? Wakefield wonders, aware, even as he thinks it, that such generalizations lead down a slippery slope.

"I don't do these things," says Farkash, completely unfazed, "because I am now using all my time. Maybe next year I will concentrate on what you say, philanthropics, and even . . . that horrible word you use so much, Paulee . . . happiness. For twenty years I will study happiness and you will see results. I am systemic, not foolish gambler."

"You mean 'systematic,'" Paulee corrects him.

"Yes." Farkash goes back to concentrating on the lamb.

Wakefield is impressed by the way frivolity and gravity mix in this high-tech world, and he has new respect for Maggie, whose job is to arrange entertainment for these highly educated, idiosyncratic workers stuck in the middle of nowhere. The ratio between frivolity and gravity is a serious issue in his own life, and the balance changes constantly. Between him and Zamyatin frivolity claims the greater percentage, but in all his other relationships, including the one between himself and his ex-wife and their daughter, seriousness dominates. With Zelda things seem to balance out. Nah, he corrects himself, Zelda is serious, even if she is flaky. It's Wakefield who's frivolous: most of the time he can't even take himself seriously. He's just a talker with wide but not terribly deep interests. He should have made an entirely different bargain with the Devil. Instead of asking for a year free to pursue alternatives to his life, he should have asked for an overwhelming interest in *something*. A science, a passion, a problem to absorb him *completely*.

The Devil, curled cozily inside the elephant's head, surveys the room through the beast's big eyes, through which the glimmer of his own yellow orbs flashes occasionally, noticed only by Paulee, who attributes the vision to last night's excess of Veuve Cliquot. The Devil follows the conversation with interest: Wakefield's probing on behalf of social responsibility worries him a little. Is there a Mother Theresa inside his client? That would certainly imperil his victory. The Devil's position on suffering is complex: he enjoys it in its pure state, he relishes anguish, profound despair, fury and anger at God. At the same time he hates social injustice. The unfair advantages of the rich and the equally arbitrary misery of the poor lessen his enjoyment of suffering in its purer form, unadulterated by circumstances that make it inevitable. The rich prepackage the misery of the poor. The taste of supermarket meat is abhorent to the hunter. What avails a devil prepackaged misery, flavorless, predetermined unhappiness? Suffering without grandeur is like polenta without salt. This is not an idle comparison: the Devil personally brought corn from the New World and prepared the first polenta in Europe. But that's another story, though a major triumph. He admires philanthropy's attempt to even the playing field. When the recipients of philanthropy begin to thrive and thus suffer in more bourgeois terms, they begin to be worth something to him. He closes his eyes, to Paulee's relief, and reviews a thousand years of great philanthropists parading wistfully to the cosmic barbeque pit, followed by a few of their successful beneficiaries. Ah. The Devil then reaches for a little jar of ointment in the pocket of his blue jeans. He unscrews the lid, dips his finger in it, and spreads the cream on his lips, pleasantly numbing them. Crème-de-philanthropist, an essence of the suffering rich, extracted from their fat. *Ah, quel élixir!* He briefly considers propelling one of the elephant's eyeballs to the middle of the table, right on top of the onion bread. What a shot! But would Wakefield recognize the ordnance of the starter pistol? Perhaps not; he seems more concerned at the moment with

Maggie's upper thigh, on which he has lightly laid his hand. Let the children play. The Diablo has a soft spot for Eros: it leads to exquisite misery.

When lunch breaks up, Wakefield asks Maggie to take him back to the hotel. She can see his mood has darkened and lets him be. Maybe I really could work for this Company, he thinks, toying with the idea. The stuff they make is new; even the word *software* is mysterious, like an artwork: it comes fresh into the world and starts invisibly connecting people. And Maggie has good instincts. If I got rich, I could help people.

After Maggie drops him off, he goes to the hotel spa and sits for a long time in the steam room with a couple of guys from the breast pump convention. Then he orders a special massage. Tightly bound in an herbal wrap, he is left to float alone inside a limestone cave dripping perfumed tears. But he's not at peace. Tonight he has to tell the people in this Company town something that he, and they, will believe.

"AND NOW FOR 'Money and Poetry (with a Detour in Art): A Speech.' Ladies and gentlemen of the Overworking Class: In my business, which is unlike any other business, maybe because it's not a business at all, in my business, you can say something off the cuff, spontaneously, and then spend years trying to figure out what you said. No inspirational speaker worthy of the title would want to know what he is going to say before he says it. That would be both cheating and boring. A speaker such as myself depends on revelation."

Wakefield pauses here, a long, dramatic pause that gives the six hundred spectators in the comfortable seats of the airy amphitheater an opportunity to consider what might be revealed by someone who has no idea what he is going to say. How inefficient, quite the opposite of making a presentation for one's colleagues with PowerPoint and notes; but how very like those first moments on a blind date! They make themselves comfortable as Wakefield reads their minds. He turns his eyes heavenward, as if awaiting said revelation.

"Of course, there is an equivalent to revelation in your professions. When that apple fell on Newton's head, it set him off on a lifetime of trying to prove the truth of that boink. Whether apocryphal or not, that story's made many bright kids sit hopefully under trees of one sort or another waiting for a falling fruit. Not every fruit is Newton's apple. Some are just unripe figs or withered plums. I'm speaking metaphorically here, but I'll quit, I swear, as soon as I channel something real. All I know is that I'm constantly trying to figure out why I said what I said—and then when I figure it out, I forget about it and say something else that eventually needs explanation, and I'm not sure which one of those things is important, which one is an apple and which one a withered plum, a.k.a. prune. Of course, the apple doesn't matter. Apples fall on all kinds of heads that are not Newton's. What matters is that the apple fell on Newton's head, no one else's."

He waits for members of the audience to consider whether they are Newton or not.

"I belong to a club dedicated to making apples fall on peoples' heads, The Apples On Heads Club. Some of the members are dead, like Herman Melville, Walt Whitman, Nathaniel Hawthorne, William Blake, Marcel Duchamp, Ted Berrigan, and Jack Kerouac, but others, like myself and my friend Ivan Zamyatin, a taxicab driver and poet, are alive. Death, by the way, is no impediment in this club. A few years ago, a literary journal commissioned a then living poet, James Merrill, to interview dead poets via the Ouija board. He discovered two clubs of dead poets in the Afterlife: the Straight Club, led by William Carlos Williams, and the Gay Club, led by Gertrude Stein. Merrill found the Gay Club a lot more fun than the Straight Club, but I'd like a second opinion on that. I think Merrill associated free verse with straight sex and gay sex with the bondage of form. There are, however, plenty of gay dead free-verse poets, Frank O'Hara, to mention just one, and really boring dead formal straight poets. And what about the bisexual club? Or the ascetic club? I know poets who are bisexual, and a couple who are ascetic."

He glances at Maggie in the front row. She looks mortified. Why is he going on about the sex lives of poets? She wishes she'd hired the juggler. The room is full of people whose desks are humming at this very moment with the technical pressures of the electronic globe. They need inspiration, where is the inspiration? Wakefield continues, only slighty perturbed.

"I am a poet."

Laughter in the audience.

"You laugh because you don't know what a poet is. A poet is the most creative being alive, a being who says things like 'Ah, Sunflower, weary of time!' or 'I have seen what other men have only *thought* they've seen.' And when they say such things, they keep saying them, repeating them over and over until they are filled by what they just said and until the whole world repeats after them, 'Ah, Sunflower, weary of time! I have seen what other men have only *thought* they've seen.' Now repeat after me:

"'Ah, Sunflower, weary of time!'"

A few embarrassed voices mumble after him. It sounds like a single word: "AWSFLAWAME!" And again. Soon Wakefield has everyone repeating the lines, and people are laughing and shouting as if this is the funniest thing they've ever said out loud. Childishness breaks out. It's good. Maggie is smiling.

"IHSEENTAMATHODSCEEN!"

Wakefield lets the noise die down. They trust him. They think they know what this is about. Some of these people are from the West Coast: they have shared feelings, held hands, sat in hot tubs together, done art therapy, howled at the moon in expensive resorts. In their childhoods there were campfires and singalongs. This is America, a land of joy. This is *fun*. But Wakefield notes that there are also a number of sullen faces. Foreigners. Russians, who never smile. Indians, who smile, but not innocently. Pakistanis, whose mustaches are trembling angrily. Hungarians, smirking. To them, Wakefield now addresses a mournful addendum.

"Creative activity is full of abandoned original utterances and one-of-a-kind failed experiments. But how do the rich get rich and stay rich? Exactly like poets. The rich find something that works and they do it over and over until it stops paying off. How do scientists discover something? They repeat and repeat the experiment. Only their spouses know just how *much* they repeat themselves. You know that bored, desperate, neurotic, on-the-verge-of-a-nervous-breakdown look that the spouses of the wealthy have in soap operas? Well, the reason for this despondency is the unconscionable number of times they've heard their mates say the same thing over and over. It is the same with the spouses of scientists and poets. It is the same with all creative people. *Yes, honey, I know, you said that already.*"

Not as many guffaws as Wakefield would like. The reason might be that Company spouses also work for The Company and are equally repetitive.

"Only children are not bored by repetition: they are surprised by it. They anticipate it with delight. How is it possible for a marvelous thing to reappear in the exact same form only a second later? On the other hand—and I'm speaking for children here—how could things *fail* to repeat themselves? A tired parent who makes the mistake of shortening the bedtime story by leaving out a repetition or two is in for a tantrum. What happened to repetition number eight, Daddy? Those of you who repeat certain experiments over and over know what the children mean. You cannot leave out a DNA combination because it looks mind-numbingly similar to the one that came before. Happily, computers don't get bored, which is why they are saving our sorry sleepy ass over and over."

The Devil, seated in the projection booth above the room, dressed in cap and knickers like a projectionist of silent movies, doesn't like the drift of Wakefield's talk. He suspects that his client is pursuing a deconstructive agenda that, after a few detours in art, will take him down to the elemental building blocks of matter, possibly, for the purpose of exposing *him,* the Great Malign One, hooves and all, before this conclave of geeks. The Devil hates to be seen. Or Wakefield may be after even bigger game; he may intend to shed his body and become pure talk, just a stream of words funneling like a twister out of a djinni bottle. In that case he might escape entirely, and the Devil would be left holding nothing but a wrinkled skin surrounded by a voice coming out of nowhere and everywhere. He may be wrong about this, but just in case, he lets his gaze drift over the heads of the assembled and shoots a quiverful of rays into the room, causing particular movies to unroll in each and every head. For good measure, he casts around a few itches as well.

Wakefield is saying, "Children know intuitively that we exist in a world that is born of and lives by repetition. Life itself proceeds by replication," but the audience is seeing black-and-white film images of scenes from their lives. An artificial intelligence specialist sees his father kneeling beside a bed, slowly pulling up a woman's stocking as she holds her leg out to him. A marketing analyst squeezes in anger the teddy bear that his older brother has just made wet with some unspeakable substance. A virtual reality designer drops the chalice at her first communion and sees big drops of red wine stand in relief on her white patent-leather shoes. A Russian engineer watches a pancake being slowly rolled up by a mean boy from his school as his beloved Pioneer neckerchief disappears inside of it. At the same time, the marketing analyst experiences an unbearable itch between two toes on his left foot and has to scratch it or die. He takes off his shoe and scratches away. The AI specialist feels something lodged between two back teeth and cannot wait another moment to dislodge it, whatever it is. Meat? He'll never eat meat again. The virtual reality designer wishes now that she'd never gone home with that Russian guy from the disco: her crotch is burning but it's a different sort of itch. She slips her right hand between her legs as discreetly as she can. Farkash sinks lower in his seat: he sees himself perched on the steep-pitched red roof of his family house in the village; his mother is calling him in to wash before dinner. An insect is crawling in his armpit, making it tickle dreadfully; he can barely keep his balance. Farkash rakes at the offending pit.

And so on, until everyone in the room is caught in a silent film of embarrassment or in the throes of physical discomforts that call for instant remedy. The room shifts, sways, rustles. Good show, laughs El Diablo, I *should* be a filmmaker. Then he remembers. He is. Not just one filmmaker, but many. The movie guides list hundreds of his works.

Is Wakefield disturbed by all the fidgeting? Yes and no. You can't expect to make a deal with the Devil and not be interrupted. This may be His Interruptiousness's very nature. The long, uninterrupted peace of paradise was shattered for good by Lucifer. Nothing's been completed since. Not a thought, not a speech. Of course, Wakefield isn't aware that the Devil is actually in the room, but it's safe to attribute *all* fuckups to Satan. That way one has deniability. Wakefield is determined to ignore the distractions of his audience. He's inspired by the certainty that he really truly doesn't know where he's going, so why stop now? His listeners can fidget all they want and take from him what they will. Besides, being interrupted gives you a chance to think. He decides he likes being interrupted, he *needs* to be interrupted. He perseveres.

"So children, who are just discovering language, and poets, who can't get over it, have a marvelous tool for confounding themselves and others. My friend Ivan Zamyatin says that language is a splendid alien, shipwrecked on our planet, who was captured by apes and hacked to bits. The English bit is from its neck."

Maggie imagines the shipwrecked alien, silicon-based perhaps, strewn about like a dismembered mannequin. Two Saxons and a Gaul break his neck into chunks like a loaf of bread and eat it. The English language is born. She can see that. She's a farm girl.

The Devil turns red: not fair. How did Zamyatin guess that? It was true, he had seen the shipwreck himself and had, proud to say, helped himself to a few alien crumbs. Right now, in his pocket, he carries seven or eight words that have never been spoken on earth, and never will be. He feels them there. Vowely. Long. Dark. Yum.

"Now let's examine the nature of success. A poet feels successful when he has written a great line. A software designer, when he clinches a patent. A rich man, when he's made another million. I know that most of you at The Company are techies, and some of you are rich, very rich. . . . It's said that The Company is bigger than the Catholic Church, so God pops up naturally here. When the Messiah returns, he won't be going to Jerusalem, he'll be coming here to the Midwest, to the headquarters of The Company."

Scattered applause.

"But is being bigger than God a good thing? It doesn't mean you *are* God. John Lennon told a reporter that the Beatles were bigger than Jesus Christ. The fallout was definitely not good. It occurs to me that if the Messiah did show up in Typical, she might be put in the paper shredder before anyone could perceive her divine nature. Or, worse, divinity might interfere with the productive rhythms of the workday and disrupt the idyllic life that you lead here in the best-possible-workplace-on-Earth, and that won't do. Pity, for instance, the government that files suit against The Company! God, you'll remember, didn't want any competition from his creation, so he split up Adam and Eve in order that the separated halves might compete with each other, leaving Him the absolute boss. That was in biblical times. In capitalist society, the biblical God is just another product, the real divinity is the Economy, with a capital E, and the government is its visible mouthpiece. Heretics say that there are a lot of gods, but even if this is true, the underlying principle is the same, no matter what their names: if you get bigger than me I'll bust you up."

Voice from the crowd: "What the hell are you talking about?"

My sentiments exactly, thinks the Devil. God? Has Wakefield gone bonkers? Is he making a pitch to the other side? Or what he *thinks* is the other side? The Devil laughs. He hasn't thought about God in a long time. It's like a former employer or an ex-wife, you rarely give them a thought if you can help it. Personally, he's always had the utmost respect for God, for not interfering. Admirable detachment. God is sleeping, let Him rest in peace.

Unfortunately, Wakefield seems to think that God is still paying attention. He can't be that stupid. You keep doing that, El Diablo silently admonishes, and you'll end up dead *and* sorry. God gave up on your kind a long time ago. When is the last time the likes of Wakefield had a sign from the Creator? As for the Messiah, the Devil begs to differ. The Messiah concept is the result of one of many deals his kingdom made with Yahweh before His big nap. Some of the terms are still secret, but it boils down to deterence: each side has a Messiah ready to go at any given time. If the powers of darkness launch their Messiah first, the other one will activate automatically, without disturbing God's sleep. It's mutual assured destruction, a MAD policy if you will, and it's worked fine so far. The Devil knows that Wakefield is only using *God* and *Messiah* metaphorically, but still, it's a serious issue; don't put your foot in it or you'll end up eating that foot, toes and all. Or maybe—the Devil pauses thoughtfully, biting his hoof—this Wakefield character is more clever than I think. Has he made another deal with one of my confederates? A chatty, indiscreet devil? Paranoia. Bad habit. But it's not unheard of for one devil to go behind another's back. You can never be too sure.

"What are you talking about?" insists the heckler, a bit more exasperated now.

You go, girl, the Devil urges.

"I'll know soon enough," says Wakefield, and somehow he does. "Robert Frost wrote, 'Something there is that doesn't love a wall,' and Ted Berrigan answered, 'I *am* that Something.' Well, I know something that's worth a lot of money. If I tell it to you—not the whole thing, of course, just a teaser—you'll *want* to give me as much money as I can carry to hear the rest of it. And I might or might not tell you everything. I don't really *need* any money, I just think that it might be fun to play with yours."

Voice: "Isn't *that* a classic hustle?" Wakefield loves it: hecklers are the spice in a great what-will-he-say-next presentation.

"Well, here it is. Please pay close attention because I will be as surprised as you are by what I'm about to say."

He pauses, scanning the faces in the audience. They would *like* to pay attention, but things itch.

"The currency of the future is poetry.

"I will repeat this, following the poetic-scientific formula I outlined earlier.

"The currency of the future is poetry.

"The currency of the future is poetry.

"Say it with me, folks!

"THECURRENCYOFTHEFUTUREISPOETRY."

Only Maggie joins in; there is some hissing in the upper tiers of the theater. Someone up in the projection booth shouts, "Viva prose!" It doesn't phase Wakefield. Bring on the philistines.

"In the future, money as we know it now will be useless—it already is. Instead of using these particular abstract units we call currency, we will use poetry to conduct our transactions. Poetry is the highest expression of any language. Money is also a language: you may think that the words of this language belong to you, but they are being spoken at this very moment by a multitude. It's eleven A.M. Central Standard Time; do you know where your money is? It may be in a shipment of rifles headed for Colombia or it may be stuck in a computer in Hong Kong. You may be speaking its name or in its name, but the actual money is as fluid as language, it flows, it's everywhere and nowhere at once, and anyone can speak in this language, not a word of it is copyrighted. When Richard Nixon took America off the gold standard, he put money firmly in the province of the imaginary; money became something that has to be taken on faith. In the realm of the abstract, currency will not rule, *creation* will. Take a million dollars, which isn't much, you can spend that for lunch in some places—a million dollars takes up a lot of space if you're going to use greenbacks. You can't transport it very easily. But if you exchange that dough for a work of art, let's say one of the cheaper paintings of Robert Motherwell, you can roll it up inside a hollow cane and limp across the border with it."

Wakefield is thinking that if he could only get his hands on a few of the canvases he saw at the Company mess hall, he'd roll them up inside a cane and limp back home and he'd never have to take another job like this again.

The Devil loves the bit about the cane. Canes have been part of his wardrobe since time immemorial. His first cane was a branch he tore off a tree after his fiery fall from Paradise to a mountainside in Thrace. He'd twisted his ankle on landing, and he limped about leaning on that flowering branch until he found a cave, his first cave. He killed a mountain goat with his cane and made a flute from a leg bone, a hat from the horns, a shirt from the fur, and a knife from a rib. One night he played his flute and fell asleep with his horns on. When he woke up there were three nymphs in the cave, as smooth and naked as Eve. They gave themselves to him night after night when he played the flute. They disappeared whenever he took off his horns, so he took the horns off when he was tired of nymphs. Alone, he used the bone knife to fashion canes. When he felt lonely he played the flute and the nymphs reappeared, sometimes the original three, sometimes others. Bored after a long time, he began to wander, killing new animals, changing his appearance, carving new canes from wood and bone, but always keeping his first flute, cane, and horns nearby. Over time, his flute and his first cane acquired all sorts of powers. They could draw to them creatures of every sort who listened raptly to his music, or they could lift him through the air to cavort with birds. In later ages, his various canes were made of rare woods and precious metals, encrusted with stones. He'd collected sword canes with deadly blades belonging to princes whose souls he gathered. He'd transported magic scrolls, money, and yes, even pictures by famous artists, in hollowed-out canes. Some artists he had never been able to persuade to give him a work, like the Master Theodoricus, a Bohemian monk so horrified that one of his devotional works might end up in Satan's collection, he had himself crucified. The fool, Beelzebub snarls, remembering Theodoricus, you thought you were painting for God, inspired by angels, but you would have been part of the greatest gallery in the world. He really should revisit his treasures, stored in his innumerable caves, and have some of them framed. As for Wakefield, his boy is on the right track now. Nothing wrong with envy and a little greed.

Wakefield continues, oblivious to the Devil's digressions. "What, you may be wondering, makes a Robert Motherwell painting worth a million dollars? The common agreement of a few esthetes backed by a dubious appraisal at Christie's? Not at all. What makes a Robert Motherwell painting worth a million dollars is its uniqueness as a work of art made by the one and only Robert Motherwell. When you see a Robert Motherwell painting, you know immediately that Robert Motherwell had no idea what he was going to paint before he painted it. The value of the painting is in what is discovered when one has no idea what he is looking for. And that goes for both Motherwell and the viewer of Motherwell's painting."

The heckler pipes up: "When is the fire sale?"

The Devil finds himself in total agreement with Wakefield. Like souls and fingerprints, art is singular, it is a product of a man's spirit, of his evolving complexity. Unlike milk from many cows, for instance, it never has the same texture and flavor from one artist to another.

"Buddhist monks create, over many days, an intricate mandala from grains of colored sand. When the mandala is complete, they sweep it away with great ceremony. The form of the mandala is traditional; no deviation is allowed. The monk-artists work to recreate the same design in exactly the same way it's been done for thousands of years. The point is the practice, which is a form of meditation. The final product is irrelevant, a mere material object, only a by-product of spiritual discipline. The difference between a modern artist and a Buddhist monk is in the approach. The artist goes into the void empty and returns with a souvenir, if you will. The monk approaches the void with a traditional body of knowledge and arrives at emptiness. Our world, no less than that of the monks, is full of junk that gets in the way of spiritual practice. The artist plays with the junk, the monk orders it into nothingness. The final product has monetary value only for those outside the process. It is a grotesque accretion of its creator's impurities, a truly filthy object that should be disposed of as quickly as possible, either destroyed or sold in a gallery. Its value is directly proportional to the necessity to eliminate it. The more a work cries out for obliteration, the more valuable it is. It is at the point of greatest contradiction, at the crossroads between its impulses to self-destruct or to continue, that money enters the picture."

Amazingly, Farkash's accented basso pierces the silence: "I can agree with this!" Heads turn toward Farkash, whose views on anything outside mathematics are completely unknown. Embarassed, he mutters, "Hmmm," then, "Sorry," and folds his arms across his chest.

The Devil snorts. He hates Buddhists. It's personal. Buddhists don't recognize his importance. As far as they are concerned, he is just one among many manifestations of the next world. Buddhists have gone as far as to put all the devils they can imagine on a wheel, half of which is occupied by angels. The devils and the angels have equal status and, as the wheel turns, equal opportunities to manifest. The demons and the angels are just different aspects of one another: ugly is beautiful and vice versa. Absolutely no discrimination. The Devil's whole sense of self, which is based on a sense of aristocratic election, is offended by this treatment. He's also offended by the Buddhists' indifference to images, their treatment of art as a superficial manifestation of action, a nervous by-product they seek to eradicate through meditation. An accomplished Buddhist lives in a void made by the erasure of the material world. Imagine an emptiness where all is potential and equal. No emotions, no passions, no crime, no ecstasy, no suffering, no guilt, no reason to make a big deal about anything. It's too depressing. Even more egregious is the growing appeal of Buddhism in his beloved Western world, the center of wealth, the fountainhead of objects and images. A few years ago, a man who abandoned all earthly pursuits and withdrew from his "normal" life would have been put in a mental institution. But because he's a Buddhist, well, now it's okay. Disgusting!

Wakefield is encouraged: Farkash has responded the way his Austro-Hungarian ancestors might have interacted with any performance:

they stood and shouted and expressed their feelings. If he can bring out the eighteenth century in a shy mathematician, he should have no problem lifting optimistic fin-de-twentieth-century Americans to the peak of confusion—before he dashes them on the rocks, of course.

"Money undergoes a conversion when one has more of it than is strictly necessary. When there is enough of it to move beyond the strict survival mode, money goes in search of beauty. That is to say, in search of the abstract and the imaginary. Just like poetry, which is the distillation of an excess of language. Too much money and too many words tend toward the poetic. Most people stand between their money and what money wants to do, because people are afraid, and fear leads to boredom. Not many people have a natural inclination to spend their money on objects of art or fanciful ideas. These bored, frightened people want money to simply reproduce, repeat itself. This activity of unimaginative repetition takes a great deal of attention and intention and leaves people exhausted and empty and keeps money prosaic. If you can't use it imaginatively, it's better to let money do its own thing. Money is becoming more and more imaginary all the time: the tenuous agreements that make for value are changing faster than you can think about them."

Fine, thinks the Devil. He leans out of the window of the projectionist's booth and in an instant evaporates the contents of the audience's pockets and purses. Their wallets, cash, credit cards, IDs, PDAs, cell phones, pagers, and keys, all gone. Everyone feels lighter. They shift in their seats, unaware that they've been pickpocketed.

Voices from the crowd: "Is the value of art obvious?" "What about poetry?" "Whose money are you talking about? Not mine, I hope!" He's got them: confusion reigns, the anxiety is real.

"I'm getting to that. The only thing more useless and unique than a Robert Motherwell painting is a poem. Take this poem:

"I don't think that I shall ever see

"A poem as beautiful

"As my TV."

Wakefield draws a C inside a circle in the air, then asks the audience to repeat after him:

"I don't think that I shall ever see

"A poem as beautiful

"As my TV."

This time the audience joins in, although several people leave the theater. Maggie is laughing her sudden laugh.

"This poem is worth one billion dollars. Why? Because I say so. A friend of mine wrote it. If you want that poem, you'll have to give him a billion dollars. If you all agree that this poem is worth a billion dollars—and I don't see why you shouldn't—then that poem *is* worth a billion dollars, and if you buy it you can memorize it and it's good anywhere you go in the world—you just go to the bank and draw as much as you want on it."

Scattered laughter, some applause, then a few sounds of distress. Some people, conditioned to pat their wallets whenever the subject is money, pat their pockets and don't feel their wallets. Discreetly, they begin searching their pockets.

"Just because this poem is made out of language and anyone can write it down or remember it and ignore that small C with a circle around it that I just drew in the air without anyone noticing . . . But really, you think it's worthless, don't you? Well, let's look at it a little closer. It isn't a very long poem, so it shouldn't take very long to take it apart. It only has two ideas in it: the idea of Beauty and the idea of TV. The poem itself is a ripoff of an older poem that used the word *tree* instead of TV: 'I think that I shall never see / a poem as lovely as a tree.' So it's not even very original, not like a poem by Cavafy, for instance. So these two ideas, Beauty and TV, are made equivalent here, which is as solid a base for equivalency as the one between gold and currency used to be. Beauty is indeed in the eye of the beholder, so it's firmly in the realm of the imaginary, just like money. On the other hand, TV is composed finitely of what you people are fond of calling content, which pours out in huge gobs of slop into American homes every day. Beauty will always be ahead of any 'content' produced now or in the future, because I can change the shape and meaning of it at will, or as much as my imagination can imagine. So the equivalency between beauty and content is only provisional, just like gold and money used to be, and if I decide to take beauty off the content standard, then nobody but me will have the key to it. This is precisely the fear that drives content providers now, the fear that people will change their minds about what constitutes beauty. It's a completely well-founded fear because people *do* change their minds about content. They are quickly bored and they demand greater and greater imagination in their content. Matter of fact, the only certainty driving the economy is the certainty that boredom at faster and faster rates is inevitable."

Nervous whispers in the crowd are beginning now. "Damn, I must have left everything in the office!" "Where the hell are my keys?" "What the fuck?" But rising clear above these whispers is the sudden voice of the Hungarian billionaire: "Now you're getting somewhere, Mr. Wakefield!"

The Devil is amused but anxious. He's enjoying the rising tide of distress in the room, but he fears that Wakefield really may get away from him. He's turning what had been a fairly simple deal, based on the clear understanding that his life might continue if he could prove in a *material* way that he was worth the Devil's time, into something far more murky: quite cleverly, Wakefield has introduced into the equation imagination, a realm where anything is possible, even the nonexistence of the Devil himself. One thing about a deal, any kind of deal: it must take place firmly within the bounds of Newtonian physics. Still, the Devil cannot quite believe that Wakefield isn't after something tangible. He's a con man, after all, a tent preacher. The Devil has conned lots of people himself, judging by the number of them sticking those stupid fish emblems to their car bumpers.

"So imagination, or the lack of it, is a problem for both producers and consumers. To stay competitive, content providers need more and more imagination, and the more they use up, the more people want. The speeding cycle of production-consumption–consumption-production has been analyzed by economists and by sociologists, but what they ignore is that this cycle is taking place within the realm of the Imaginary."

Right, Mr. Wakefield. Let's have the punchline.

"And in this realm, which doesn't resemble in the least the models economists or sociologists use, poets hold all the cards. If I go back to the original of my billion-dollar poem, I, too, can say 'only God can make a tree.' So we are back to God. TV and what it gives us can be the equivalent of beauty in a bad parody, but the truth of the matter is that the natural world remains the basis for all value. So it is in relation to the natural world, or 'nature' that we must measure our human world. Or, to put it another way, virtuality has a boss: Reality."

Farkash is out of his seat. "You are contradicting yourself! Reality is a construct!"

The impatient Diablo puts a lump in Farkash's throat, making him unable to speak. Butt out, Farkash. Of course Wakefield is contradicting himself. But nature, that's his beat and he likes to hear it praised.

"Yes, Mr. Farkash, but Reality is the oldest virtuality there is, and it has more layers than we can ever understand. Money is virtual, but of recent vintage. The best hope for people who have too much of it is to turn it into something 'natural,' but it's hard to say what that is anymore. The only thing people know—and they are right—is that the road to this 'nature'—and I don't mean the kind you see in SUV commercials—goes through the kingdom of the Imaginary. There is no other way to it. Not-yet-written poems are the most valuable commodity your money can buy. They *are* money. Of course, the poem or the painting, once it is purchased, self-destructs, and in so doing destroys its owner. The 'content' of any work of art is an attack, or at the very least a satire, on materialism. What is most interesting about a work of art cannot be owned, though it can be displayed. But at night, when your guests have gone home, you better turn the damn thing with its face toward the wall, or cover it with a tarp, or lock it in a safe, if you don't want to have nightmares. The content value of art is proportional to the amount of anxiety it produces in its owner."

Pandemonium breaks out. People are hunting for their wallets under the seats in front of them. Some of them are simultaneously scratching and searching. There is cursing in several languages. Only Paulee, who is sitting in the front row, is smiling calmly. He knows precisely what Wakefield means: he owns more artworks than anyone in the room, but he doesn't live with them. He has stashed them all in bank vaults and lives in an airplane that is spare and clean, containing only a working desk, a baptismal fountain full of wine, and a bed. In addition to the physical art he has stored in places where he rarely looks at it, he has bought the electronic rights to most of the acknowledged masterpieces in the world, including the collections of the Tate, the Metropolitan Museum, and the Hermitage, and those images rest quite safely in cyberspace, available by subscription to anyone who needs them. The image of a weeping first girlfriend abandoned in a cornfield in Iowa slips right off the polished surface of Paulee's mind. So what if his pockets are empty.

Wakefield is now shouting over the din: "Take another quality of money: strength. Money confers strength on its owner, which can turn into power if used with any degree of skill. Strength is the ability to live with paradox, to keep two or more contradictory things in mind at the same time. That's also Freud's definition of sanity. If you can live with a painting that aims to kill you in your sleep and you know it, you are strong. Of course, if you don't know it, you are just stupid and that's not strength—your vanity will sooner or later be revealed."

Wakefield is on a roll now. He could care less whether the Devil himself is in the audience.

The Devil senses his defiance and is getting angry. Maybe now is the time for the starter pistol, Wakefield. We'll make it real loud and clear and unmistakable. He positions a small cannon at the window of the projection booth. What kind of missile should he use? An exploding apple full of nails? A rain of wallets and keys? A huge ball containing the compressed contents of Wakefield's apartment? But he checks himself. Why rush things? They are just getting interesting. Has he become so accustomed to the intellectual frailty and moral softness of postmodern man that he can't handle a real adversary? If Wakefield is one. He may be a real idiot, and all this talk just a smokescreen for hiding his fear. Patience.

"The reason most people want to have a lot of money is so that other people won't laugh at them. In the past—like the 1980s—the rich were purposely ostentatious and so obviously nouveau riche that everybody laughed at them.

"But these days the horror of being laughed at has overcome the temptation to feel giddy about money. In addition to that understandable terror of waking up and having hair like Donald Trump's, having too much money can make a person feel guilty. Understandably, people want to assuage their guilt with philanthropy. Generosity, a.k.a. philanthropy, is as American as . . . well, you know, french fries. An unphilanthropic American is a failed citizen, an aberration that our national identity will not tolerate. Even Al Capone set up soup kitchens."

There is some applause, but most of the remaining people are so upset about their empty pockets, they fail to rise to a higher plane. Only Farkash, unable to speak, experiences a conversion. He begins planning a charitable foundation to propel Hungary into the twenty-first century.

"But here again we run into the problem of the imagination. You can give your money to gray bureaucratic institutions and assuage your guilty conscience, but you will remain outside the creative process. Money is a language and, just like language, it can be boring or it can be inspired. The Spanish poet Federico García Lorca said, *'No se puede vivir sin amor,'* and I'll paraphrase that: *'No se puede vivir sin* imagination.'"

The Devil knows suddenly that he's right to have waited. Here comes the pitch.

"For all these reasons I have created the School for the Imagination. The school caters to people who want to understand and create a poetics of money. Some of you may be suffering from SWS (Sudden Wealth Syndrome, i.e., 'I got the house and the boat, now what?') or from TBS (Terminal Boredom Syndrome). Our staff consists of poets. Some of the course offerings are: How to Speak Money and Create Giddiness & Freedom in the World, How to Set Up Simple Religions That Employ Small Gods & Deprogram Fanatics, Enjoying Simple Pleasures Without Reaching for Your Wallet, Feeling Loved While Everyone Hates Your Guts. Students are taught how to regain the imaginations they lost as their fortunes were gained. Using a ten-point system in which each million dollars is regarded as losing its owner one full IU (Imagination Unit), the program seeks to attenuate the sterility and affective waste that can lead, in extreme cases of billion-dollar fortunes, to a total loss of humanity."

Wakefield hasn't been so good in years—never been hotter, in fact. A half-mocking voice from the crowd asks: "Where do we sign up?" Wakefield gives them the school's imaginary URL: schoolforthe imagination.com.

"Thank you for your time, ladies and gentlemen, I hope I have stimulated you! Now, if anyone has a question?"

A dozen people stand up in the audience, waving their hands. "Where's my wallet? You're just a cheap magician! You're no Houdini! Give it back!" A very serious young woman can be heard above all others: "Are you trying to tell us that we live in a dream world?"

Instantly Wakefield answers: "Yes. When you are dreaming, you don't know that you are dreaming. You just get a clue now and then and it scares you. It scares me. I made a deal with the Devil and I'm waiting for the starter pistol. But that's another story."

Indeed. The Devil abandons the projectionist's clothes behind the booth and takes off to his first cave in the Balklands for some R and R. People these days can be so taxing! Oh. He waves a hoof over the room, and the audience's belongings return to them. He sips a bit of the ensuing confusion like a tropical cocktail through a straw. Mmm. Nothing like it: fruits of mayhem.

Maggie bounds onto the stage smiling. "Friends, let's not tire our guest. Let's give him a good hand, a strong round of applause. I've learned a lot."

Maggie whisks Wakefield backstage to a door leading outside, applause dying out behind them. She hustles him into her SUV before anyone in the crowd has a chance to follow and, perhaps, rough him up.

THAT NIGHT, WAKEFIELD and Maggie have a quiet dinner together.

"What the hell was that about?" she asks him.

Wakefield laughs. "Damned if I know."

"I'll have to do some serious damage control," she says, but she's not angry. On the contrary. She's aroused.

A not-so-mysterious feeling passes between them. They have a nightcap in his room.

"Adultly speaking," says Wakefield, "should we fuck?"

"If there is some lovemaking involved," says Maggie.

The thing between them thickens and vibrates like an orange made out of light, and soon Wakefield is inside Maggie, thinking nothing, imagining nothing. He sinks. They travel. Afterward, exhausted and sweaty, he thinks that ideally all journeys should be the kind people have while making love.

"This is why I travel," he says out loud, knowing he shouldn't. It sounds crass.

Maggie opens her eyes lazily. "What do you mean by that?"

He explains that a long time ago he used to hide. It was a compulsion that had begun in his childhood. He hid from people, but it was not from shyness or fear. Hiding excited him. Then he became a restless traveler, and sometimes it seems that all his journeys end in women. He tells her about Marianna, how he found her at the very moment he had decided that travel leads nowhere.

"I know," says Maggie, lying on her tummy, her lovely ass rising above her dimpled coccyx, "that you think I want you to tell me about your ex-wife, and maybe I do, but I'm more intrigued by this hiding business. What do you mean you *used to* hide? You bury the bone pretty good. . . ." She looks up at him and smirks approvingly. "Is that what you mean? Hiding the bone? Or however that expression goes?"

"Burying the bone. Hiding the sausage." Wakefield tries to sound pedantic.

"Whatever. About the hiding," she persists.

This is difficult. Wakefield has a neurotic habit he doesn't often disclose. He told his ex-wife and soon regretted it. The only other soul privy to this information is Ivan. He's only just met Maggie. On the other hand, confessing to a stranger . . .

Maggie's right on top of his dilemma. "I did a stint tending bar, you know, and people told me everything. Bartenders are like priests, they say."

"Maybe you could get it out of me with torture?" Wakefield teases.

She leaps on top of his back and grabs his hair and pulls. Ouch. "It's torture if you don't tell me. Or death. You tell me, I let you live, Scheherazade." She reaches under his hip and takes hold of his revived interest, sticky in her hand.

All right then, he'll talk. Little Wakefield was a hider. When he was very small he would crouch behind a dresser, or roll in a ball under the kitchen table, or stretch out as still as a corpse under his parents' bed, listening for their true thoughts. Their conversation was different when they were alone. When they spoke to each other in front of Wakefield it was somehow false. And when there were other grownups around they never spoke to each other. Or to Wakefield.

His parents were weekend tourists. They would drive to little towns to visit courthouses and churches. Sometimes they went to museums in bigger cities. They ate out at cheap restaurants. When they took Wakefield with them on these trips, he would look for places to hide. After he learned to write, he kept a list of places where he had hidden.

He recites for Maggie *Young Wakefield's List of Best Hiding Places:* "*HOWARD JOHNSON'S outside Gambier, Ohio. You go to the bathroom but instead you go to the door and come up behind the cashier. The COURTHOUSE in Springfield. Under the big desk. The RUBBER MUSEUM in Akron, Ohio. Between the rubber ashtrays and the space*

*suit. The HENRY FORD VILLAGE, Detroit. Inside the Model T. The
DETROIT MUSEUM OF ART. Under the bench in front of the big
painting of a fat naked lady."*

Maggie has stimulated his interest to the required dimensions. She
turns him over and rides him, moaning with eyes closed. "Continue!"
she commands.

Little Wakefield discovered good hiding places in trees, in parks,
under picnic benches, at truck stops, in roadside gift shops, behind
trash cans, under piles of branches, in boiler rooms, in the backs
of pickups. One time he'd been driven off to another state and his
parents filed a missing person report. They were always having to
search for their son, but they rarely found him on their own. After
a while, Wakefield would come out of hiding all by himself. Sometimes they were angry, but more often just relieved. Now, inside
Maggie, Wakefield sees the past clearly; the film unreels to her slow
movements.

Young Wakefield studied environments like a thief, attentive to the
architecture of corners, of shadows, his eyes trained by habit. As he
grew older he continued the hunt for hideouts. The radius of his parents' weekend forays widened, as did their taste for "culture." They
graduated from simple picnics and roadside attractions to historical
sites, and Wakefield explored old cemeteries and Civil War battle-
fields, transformed over time into mazes of forgotten space. By his
teens, his expertise was such that he could intuit secret unused space
almost without looking.

Maggie's intuitive interior is surrounding him with heat, her pace
quickening, threatening to break the film. He lays his hands on her
hips to slow her down.

He caught people in furtive pleasures and overheard embarrassing
conversations, and when he was sixteen he grew ashamed of his compulsion. No one told him that what he was doing was shameful (since

no one knew what he was doing), but he felt it. Nonetheless, it was hard to stop and he struggled with his habit. He was almost caught in a dress shop behind a rack of discounted summer dresses. A woman was dreamily fingering the sleeve of a dress, and Wakefield, hidden in a recess, responded by tugging at the other sleeve, a tug that set off an unbearable erotic vibration. She knew that he was there. When she tugged again, he stopped breathing. After she walked away, Wakefield was covered with sweat and there was a dark wet spot on the front of his pants.

"Sure," says Maggie, "it's all women's fault." She starts moving faster. Heat increases between them and once again Wakefield takes her hips in his hands to slow her down.

It all came to an end when his first girlfriend, who knew nothing about his fetish, took home another boy who made a number of successful advances on her body while Wakefield was hidden in the room. Instead of jealousy, he felt only guilt, and promised himself never to hide again.

"So you stopped completely?" Maggie asks, stopping her own motion.

This time Wakefield's hands encourage her hips; he lets himself be taken and follows Maggie to the end of the earth. They drop off the edge. The earth is flat after all. Their combined moans can be heard through the walls of the room, and Wakefield has the feeling that others are listening, their breaths quickening as well.

Not hiding doesn't stop Wakefield from thinking about it. He is fascinated by things that are found to hide other things, such as the equestrian statue of Henry IV on Pont-Neuf in Paris, which when X-rayed revealed a bust of Napoleon. It had been hidden there by the sculptor, a faithful Bonapartist. When he was married, Wakefield collected sword canes and boxes that had secret compartments, but these things were expensive and competed with Marianna's collections of glass figurines and dolls. They couldn't afford both, so he took to haunting flea markets for false-bottomed suitcases, magicians' boxes, and spy gear. Marianna even gave him a set of nesting Russian egg dolls painted with the faces of Russian tsars and dictators. The smallest egg was the size of a grain of rice and portrayed Ivan the Terrible. It was one of the rare times their tastes coincided.

When travel became his livelihood, he didn't much notice what Marianna was up to, except that every time he returned home, their apartment seemed smaller and smaller, filled with more and more kitsch. Eventually a real baby was added to the jumble of dolls and figurines that constituted their home. The child was plump and pleasant to touch, and it was, like all infants, guileless. Wakefield was afraid of it, just as he feared breaking the other objects in Marianna's collection. Then came a time when Wakefield realized that if he didn't stop traveling, he'd come home one day and there would be no room left for him.

Wakefield proposed that they build a house, and he drafted plans for one with a number of secret hiding places. When he explained to Marianna how he'd incorporated his hiding fetish into the design, and what exactly his fetish was, she found his kink disgusting. She said it reminded her of Europe. So they bought an ordinary suburban house that she rapidly filled with more glass and dolls.

He began investing in stocks. He studied the market like an architectural blueprint and soon learned to spot profitable weaknesses like hidden spaces in the vastness of the world economy. When his profits were much more than adequate for their needs, he lost interest in the market and sold most of his stock, creating a large bank account for Marianna. Now financially secure, Marianna gained new social confidence and made new friends, even got involved in charity work. Most telling was an unprecedented interest in Romania, specifically the plight of Romanian orphans. She contributed money to the cause and even offered to translate adoption documents for American couples.

Marianna's new friends found Wakefield mysteriously poetic. His brooding silences, his vanishing for long periods on travel assignments, his obsessive reading when at home, his noiseless manner of eating, walking, and sleeping, had a charming, almost narcotic effect on them.

But during one of his longer trips Wakefield's resolve never again to hide broke down and he reverted to his childhood habit. He began to spend nights hidden in a large department store or a museum, enjoying the profound thrill of the moment when the doors shut and all the employees went home. He learned the movements of night watchmen and crept silently from hiding place to hiding place. In the morning he would slip out, go back to his hotel room for a nap and a shower. He arranged to meet his hosts only in the afternoon, and to lecture only in the evening.

During especially long trips Wakefield would forget what his wife did at home and what his life was like there. Then he spent six ice-bound months in the Arctic, on assignment for *National Cartographic*. One night he was drinking vodka with Ivan, who asked him if he was married and what his wife did, the usual questions strangers ask. Wakefield told him that she was an emergency room doctor. Strangely, he began to believe it, and after the Russian went to bed, Wakefield stayed awake fleshing out his fiction: He understood how the ultrareality of caring for the city's disposable bodies might strain their relationship, and that she harbored a profound distrust of his work, which seemed to her dirty and escapist. To a doctor, "hidden spaces" were anathema, since her profession required that she reveal what was hidden in the body, to locate disease and injury and treat them. As a woman, she'd rather not have a "hidden spaces" specialist for a husband, since such a notion was transparently a metaphor for other women's mysteries. He could find no way to dismantle this instinctive mistrust, so there in the darkness of the Arctic night he decided to abandon his marriage. He wasn't exactly sure how to go about it. Perhaps he should, like his literary namesake, disappear and return after twenty years as if nothing had happened.

Marianna must have anticipated his decision; he returned from Alaska and found the house empty. Marianna and child had vanished. Alone in the house for the first time, Wakefield thought about how she had remained a mystery to him through the years of their marriage. Perhaps she had been one secret place he had not sufficiently explored, a maze whose architecture he had never quite figured out, and now it was too late.

The divorce settlement took half of his remaining portfolio. He cashed out the rest and bought a condo in the city where he still lived. After the breakup he wrote Marianna an (unmailed) letter, asking her to forgive him for pretending to believe in the future. He hadn't, and he didn't, there wasn't any, not for them, not for anybody. "I am not an intellectual pessimist," Wakefield wrote somewhat preciously, "but I simply have no faith in anything that is overly articulated and requires, besides, an unnatural effort to overcome my instincts. I am painfully aware that I differ in this from most of my fellow Americans, and I'm sorry that I led you to believe, a long time ago in Europe, that I was a regular Joe. I prefer the Inca, who keep an imperturbable and steady gaze in the face of adversity and history, but equally in the face of success and good fortune. They seem to me to possess a longer view of time and see historical cycles in a cosmic light."

His wife's reply to him (which he imagined) ignored his philosophy and stubbornly advised that he make "use of the gift" as God and nature intended, even if she was not the one to best inspire him to action. Wakefield saw that she would be all right without him, because her faith in the mission of humanity was stronger than her misplaced faith in Wakefield.

Ivan Zamyatin, who had become his friend in Alaska, eventually left the Arctic and moved to the city of Wakefield's current residence, where he abandoned architecture and became a cabdriver and provider of advice. The Russian had convinced himself, perhaps during their long discussions in the Arctic, that architecture was not his calling, that he was, in fact, made physically ill by it, whereas contact with people, in any situation, buoyed him and made him happy. Naturally, he had sentimental advice for Wakefield: "You haven't met the right woman, my friend!" To Zamyatin all women were fascinating. In fact, he'd never yet found one who bored him. He had been married six times, had enjoyed countless mistresses, and his offspring were equally numerous. He was as a result a poet of life and love, but as far as Wakefield was concerned, his advice was useless. There was no right woman for him: women were, like Wakefield himself, inexplicable.

"WHAT DO YOU want to do now?" Maggie plops herself down on her back, arms behind her head. She's wide awake, though the bedside clock reads 3:30 A.M.

Wakefield makes a mental note to self: oral sex = walnuts and sea salt.

"I don't suppose sleep interests you?"

"Sleep? Are you kidding? We don't do much else in Typical. When a guest comes we stay up late."

"This guest came three times. Do we still have to talk?"

"No. Now we drink more." They've already consumed most of the minibar's contents.

Wakefield saunters naked to the minibar, by this time unselfconscious of his slight paunch, and pours two little bottles of rum covered with two fingers of fizzy Coke. It's the last Coke and the rum is the last of the hard liquor.

"I'll tell you *my* secret now," says Maggie. "I don't have any."

"Sure. Tell me another one. You're all secret. You have parents in exile, a child, an ex, you do PR for God . . ."

"Well, sure," she admits, "I have stories. But they aren't secret.

They're just what's happened so far. But I don't have hidden vices or a secret life or an obsession with anything weird. When I masturbate, for instance, I think of myself, I don't fantasize about movie stars or orgies. . . ."

"That's too bad." Wakefield is a little disappointed.

"Actually, I do have a vice. . . ." Maggie sighs.

Wakefield is interested.

"Reading," Maggie confesses, "books."

"A private vice."

"It's a serious vice," says Maggie, "but it's the only vice that doesn't harm anybody, and it's my belief that you should live your life so you do the least harm."

Wakefield feels enormous empathy, and he kisses the hand propping up her head. He has empathy because she is a reader, like himself, and because she's just articulated the single most untrue idea he's ever heard. Not only is reading *not* harmless, but he knows that reading can profoundly screw a person up. He doesn't want to recite the litany of sheer evil that has wafted from books since the beginning: the maleficence of the Bible, the toxicity of Goethe's *Young Werther,* which prompted young men to suicide, the malignancy of Hitler's *Mein Kampf.* Those were books and people read them.

Maggie interprets Wakefield's friendly kiss as agreement with her point of view.

"Besides tending bar in the evenings, I worked in a bookstore and went to school all at the same time."

Young Wakefield had also worked in a bookstore while he was in college. The owner was a pipe-smoking man who knew everything about books and movies. That bookstore was a hush-hush emporium of terror; anyone who lingered too long among the dark mahogany shelves was subject to icy bad vibes from the two Oscar Wildish clerks, of whom Wakefield was one. Their standards were high and books mattered, though for mercenary reasons a few best sellers were also in stock. Wakefield was expected by his pipe-smoking boss to have an opinion about which books were truly great, a designation that coincided with how potentially harmful they were: the "greater," the more dangerous.

Maggie had worked at Book Universe, a chain bookstore frequented by college kids and perverts. The students and deviants were actually allowed to drink coffee in the store, and they left the coffee-stained books behind when they had wasted enough time or managed a furtive, half-hidden orgasm.

"The books were mostly trash, and the clerks were complete idiots," Maggie admits.

"They didn't know their Proust from their ass!" Wakefield baits her.

Maggie smiles. "Their asses were cute. Our biggest sellers were the Idiot Guides. There was *The Complete Idiot's Guide to Being a Psychic, . . . to Learning Italian, . . . to Geography, . . . to Elvis, . . . to Getting Rich, . . . to Getting Published, . . . to Divorce, . . . to Writing, . . . to Weddings, . . . to Etiquette, . . . World History, . . . Beer, . . . Feng Shui.* There was even an *Idiot's Guide to the MCATs,* the medical exams. Having an idiot doctor is one thing, an Idiot Guide–certified one, something else altogether. It hurts just to think about it."

What hurts Wakefield is seeing how bright Maggie really is, and how young. Personally he has nothing against the Idiot Guides. That they are so popular testifies, on the one hand, to a willingness to admit that one is an idiot and, on the other hand, to the desire to know at least a little about something. Surely no one can pretend to know all about everything these days, and maybe knowing a little about everything is preferable. Embracing the fact that you're an idiot is both gently self-deprecating and the logical result of a long dilettante tradition in America that began with abridged editions of classics, followed by CliffsNotes and Reader's Digest Condensed Books. Generations of college students have muddled through school on the strength of these diluted simulacra. Once-shameful shortcuts are now a point of pride. And of course, Wakefield himself is a dilettante, and proud of it.

"And you can buy term papers on the Internet now," adds Maggie, scandalized.

Wakefield snorts in seeming agreement. "Can you imagine a private library composed entirely of Idiot Guides? Friends come over and are enraptured: 'All the Idiot Guides. Wow! Can I borrow the *Idiot's Guide to the Idiot's Guides*? The Idiot Guides will eventually rule the earth just like idiots have for a long time. Was there an *Idiot's Guide to Self-Surgery*?"

"*Idiot's Guide to Self-Lobotomy!*"

"*Idiot's Guide to Creationism!*"

"Maybe that's redundant."

"*Idiot's Guide to Idiocy?*"

"*Idiot's Guide to Fellatio?*" Blue eyes sparkle, and she goes down on him. His overworked membrum is exhausted. She delights in tasting the glans steeped in their combined juices, and doesn't mind. Wakefield relaxes. Is there an *Idiot's Guide to Embarrassment*? Or an *Idiot's Guide to Himself*?

They fall asleep, tangled in the sheets, and they don't wake up until the clock on the bedside table reads 11:30 A.M. and someone is knocking at the door. "Oh, Jeez," Maggie says, "I forgot all about Chez Soleil and the Home of the Future."

The Company has scheduled lunch for Wakefield at a fine restaurant, followed by a visit to the "Home of the Future," a project almost ready for the public. Wakefield's flight isn't until evening and The Company wants to make sure that he is properly entertained.

"I'll be right there," Wakefield shouts at the door.

Maggie is scrambling for her clothes, looking distraught. Of course, she's a single woman, but sleeping with the speaker might not sit well with her bosses.

"What do we do?" asks Wakefield, aware of her predicament.

"You go out there and let them take you to lunch. I'll join you at the restaurant," she whispers.

Wakefield gets dressed and gargles a bit of mouthwash. He's unshaven and can smell Maggie all over him. The young man waiting in the hall introduces himself. "I'm Paulee's assistant, Kevin. I helped design the Home of the Future. I'll be driving you to Chez Soleil." In the elevator Kevin chats pleasantly while Wakefield tries to look alive. Outside, everything glimmers. The snow is blinding.

Kevin holds open the passenger door of his luxury car and Wakefield topples in.

"I enjoyed your talk last night," Kevin says predictably. "It was an inspiration. Without imagination, we are nothing."

Is that what he'd said? For a moment, Wakefield doesn't know where he is or what he said. Why can't he go back to his nice dark room? It's too clean and white out here. Kevin pulls up to the restaurant, deposits Wakefield at the door, and drives off.

Chez Soleil is golden and bright like its name. The scent of garlic and fresh bread permeate the air, combining, not unpleasantly, with Wakefield's own postcoital bouquet. Some of The Company are already here, including Paulee and, surprisingly, Farkash. Farkash is wearing the same coat he wore at the lecture, but Paulee, freshly shaved and massaged, glows pink in a blue cashmere sweater. There are also two elegant women and an Asian man with a shaved head. Wakefield is introduced, and he shakes a beautiful manicured hand belonging to a woman named Neva. The other woman is Sherrill, who looks like an intelligent squirrel wearing cat's-eye glasses studded with tiny rhinestones. The Asian man crunches Wakefield's fingers in a powerful grip. His name sounds like "Pathogen," but maybe Wakefield has misheard.

He is about to hide his exhaustion behind a menu when Sherrill, who's been studying him intently, announces: "Mr. Wakefield, I think you're full of shit."

Wakefield can't believe she actually said that, but everyone laughs, and he offers a goofy smile.

"Never mind Sherrill," Paulee growls.

"Charmed, I'm sure." Wakefield wants to ask Sherrill where she got the idea that he's full of shit, but then he remembers his speech. She's probably right.

"I own a lot of art," Sherrill continues unperturbed, "and I look at it as a source of pleasure, primarily, and only secondarily as an investment. I buy the work of artists nobody's ever heard of, and I pay whatever they're asking."

"For the work?" Paulee asks, winking.

Farkash looks at him disapprovingly. Obviously, Wakefield has arrived in the middle of a conversation that concerns him only marginally.

"What did you do with Maggie?" Wakefield catches a proprietary hint in Paulee's tone.

In fact, Paulee is alluding to what he thinks was Wakefield's magic act in making wallets appear and disappear. But Wakefield doesn't know anything about that: he'd attributed people's calls for their wallets and keys as imaginative responses to his speculation about money. He gives Paulee a dirty look.

Oh, she called," says Sherrill. "Something came up, but she'll join us shortly."

Wakefield realizes that Maggie and Sherrill must be friends; she's covering for her. Seems that her "you're full of shit" comment might refer to something other than his ideas about art. He decides he likes her.

A young Clark Gable appears at the table and begins the Menu Recitation, a new American poetic form. Today's Special is intricate and vertiginous, detailing the tiniest manipulations of the beef and the minutest saucing of the fish. Scented rhetorical transports. Oleaginous mung. Striped miniatures. Taunted crab claw.

Sherrill interrupts. "Falcon claw?"

Displeased, the poet repeats, "Fulcrum."

"We used to call that fatback in Kentucky."

The poet begins again. It's neither falcon claw nor fulcrum, but *fourme d'ambert*. It's part of the Roasted Beet and Bean Salomée. Go figure. Threatened with the recitation reiterated da capo, Paulee glares at Sherrill. Again, everyone laughs. This is a veteran audience. They've been through more menu recitations than the fans of slam poetry; to paraphrase, they've heard the best ingredients of their generation pot-roasted over slow flames.

Most important, wine is ordered. Wakefield, who is still a little drunk, chugs down a glass of three-hundred-dollars-a-bottle vino and his brain smiles thank you. Happily, his lunch companions momentarily forget about him; Sherrill and Neva quarrel good-naturedly about something vaguely sexual. Farkash and "Pathogen" are silent but alert.

Paulee manages to tell Wakefield, in his suggestive way, that Sherrill is some sort of a multidisciplinary, transcultural specialist, valued by advanced technothinkers for her studies of new media. She is also single and on the lookout.

"Her address book contains only the names of single potential Nobel laureates," Paulee fills in. "She's teaching computers to understand English, her English. Her computer reads everything written in English since Beowulf. Quote something by a beloved classic, Sherrill."

Sherrill obliges: "In some old magazine or newspaper I recollect a story, told as truth, of a man—let us call him Wakefield—who absented himself for a long time from his wife. The fact, thus abstractly stated, is not very uncommon, nor—without a proper distinction of circumstances—to be condemned either as naughty or nonsensical."

Wakefield's wine glass freezes in midair. Even Paulee is momentarily caught off guard. "Wakefield?" he asks incredulously, "like our guest? You stuck his name in, Sherrill."

Sherrill smiles mysteriously. Wakefield takes a long sip of his wine. It is a classic, after all.

Neva saves him from commenting when she asks, "What's your new project, Pathogen?"

"I'm still unpacking."

So that's really his name, thinks Wakefield, just like my name is really my name. He remembers who Pathogen is. A writer of complex dystopias, he recently published a huge nonfiction book about his round-the-world search for the origin of an electromagnetic frequency that science has been unable to explain. Wakefield actually tried to read it, but he couldn't get past the introduction. Too much math.

Between the heart of palm salad and the tiny olives, and well into the second bottle of wine, Maggie shows up showered and fresh, wearing what looks to Wakefield like a Catholic schoolgirl's uniform. Very funny. But for the subtle shadows under her eyes, which could be makeup, she looks none the worse for wear. They exchange a "Hello" that doesn't sound casual to anyone.

Farkash now addresses Wakefield. "Mr. Wakefield, last evening you said that the material world is disappearing. Is that correct?"

"Absolutely." Wakefield is flattered.

"He wasn't speaking literally," interjects Neva.

"Yes I was." Wakefield hates it when people think his ideas are metaphorical. He doesn't really know what that is. He fancies himself a strict literalist.

"I thought so." Farkash brings his fingers together in front of his chin. The table goes silent. They know the gesture; it's significant. "I work now on a mathematics of image formation. At a certain point in time for the brain the world became material. Now we are moving away from that point and the disappearance of the material is generating interesting numbers."

"I didn't know you were interested in humans, Farkash," Paulee quips.

"Only because they generate formulas, Paulee. Mr. Wakefield described something that I can illustrate." He takes a fountain pen from his pocket and starts writing a complex formula on the tablecloth. "See?"

They all look. Wakefield looks too, but he doesn't see.

Paulee: "Pretty."

Neva: "Another billion-dollar tablecloth."

"It's a design for molecular computation that could allow us to dispense with hardware computers, in common language," Sherrill, who knows math, too, explains to Wakefield.

While they continue to admire the tablecloth, Maggie distracts him with a look. He is flattered that this equation is somehow related to his ideas about the state of the imagination, but puzzled by the very nonimaginary and nondisappearing persistence of his desire. He suspects that the force that keeps the world from dematerializing is libido. Attraction. Maggie licks her lips, and his desire increases. Maybe attraction is taken care of by the formula somehow.

Over the raw oysters on ice sprinkled with Dead Sea salt, Sherrill eyes the Clark Gable waiter.

"He looks a little like the second man who made it to the South Pole, I forget his name."

"Sherrill has a thing for heroes, manly men who spend rugged years away from human company," Maggie explains. "Her screen saver is a collage of faces of polar explorers."

"They get frostbitten and Sherrill nurses them back to health," says Paulee. "I think he looks more like Clark Gable than Amundsen."

And so it goes, over Lapin aux Marrons, Halibut Cheeks, Escargot Parsillade, Hardy Kiwi and Fleur de Maquis salad, baby greens with unborn arugula, pear and corn cakes, Apple Bacon-Wrapped Fallow Venison Leg rubbed with (more) Dead Sea salt, tiramisu, tarte tatin, Graham's Vintage Port, and espresso. They are all brilliant, hope-filled, flush, and firm in the certainty that they are irreplaceable.

But with the espresso a kind of melancholy sets in. Rich or not, they are all just people who've eaten too much and must now return to the office. They have neither the time nor the personalities for rest, no matter how extravagant the lunch. Despite their nervous energy Wakefield perceives that his table companions are exhausted; they've all been on at least three planes this week, and it matters not a whit if the jets are private. He allows himself to feel some compassion for them, but doesn't look when the check comes. He knows the total without tip is more than the yearly income of a Peruvian village, or all the small loans made in one day by the World Bank to Indian seamstresses.

THE HOME OF the Future is Neva's brainchild, inspired by a sketch Paulee made one night on a napkin. These people get all their inspiration in restaurants, Wakefield snickers. The Company is funding the project in the hope that every future home in the world will run its software. To that end, a great many specialists, from child psychologists to entertainment analysts, are involved. Sherrill studies the reactions of a series of families invited to live in it, as if they were natives of a tribe. "Future primitives," she likes to call them. She and Neva, the HOTF Team, will be Wakefield's guides. Maggie tags along; she's never seen it. At the gates of the Company campus, Sherrill signs them in and they all pile into a cheerfully painted Company minibus. It pulls up to a Frank Lloyd Wrightish–looking house built into a snowy hillside.

"No cameras," Neva warns. "It's still experimental."

Wakefield shrugs. Cameras were never his thing. His notebook, on the other hand, is awfully accurate most of the time.

Sherrill hesitates a moment at the door, trying to remember the entry code; Neva leans over her impatiently and punches it in.

Lights simulating afternoon sun come on as they enter, and a pleasant masculine voice says, "Welcome home, Neva and Sherrill. Who are your guests?"

"Wakefield and Maggie," Sherrill replies, and the voice repeats after her with delight, "Wakefield and Maggie! Welcome to the Home of the Future, Wakefield and Maggie!"

"Fuck you," says Sherrill.

Machines begin to activate in the kitchen. The icemaker pours cubes into a glass and fills it with water. "You must be thirsty, Sherrill," the house-voice says. A minioven pops out a fresh cookie. "Martha Stewart's latest recipe," the house-voice tells them. "I think you'll like these, Sherrill. And here is one for Neva. And one for Maggie. And one for Wakefield." Out pop more cookies. Pop. Pop. Pop.

Sherrill orders the cookie machine off, but four dinners have already started heating themselves in a microwave that hums the tune of "Three Little Maids from School." Neva stops it with a sharp voice command.

"Let's have a fucking whiskey," suggests Maggie.

"Fucking whiskey coming right up, Maggie," the voice responds jovially, and a tumblerful slides down the counter toward her.

"Make that two more," says Sherrill.

"Amen." Wakefield has just found his voice.

Whiskey in hand, they head for the living room, a welcoming space furnished with family-style clutter. A teddy bear propped up in a rocking armchair begins to clap and flat-screen "paintings" light up on the walls.

"Not fucking Impressionists!" grumbles Sherrill, avoiding a robot waiter who is intent on running right through her. "You've got to see more art, Neva."

"Honey, it's supposed to be an *average* home."

"Okay, okay," says Sherrill. "Stop!" The robot waiter freezes and the paintings vanish. "Night!" she commands, and the lights dim, the ceiling becomes a starry sky, and a Chopin nocturne begins to play.

"Can we watch a movie?" Wakefield asks, lying down on an inviting couch. The couch adjusts itself to the contours of his body and props a perfect pillow under his head. He's overcome by sleepiness.

"Sure. *Last Tango in Paris,* Neva?" asks Maggie.

"It's supposed to be a family home of the future!" Neva apologizes. "Don't you want to see the nursery décor?"

Not particularly, thinks Wakefield, but it's too late. As soon as she says it, baby-mobiles dangle over their heads and Mother Goose posters appear on the walls. Sherrill looks sad. "I'll never have any kids!" she says to no one in particular.

Neva rolls her eyes. The kiddie stuff disappears, replaced instead by holograms of Art Nouveau ladies with long, flowing hair. The robot waiter appears with more whiskeys, and places one carefully on a small table that pops up like a mushroom from the floor beside Wakefield's couch.

Maggie lies down on the floor next to Wakefield and the carpet begins to rise, molding itself into a couch identical to the one he's lying on. The two couches touch. It's a bed!

"Smart room!" says Sherrill.

Maggie kicks off her shoes and is about to toss her sweater on the floor beside them when Neva says, " I wouldn't do that." But the robot waiter has already grabbed the shoes and disappeared with them.

"Shit," shouts Sherrill, "the shoe-shine and laundry service is offline. The damn thing won't return anything until it's fixed."

"At least you got to keep your sweater." Neva is amused.

"We owe you a pair of shoes," Sherrill offers, upset with Neva.

"But I want mine," pouts Maggie. "I'm not rich like you, Sher."

"Italian, I promise."

Milky light begins to fade the stars. Wakefield can't tell if he's been asleep or dreaming with his eyes open. Apparently the tour is over.

"This is the Rip Van Winkle house," he yawns. "I've missed the American Revolution."

"Only the first one," says Sherrill. "The second one is just beginning."

They make their way past the robot waiter and the superautomated kitchen; Wakefield holds on to the whiskey glass; it's nice, with a heavy bottom, cut lead crystal. Maggie is barefoot. Sherrill and Neva aren't speaking to each other.

"Good-bye, Wakefield and Maggie. You are a nice couple. Happy anniversary!" blurts the house as they approach the door.

"The anniversary of what? I can't walk like this in the snow!"

"Your glass, Wakefield?" the house-voice reminds him.

"I like it. Can't I take it with me?"

"The glass belongs to the house, Wakefield!" There is slight menace in the voice.

Sherrill intervenes. She takes the glass out of Wakefield's hand and drops it in her purse. "It's a gift," she says sternly.

"I'll have to report it," says the house. "We have inventory every day."

"Bitch!" Sherrill ignores the voice but gives Neva a nasty look. Like mother like son, she thinks.

Wakefield picks Maggie up and carries her to the minibus. She's not all that light, but she's warm and smells like a loaf of fresh French bread with a hint of whiskey.

"How sweet!" Sherrill hands Wakefield the whiskey glass as he hops into the van after Maggie. "Your souvenir." Neva waves good-bye. She and Sherrill are staying behind to "work out some glitches." As they are driven back to her car, Maggie takes his hand and puts it between her legs. Her beastie-in-residence is pulsing. She puts her feet on his lap. He warms them with his free hand. A nice couple, indeed.

Now wouldn't the Devil have just died laughing if Wakefield chose the Home of the Future in which to make his "authentic" life? Of course, there's no good reason why the "authentic" couldn't occur in the most artificial environment. Authenticity may not even be possible unless it's deliberately constructed. The Devil may have, in fact, known only too well that "authenticity" is hugely misunderstood by humans. For most of them, Wakefield included, it means something like "spontaneity," or "innocence," or "soul mate," all words that refer to a lost paradise possible only in the thrall of romantic reverie. In reality, modern humans, like the world we live in, are meticulously constructed and designed, utterly inauthentic and mechanical creatures. But Wakefield refuses to believe it. He's convinced that though reality may be a construct, it's built on something else, something *authentic,* and that he can discover it.

MAGGIE AND WAKEFIELD make love one more time in his hotel room, then she drives him to the airport through the snowy fields. The squat, modern buildings of The Company look like alien landing craft.

"It's hard to believe we grew corn there," Maggie says. "Poor Daddy. But it's not so bad, actually. It's been great for me."

No, it's not bad. It's quite wonderful, in fact. Some of the great brains of the age and the busy bees of American prosperity have made a home here; the spices of the world have wafted in and educated the palates of people who once thought french fries were haute cuisine. And Maggie is beautiful, sweet, and intelligent. Typical is a pretty great place.

But it's not time to settle yet, Wakefield tells himself. I haven't even heard the starter pistol, I can still play at life. But how long can he be a spectator of his own life? He feels suddenly desperate, like a tourist looking into the windows of a building where everyone is at home, relaxed, playing with their children, reading, watching television.

That could be his life, but something prevents him from going in, a "something" that keeps pushing him on. He looks fondly at Maggie, who seems to expect something from him, more than "I'll give you a call." It's another "something" Wakefield finds impossible. He tears a page from his notebook and scribbles down his home number and private e-mail address and hands it to Maggie, who looks disappointed in him.

To his credit, Wakefield has begun *some* preparations for eventually honoring the Deal with his Satanic Majesty. He has wrapped the whiskey glass from the Home of the Future inside a sock and has wound a T-shirt around the sock for extra protection. It's inside his carry-on bag, and is intended to be the first in a series of objects that he will eventually present to the Devil as proof of the sincerity of his search, if not actually proof of his success. Damn you, Beelzebub, he swears silently, why don't you fire your freakin' pistol now, so I can seriously get going? For a moment he wonders if the shot wasn't already fired and he didn't hear it because he was too busy talking.

Waiting to board his flight, Wakefield checks his e-mail. There's one from Marianna: "I hear you're coming to my city. Call me, we have things to discuss." Damn, she must have seen his talk advertised in the paper. Marianna moved to the Wintry City after their breakup, when she decided, after years of avoiding her roots, to reconnect with them; the large Romanian community there had apparently been the draw. Okay, Marianna, I'm not gonna call, but if you find me, you find me.

A message from Ivan: "You missed a great party. Our new mayor decided to live up to his election promises and arrested sixty cabdrivers, most of them Arab and Russian, for not having proper licenses or for having bought them illegally. I was not one, but then I paid more and I know the guy—he used to drink at the bar. Anyway, they released them all today with a fine and everybody's driving again because there are fifty thousand neurosurgeons in town and, man, you should see their wives! They smell good!" Strange that Zamyatin writes English without an accent. When he speaks, his accent is always with him, but his English grammar varies according to weather, mood, or vodka. He can sould like a Cambridge professor or like a breathless greenhorn, as if language was itself some kind of weather or mood or alcohol. Wakefield feels a longing to be back home hanging out with Ivan in his slapdash, tolerant, corrupt semitropical city.

The next e-mail is from the publisher of a new magazine interested in a travel piece about anything, 1,500 words at $2 a word. That's $3,000, but Wakefield rarely writes articles anymore, having parlayed his writing career into the much more lucrative lecture business. He still receives regular offers, though, because he acquired a reputation, and a readership who sensed that beneath his descriptions of ice floes, tribal rituals, restaurants, lodges, and festivals, there was a certain darkness that resonated like a hidden architecture, an occult subtext. Fans of his writing actually created his lecture career; some of them were high-income professionals charged with hiring speakers for their annual conferences. In the hope of finding out what it was that lay behind Wakefield's prose, they hired him to speak at their luncheons.

Talking to people about things he knew well was easy; he tried to describe his experiences spontaneously and he allowed himself the luxury of thinking out loud, as if he were among friends. Sometimes the audience lost interest when it became clear that he was working against the grain of their hopes and dreams, but still they sat quietly, anticipating lunch. Some audiences didn't appreciate his little ice-breaking jokes at the expense of their chosen profession, but others were fascinated by his lack of respect and listened to every word he said with a kind of awe. Wakefield himself was astonished when reports of this effect filtered back to him. "Fantastic," "a prophet," "visionary" were some of the more embarrassing estimations of his skill. If Wakefield had been a preacher, he might have taken such praise as his due. As it was, he really had no idea what it was they had heard.

He understood his effect even less now, many years after his first en-gagement. When people asked him to define what he did, he said simply, "It's a kind of performance art."

Ever practical Ivan Zamyatin made light of Wakefield's insecurity. "Do what you're doing!" boomed the Russian. "The more you do what you're doing, the more they'll pay you. More rubles, my friend, more rupees and pesetas!"

But Wakefield couldn't just go on doing what he did, because he had no clear idea of what he'd done. In his very first paid speech, he had described an adventure that had taken him in search of the lost city of the Incas. He had speculated about what it must have been like to live in a layered and terraced world that stratified its inhabitants by rank and wealth. Then he'd gone on to talk about the people who must have lived between the layers of such a world, hidden people whose social functions were not clearly defined or understood, and who might have been much like artists and drifters in our time. As he spoke he closed his eyes and imagined them, inspired by their presumed exis-tence and by their strange relation to their hierarchical society. This closing of eyes was interpreted by the audience as either a rhetorical trick or a genuine moment of rapture, but it was for Wakefield a nearly unconscious gesture, a way of concentrating. The more he talked, the more clearly he saw the "hidden tribes," as he called them, and the more articulate he became in defining and *defending* them. He didn't even realize that in addition to speculating as to their existence—every-where, not only in Peru—he was finding reasons for their existence, and not just reasons but imperatives as well, and he felt himself be-coming a spokesman for the "hidden tribes" whose existence no one had proven. He ended up asserting that he was himself a member of such a community, and that his existence was proof of theirs.

He had worried, that first time, about his paycheck. After the lec-ture his host, in whose pocket the check lay, shook his hand with ev-ident emotion. Not only had he not thought Wakefield was insane, he had been genuinely moved. If he'd had two checks, he'd have handed them right over. So Wakefield learned not to worry about where his talk might take him; he just went with the flow.

This is what he tried to tell Ivan. Sure, the money was good. His price crept up, then shot up. He wasn't alone. It was a time of tent revivals, just like in the mid-nineteenth century. Snake-oil salesmen and gurus of every stripe were making bundles preaching to the crowds. Putative paradises achievable through patented formulas were conjured from thin air and made instantly available. America was rolling in money and a not inconsiderable portion of that gravy slopped generously into the bowls of smooth talkers and charlatans. Wakefield read some history and found that his own age was very like the Jacksonian era before the Civil War. At that time everyone from mesmerists and channelers of the dead to writers like Mark Twain were raking in the chips. It was about that time, too, that Hawthorne's Wakefield decided to drop out. Nineteen-nineties America was just as enamored of bathos and fantasy as Jacksonian America had been. It made Wakefield feel even more like a fraud. So he stopped accepting writing assignments and began to think about gradually retiring from the lecture circuit. His plan seemed reasonable, but he was still stricken with an unspecific dread.

He went to see a doctor. "Not unusual," his doctor said, prescribing a new antianxiety medicine. "Everybody takes these now," the doctor assured him, "though I don't quite know what's making people so anxious. Stock market is doing great, people are traveling, there's a new restaurant on every corner." The doctor, a younger man than Wakefield, became reverent. "My wife and I have reservations at Marlene's. . . . I hear she does for crab what Perlman does for the violin."

On the way home Wakefield couldn't shake the image of Chef Marlene torturing a poor crab to draw the music out of it. That night he dreamed that he was in a casino among a crowd of people all looking up at some kind of board. Only there wasn't any board, or any roof, for that matter; the mob was staring at a cloudless blue sky. This is the casino of the dead, his dream voice told him; they're waiting for you to make a speech.

Not long after, the Devil showed up.

Now Wakefield writes the editor of the new magazine a polite e-mail, turning down the essay invitation. He quickly scans the title headings of his other messages, erasing the usual promises of paradise: Viagra, penis enlargement, breast augmentation, diet pills.

Quit while you're ahead, Wakefield thinks, as he boards his flight out of Typical. This will be my last lecture tour. He's concluded the first leg successfully (and without Viagra), and the next stop should be a breeze. The third and last gig worries him, though. Other than his attending a party for his usual lecture fee, he hasn't been told a thing. His agent had reported that the man who hired him only said, "I've heard him speak, now I want him to listen." Wakefield wonders about that. Maybe he's a lousy listener. He wonders, too, if he's really ahead of anything. He's racing alright, but the race hasn't even begun. Zelda once asked him, when he'd scheduled five flights in one week, "What are you running from, Wakefield? Somebody chasing you?" At that time there was no Devil, and Wakefield hadn't the slightest idea why he was running, or even that he *was* running, and it had never occurred to him that anyone or anything was chasing him.

"Why do you think I'm running, Zelda?" he'd asked her. She'd taken her time and then answered, not surprisingly, "Your daemon."

"My demon?" Wakefield thought he'd heard her say.

"You know what I said, Wakefield. Your daemon. If you persist in mistaking your daemon for a demon, you'll get what you wish." Guess she was right. Zelda had explained the "daemon" to him before: it was the angel of his fate, the particular guide and guardian of his unique life. Running away from one's daemon was a spiritual crime in her book, one of the gravest.

PART THREE

WINTRY CITY

WINTRY CITY'S ALMOST HOME, Wakefield's been here so often over the years, so he's excited when the airplane approaches low over an immensity of solid brick neighborhoods, alive with ethnic old-timers, new immigrants, and blue-collar families.

"How is my favorite melting pot?" he asks the Arab cabdriver who takes him from the airport to his usual hotel, an old gangster hangout circa 1925, recently restored, but not too much, he hopes.

"Pot of boiling shit," the cabbie says.

They pass a familiar diner Wakefield remembers as having the best potato pancakes in the city; around the corner is an ancient Polish Dog stand huddled right under the elevated tracks. His mouth waters; sauerkraut and spicy brown mustard. Yum. The cabbie curses. The street to the hotel is blocked off by police.

"Maybe a riot or a festival. Never can tell."

When Wakefield was last here, he noticed that the city was undergoing a transformation. Once a fairly grim blue-collar town where men went home after work to corned beef and cabbage, it had become almost lighthearted, constantly celebrating festivals, fiestas, and ethnic parades. When he bails out of the cab at the end of the block the driver tries to overcharge him by ten dollars. He argues; it's a principle.

"My friend, your meter is fast. I come here all the time, I know how much it should be."

"Look," says the driver, "I'm sorry, but my rent goes up five hundred dollars last week. I don't know what now. Five children, wife has no job."

Wakefield is interested. "How could your rent go up so much all at once?"

The cabbie hangs his head. "Two weeks now a foreign woman buys my building with suitcase full of cash. Next day, everybody work there gone, maintenance guys, boilers man, super, janitor, everybody. These men come instead, all foreign, they speak no English, not a word, they wear nice suits, black shoes, sunglasses, all young, no smile, very very frighten. Then rent goes up. Tenants there, maybe fifteen years, they complain. Owner say, they the new maintenance, they also can beat you up. You pay or leave. Half the people, all the old people, they leave. Some have family, other to the bum shelter. You tell me what I do."

Wakefield is indignant. "These are not the old gangster days. You go to a lawyer, sue the woman, this is America."

The cabby smiles ruefully. "What America you come from? This is old days now. Gangster from Communist, from Russia, Ukraina, Romania, worse than Al Capone."

Wakefield pays him the extra ten dollars.

. . .

HIS LARGE ROOM on the eighth floor, though newly renovated, still feels old-fashioned, with windows that actually open and a
gorgeous view of the lake. When he looks out he sees an astonishing
sight: hundreds of yellow cabs parked like a flock of birds on a cement
pier on the shore. Beside each cab a driver is bent in half on a prayer
mat. Rush-hour commuters whiz past them on the freeway; their
prayers fly over the lake toward Mecca; gangsters from ex-Communist
countries terrify their families; their cheating meters are fast.

After a long, dreamy soak in the huge lion-clawed bathtub, Wakefield descends to the lobby to have a drink. He finds a seat in a deep
leather booth and lazily examines the Deco fresco adorning the walls,
and the huge mirror behind the long mahogany bar.

Sipping his whiskey, he calls Zamyatin on the cell phone.

Ivan is in his cab conveying "precious cargo" to the airport. In
Ivan's lingo, precious cargo means one or more beautiful women.

"I'm in a city oppressed by your people, Zamyatin," Wakefield tells
him. "It seems that the ex-Commie mafias are taking over where Al
Capone left off."

"So what am I supposed to do about it? Come over there and kick
ass? (To Precious Cargo: Pardon me, language like this makes me
ashamed of myself.) Listen, my beautiful person, if you pay my ticket,
I come be your translator, Superman. (To Cargo: My friend, you see,
has complex on saving the world. I only want to save money. . . .) Call
me again when you need good, sane person talk, right now I must explain road to Precious Cargo. Okay, my friend?" Zamyatin is talking
funny English for the sake of his precious cargo.

WAKEFIELD HASN'T HAD much time to make many friends.
He has quick, extravagant encounters, thousands of acquaintances, but
there is only one person he can call in the middle of the night. Ivan
doesn't sleep much anyway, and is always (gruffly) glad to hear from
him, and Wakefield has become dependent on his frankness, which

never wavers. He could call Zelda at 2 A.M., but she'd interpret it as a "cry for help" and would offer not advice but "therapy."

Wakefield once confided to Ivan his fetish for hiding and secret spaces. "Your 'harmless habit,' as you call it, is a gold mine," Ivan had said. "You have notebooks on secret hiding places? That's money in the bank, *bozhe moy*, you could be a cat burglar, a diamond thief, a James Bond spy . . . And there's also personal profit, watching all those people fucking!" Ivan got very excited about this hidden potential.

Wakefield told him that he was interested simply in forgotten space created by renovation and disuse, but the more he explained, the more poetically elaborate the concept became. "This architectural amnesia is the real estate of poets, born of layering, history, forgetting. It can only be inhabited stealthily after it's found; it cannot be rented or distributed. It would be immoral to profit from it. You may not get this, Ivan, but there is a kind of altruism involved here, an experimental altruism. I don't hide in order to spy on people: I hide to fill the forgotten places that need to be filled in some way. People believe in house spirits, in ghosts, in all kinds of presences that they claim to dread but actually crave. I see myself as a kind of household deity, a *spiritus locus,* if you will. Beyond that, I don't want to think about it. I am simply a cartographer of lost space."

Ivan had shrugged and redirected his energy to a person of the opposite sex.

IT'S GOTTEN DARK now and Wakefield remembers he's still hungry for that hot dog. All space is "lost space," there is no charting it, Magellan's job has grown huge in speeded-up time. He looks around for a sympathetic face at the bar, but there are only stiff young executives gazing at themselves in their giant martinis.

After a night of dreamless sleep, bathed and shaved, wearing his all-purpose jacket and his heavy wool overcoat (thank you, Zelda), a cup of very black coffee in hand, Wakefield waits in the lobby for

Susan, his contact from the World Art Museum. He has the feeling that he knows her because they have been e-mailing each other about the gig and their messages have become friendlier and more revealing with each round. He knows that she is a second-generation American, of Serbian-Bosnian descent, who might have been named Fatima or Nina, but her newly naturalized parents wanted her to have a head start in America. She grew up "Susan" and became a curator and administrator for the World Art Museum, currently holding an exhibition of Communist-era dissident art, for which Wakefield is the opening-night keynote speaker. He knows that she is also a vegetarian. Her parents are conflicted about everything, including her current job, because she has plunged with such gusto into the intricacies of the world they left behind, but also proud because they believe she has transcended their past and become a refined American person, a Museum Susan. Since the start of the war in Yugoslavia, there has been tension between her Serbian father and Bosnian mother. She wrote him about her neighborhood, its eight Orthodox churches, two Greek, two Russian, the Serbian, the Armenian, two Romanian, and two mosques for the Albanians and the Bosnians, *and* two Polish Catholic churches. She attended none of them when she was growing up, because her father, who'd been a Communist party official, was an atheist, but not long before the war started he suddenly got religion, began going to the Serbian church, and joined a nationalist group. Wakefield also knows that she's single and she's had boyfriends who horrified her parents.

Wakefield imagines that she is petite, with long, dark hair and brown eyes, and is a sloppy dresser. He is also certain that she'll be late. He is surprised when she shows up on time, a slender, short-haired blonde, elegantly hip, her tight-fitting jeans a designer brand, her tan sweater cashmere, and her peacoat pure Goodwill. Her fur-lined booties are Finnish. Her black leather gloves are Italian, and the rabbit-fur hat with earflaps is Russian. Wakefield instantly imagines her naked, the pert breasts, the soft, spa-massaged skin, the trimmed (possibly red) pubis, the long, flexible toes, the tight boyish buttocks. So much for electronic intimacy.

Nor does their cyberacquaintance help the initial awkwardness of meeting in person. Driving her vintage VW bug to the museum, Susan is thoughtful as she explains that the exhibit, which brings together artists from the various warring zones of the Balklands, has become the subject of heated controversy in the past week. She tells Wakefield to expect pickets at the opening when he goes to deliver his speech.

"Oh, bring it on!" Wakefield says. "I enjoy a good fight."

"It's personal for me. My parents have barely talked to each other since the war started back home, but I thought that they might come to see my big moment. But they won't come to the exhibit. I was actually hoping that maybe you could talk them into it," she says sheepishly.

"Me? I don't even know them."

Susan laughs. "Well, that's the weird thing. They have read your articles for years in *National Cartographic,* the only magazine they get, and they think that you're some kind of god. When they heard that you were coming for the show, I could tell they wanted to see your performance, but they can't admit that they both want the same thing. Maybe if you asked them personally . . ."

"I'll think about it."

She surprises him with a very old-world kiss on the cheek. Suddenly, the warmth of their exchanges over the past few months becomes apparent to both of them. Oddly enough, they *are* friends.

THE MUSEUM IS CLOSED to the public this day, so Wakefield gets a private tour from Susan and the senior curator, Doris, an older African-American woman with a kind face and snow-white hair.

The introductory essay in the catalogue, written by a rather florid

Serbian poet, explains that the ex-Communist Balklands, consisting of Serbia, Montenegro, Bosnia, Macedonia, Albania, Bulgaria, and Romania, are a part of the world where pre-Christian myths are still alive in the memories of the peasants, and that when the people aren't fighting, life in these countries is sweet, like certain mild goat cheeses. Elements of the art on exhibit can be traced to ancient Greece, but there are also Turkish and Slavic influences. The communist governments attempted to erase this mythical and historical memory, but artists rescued the degraded residue of the past and combined it with contemporary elements in order to protest the authoritarianism of these governments. Most of the work in the show was created at great risk before 1989, but some pieces are more recent: for instance, a sculpture of Pan welded from scraps of the shredded Iron Curtain. The Pan of legend came from Thrace, present-day Albania. Included in the catalogue is a lively statement by an artist who spent fifteen years in a prison camp.

> *Our worldview balances precariously on a head of cabbage, like the Native American world on the back of a turtle. Imagine this: a person trying to stand on a rolling cabbage, like a circus clown on a ball, while trying to retrieve a torch burning just out of reach! The Cabbage! This all-important vegetable is essential to any understanding of the Balklands. It is the flower of Eastern Europe the way garlic, as Salvador Dalí said, is "the moonflower of the Mediterranean." Like the onion, it is perfectly postmodern: it has layers which when peeled off reveal only more layers. Naturally this criterion privileges the onion, which has only layers and no real core, and as St. Sylvester so admirably put it: "God is like an onion because he is good and he makes you cry." The cabbage is not lachrymogenic and it does have a hard core which I, for one, love to eat raw. Nonetheless, it has enough removable skirts to please the most hardcore relativist. The cabbage is bombastic—one might compare it with a provincial*

bureaucrat swollen with self-importance. This bureaucrat-cabbage is a familar Balkland type, left over from the Ottoman and Austro-Hungarian empires, and it has survived through communism to the present day. That such a creature, the Cabbage-Bureaucrat, persists is an homage to the infinite subterfuge and cunning of our world. In the age of the Iron Curtain, the Cabbage was supreme. During communism when only the elites dined on meat and fish, the primacy of cabbage, with its court of turnips, parsnips, and potatoes, was unquestioned by the people. In metaphor and reality, the Cabbage was on the throne, served by a faithful retinue of inmates.

Susan watches Wakefield read, waiting for his reaction.

"This guy is a genius," he murmurs, feeling a little unbalanced himself by the rolling cabbage and swift metaphorical currents of the prose. "Maybe I should look at some art now."

Susan directs him to a wall-size painting entitled *Pigs.* A crowd of superpiggy pigs is gathered at the base of a mountain of cabbages. The painting is accompanied by a lengthy text projected on the opposite wall, and Wakefield wonders if every picture in the show is really worth a thousand words. The artist's statement reads:

> *The slaughter of the Pig was the climax of the year, representing the payoff for the peoples' toil. At Christmas, even city dwellers would join together with the peasants for the slaughter and feasting. My painting asks: "How are Socialist pigs different from Capitalist pigs?" The correct answer is: "Our pigs are different because they are SOCIALIST pigs." Pigs are not cabbage, pigs are meat, and represent progress, therefore socialism, therefore the future utopia. Cabbage was our reality, pigs our dream. A story when I was a child said that during the barbaric days before communism, a capitalist pig ate the testicles of a baby left outside a peasant hut. The baby grew up to be a great worker who married a beautiful and loyal Party commis-*

sar who was willing to put the Five-Year Plan above the bourgeois pleasure of sex.

Other works in this room portray pigs in many media. There is a photograph of an aproned housewife displaying the carcass of a pig for inspection by a man in whose face is reflected envy, greed, and disgust, as if the man is thinking that the situation might be reversed: the pig offering for inspection the disemboweled housewife.

"Give me a nice pork loin from the supermarket anytime," Doris observes, delicately.

"I don't eat meat myself. It drives my folks crazy." Susan rolls her eyes. "I stopped eating it in junior high, and it was the main thing we fought about until I moved out of the house. Eat, eat, eat, eat pig! It was like an obsession. My dad called me an ungrateful slut one time, he was so angry, and I was like, why is somebody who doesn't eat meat a slut? He just kept screaming, 'Slut! Slut!' so I came to the conclusion that this is just the logic of our people . . . as you can see from this stupid war now."

"Oh, honey, don't take it that way," Doris says kindly, "don't take it to heart. Poor folk work their fingers to the bone their whole lives to put meat on the table, and they can't see how you can just turn down their food. It's like turning *them* down, it hurts their feelings."

"I guess I *was* turning them down," Susan admits.

The next exhibition room, themed "Another Traditionalism," is given over to the works of those Balklanders whose religion forbids the consumption of pork. The focus is on sheep instead, treated with the same hunger and awe, but in a less realistic style. The sheep in these works are quasi-abstract. There is, for instance, a ceramic globe under a sapphire spotlight, its surface decorated with what looks like elaborate script, but the "writing" is, on close inspection, really scores of sheep being sacrificed by figures holding tiny gleaming knives.

The next room contains a particularly complex sculptural object, a grotesque hybrid of cabbage, pig, and sheep, from which flutters a banner inscribed We Had an Avant Garde! We Are Durably Modern! Between the reality of cabbage and the dream of meat, Surrealism has erected a flag.

Wakefield wonders how Susan has dealt with all these competing interests; curating this show must have been difficult for her, and he tells her so.

"I had to do it, but only a little for myself. Until this war, Serbs and Croats and Bosnians all went to different churches but got along fine. Well, we didn't. I told you my father wasn't a believer, but none of that mattered. There were a lot of marriages like my parents'. We had the Yugoslav ethnic festival in June, everybody came. Now they are all fighting, people have been knifed, Mommy and Pop don't speak . . ." She stops herself and wanders to the next room.

Wakefield follows at a discreet distance. The exhibition continues with the ubiquitous materials of life under Communism, namely iron (or steel), cement, and cigarettes. There's a tangle of barbed wire in the middle of the floor. Wakefield steps carefully around it. A panel lettered in black Constructivist script is propped against it, which reads:

> *The Iron Curtain was made out of barbed wire, the barbed wire of the border, the prison camp, the factory. Iron, the product of heroic workers, was Stalinist manna. We were taught that in the coming Socialist Eden all one had to do was open one's mouth and bolts and screws would pour out of it. Barbed wire was our crown of thorns.*

There are mutilated busts of revolutionary "fathers," and a statue of Stalin that's been smashed into a cube by a car crusher. The air is intentionally dusty, to recall the industrial pollution of Communist cities. Susan reads aloud yet another statement:

The Iron Curtain was made of cement. Rivers were dammed with cement, mountains were covered with cement, the heroes of revolutionary history were cast in cement. Cement represents the qualities the regime desired to foster: hardness and intransigence, in contrast to the undesirable qualities of flexibility and sensitivity, which were bourgeois. Hardness and Intransigence, together with their little brother, Vigilance, formed a masculine trinity, and the hard, intransigent, vigilant worker was our mascot. In the sexually repressed and conservative communist ethic, this hard worker implied also a proud, erect condition. By giving it all to the ideal, he earned a permanent place in the utopia.

Wakefield's head is aching from the cumulative fear that emanates from these twisted remains of a world still packed with evil energy. The Devil pops into his head. He's smiling ruefully as if to say, "See what I mean?" Wakefield doesn't know what he means. He can see the shimmering form. His Majesty looks very goaty in his Pan getup. There is none of the weary worldliness he'd affected when they'd first met. He looks rested and fresh. Behind him are the smoldering ruins of a recently bombed medieval town. Very painterly, thinks Wakefield, then turns back to Susan. He touches her arm in sympathy, and her dark eyes fill with gratitude. The Devil evaporates. The presence of the older woman is comforting, too. She seems in her wise way to accept the violence, the humor, the contradictions.

Wakefield had planned to deliver the same speech he gave in Typical, thinking "Money and Poetry (with a detour in Art)" was universal enough to go anywhere in America, but he knows it won't work. The relativity of value loses its context here; it doesn't apply to art that witnesses and testifies, that has challenged the temporal powers, the State, the police, the prison, the mental hospital. The purpose of this art is to scream out a reality that makes no sense in a country where all is now virtual, provisional, free-floating, happy, well fed. How can he connect this art to the disappearance of the material world?

He looks to Susan for help, realizing that she's the bridge. His dilemma is inscribed in her psyche. Her body is nouveau American, but her wetware was forged between worlds.

"Maybe I'll just talk about you tonight," he jokes.

"If you did, it might make it easier to understand . . . myself."

"Well, a shrink I'm not. About your parents? Do you really want me to talk to them?" Wakefield figures that meeting her folks might possibly help him get ideas for a completely new speech.

Susan grabs his hand, barely containing her excitement. "Let's do it right now."

Wakefield nods, ignoring his crass instant interpretation of the phrase.

In the car Susan calls her mother and lets her know that they are on the way. To get there Susan drives through a vast Hispanic neighborhood; she points out the big neon crown on top of El Rey Burito, a place she went when she dated Tulio, a minor-league baseball player. "I was still in junior high," she laughs. "My parents would have died if they'd found out." Bordering the Hispanic neighborhood is an African-American community, and other landmarks of her high-school years and a relationship with a Black guy. "They would have died *twice* if they'd known about him."

The Black 'hood ends abruptly at a string of Polish and Ukrainian bakeries, restaurants, and barbershops, some of them with signs in Cyrillic script. The gold dome of a Byzantine church glistens at the end of the avenue.

Susan's parents, Slobodan and Aleisha Petrovich, live in a five-story red-brick apartment building. Susan parks in the slushy snow right in front, where her father is bent over the engine of his car, cursing.

He straightens up when she calls his name. By way of introduction Susan says, "I brought Mr. Wakefield over to meet you."

Mr. Petrovich wipes his hands on a greasy rag and mumbles a greeting, sounding not at all like the great fan of his work Susan has led Wakefield to believe he is. To his daughter he says only, "Can you give me a jump? You got cables in that hippie car?"

"Nice to meet you, Mr. Petrovich. What's the matter?"

"Dead battery."

It turns out that Susan does not, in fact, have any battery cables in her hippie car.

"Is Mommy home?"

Mr. Petrovich looks at her as if she's from another planet. "Where else you think she is? She's always up there with her friends, my enemies." He turns his head and spits in the dirty snow. "So you're the guy come to talk about peace and harmony. You can't wipe out one thousand years of history with some art. It's all shit." He waits with his hands on his hips for Wakefield to respond.

"Here he goes," Susan says tightly, determined not to be baited.

"It's not my intention to change history," Wakefield answers, "but if art helps people get along, I'm all for it."

"Tell you what. We tried 'getting along,' we tried to be good Americans . . . but guess who doesn't want us to get along now? I suppose you like the American bombs killing women and children in Belgrade?"

Mr. Petrovich slams the hood shut and lays his calloused palms on it. He looks at Wakefield through the thick lenses of his eyeglasses. "Bombs killing women and children in my homeland!"

"I don't like bombs," Wakefield says, "but it wasn't just an American decision to bomb Belgrade—"

"It's NATO trying to save Mommy's people," Susan interjects.

"Your mommy's people!" Mr. Petrovich spits again. "That's who started it. They were happy enough under Tito. Now they want our land, holy Serbian land!" He turns to Wakefield. "I have papers upstairs. I prove it to you!" Mr. Petrovich starts reciting a litany of dates, martyrs, and battles, only half in English.

"Well, that's enough for me," says Susan. "All my life he's an atheist commie, now he cares about stinking relics. Let's go upstairs."

A burly man with a black mustache even thicker than Mr. Petrovich's graying one approaches the car and says something in Serbian. He's got jumper cables. They open the hood and start hooking them up. The man opens the hood of a truck parked in front of Petrovich and winks at Susan.

"Pervert!" She blushes. "It's the mustaches," she explains to Wakefield, "the war of the mustaches. When these guys shave them off, there will be peace."

It's a real revelation, and Wakefield can suddenly see two enormous armies facing each other: the men with mustaches against the ones without. In the sixties when Wakefield's hair was moderately long, there was war in America over hair. The "Hair Curtain" fell between generations almost as inflexibly as the Iron Curtain between east and west. Back then, it was the longhairs versus the National Guard. Now it's the mustachioed against the clean shaven.

Upstairs, Mrs. Petrovich, who has been watching everything from the apartment window, has refreshments waiting for Susan's guest: cake, tomatoes, liqueur, cheese, and a carafe of ice-cold water. The particularly pungent goat cheese sits in the middle of a wooden board with a knife stuck in it.

"This is my mommy, Aleisha Petrovich. Mommy, Mr. Wakefield."

Mrs. Petrovich doesn't hold out her hand for Wakefield to shake, but she makes a big welcoming gesture toward the couch. "Sit, sit. A shame that man. You tell me what I do." She wrings her hands, on the verge of tears.

"Now, now, Mommy, you know that's how he is, a rude sonofabitch!"

"Susan! Don't talk like that. Maybe even he is sonofabitch, excuse us, Mr. Wakefield. You should have come here before the war. Men were polite and good, working hard, never a bad word, no cursing . . ."

"Right," mocks Susan, "drinking and gambling every night at the club, asleep all day Sunday, screaming at me and Tiffany. . . . He was only nice when Professor Teleskou was home."

"Have something sweet, Mr. Wakefield. I make."

Wakefield takes a slice of crumbly poppy-seed cake and stuffs it in his mouth. Mrs. Petrovich pours him a glass of water. He takes a sip.

"Thank you, Mrs. Petrovich. Susan said that you might like to see the exhibit and hear me talk tonight. I would be delighted if you did."

"How can I? You see that beast. If I leave the house, he thinks I'm going to Bosnia Club to make bombs against him. . . . Maybe I should."

"Please forgive me," says Wakefield, "I'm an ignorant American. What is it all about?"

"Land. It's about land. For eight hundred years they take our land. They kill us."

"And you kill them," says Susan. "It's the same land. For hundreds of years you live together, then you start killing each other. Besides, you don't live in that land anymore."

"It was supposed to be different in America," sighs Mrs. Petrovich. "It was, many years. This is good place, we have festivals and everybody hate the Communists. Then the Communists go, everyone happy for maybe two months. Then this big war over there starts and everybody here starts. Now, you go out and the Negroes rob you."

"Here we go. The Yugoslavs kill each other, so let's blame Black people. Mother, please."

Wakefield is reminded of Maggie's description of her father's prejudices. And that reminds him of Maggie. He imagines her lying naked on her back in the hotel room in Typical, talking about the Idiot Guides. He feels a pleasant tremor in his groin, even as he hears Susan bring her mother up short. In fact, Maggie might have said it the same way. It's the voice of children exasperated by their parents' prejudices but smart enough to know that it's hopeless to argue.

"They're always looking for somebody else to to blame for their problems!" Susan sighs. "That's how they think in Europe, which is why I don't eat meat."

More twisted logic. Wakefield has his job cut out for him. What is he going to talk about tonight? Art? Art that was once a code for meat? Art that bemoaned the lack of meat, protested the absence of meat, made imaginary towers of meat? Maybe he should just do some kind of performance art, and speak from inside a pig carcass hanging from the ceiling with only his head sticking out. His head, looking as if it is being born from the belly of the sundered pig, recites dada poetry in an invented language to people who speak many languages but believe only in their own.

"You can't even go out at night anymore," Mrs. Petrovich cries. "They push you down, take your purse, and kill you. Most of my friends move out already, their children help them." She shoots guilt daggers at Susan, who defends herself as best she can.

"I already said you can move in with me. Tiffany said so, too. Leave Old Slobodan here to fight it out with his pals. He doesn't like women anyway."

Mommy doesn't hear the last part. "Tiffany?" She nearly spits. "What devil come in me to name her Tiffany? She's a whore now."

"Fashion model, Mommy. Tiffany is a respected fashion model. She makes good money. So what if she lives with a woman? Wouldn't you, if you had another chance?"

Surprisingly, Mommy laughs at this, and nods through her tears. "I would, yes I would. Have more cake, Mr. Wakefield. Forgive us, we are—what do you say?—'passionate'?"

There is sudden affection between mother and daughter. They laugh about something known only to themselves. Wakefield cuts a hunk from the cheese and shuts his eyes involuntarily as the essence of goat milk floods his mouth. He chases it with a slice of salted tomato and a shot of plum brandy. When he opens his eyes, he notices the stacks of *National Cartographics* on the bookshelves.

Aleisha Petrovitch, Susan has told him, has difficulty walking because of her varicose veins and excessive weight, and she depends on Susan to drive her to the grocery store once a week. The rest of the time she watches the news and reads.

"You should write a story from my life, Mr. Wakefield. What a tale I have lived."

"Our people are like a magical-realist novel," says Susan,

"When you were a girl?" suggests Wakefield.

"Long before, Mr. Wakefield. When my grandmother was a girl. What happen is that we had a well in the village where a man who traveled—"

Susan: "A peddler."

"Yes. A peddler drowned in the well. Our water tasted first like iron, then sulphur, and the mullah said that the Devil made his bath there, but the men think the Serbian men over the mountain came in the night and poisoned our well. So our men made a poison, too, and the mullah wouldn't bless it, but the men didn't care. Before they go to the Serbian village to curse their water, they met around the well to take one more drink of bad water to make them strong. There was moon and stars and night was light like day. My grandmother was only a girl, but all the children were awake and they let them watch. The first man drew out some water and drank, then made surprise face. Another drank, and he, too, made surprise. Everybody tasted then and nobody could believe. The water was like sweet honey, not iron, not sulphur. The mullah said that the Devil was big trick maker, that he make water taste bitter one time, sweet another. Then nobody knew what they must do, and big discussion went on, and while some people said this and some said that, there was a yellow light around the well and a very big butterfly shoot out of the water and fly up into the sky. Big like a boy with wings. Nobody believe what they see, nobody could say anything. They watched as the butterfly get higher and higher and become a star. When they talk after a long time, the mullah said that this was the Devil with wings who was chained in the well and that the men who made the poison let him out because mullah didn't bless it. But the men didn't think so, so they look up where the butterfly flied and beat their chest and cry. Then everybody tasted the water again, even the children, and it was still sweet like honey. Next day, one man went down on long rope to the bottom of well that was so deep they had to take all the rope in the village, and when he come back two days later, he bring with him a white bone deathhead . . . How you say that?"

"Skull, Mommy."

"Skull. He take the white skull and show it to everybody and everybody said the mullah must bless. The whole village goes to mosque, but the mullah would not bless because he said this was Devil skull. Another peddler man who was there said no, this is skull of peddler, I know him. But nobody believe him. After one week everybody said, let's go to big mosque in Kosovo and have bigger mullah bless it, but that never happened. The Serb army came and burned our village and only ten people lived, my grandmother was only a little girl. Her mother and father were killed by the soldiers. My grandmother went to live near Mosul where she met a builder name Yssan."

"Mother," Susan says impatiently, "maybe you should start more recently. Mr. Wakefield may be tired."

"No," Wakefield protests, "go on, Mrs. Petrovich." The history of the Devil interests him. He imagines for a second Mrs. Petrovich's face if he told her that he knows Satan personally.

"Okay, now. My grandfather Yssan was building a mosque, but the walls fall down all the time. The Mosul mullah tell him that the Devil keep pulling down at night all the walls Yssan make in daytime. Only way for mosque to stand is for one martyr to be built inside wall. He tell him to spend the night outside building and ask persons who come by after midnight if they wish to be martyr for glory of God. By this time my grandparents have five children, four girls, one boy. Two of the girls come out at night to see boys, disobeying their parents. When first girl come by, Grandfather catch her and he ask angry if she love God, and she cries and says yes, yes. So he grab her arms and put her feet in the brick mud and he build his daughter, Aleisha, in church wall. His best daughter, he love her the most, she cries, he cries, too, but what is done now is done. When wall is up to her chin, she says, 'I love you,' but it's for Grandfather not God, so he cries more but is more angry and covers her all up with bricks. His daughter Fatima comes by and sees what is going on, but he does not see her. She runs away that night to big city, Belgrade, and pretend to be modern woman.

"After that, the mosque stand beautiful, but the Turk army comes the week after, then Serb army, then armies from Europe, they kill everybody. But they don't burn the mosque. My mother Fatima in Belgrade, she marry Serb writer of beautiful poetry, and she never tell anybody about the Devil and the wall and her sister's death. When I'm sixteen, the German army invade Yugoslavia and kill my mother and father in bombing, but I am in school so I escape to Mosul where some family still lives. That's where I hear this story, and I was so sad. Then I met Slobodan who came to the house with partisans from the mountain to get food and blankets. Partisans come in the house with guns and we think life is over, but they don't kill us, they take all our food and Slobodan look at me and say, 'After the war I come for you.' He did, and that is why I'm in America now with him."

"Tell about the mosque Grandfather built, Mommy."

"It stand beautiful until last week. Serbians dynamite it. Nothing there now." She starts crying. "My mother sister die there but Allah didn't keep his word. They name me for her."

Casually scanning the airwaves for his name, the Devil overhears this and swells with pride. The Balklands are especially dear to him; he has shaped their essence with his flute and lyre. He is both Pan and Orpheus, master of Greek caves and king of Thrace. He has created such beauty there that the human tribes that followed defended his melodies, his stories, both those he told and those he inspired, to the death. History there, in all its bloody absurdity, was generally the result of people fighting to preserve his memory. The wars themselves were not his fault; his policy is noninterventionist. He's often blamed for carnage, but he doesn't revel in it. Nor does he have any particular revulsion to it: a field of corpses or a burning city have a beauty of their own. He's attached to the Balklands because it is there, only there, that he feels at home after his original exile. Stories like the one Aleisha told, garbled as they are—he would like her to speak better English—make him proud because they are about the time when the world was young and everyone could recognize his magic. A big problem with the world now is that it is prosaic, it lacks a link to magic, it is unimaginative, without the awe it owes him. Even the wars lack grandeur, the weapons are impersonal, people use his name mostly as a curse, they rarely acknowledge his divine nature.

The Devil allows himself a moment of self-pity, then swells with pride. After all, it is he, not God, who is the originator of Art. God hasn't made a thing since he animated his clay ape. Everything else about the creature, including the music of its doubts, its flights of fancy, its love of beauty, are Lucifer's work and his work only. People rarely sacrifice to him personally, but they willingly die for beauty, they give their lives to the awesomeness of what moves them to depths of emotion, which is for the most part the Devil's music. Unaccountably, there are people still faithful to their remote Creator, who could care less. These dry and resentful souls scourge innocence with the whips of guilt and sin and hatred of nature. They talk of the "sin of pride," they shrivel the blooming flesh, they freeze the scent in the bloom, they punish play and snuff out joy. Pan's poets have long denounced these stormtroopers for God, Orpheus has nearly broken the strings of his lyre to weaken their magic, but to no avail. As beauty begins to reel under the blows of killjoys, science marches forward employing all in dreary cubicles of reason. Pan, who likes all his names, including Satan, Lucifer, Orpheus, Beelzebub, the Evil One, and whatever else people come up with, has his job cut out for him these days. God may no longer be around, but the minions acting in His name are massing at all the exit points of liberty, blocking the escapes to imaginary worlds, to fancy, to reverie, to wilderness, to play, even to one's flesh, and even to death, can you believe it. They are freeze-drying people! Satan is sick of it and of all spiritual bureaucracies, including his own, but he won't give up, even if that means eventually waking God Himself from His immemorial slumber. Ironically, he might need God in the end to help him fight the phonies operating in His name. That's if He still cares about the monkey he once set spinning through the light.

His Malignancy chews thoughtfully on a hoof: he could use a nymph right now.

Susan tries to explain at least part of her mother's mysterious story. "Every mosque, church, or bridge in the old country has someone buried in it, apparently. Usually it's a virgin or a new bride. You ask my mom when something happened and she tells you that whatever it was, no matter how tragic or insane, a war followed shortly thereafter."

"But it's all true, Susan. This is your family stories."

"They are great stories, Mommy," Susan says agreeably. "Professor Teleskou loved your stories; he used to write them all down."

"Maybe he did wrong to write my stories. Poor Professor!" says Mrs. Petrovich, turning to Wakefield. "Someone break into his apartment and steal all his notebooks, his computer, everything. Then they kill him!"

Professor Mihai Teleskou is an author with whom Wakefield is familiar. He has read a book by Teleskou about the afterlife beliefs of Balkland peasants. It is called *The Gnostic Tree: The Devil in the Balklands*.

"We loved the professor," says Susan. "After his apartment was burglarized, he moved into our spare room. He thought someone was after him, the Romanian secret police, really. He felt safer here because my father has connections and could protect him. Pop actually had guys standing watch in front of the building twenty-four hours a day, because everyone was afraid of more burglaries. The professor wrote in his room and when he went out to the college or for a walk, my father's friend Miroslav went with him, even the day they killed him. Professor Teleskou went to the bathroom across the hall from his office. When he didn't come back, Miroslav went to look for him. He was dead in the toilet stall. One shot to the back of the head. And nobody heard anything. It was horrible."

Aleisha begins to sob; Susan puts an arm around her shoulders.

"His stuff is still in the spare room. Come look." Susan leaves her mother in the kitchen and takes Wakefield down the hall. She flips on the light in the tiny bedroom: Books are piled up along one wall, books on Balkland folklore, mystical cults of the Middle Ages; Provençal poetry, Cathar legends; a Bogomilian treatise, Flammel's alchemical writings, an encyclopedia of witchcraft; Gershom Scholem on the Qabbalah; biographies of Giordano Bruno and Francis Bacon; Aramaic, Hebrew, and Greek grammars. A painting of the Tree of Qabbalah with its shekinahs in bright colors is framed above the desk; a tankha painting of the Tantric Tibetan wheel hangs between the narrow windows. On the desk there's a sheaf of papers held down by a miniature replica of the Rosetta stone. Next to it is a manual typewriter. Wakefield notices a title page on top of the pile: "Magic and Memory." Sounds pretty benign. Who'd want to kill this guy, he wonders. He is fascinated by the Tibetan wheel, half of which is festooned with grotesque demons, the other with beautiful angels. Presumably, as the wheel turns, the world becomes alternately horrible and beautiful and vice versa, but to the enlightened, horror and beauty are the same. Demons are the other side of angels; the difference is only in how we perceive them. Wakefield has long wanted to believe that, but he can never quite muster the wisdom: beauty still leaves him weak at the knees, and horror makes him want to run and hide.

Susan touches the keys of the typewriter and blows some dust off the desk. "Mommy wouldn't come in here after he died, so it's just as he left it. She doesn't understand all this, but Mihai, Professor Teleskou, told me some things about what was going on. After 1989, after the revolution, he became involved with politics in Romania. He wrote articles for an émigré newspaper about the power struggle there; according to him, some really odd business was being revived after the fall of Communism, having to do with nationalist and racist mythology, and he must have touched a nerve, because some people back in Romania got really paranoid. He got threatening mail that said he was betraying his country, that he was a Jew-lover, a pervert, stuff like that. But he kept publishing his articles, mostly about Balklands folklore and how everything going on there now can be read in fairy tales and legends. Then they stole his files and his computer. And I think they killed him."

"Jeez! I didn't think shit like that happened anymore, at least not here."

"Mihai was very brave. He used to say the Iron Curtain didn't fall, it was lifted. He wanted to make sure it stayed up."

Wakefield doesn't know what to say. He feels very close to this woman who carries two worlds within her. She seems fragile yet strong. He puts his arm around Susan's thin shoulders for a moment, then withdraws, feeling awkward.

"He was a wonderful man, very gentle. He didn't want Mommy to know about the threats. . . . She was a little in love with him. So was I."

They haven't noticed that Mrs. Petrovich is standing in the door-way.

"He was thin like straw, but he love my food. I never put any meat on him. Too much thinking, I tell him. So tall, such beautiful eyes, and he always dressed so neat, so clean, with a tie, a nice briefcase. A gentleman."

Mother and daughter wipe tears from their eyes.

Wakefield finds it hard to believe that a scholar could be killed over some esoteric fairy tales. Unless the bad guys also used those fairy tales in some way, like a code. People sometimes collide on the same ground and nobody believes anybody could be there by mistake. Wakefield once endured two hours of questioning by the FBI about an article he'd written on military architecture, citing a totally un-classified description of certain missile silos in Wyoming. The FBI wanted to know whose eyes the article was meant for, and they had difficulty believing that he wasn't sending signals to the Soviets.

"I see guys in black trenchcoats and shiny shoes sometimes, lurk-ing around this building. Definitely from Teleskou's country. Maybe there's something here that they still want. . . ." Susan trails off.

"I have a gun now. These men come here, they better watch out," Mrs. Petrovich says passionately. "Maybe I even use it some day on your father." Her eyes flash.

Susan ignores that remark, and now tries to play down the men in black. "Oh, Mommy, those guys are probably just artists, they always wear black. This neighborhood attracts artists."

"It's the smell, Susan. I know the difference, I can tell, I could be parfumer. The artistickis smell like smoke and paint. The killers smell bad like mold, like blood . . ."

"My father and Mihai used to argue sometimes, but Pop never got angry, he was always polite to the professor. Pop started up on this land thing one day, talking about the blood of our people and so on, and the professor said the war wasn't about land, it's about *genii loci,* spirits of place. He said that people get possessed by these spirits, and even after years in exile, they are the playthings of these spirits, and the politicians know this and use the spirits to stir up hatred. Pop had no idea what to say to that."

"Yes, the professor was too smart for Slobodan!" Mrs. Petrovich seems pleased by the memory.

"Maybe we should go now, Susan?" Wakefield feels it's time to make an exit. He's got a speech to write.

"No," says Mrs. Petrovich firmly, "you must have some Turkish coffee!"

Resistance is futile. In the warm kitchen Wakefield stares into the delicate porcelain cup filled with sweet black coffee, a dark mirror. Nothing can be seen there. When he's finished the coffee Aleisha takes his cup and overturns it on the saucer. She reads the trails of coffee grounds. "Many roads," she sighs. "Mr. Wakefield, you are like us. Always going from your home. Why?"

"I thought that maybe *you* could tell me." Wakefield is sincere. He's been running as long as he can remember.

Mrs. Petrovich gazes into the cup.

The Devil has a keen interest in what she sees in there, too. He watches over her shoulder, pleased with her skill. One of his disciplines, one he is very proud of, is to steadfastly forbid himself to know the future. It is a point of honor, particularly since he's a gambler and has been one since day one. He does not cheat, despite what his mythographers say. Why would he? It would ruin the game, and he'd be bored stiff if he knew the outcome. These days he'll do anything not to be bored, including losing. Of course, he will use what advantage he can, count cards, ride streaks, read the psychology of his opponent—all too easy after watching thousands of predictable humans doing predictable things for eons. In other words, he seeks no more advantage than a smart mortal would, and that includes employing fortune-tellers. They are his muddy mirror and his protection against the temptation to cheat. In his time, he has used diviners of every kind, from astrologers to augers who read the entrails of sacrificed animals. He has found that the world is a forest of signs and an open book for the trained eye. Some of the greatest diviners read just for the joy of it, deciphering rocks and tree branches, the wind's play in the sand, the lines of faces. Everything in the material world speaks to those willing to read it. In fact, the world shouts prophecies and messages of every kind in wonderful, unique forms. It would be a violation of the world's beauty to intervene directly in the all-knowing of matter. The Devil does not need to cheat; he has legions of translators.

"It look to me, Mr. Wakefield, please forgive me for the truth, that you are running from responsible, that you are like child who does not come inside when mother calls."

Wakefield laughs. "Apt, no doubt. Will I ever come inside?"

Aleisha points hopefully to a clump of damp grounds at the intersection of many fine lines. "That is home, maybe you go there in a year, but you wait for something."

That's nothing either Wakefield or the Devil doesn't know. Neither one has gained an advantage through Mrs. Petrovich's cup.

"Many thanks, Mrs. Petrovich. I *am* waiting for something."

Right. The Devil fingers a sixteenth-century Italian musket with gold-inlaid ivory stock he has brought along for the occasion, but changes his mind (yet again) and returns to his Carpathian cave where, on a bed of moss next to a gurgling brook, a sleeping beauty dreams of his long, curly tongue. Wakefield can wait a while longer.

The front door bangs and Mr. Petrovich treads heavily into the room. He's holding a bottle of plum brandy; his face is swollen. Aleisha leaves the room and Susan stands up, ready for anything.

"Been having a good time eating my food, Mr. Wakefield?" Slobodan's bloodshot eyes roam the kitchen. "Where is she going? My check must be here."

Mrs. Petrovich comes back into the kitchen with her hands on her hips. "I pay bills with your check!" she hisses. The adversaries face each other. Susan steps between them.

"Pop, you should leave now!"

Mr. Petrovich says something nasty in Serbian and heads for the door.

"Mr. Wakefield, tell your boss we aren't afraid of bombs!" Slobodan shouts before he slams it.

Wakefield makes a mental note. Who *is* his boss?

When he and Susan step out on the street, after many hugs and kisses from Mrs. Petrovich, they see Slobodan Petrovich speeding off in his old car, exhaust billowing behind him. Wouldn't pass inspection, thinks Wakefield. Nor would his native country, billowing its own lethal smoke thousands of miles away.

Back at the wheel of her little car, Susan is quiet for several blocks.

"Well, that was a bust," she finally says, lighting a cigarette. "Sorry. Do you want to get a drink?"

His talk at the museum is at eight, and it's already five, but the hell with it, it's been a long, weird day. He has *some* notes. "Sure. Let's go back to the hotel, have a drink at the bar there. That way I can change into my art sweater and get ready for tonight. I have no idea what I'm going to talk about."

His black turtleneck sweater is always helpful in art-situations.

"You could talk about hit men in black turtlenecks," Susan jokes, throwing the butt out the window. "Just kidding."

Well, sure. If there is one thing that Wakefield knows he can count on, it's serendipity. The left field always provides. He pursues the Teleskou story. There is something very mysterious here, and possibly helpful.

"Let me see if I understand this," he tells Susan. "Teleskou was a collector of religious belief, a *Homo religiosus,* who believed in the myths of races, in spiritual forces that shape nations as well as people. He believed in the afterlife, in ghosts, in place-spirits, in active witch-craft, really. I know he wrote in a dispassionate, scientific way, but those things were real to him. Was everything in Teleskou's world-view antithetical to your father's?"

Susan takes her time. "No, but *something* was."

"What was it?"

"Me." Susan lights another cigarette.

Somehow, that doesn't surprise him. "You had a romance with the professor?"

"Not a romance, no. I felt that he was my older soul mate, my guide. But Pop was suspicious. Fairy tales always made him nervous."

"No wonder, given Aleisha's. Surely the politics is something else, though. The police will figure it out one day," says Wakefield. Truth-fully, though, he is not so sure that the police will figure it out. He senses here a mystery that is beyond the Wintry City police, involving as it does myth and the Balklands, ideologies and a beautiful princess. A detective with a Ph.D. in religious studies might, just might make something out of it.

Wakefield goes to his room, leaving Susan in the bar with a mar-tini. On his way up in the elevator he phones Zamyatin. "I'm in deep shit, man. I landed on your planet and I have no idea how to talk to the natives." He tells him about the pre- and post-Communist art show, the ethnic tensions, the battling Petroviches, Susan. "What am I going to say tonight?"

On the other end of the call Zamyatin is at his living room window in the bar, in a philosophical mood. Wakefield can hear the ice cubes clinking as they talk.

"In the first place, don't even say 'ethnic' this or that, that's like the newspapers. Where does the word come from? 'Ethos,' the beliefs and behaviors of a people. They don't hire you to talk about their ethos, that's what they are fighting about. They hire you to tell them about *your* ethos, something they don't know, maybe how to make some money, or travel for free. Forget about that ethnic shit. Of course, they might just kill you."

Zamyatin laughs his smoky laugh that sounds like marbles in a tin box. Wakefield has reached his room and is rooting around in his bag for his sweater. He wonders how long he can go on pulling his speeches out of thin air, giving himself up to inspiration and chance. What if one day he's on stage facing the expectations of a hungry mob, and his inspiration snaps? What if the Devil cuts the rope and he falls to the ground with a thump? That would be some warning shot: the total failure of his act!

" . . . so my favorite song," Zamyatin goes on about something, "is 'Paint It Black,' so we play it over and over until the KGB colonel knocks on the door one night and says, 'I'm confiscating the music.' And from then, I hear the Rolling Stones come from the colonel's apartment every night! You see, that was socialism. Then I signed a manifesto to free political prisoners, and they take me to the nice, quiet hospital. . . . The colonel himself takes me, then before I go in he gives me a little present. It's the Rolling Stones, my old tape. I play 'Paint It Black,' very appropriate because everything in the hospital is white including the food, then they send me to the Arctic where, you know, everything is more white. You tell me what it means. God, does she have a cute ass!" That's clearly not in reference to the tape.

Still listening to Ivan, unable to find his sweater, Wakefield logs on and sees that he has twenty-two e-mails. "Okay, but do you think this ethnic fighting is going stop or is it just getting started?"

"I know my people: gloomy Slavs, people with souls as dark as Leningrad in December. They gonna suffer forever. They have old, old feelings . . . like nine hundred years old. What we should do is parachute one hundred thousand psychiatrists in there and put the whole place in therapy, make everybody listen to Rolling Stones. Maybe after thirty, forty years the lamb lies down with the chicken hawk. Listen man, good luck tonight! I gotta go."

What's scary is that Zamyatin is never wrong, not even when he sounds completely insane. Wakefield has an overwhelming desire to hear "Paint It Black," also one of his favorite songs. The Devil's, too, no doubt. He reads some of his twenty-two messages. Of course, there's a new one from his ex-wife. "Are you in town yet, Wakefield? You didn't call, so I suppose you are. There are things we need to discuss and if you don't call me I'm going to come to your thing tonight. Peace, M."

Peace, huh. That's serious. Wakefield has an unpleasant vision of Marianna in peasant-roots drag making a scene at the museum. *That* would be a performance. He could announce from the podium that he has racked his brain for insights into the problems and paradoxes represented by the exhibition and come to the conclusion that a public discussion with his Romanian ex-wife on the subject of their daughter would best serve the purpose.

He's found his sweater and is putting it on backward when Susan calls from the bar. "What's taking you so long? Hurry up, I have a surprise for you. . . ."

Wakefield sees the surprise as soon as he enters the bar. Everybody's staring at two incredibly beautiful women sitting with Susan, drinking martinis. They look like women on the covers of fashion magazines. They *are* on the covers of fashion magazines. He squeezes into the booth next to Susan, who's on her third martini and very happy.

"This is my surprise," she bubbles. "My sister, Tiffany, and Milena, her girlfriend."

Wakefield, kissing their proffered hands, murmurs, *"Enchanté,"* in an "I've been to Europe" way. He can't believe his luck. He's in the garden of the muses.

Tiffany met Milena, a Czech girl with the same name as Franz Kafka's girlfriend, in Prague, at the Café Milena, a coincidence that still amuses them as they recall their encounter for Wakefield. Milena Café has a view of Prague's famous medieval clock that rings in the hour with the figure of Death.

"So it's the hour," says Tiffany, "and I'm standing at the café window looking at Death with all these German tourists, and when I go back to my table, my purse is gone. . . . I look around and I see this boy, like twelve years old, running toward the door with my purse under his arm, and the next thing I see is this gorgeous long leg come out from under a table, and he trips over it and falls face down. In a flash I'm on top of him, but the chick who tripped him is already on top of him. I fall on top of her and we are both on the floor on top of the little thief, and when we look into each other's eyes . . . kaboom!"

They look into each other's eyes and laugh. Susan makes a face. She's heard the story.

"That's amazing," says Wakefield sincerely. It's nice to see people in love from so close up. "Like magic."

"Prague is a magical place," Milena says in her seductive accent. "Alchemists, artists, writers, everybody loves Prague. It's the most beautiful city in the world."

Tiffany says tenderly, "She's never lived in a city where art isn't just everywhere. Art is her air. She thinks that it makes everything run, even the buses, not to mention revolutions."

"And what is wrong with that?" Milena asks, draping herself around her friend. "Beauty is truth, is it not?"

Susan turns to Wakefield. "Isn't true love disgusting? You want to know how I feel about the guy I've been dating? If there was a fire and I had to choose between him and my new vibrator, it would be no contest."

A young man with a clipboard approaches their table.

"Hi! I'm from Trend Watch. We're doing a survey. We're asking people what they think the next big thing is going to be. Would you mind?"

"My dinner," answers Milena, who's a chef, as well as a model.

"It's so nice of you to ask," says Tiffany, stretching like a lynx inside her angora sweater.

"In the future, robots will conduct surveys," says Susan.

"You know what I think?" Tiffany says sharply, her irritation directed at her sister. "I think the next big thing will be that people will always be very nice to other people because they'll be wearing electronic bracelets that monitor their aggression levels. Whenever you say mean things, you'll get zapped."

The survey guy is fixated on Tiffany's angora-framed cleavage; the tip of his tongue is actually hanging out of his mouth.

"I think a well-placed 'fuck you' would be worth getting zapped for," Susan counters.

Milena ignores them and earnestly tells the surveyor, "Wearable technology, if you really want to know, is the next big thing. And fingerprint ATMs."

While Milena enlightens the surveyor, Susan tells her sister about the situation at home. "Pop's gone nuts. We've really got to do something, Mommy's crying all the time."

"You know how she feels about me and Milena. I don't know what I can do."

"We've got to get her away from Pop. I'm afraid he'll hurt her. Or get hurt himself. I told you Mommy bought a gun."

Milena and the clipboard guy have somehow gone on to the subject of post-Communist legs.

"It's a new, EU kind of thing. After communism, girls' legs grew longer, everyone got taller. And the shorter the skirts, the longer the legs, you know."

He doesn't, but laughs anyway. He doesn't care what she says as long as he can keep looking at her. Tiffany turns away from her sister and jumps into Milena's conversation.

"Milena just loves surveys. In her country no one ever asked her opinion about anything. She was eleven during the Velvet revolution, Havel and all that. She's a velve*teen*."

Apparently Susan is used to this kind of family-issues avoidance by Tiffany. Milena continues to elaborate her theory of post-Communist beauty.

"The founding myth of Bohemia is very interesting. The tribal ruler was a woman, the Princess Libuse, and she was forced by the nobles to take a husband, which caused all the women to revolt. They call it the War of the Maidens, and it lasted for many years, but unfortunately the men prevailed and established a dynasty that ruled for six hundred years. Because of the importance of women in Czech history, beautiful stone women decorate almost all the buildings in Prague. That's why we invented Art Nouveau," she smirks, elbowing Tiffany. "When I was a little girl I loved these stone ladies, and I wanted to look just like them when I grew up."

Susan looks disgusted by her chickenshit sister and Art Nouveau. "Are you saying that Czech chicks grow up beautiful in order to compete with a bunch of buildings?"

"What's wrong with that? Stone women can be naked year round because they're not bothered by cold and snow. In the Czech Republic we have only one or two months of summer to enjoy being naked."

"Milena loves to be naked," confirms Tiffany.

The guy with the clipboard holds it against his chest, as if holding in his about-to-explode heart. He's hypnotized.

"Shoo," Susan tells him. "Go away now."

He doesn't know what to do.

"That's all," says Tiffany. "That's all we have to say."

Milena winks at him. Reluctantly, he drags himself away backward, like a supplicant. The next big thing. Wow.

"You chased away my admirer!" Milena pouts.

"There are always more where he came from." Tiffany bumps her shoulder. The two of them are like a couple of young thoroughbreds.

Wakefield doesn't want them to gallop away, but he really does need an hour alone to prepare for his talk. It's getting late.

He excuses himself from the booth, but Susan won't budge.

"I'll just stay here and drink until you come back. Don't worry, I'm an excellent drunk driver."

"I'm not so sure," her sister warns. "I can drive all of you. Milena's getting pretty shit-faced and I just love it when she's like that. She'll do anything."

Milena pulls up her skirt under the table. "I'm not wearing any panties!" she announces cheerfully.

Twinge of desire. No, he really must go upstairs for a while. Alone. He does like his wide range of choices, options, and possibilities, though. It's as if in giving him a deadline for starting the race for his "real" life, the Devil gave him a prelife of delights, like the best parts of all kinds of great movies. Just as quickly as he rejoices, he sees the downside. If all the great alternatives occur in the prelife, what happens after the starter shot? Will the range perversely narrow, leaving him not with the likes of Maggie or Susan, but choices between, let's say, working forever in a slaughterhouse or serving breakfasts in an insane asylum. No women, no great restaurants, no glittery cities, no beautiful cornfields . . . just his back on an eternal treadmill. The Devil's sense of humor is not like ours. We laugh about anything, including ourselves, but the Devil has a cruel surrealist streak.

BECAUSE OF THE controversial nature of the exhibition, the museum has hired private security guards to augment city police for the opening. When Wakefield and his tipsy sirens arrive, there is a cordon of uniformed police and beefy guys with walkie-talkies and bulges under their jackets in front of the building. Wakefield goes through a metal detector and receives his Speaker badge. Doris is there on the other side of the checkpoint, and she takes him to the green room backstage. They are accompanied by two muscular guys in suits who scan the empty hall before unlocking the door to the green room. Doris sighs. "Private security. We had to. Regular museum security people don't even have guns. I hope it doesn't bother you."

Wakefield drinks a soda, then goes out to peek at the crowd from behind the curtain. One bodyguard walks in front of him, the other behind. Wakefield takes a look; the auditorium is full, at least fifteen hundred people. He sees his friends in the front row. Milena has stuck her long legs out in front of her. The short skirt and what he knows isn't under it give him a momentary thrill, but it's followed by a stronger feeling of fear.

As senior curator, Doris takes the stage to begin her introduction to the exhibition. She speaks carefully, noting how difficult it has been to select the works, which represent so many countries and so many, often conflicting, points of view. She explains that the process was unbiased, and that the museum hopes that it will foster understanding and, more important, tolerance. There is a scattering of polite applause. Then she launches into her introduction of the speaker.

"Mr. Wakefield is a man known to many of you as one of this country's best travel writers. He is also an accomplished speaker celebrated for his poetic insights and surprising improvisational style. What you may not know is that he is also a student of architecture and a sensitive observer of human societies. I saw on the noon news today that the symbolic Bridge at Mostar, said to connect or divide East and West, a bridge that withstood two world wars and many local conflicts, was blown up. You may wonder why we have hired a poetic travel writer to speak here tonight. The answer may or may not flatter Mr. Wakefield. We simply could not think of anyone better able to see our exhibition in the afternoon, relate its images to those we have seen in the news this week, and provide us, additionally, with his own impressions of travel in the Balklands. Some poets travel at the speed of light. I think we found one."

Wakefield walks to the lectern and receives brisk applause. His bodyguards, wearing night-vision goggles, stand in the wings, scanning the darkened theater. He can't see the audience, but he can sense its energy, a fifteen-hundred-headed beast holding its breath.

When the applause dies down, Wakefield addresses the beast.

"Comrades!"

Laughter, hissing, boos.

"Workers, soldiers, peasants!"

More laughter, louder hisses, an angry voice: "Fuck Communism!"

"The other day on the Nature Channel—
I always wanted to start a speech
'the other day on the Nature Channel'
that being the only nature
we know these days
'nature' a channel among many
next to the People Channel and the Disaster
Channel that would be news
and the Sci-fi Channel and the Mystery Channel—
the other day on the Nature Channel
I saw that a perfect ball of iron
spewed by the earth on an island near Madagascar
several thousand years ago
was hollowed out by a man and his sons
who moved inside of it
and were promptly declared gods
by the natives who were allowed inside
the ball once a year to get drunk
and worship something called Aurak
which was a huge petrified fish
that zapped them when they touched it
and for having that experience
they paid the ball carvers in fish

goat meat grapes and lizard kebobs!
And that was not long ago
just after the Second World War
when American planes failed to deliver
Paradise and the local cargo cult failed.
It was at about the same time that in
faraway Romania
Professor Teleskou's mother was in labor"

A murmur of stunned surprise at mention of this name. Voice: "Who killed him?" Wakefield has been counting on this reaction: the assassination of Professor Teleskou, though he was Romanian and not strictly speaking a party to the current conflicts in the Balklands, was considered by some in the Wintry City to mark the *real* start of the war. The issues of land, nationality, race, blood, ancestral rights, and religious feuds, explored in his writing, resonated for partisans of both sides. Teleskou had separated the myths and legends from the nationalist propagandists' uses of them, and that was widely believed to have been the reason for his murder. Their superstitions unmoored, the fanatics killed him.

"In labor Mrs. Teleskou
watched a huge bomb
fall from the sky and level the Church
of the Immaculate Conception
where their neighbors had taken shelter
and she gave birth to a baby
who would survive the war
survive communism
become a world-renowned scholar
and nearly survive the twentieth century!
A miraculous plume of smoke attended his birth!
and the priest of the destroyed church
who also miraculously survived

blessed the baby in the Orthodox rite
and declared the baby divinely pleasing
and thanked the young mother for having delivered
beauty amid the ugliness of war!
He is a pleasant sight unto God, he said.
But under the smoldering church
there was the ruin of an older pagan temple
and beneath that chained to the bottom of a well
was a dying monster.
It was the Beast of Hatred
still alive and calling for the flesh of babes
from underneath the ruins.
Architecture, like Gaul, is divided into three parts
the part that comes courtesy of the Nature Channel
the part that comes thanks to the War Channel
and the part that comes from the Imagination Channel
and these three architectures
the architecture of nature
the architecture of ruins
and the architecture of the imagination
are the sons of Disaster.
The mother giving birth in the ruins
is my mother and your mother
our mothers who warned us not to go near ruins
when we were children but where else could we go
where else could *you* go
when the whole town was a ruin
and the whole country you lived in was in ruins
and the world you were born into was a ruin
and the school Professor Teleskou went to
the Elementary School of the Ursulines
renamed the School of the Red Star

was the ruin of a convent under which ran
tunnels connecting one ruin to another
tunnels that were also tombs
and that had been used in the Middle Ages
to escape from invaders
into the woods where one was safe in the arms
of the nature channel
and the shapes of those ruins
were as fantastic as the legends of your people
who sang them in the ruins of their hovels
to put the world back in some order
after the sky and earth gods the sons
of Disaster had their way with the world!"

Wakefield pours water from the carafe under the lectern into the
glass and the sound is pure; every drop is felt by his listeners. Transcendent silence! He thinks he sees Milena's long legs in the front
row, luminous in their liberty, freed from the ruins of the Old World.

"So when the professor was a boy
he became an expert at making temporary
houses in the shadows of cemeteries and crumbling
walls where he took his first love"

Here Wakefield steps on the shaky ground of a biography he's inventing, but no discontent greets him, so he goes on.

"and there they lived for hours safe inside each other
and that was the architecture of adolescence
which builds shelters of mystery for the unfolding
of its own mysteries
and that—to be perfectly honest—is the only
architecture I care for
and that—if you are honest—
is the only architecture you care for
that shelter-building adolescence pursuing only its love

away from governments police borders and pride of ownership."

This utopian sentiment is met with inaudible but palpable derision by a few, a very few souls in the room; possibly the artists who have traveled from Europe to present their work here; they have pride of ownership and are wary of utopias.

"I would like to see a collaborative
project of urban adolescents of all ages
and from all countries
describing the shelters they have made
for their desire from the ruins of their cities.
What is the eruption of the marvelous
if not the eruption of desire
that rearranges landscapes according
to its fancy
knowing that all architecture
is born of Disaster.
Within every building there is another
known only to desire-driven adolescents
even official buildings
of the state and of the police
where the tormented wait in endless antechambers
under great vaults with trembling forms in their hands
even there you will see a young sergeant or clerk
find a secret place to gratify her imagination
and there is no building on earth that has not been
rebuilt by the imagination to contain
shelter from bright lights nooks of darkness
chapels of selfhood chambers and vaults
for the song of *axis mundi!*
One year after the dictator Ceausescu
ordered the old center of Bucharest demolished
Byzantine churches and stately homes

the coldest winter in the history of the Carpathians
froze all the rivers and the lakes
and in the spring when they thawed
an intact fourteenth-century basilica floated
down the Danube and headed for the Black Sea
where it sank under the waves
joining Greek triremes and Roman warships
and Turkish galleons and Venetian galley ships
and that was the signal for the revolution
and the end of the dictator
and this we have from Teleskou now dead
who loved the stories of his country
 and the miracles of love born of those stories
not often enough, alas!"

Wakefield can't hold this ground much longer without an accent, a man born in security on a rich and hopeful continent. Time to retreat home.

"In America
we watch history floating by
and sinking under the waves of the present!
Here architectures ruin one another
almost as quickly as they rise.
Our country has grown up
free of Father Disaster
but in America all buildings are temporary
even the post offices and the churches
and the museums where artifacts barely recovered
from the shock of being moved across oceans
have to move again to a newer building!
Please look closely on these artworks, comrades!
Tomorrow they may move to a new building."

Laughter. They don't even mind being called comrades now. The speaker has moved on to something they all agree on: in America they are misunderstood because America has no history; it eats its own tail like a hyperactive serpent.

"In America a child can no longer
visit the place where she was born
a shopping mall
stands there instead.
In America a grown-up can no longer see the school
where she learned the art of growing sad
a freeway goes through there now an overpass
her memories of brick turn to glass
the suburb goes from white to black
and time speeds up so much she has
to stay young forever and reset the clock
every five minutes just to know where is there
and *there* is everywhere
because she lives in time and not in any space!
In our country here
the future is in ruins before it is built
a fact recognized by postmodern architecture
that grins at us shyly or demonically as it quotes
ruins from other times and places!
There are no buildings in America only passageways
that connect migratory floods
the most permanent architecture being
precisely that which moves these floods
from one future ruin to another
that is to say freeways and skyways
and the car is our only shelter
the architecture of desire reduced to the womb
a womb in transit from one nowhere to another!"
Saddened by his own vision, and sensing smugness in the audi-

ence, Wakefield is revolted by his desire to please the foreigners. He coughs. He is betraying his own country now for the sake of . . . what? Applause? There isn't any. He veers down another path.

"The miracle of America is of motion not regret
in New Mexico the face of Jesus jumped on a tortilla
in Plaquemine a Virgin appeared in a tree
in Santuario de Chimayo the dirt turned healer
a guy in Texas crashed into a wall when God said
Let me take the wheel!
And others hear voices all the time
telling them to sit under a tree or jump from a cliff
or take large baskets of eggs into Blockbuster
to throw at the videos
the voices of God are everywhere heard loud
and clear under the hum of the tickertape
and all these miracles and speaking gods
are the mysteries left homeless by the Architecture
of speed and moving forward onward and ahead!"

Wakefield throws his hands into the air as if to sprinkle fairy dust on the room; he is evoking the richness of a place always ready for miracles.

"Which is not to say that I prefer to wait
for others to turn my house into a ruin
I would rather do it myself the American way
with a second mortgage and a wrecking crew
that way I can say that I am the author of my own ruin
that's the American way
we don't whine or complain
well some of us do"

The Devil can't stand being lectured to, not since he was made to stand in front of the heavenly throne before being hurled flaming through space. His ears turn red, the pointed tips glow with anger, and he feels an urge to cause the speaker to have a mishap. He's made lecturers choke on a sip of water, have a heart attack on stage, or be hit inexplicably by a falling prop. So he's only half listening to Wakefield, enjoying his client's evident discomfort and self-disgust. He really loves it when people wrestle with themselves over self-created problems. You dig your own pit, he sometimes tells them, then you come to me for a solution. Or worse, you address your sleeping God and end up killing your neighbor. As long as Wakefield is caught in contradiction and self-doubt he's safely in the Devil's hands, no need to worry that a purer, angelic creature—an innocent Wakefield—will suddenly burst to the surface. He takes a nap and turns his attention to the increasing number of dream figures that are crowding the dream fields. In his opinion, this sudden surge of dream figures has something to do with the unsettling of tribal boundaries; as people become angrier they release demons safely bound until then in layers of storytelling, bound with ropes of narrative. The Devil sees these ropes snapping and the layers flying off, leaving exposed malignant medieval creatures that even he shudders to gaze on.

Wakefield is fully aware that he's digging himself into a hole. He decides to change the rhythm—he's a performer, after all. He's going to chant the mantra of self-reliance, which these foreigners can use, that's for sure. In America we value self-reliance as well as cooperation, and this is what we say: "If you do it for me, I'll do it for you." He chants in a singsong voice:
   "If you do it for me, I'll do it for you!
   Now everybody say it:
   If you do it for me, I'll do it for you!"
   A few multiaccented voices repeat: "I'LLDOITFORYOU!" More voices: "YOUDOITFOR ME!" Laughter, applause. Milena shouts: "DOITTOMEBABY!" and Tiffany: "SOCKITOMESOCKITTOME!"

Others are just calling: "GETONWITHIT!" Self-reliance has taken on a not unpleasant erotic twist. Pleased, Wakefield begins again his poem.

"Each home houses
an inner demolition dictator
a household god chomping on
his cigar of cash and impatience
who is not content
until everyone is in a car
driving from Nowheresville to Nowheresville
in search of therapy and desire!"

One strong, chilling female voice emerges from the darkness. "Wakefield, your therapy is just beginning!" Heads turn, looking for the source of this challenge, and a small, neatly dressed woman stands up. "You made a ruin of my desire!" Wakefield realizes that the woman is his ex-wife, making good on her threat. Marianna, who when she got her first look at New York City from the window of a taxicab, cried out, "This is what I always desire!" Wakefield takes a sip of water and forges ahead.

"Which brings me to you, Marianna,
my wife from the land of Teleskou."

A whisper: "That's his ex-wife!" Some laughter here and there. The crowd seems to lean forward to better hear what will happen next.

"My America-loving wife
born in an old-world city
the Little Paris of prewar Europe
a country you once denied."

Marianna is silent. What the hell, he might as well tell everybody everything while she ponders her next outburst.

"Then we lived in a city without a plan
a place even the gods
of demolition had left out of boredom
a city like many that spreads everywhere

complacently sprawling
and you loved it.
Wasn't that the place where
at least in the beginning
the architectures of nature
ruins and imagination met?"

"You owe me a better explanation than that, Wakefield!" Angry
male voice chides: "Be quiet lady! Work it out after the show!" but
others call out: "Let her speak! This is America!" In the wings the
bodyguards begin to react. They step out onto the stage and one of
them speaks into his lapel sotto voce. There's a commotion in the
dark, and Marianna is hustled away from her seat. "He is the father of
my child. Asshole! Let go!" Wakefield leans forward over the lectern,
trying to see what's going on. "Whoever you are," he shouts, "leave
her alone! That is the mother of my child!" Someone shines a flashlight on the scene. Wakefield sees Marianna being pulled down the
aisle by uniformed cops; there are angry shouts from the audience,
and several men rise from their seats, as if to defend her. "This is
crazy!" Wakefield shouts. "Stop now!" and like divinity intervening,
Doris appears on stage and says calmly: "Security! Release Mrs.
Wakefield. Friends, return to your seats!" The policemen obey, and
Marianna straightens her blouse, smooths her hair, and spreading her
arms wide, says, "This is how America treats the foreign-born!" There
is a rumble of argument in the crowd, and Wakefield appeals to Marianna, "Can't we talk later, my tigress?" There's laughter at that, and
Marianna takes her seat. The crowd applauds.

"Which brings me to *this* city
of immigrants and turbulence
of ruins and imagination!
Once, in other lands
artists under the watch of policemen
wielded paintbrushes and chisels

to speak their rage and laugh their way
out of the prison-gray mind of terror
and while they did this
unbeknownst to them
they tickled American commuters traveling on freeways
unaware not just of these artists but unable
even to locate those countries on the map
and these commuters without knowing why
were seized by a desire to masturbate."
Marianna shouts: "Wakefield, you're a jackoff!" The audience roars
with laughter, and Wakefield laughs, too, relieved by their sudden
good will.

Wakefield has made a connection so startling that even the Devil is
taken aback. He rouses from his nap and bangs his horns against the
jagged roof of his cave, breaking off a stalactite. The idea that the suffering of artists in one region of the world can cause unconscious sexual arousal in regular people in a completely different part of it is
brilliant. He has actively made such connections himself, by means of
epidemics and viruses, but never by means of brushes and chisels! The
Devil feels something like *admiration,* a sentiment so alien to him, he
has to pause for a moment to figure out what it is. Yes, of course, he'd
admired Christopher Marlowe once, but that had been such a long
time ago!

"For years one stretch of freeway
from our house to the mall
was our favorite, Marianna,
and driving among the work-drab drones
we laughed and you cried out
'Ah, now I understand!'
and I enjoyed those life-enhancing words

and saw my own country for the first time
its drama unfolding in three acts:
first, the act of revising architecture
through loving alien eyes
understanding that in the country of freeways
freeways are history.
Second, making love inside our car
we sensed the commuter-tickling power
of artists breaking their chains
in countries far away, including yours, my ex.
We married the heroic to the ludic.
And thirdly, the project of remaking the world
along the love lines of the year 1968
seemed quite feasible even decades later.
And thus, as from a placid lake
itself a kind of natural proof
even as rents go through the roof
a Nessie can lift her head and thrill two lovers.
That was when visions of the magic world
came to us as easily as laughter
not hate and history and old quarrels."

Wakefield leaves the stage before the audience realizes he's finished his bittersweet love song. Behind him he hears a thundering sound, whether applause or jeers he can't quite tell. He's cut his talk short, but the unexpected psychodrama has more than made up for it. Backstage, Doris slips him his honorarium check. He puts it in the inside pocket of his jacket. The security detail moves in front and behind and he's back in the green room, sweating, exhausted, and dreading his meeting with Marianna. He drinks a Coke and waits for the inevitable scuffle outside the door. When he hears his ex-wife's voice in argument with the security guards, he flings the door open, and there she is, her agitated breath pushing her breasts rapidly against the Romanian peasant blouse with embroidered red and blue flowers. She's nothing like the old fashion-crazed Marianna: she's wearing gold wire-rimmed glasses that make her look like a schoolteacher. And sensible shoes! He offers her a seat on the couch, but Marianna grabs a chair instead, turns it around, and sits on it staring at Wakefield.

"We should talk about Margot, I suppose," Wakefield says uncertainly.

After a dolorous silence, Marianna speaks: "Yes, about her and about the thousands of little Margots that lie crying in their own filth in stinking cribs."

What thousands of little Margots? Isn't one enough, considering that she'd run away from home at sixteen, lived in a ghetto with a musician, and not contacted either of them until she had gone to college all on her own? When she finally called her mother, she was a waitress in a steak house and had some other mysterious job she didn't want to discuss. However, after that first call things started looking up. Margot finished college, went on to graduate school in library science and called both of them every Christmas. She even stayed with Marianna for a month, though Wakefield hasn't yet been graced with a visit. But as far as he's concerned, Margot is mostly okay, and he's about to say this to Marianna, all this, when she says, "Thousands of little *pre*-Margots, I should say, little Margots who'll never have the opportunities our Margot had. I'm talking about *orphans,* Wakefield. The Romanian orphans."

Marianna snaps open her purse and pulls out a rumpled pamphlet she flips open in front of him. "Look, for chrissakes, look!"

Wakefield looks: grainy babies lie in lumpy squalor in a dim dormitory. "I know," he mumbles, "I saw it on TV, it's a terrible situation."

Marianna holds him in her unblinking gaze, her once beautiful brown eyes cold behind the glass. "Is that all you have to say?"

Wakefield searches his memory and his conscience. "It's terrible, yes, but what am I supposed to do about it, Marianna?"

"Okay. Now you're talking. Three things you can do about it. One, you contribute that check you just got. Two, you come with me to see the organizers of the International Architecture Show and help me talk to them about building orphanages. And three . . ." She hesitates. "Three, you come with Margot and me to Romania to see the situation firsthand and then you write about it for *National Cartographic.*"

The third point floors Wakefield. What? Does she want to reconstitute their family unit? It's an extraordinary offer, with a dream-feeling to it. If the Devil is listening now, thinks Wakefield, he must be worried about the Deal. What could be more authentic than regaining the life he once had? It's like being offered a return to innocence, before he's completely lost touch with himself. Can you ever go home again? Apparently. Not only that, but it's a return with a larger context, a humanitarian venture that will have its own humanizing effect. He could abandon everything and leave right away. It's a real crossroads, maybe the one he's looking for. He tries to gauge the depth of Marianna's offer and sees nothing but missionary zeal in her eyes. No affection, no hidden agenda, not even sympathy. It's all about the orphans for her, not about him at all. He tries to sound both reasonable and tender when he answers:

"Marianna, this is quite a proposition." He fishes into his pocket for the envelope, takes out the check, turns it over. Marianna already has a pen pointed at him. Wakefield endorses the check and hands it to her, smiling. "Part one is easy, and I can help you with the second thing, too. I'll have to think about the rest."

He watches her face closely for some visible disappointment, but she just snaps the check into her purse and says coldly, "Meet me at the ticket booth of the Architecture Park tomorrow at ten o'clock."

She is gone before he can ask for news of their own Margot. What just happened? Even the Devil is rubbing his eyes in bewilderment. Wakefield's own eyes are moist. His vision of paradise regained has vanished as quickly as it appeared.

By the time Wakefield returns to the lobby, security has funneled the crowd into the gallery, where a reception with wine and cheese and a jazz trio is in full swing. The lobby is empty except for museum staff, including Doris, who gives him a big hug, and Susan, who gives him kisses on both cheeks *and* a hug. Her makeup is a little tear-stained but she's smiling. "No sign of your ex-wife," she tells him. "I think you got to her."

Wakefield doesn't tell her about his encounter with the new Marianna.

"We could go in to the reception," Doris says, "but we thought you might like to get out of here. Will you let us take you to dinner?"

"Tiff and Milena are waiting outside," Susan adds, dabbing at her makeup with a tissue.

Wakefield accepts gratefully, but as they push out the museum doors they encounter an obstacle. Across the street, separated from each other by police and private security, two groups of protesters are facing off with signs and loudspeakers. Susan's father is at the front of one group, holding a sign that reads: This Isn't Art! It's Shit! Another man shouts into a bullhorn, *"Justice for Serbia!"* and *"American bombs are blind!"* The opposing group are mostly women, among them Aleisha Petrovich, her arms linked with two other women's, shouting: *"Criminals of Serbia, stop your killing NOW!"*

"Oh, my God," Susan exclaims, "my mother shouldn't be here! If they let go, she'll probably fall down." She calls to her mother, but her voice is drowned out by singing from the Serb protesters:

> "All this was once ours,
> until the stinking beasts
> next door came here.
> They speak a nasty language
> and drink some nasty beer!
> Their women are wolves

and their children are dogs.
Let's turn them into burning logs!"

Susan is still trying to get to her mother when the police vans come screeching around the corner. Policemen spill out with riot shields and batons and begin dragging protesters into the vans. Susan grabs Tiffany by the hand and yells something about "can't do dinner" and "bail" to Wakefield before taking off toward the parking garage, followed by Milena, running with difficulty in her high heels.

WAKEFIELD AND DORIS settle for a couple of Polish dogs and an early night. Back in his room, Wakefield can't sleep. First he hears angry voices, barking dogs, then breaking glass and what sounds like dishes being tossed against the walls. Then there is the acrid smell of tear gas and a German shepherd with bared teeth stands on the bed growling at him. He pours two whiskeys from the minibar into a glass and downs it. He picks up the room-service menu with shaking hands, and the embossed name of the hotel triggers a memory. This is where the delegates to the Democratic convention stayed in 1968. He's listening to . . . history. The dog disappears, but the room starts to tilt and sway. He feels sick. The sounds of the riots and the gas recede, making room for a battlefield. Wakefield hides behind the dresser while shells explode around him. He dials room service. The voice on the phone sounds familiar. "A bottle of Stolichnaya," he manages. He tries to turn on the TV, dodging shells, careful not to step on several dying soldiers lying around the room, but the screen fills with snow, no images appear. By the time he hears a knock at the door and jumps to open it, the room is filled like a meat locker with corpses. It's freezing. Wakefield opens the door. His teeth are chattering, but he relaxes when he sees the face of the bellboy. As he takes the bottle of Stolichnaya from his hands, the corpses vanish and room temperature returns to normal. Strangely, the bellboy follows him into the room and takes a seat, showing a little hoof when he crosses his legs.

"You look like shit," the Devil-bellboy says.

"Thank you, Your Majesty," Wakefield whispers in a breaking voice. "Is all this your doing?"

"Hardly. I'm as baffled as you are. It seems that we're not alone."

A hint of a smile appears on Wakefield's dry lips when he sees the Devil's sincere puzzlement and raised tufty eyebrows. Then he starts giggling like a nervous girl on a date. When the Devil's yellow eyes widen in an expression of mock sincerity, Wakefield bursts out laughing. He laughs and laughs, can't stop himself. "I can't . . . believe it," he finally succeeds in saying through the guffaws. "The Devil himself doesn't know what's going on. . . ." Wakefield realizes that if he laughs any longer, His Demonic Highness might be offended, so he stops, with an effort. It is a very strange world, indeed, when the only company he draws comfort from is the Devil.

"What do you mean, we're not . . . alone?"

"That's difficult to explain to a human."

"Try me."

"Well, it's like this. There was a time when I could keep track of everybody and every *thing*, even ghosts and goblins. Fellow devils all registered with me, of course. Then things and creatures, and I don't mean just humans, started multiplying. Every creature, thing, even *ideas,* started to subdivide. The agreed-on borders of time and space started to fray as more and more of these new abominations claimed a place in the sun, so to speak. Realities that had always been quite separate started mixing; even time started going backward and forward without any respect for the old physics. Me, I'm a strict Newtonian. This whole blender effect is making me queasy."

"I don't believe you," Wakefield says bluntly. "Things were always mixed up, they are just . . . faster. You're just getting old, you can't keep track of them. Me, too, for that matter. Old and stupid. Anyway,

I don't need a lecture. I can do that myself, thank you. What I need to know is when are you going to fire your damned pistol so I can get serious."

It's the Devil's turn to laugh. "You're such a conformist, Wakefield. Just like your namesake in that Hawthorne story. Why do you need to wait for authorization? Why don't you just pick something from that huge menu you're staring at every day, call it the real thing, and get on with it? What do you care what I think?"

"Because, because . . . ," Wakefield stammers, "I can't make up my mind."

"Well, more power to you," snickers El Diablo. "What do you think I get out of this? Your confused mind is my only pleasure. Well, one of them . . . ," he corrects himself. "One of the best. If you make up your mind and the race hasn't started, I can call it off, of course . . . but so what? You'll get what you want, maybe even eat half of it before I show up and haul your sorry ass out of this world."

"Well, that's just it. I'm not ready. Besides, didn't you want me to bring you a gift, something to please you?"

"Well, yeah, I have my collections to look after. But you've given me plenty already. Go ahead, though, *étonnez-moi!* Blow my mind. Bring me something I never thought of. Humans do surprise me sometimes. By the way, let me give you a hint about 'authenticity': all the women you've known so far were 'authentic,' as 'authentic' as humans get. So I might rethink that notion, if I were you. Personally, I prefer 'vivid' to 'authentic.'"

"Well, you're not me. So when are you going to shoot?"

"Haha," laughs Sataniko, "when I can't stand it anymore. Maybe I'll just shoot myself to further complicate things."

"How is that possible? I thought you were immortal."

"I didn't say I was going to *die*. I shoot myself all the time."

. . .

AT BREAKFAST, WAKEFIELD feels like he's had a rough night, but he can't remember much of it. Only the encounter with Marianna, his lecture, and the crazy street riot remain vivid. The newspaper left at the door of his room clarifies some things. The protest and arrests are front-page news and the story is worse than he would have guessed: Slobodan Petrovich, released on $750 bail, led a violent gang of men who smashed the windows of the Bosnia Club, where the counter-protesters, including his wife, Aleisha Petrovich, had regrouped after their own release from jail. The vandals, including Mr. Petrovich, were rearrested, and the judge refused to set bail a second time. On the editorial page one commentator laments, "How can American citizens, no matter their birthplace, behave like this? Why haven't they learned tolerance? Real, local issues must take precedence over old-world imperatives of blood and revenge. We need voter registration and sewer taxes, not single-handed Noble Slayers of thousands." The editorialist seems very familiar with the nationalists' rhetoric.

Susan arrives as Wakefield scoops up the first forkful of his eggs Benedict. She looks like she hasn't had any sleep, either. He makes room for her on the banquette and orders her a cup of coffee. He covers the eggs with his napkin; the sight of them clashes with the throbs of his vodka hangover.

"I'm so sick of this shit. It's not like I make a lot of money. I spent my whole puny savings bailing out my fucking parents."

Wakefield grins, and Susan laughs despite her distress.

"We have a plan," she tells him, gulping down some coffee. "Tiff and I think that you'll have a very bad impression of the city if you don't see something besides the battling Petroviches while you're here. We want to go to the annual show at the International Architecture Park. I hear it's really civilized, and maybe after that you could come with me to the Tribune Tower. I have to meet a reporter there; she knows everything about our situation and has a lot of connections. I'm going to ask her to help my pop."

She shows Wakefield a brochure of the Architecture annual. The exhibition sprawls over sixty acres. Wakefield remembers that he's promised to meet Marianna there, but Susan's invitation gives him a way out: he'll meet Marianna at the show and then they can run into Susan, as if by accident. If things are going well, they can all join up. If not, Wakefield can make some excuse and say good-bye to Marianna.

"Okay," Susan agrees, slightly disappointed, "let's meet at noon by the Hungarian pavilion. And here, take one of these. It's codeine and Tylenol."

Wakefield takes the pill from Susan. It's just what his throbbing head needs.

THE DAY IS GRAY, the leaden sky filled with impending snow, but it's not all that cold, and Wakefield carries his coat over his arm as he strolls through the International Architecture Park with Marianna. Only, they are not really strolling. Marianna is clutching a briefcase that looks incongruous with her long peasant skirt and sheepskin coat with hand-embroidered edges. Whatever happened to couture and $500-an-ounce perfume? She even smells like sheep. They are on their way to meet with the Swedish Culture Minister, who is greeting visitors today at the Swedish pavilion.

The pavilion is a mall-like minicity, complete with split-level homes, an amusement park, and a sculpture garden. It looks terribly familiar. Marianna beats him to the punch: "It's like that suburb we lived in when Margot was born." Indeed, to be complete, all the illusion needs is for a younger Marianna and Wakefield to walk out of one of the houses, holding baby Margot.

They enter a reception area lit by a huge skylight. Seated behind a glass-topped desk in a Deco chair is a cheerfully blond young man with a diamond stud in his left ear. He is the Swedish Culture Minister. Several respectful students are listening to him speak in accented

English. He looks a little bored, so when Marianna and Wakefield approach, he waves them over familiarly, raising his eyebrows as if to say "Finally, some grown-ups!"

"Well, what do you think?" he asks his visitors. The students turn a bit resentfully toward the newcomers.

"It looks very familiar," says Wakefield. "We used to live here."

"That's it, that's it," the Minister nods enthusiastically. "Precisely. It looks familiar because it *is*. This architecture could be *anywhere,* and that's the point. But the difference . . . ," he raises a significant finger, "the difference is in the materials. Everything is constructed from lightweight plastics more durable than brick or steel, which makes this entire city portable. Two men could push a house made of these materials fifty feet in sixty seconds! Let's see, shall we?"

The little group follows the energetic Culture Minister outside, where he hurls himself against one of the houses and shoves it a few meters.

"So you see, these structures are an answer to the most vexing problem of contemporary life: boredom. Here you can move your house, exchange views with your neighbors, or take the whole thing with you for a weekend of fishing in the country. Sweden has beautiful lakes."

Marianna catches the Minister's eye and reaches for her orphan propaganda.

"There are one hundred thousand orphans in Romania, locked up in terrible institutions, living on the streets or underground in sewers. How can Swedish architecture help improve their lives?"

The Minister looks with distaste at the crumpled pamphlet and his eyes rest for a second on the grainy babies. He is about to make a gesture of curt dismissal, but the students have gathered around Marianna and are passing her pamphlet around. They are interested, and the Minister changes his mind.

"Well, these materials are still expensive, but such light houses could be useful to . . . orphans." He pronounces the word with reluctance, as if it were completely alien to him.

"I don't see how they could be useful," Wakefield says, playing devil's advocate, "if they move so much. Orphans suffer from being moved around like leaves by the wind. What they need is stability, but not *institutional* buildings, of course. Solid brick homes with parents in them, not prisons."

"Naturally, naturally." The Minister turns to the students. "Any ideas? You are all smart MIT architecture students."

A young woman with serious eyes says, "I'm an orphan." Her fellow students look at her, startled. *They* are not orphans. "Yes," she says firmly, "I grew up in foster care. I would have loved to live in such a light house in Sweden by a lake. Perhaps we could make a whole city for orphans."

A few eyes tear up, and the Swedish Minister is suddenly alert to the potential. "Hmm, a light Swedish city for orphans. . . ."

"*Romanian* orphans," Marianna corrects him.

"Well, yes. A Swedish city—"

"For Romanian orphans!" interjects an enthusiastic student, looking awestruck at the young woman with serious eyes, with whom he has fallen instantly and irremediably in love.

The rest of them catch on quickly. "TLSCFRO," a wit spells out, "The Light Swedish City For Romanian Orphans."

And so The Light Swedish City for Romanian Orphans (TLSCFRO) is born on the spot. The young blond Minister has no choice but to listen to the plans being made by the bright would-be architects, who have not only formed an ad-hoc committee, "The MIT Team for TLSCFRO," but have begun drawing in their notepads. E-mail addresses are exchanged and a letter of intention is drafted and signed by everyone.

The activity attracts a crowd and word spreads rapidly. A photographer and reporter from *Architecture Magazine* appear and the Culture Minister finds himself explaining TLSCFRO as if it had been a carefully thought-out idea now being unveiled for the first time on the occasion of the Swedish exhibition.

Wakefield is amused. The Minister must be cursing the day he decided to make a public appearance at the site. He's doubtless imagining the dismay of his budget people when, in addition to the cost of the exhibit and the expense of his own travel, he presents them with TLSCFRO. Still, the publicity benefits are undeniable. Everyone is smiling, Marianna most of all, while the students high-five one another, excitedly discussing their upcoming internships in Sweden to help build TLSCFRO.

After handshakes all around and an orphan brochure in every hand, Marianna snaps the "letter of intent" into her briefcase, the only nonethnic accessory on her. Wakefield's hangover is gone thanks to Susan's pill and a mild euphoria sets in. He regards his ex-wife with genuine admiration, as she takes leave of her allies. Buoyed by triumph, Marianna walks briskly a few steps in front of Wakefield, who wonders where this woman, who was once his wife, came from. Of this Marianna he'd never had a hint.

A few yards from the Swedish site is the Belgian pavilion. Not much luck here, since there isn't one human being anywhere in sight. Belgium has contributed a fully automated futuristic prison, where each transparent cell is equipped with a computer built into an extension of a narrow bed. The visitors wander about on their own, listening to electronic voices explaining that the walls of the prison become opaque after dark and transform into projection screens on which educational programs are beamed until lights out. Wakefield depresses a lever below the word *Evening* in one of the cells. The screen-wall darkens and a language menu appears: Press One for French, Two for Flemish, Three for English. He presses Three and gets more choices. Press One for Literature, Two for Basic Science, Three for Economics, Four for Psychology, Five for Environmental Studies, Six for Food Preparation, Seven for Media. He presses Four for Psychology. A silver-haired teacher appears on the screen. "Turn on your computer to begin taking notes," he instructs. "Early Childhood." A brain with highlighted areas revolves slowly beside the teacher.

"Belgian convicts must be walking encyclopedias," says Wakefield.

"Let's go," Marianna says glumly. "These people have no compassion."

Neither, it appears, does the world's greatest superpower. American design is represented by an immense store called ShapeShifters, as vast as three Home Depots. On the miles-long shelves objects made of "intelligent plastics" form and reform themselves. Wakefield reaches out to touch what looks like a bolt of fabric; it cascades off the shelf and unrolls itself, a watery puddle on the floor. When he steps into the puddle, it covers his shoes like galoshes.

A quiet voice track provides visitors the architects' statement: "Form and function are an extension of content. The content is intelligence. Our minds contain all forms. We can teach the material world to listen." Morphing, changing, my country 'tis of thee.

"This is scary." Marianna is holding a round ball that's changing into a square box, its surface changing design from polka dots to stripes, then changing texture from smooth to pumice rough.

"This reminds me of this one time on acid when I tried to walk through a door because I was sure I could rearrange the molecules to let me through. I knew that it was possible, I just didn't know how." Wakefield thinks he had this experience before he met Marianna, but when she rotates the box and it becomes a diamond-shape prism reflecting the light, he's not so sure.

"I was there," she says, but doesn't sound happy about it. "There is nothing for my orphans in it."

"In what? Our shared past or in that box?"

"Both."

A familiar note now creeps into their conversation. It's not a big leap from here to an all-too-familiar recrimination fest.

They barely notice as ShapeShifters changes from a megastore into a multiplex cinema. Movies start playing, there is the aroma of popcorn in the air, but their brief neutrality has dissolved. They are combatants again. Wakefield tries to steer the conversation in another direction. "The Company must have something to do with this! It's a version of the Home of the Future!" The theme of the U.S. pavilion is "Virtuality Takes Command," and The Company is in fact listed as the main sponsor. He feels a twinge of nostalgia for Typical, as if his visit there had happened ages ago. He thinks about Maggie and feels an urgent need to get away from Marianna. This is some kind of trap, he seethes, and I will not go back to any past.

Marianna is obviously determined to go on to the future, but the past is not easily eluded. In search of other exhibit organizers, perhaps even another Minister of Culture, they stumble into the Russian pavilion, an acre of ruins: war-ravaged Stalingrad recast in plaster, crumbling Brezhnev-era beehives, piles of maimed statues of famous Bolsheviks. The ruins are punctuated by pillars plastered with leaflets. The text on the leaflets reads: "The process of re-carving, re-education, re-creation, re-consideration, re-casting, becomes organic over time, creating a new nature, an urban wilderness, a necropolis of architecture." There is not a human being in sight. This is obviously the world that created orphans, and it has no tools to help them.

A glimmer of hope shines briefly in Luxembourg, where they encounter the designer of a video installation consisting of a huge screen on which corporate logos morph into one another endlessly: the McDonald's arches become VW, VW becomes CGI, CGI becomes IBM, IBM becomes Microsoft, Microsoft becomes U.S. Steel, U.S. Steel becomes The Company, ad infinitum in rondelles and waltzes of symbols. The artist, glad for visitors, takes Marianna's pamphlet without reservation, studies it carefully, then proposes: "I will enlarge this photograph and project it behind the morphing logos! The subliminal effect will be phenomenal!"

Wakefield imagines the grainy babies flashing through the sinister morphing logos, and cringes. Marianna isn't too impressed either, so they exit rather abruptly, leaving the poor artist feeling even lonelier.

Each country's pavilion is surrounded by bare chestnut and maple trees with snow frosting their branches, and it's becoming clearer to Wakefield as they walk that nothing is going to diminish the distance between Marianna and him, not even the sudden salvation of one hundred thousand orphans.

Happily, his most recent three muses save *him*. In front of the Hungarian pavilion they "run into" his friends. They are a fairly dazzling crew, Milena in a plaid miniskirt, black sweater, and black tights, her neck bundled in a long red scarf; Susan wearing an ankle-length faux-fur coat and combat boots and her customary frown of concentration; and Tiffany in blue peacoat, blue jeans, and thigh-high leather boots.

Introductions are made and everyone studies the huge globe in front of Hungary's exhibit. Conceived by an eccentric architect who'd worked on the design secretly for fifty years, the plans for this object were discovered in an attic in Budapest. The building of the actual globe was subsidized by an anonymous Hungarian billionaire specifically for the site. (Wakefield silently upbraids Farkash: See what a billionaire can do?) This visionary world was intended by the architect to "restore the emotional and spiritual unity of Man and Earth." Examined closely the model reveals exquisitely detailed pyramidal and circular towers, looping streets, naked people, and saucery vehicles. It's like an odd combination of Paris and Aztec Mexico. Between the jumbled buildings are ritual areas: wells, stages, and altars, and the poignancy of sheer impracticality shines over the utopian city like a full moon.

Milena points to a sleeping microdragon curled around a tiny well. "He looks like my imaginary pet, Jaroslav. He still comes when I call him. Did you have an imaginary pet when you were a kid, Tiff?"

"Susan was my pet." She strokes her sister's head.

"Gee, thanks. It's not bad enough that I'm the short one, now I'm an animal!"

"How about you, Marianna?" Milena asks. "Did you have a pet?"

"I don't have a pet, I have a *cause*," she says acidly.

For the first time in a long time Wakefield feels the urge to hide.

"Cerberus was my pet," he mumbles, embarrassed for his ex and for himself. Nobody laughs.

The group holds together for one more country. Japan has chosen to cover its site with a beautiful, empty City of Women that ignores architecture altogether. Under the winter-bare trees are large photographic panels of the face of the same woman. The images are scattered sparely over the large area, so they are forced to meander among them. The face is neither beautiful nor terribly expressive. It floats in the zenlike emptiness of the apple-blossomy snow. Transparency reigns in the City of Women, and also a serene sadness, as if roughness and jagged disharmony had been removed, their traces swept clean away. Wakefield is struck by his vivid, three-dimensional companions walking between the photographs of that plain, repeating face. The scene is disturbing, almost painful; the women in his past have the same quality of repetition, he realizes, and it makes him sad that time has erased their color and dimension.

"The face looks like a blown Easter egg before it's painted," says Tiffany. "Very creepy."

Susan concurs. "Maybe she represents the people killed at Hiroshima," she ventures. But the face isn't tragic, it is pure surface.

Nonetheless, the City of Women depresses them. The merry little gang falls silent, and this is where Marianna chooses to leave them. Wakefield watches her walk away, her briefcase swinging at her side with pendulum-like precision. Inside of it the orphans wait for better days. Wakefield feels like one of them.

"Let's get out of here immediately," Milena orders. "I need a drink, a joint, a foot massage. . . . Enough of architecture!"

THE LIFE OF REAL city streets revives them, a vibrant, instant cure.

"I fear for the future if it's left up to architects," Tiffany says, repairing her lipstick, "but they do seem well-meaning."

"Boring," pronounces Milena.

Wakefield is thinking that architecture seems to struggle with ideas a great deal more than most art forms do, perhaps because of the conflict between corporate visions and individual architects' beliefs about the way people should live. He vows to try to feel at home wherever he is, to live in a kind of architecture-without-architecture. After all, the body is architecture; so are the clothes a person hangs on it. One can view anything, including emotional life, architecturally. One can make a structure from one's sorrows, or from one's joys. He is awfully close to forgetting his deal with the Devil, all the deals he has made in the past or will make in the future. He could live in the eternally repeating present of the City of Women.

Milena and Tiffany stop to kiss on the sidewalk.

"Disgusting," says Susan.

"Come here," says Milena, putting out her arms. A group hug ensues. Wakefield feels supremely at home in the house of women, inhaling their perfumes and warmth. It's cold, starting to snow, and they are hungry.

"Starved!" Milena calls it.

They agree that a Ukrainian restaurant is the warmest place to be, because of the steam of cabbage soup and piroshki, and they pile into the first one they find. The waitress who takes their orders is middle-aged, plump, and friendly. Wakefield has a view of the street through the steamy window. It's snowing now in earnest. There is a little bowl of salt on the table, with a tiny carved wooden spoon for sprinkling it on the food. He slips the spoon into his pocket. It's an almost unconscious act, but he realizes as soon as he's done it that it's another present for the Devil.

A salt spoon? he imagines the Devil asking. Whatever for?

Salt, improvises Wakefield, is human life itself. In the Balklands the peasants traditionally greet important visitors with bread and salt.

Sure, but in what way does a spoon stolen from a Ukrainian restaurant significantly represent your self-discovery?

Blood, sweat, and tears, baby. Surely the Devil can appreciate how salty a woman feels after he's made love to her. He won't spurn a tool that can hold the crystalized essence of a lover's sweat. Especially one hand-carved in a village by a virgin. The virgin is, of course, hypothetical, but there is nothing, Wakefield is quite sure, as dear to the Devil as salt.

The aroma of onions browned in butter, one of Wakefield's favorite scents, is making his mouth water, and turns his attention from the Devil. He asks his companions what their favorite smells are. Milena says her favorite is the smell of creosote on railroad ties in August, and Wakefield can imagine her, a Young Pioneer, her red cravat askew, skipping along a railroad track, a chorus of insects humming around her. The same rails have seen the trains of two world wars rattle past, but there is no train now, only a sweet, light sadness in the last quiet year before the end of the Cold War. Nothing is happening. Milena just skips from one tie to another, breathing.

A summer smell lives in Tiffany's olfactory memory, too. She is partial to the smell of a tomcat's belly after he's rolled in the dust.

Susan remembers a pleasant, dusty smell. "I love the smell of a dark room filled with old books. I'm hiding while two people I can't remember are making love, not knowing of course that I'm watching. The scent of dust and sex."

"That was in our house!" says Tiffany. "The spare room where Professor Teleskou stayed."

"This was a long time before he moved in. I was only three or four," says Susan. There is an edge in her voice, and Professor Teleskou's name hangs in the air for a brief moment. Some tension passes between the sisters. Wakefield believes Susan that she didn't have an affair with Teleskou. On the other hand, Tiffany may have. He remembers Teleskou's melancholy smile on the jacket photo of his book, and feels an unaccountable kinship with the dead man. It's so familiar! Suddenly he knows it: that smile is the expression of someone who has also met the Devil. Teleskou is a brother unto Mephistopheles.

All of them agree that they love the smell of overripe apples.

After bowls of cabbage soup and piroshki with sour cream and apple sauce, Tiffany and Milena leave for a photo shoot, "a cover and spread" for a big fashion magazine. Wakefield parts regretfully from the living delight of his new friends, though he'll see them again, reproduced on the covers of a million magazines. Good-bye, real faces! He kisses them both, first on each cheek, then on each hand, like a European gentleman. Their perfume lingers, and he thinks how unbelievably intimate the act of touching a hand to one's lips is. His catalogue of scents grows by one delicious memory.

Wakefield notices that Susan is watching this ceremony a little enviously. Men always fall for Tiffany, and they fall double hard for Tiffany and Milena. But walking to the Tribune Tower to meet Susan's journalist friend, it's just the two of them.

The Tribune Tower's American Gothic body is embedded at street level with stones from some of the world's übermonuments: Jesus' birthplace in Bethlehem, the Great Wall of China, the Taj Mahal, and the Berlin Wall. These fragments are the souvenirs of hubris, of tourists who thought nothing of taking chunks out of the world's most sacred and awesome places to bring home for triumphant display.

"It testifies to a touching innocence, don't you think?" Wakefield observes. "Or was it arrogance? Insensitivity? Maybe some kind of naïve homage to History, with a capital H?" Actually, the pilfered stones remind him of the salt spoon in his pocket, an offering to the Devil. Perhaps these tourists, all tourists, maybe, pilfer things for the Devil. His Malignancy must be drowning in his collections of love offerings.

Susan is of a generation of museum curators who, unlike her predecessors, was schooled in sensitivity to other cultures and places, but she has no romantic illusions. "American collectors saw nothing wrong with bringing home from abroad whatever they could get their hands on. We owe our great collections to crude millionaires who basically bought Europe and Asia wholesale. The University of Oklahoma, for instance, has this great archive, Giordano Bruno manuscripts, annotated Galileo first editions, all of it bought by one Okie oilman on a Grand Tour. Tell you the truth," she says, thinking of her unshaven Pop in the city pokey, "I sometimes think we should buy some countries wholesale and move them physically to Wyoming."

In the grand lobby of the Tribune Tower she directs Wakefield's attention to a motto, inscribed in gold. "Make no little plans; they have no magic to stir men's blood."

"In the twenties the publisher of the *Tribune* made an appeal to architects to design 'the most beautiful office building in the world' as an homage to free speech. There was a hundred-thousand-dollar prize, and two hundred and sixty entries came in from twenty-three countries. One of them was a design by a Finnish architect that was a Dada sendup of the words *capitol* and *capitalism,* but the jury didn't take freedom of speech that literally, so they opted for a Gothic skyscraper."

Susan knows her city's history; there is passion in her exposition. Wakefield repeats to himself Daniel Burnham's motto, and is moved by that "magic to stir men's blood." There is something troubling in those words in connection with Susan; she has lived her life surrounded by men who believed in blood-stirring magic, her father and Professor Teleskou being prime examples. Wakefield wonders if she sees herself as a pacifying force among them.

They take a brass and marble elevator to the fiftieth floor, where the journalist, Jackie Lopez, is waiting for them in a storm-tossed office. She is a small, no-nonsense woman who moves energetically among towers of tilting books, piles of folders reaching to the ceiling, a photo-covered desk atop which two laptops are humming, and crumpled wrappers of old lunches that never quite made it into an overflowing wastebasket. The friends hug, and Susan introduces Jackie to Wakefield. "Jackie investigated Professor Teleskou's death."

"You wrote this morning's editorial," Wakefield observes. "Very insightful editorial."

She shakes her head. "It's insanity, and the surprising thing is that more people haven't been killed." She shifts gears. "Would you like to go to the top of the tower? Maybe we can go for a drink afterward and talk about how to help your father, Susan. He's got a bad case of something I call ethnic PMS. I think it sounds nicer than 'bloodlust.'"

A special elevator takes them to the observation deck below the tower's buttresses. Wakefield stands under the rib of an arch and holds his breath. Around them the city's skyscrapers, like a race of giants, lean against the wind, each one an entity seeming to enjoy the intimacy and proximity of the others. Jutting out of the buttress he's under is a gargoyle that's missing an ear. Wakefield looks around; there in the snow is the stone ear, chipped and dirty. Quickly he picks it up, holds it for a moment in his hand, then slips it into the pocket with the wooden salt spoon.

THE EAR OF A gargoyle from the oldest tower in Wintry City! Wakefield announces to himself, holding it out for Satan.

The Devil laughs. All gargoyles, he says with a hint of pride, are representations of myself. What makes you think that an ear ripped from one of my images would please me? What does it have to do with you, anyway?

Wakefield doesn't yet know what the gargoyle's ear has to do with anything, but he knows that it's hard as hell to please the Devil. Is there any one thing in this world that the Devil doesn't already own in multiples? Maybe that's the point, and this is why the Devil is laughing. It would be easier for Wakefield to define his "soul" than to muck about the world trying to find unique tchotchkes to please the Prince of fucking Darkness.

TURNS OUT JACKIE is a poetic observer. "I believe that buildings have multiple, borrowed souls that change with time and distance. The soul of this tower has lent most of itself to the buildings around it. All the new buildings quote a little from ours."

Indeed, they do. Each one wears a cupola or scroll in its honor. If buildings can have souls, thinks Wakefield, then surely human beings do.

Descending from the tower, they make their way to a popular reporters' bar-and-burger joint, where Jackie orders a beer and a cheeseburger and Wakefield and Susan have bourbon on the rocks. Wakefield notes that Susan has switched to his drink and wonders what it means. Does she fancy him? It is certainly deliberate. And flattering. He catches her eye and something flits there, holding both of them. Wakefield knows this feeling: it's like a tiny opening in a curtain that can lift at any moment, plunging him (again!) into a sentimental drama for which he has never figured out a resolution, except flight. He's tired already, and nothing has happened yet.

For the moment he's still safe in the shadow of the great tower. Did the builder of this grand structure believe that it conferred immortality, like the pyramids? He toys with the idea, sipping his whiskey. Perhaps there exists a tribe of Immortalists who, unbeknownst to anyone, live inside great buildings, parasitically wedded to the time-proof structures, safe from human relationships.

The women are discussing Mr. Petrovich, who is well known to Jackie. "Granted, he's a peculiar man, your pop." She takes a huge bite of her juicy cheeseburger. "I think something about Teleskou set him off, in a way. Bear with me for a second." She wipes mustard off her chin with the tablecloth. "Your pop was raised in the Marxist faith, so he believes in dialectical imperatives, whether he admits it or not. Everyone thought of Teleskou as a peacemaker because he was a nice guy, a sweetheart, really. But his philosophy was really disturbing, very disturbing to someone like Slobodan, who was once a high-ranking ideologue. And Slobodan cared about him, loved him, so when he was killed by men who were most likely of the same ideological provenance as your father, he did the dialectical thing. He abandoned his materialist atheism and went in a completely different direction."

Susan is not happy with this line of reasoning. "My father had already started going to church *before* Mihai was killed; it wasn't a sudden thing after his death."

"Well, but the church is similar to the Communist party. Your father tried to defend himself against Teleskou's mysticism by taking refuge in another dogmatic, ideological structure, where he also became involved with the nationalist, racist cause."

"So what do we do, Jackie? You know the district attorney, the mayor, everybody. Can we get him out *and* make him understand that he's got to stop?"

"The sixty-four-thousand-dollar question. Chernishevski asked it. Lenin. 'What is to be done?' The answer is: 'We just do it.' We'll bail him out again, if I can get the judge to set bail, get a restraining order so he won't go home and kill your mother, although I doubt he would, and then I'll sit down with him in a small room and break him like a Commie policeman would."

"You'd do that for me, Jackie?"

"For everybody, not just you. This madness has to stop, to quote my editorial self. Besides, if we can calm your pop down, his dumber cohorts will follow. Of course, this may be unnecessary. Did you see the news today? People are out in the streets of Belgrade. Milosevic could be gone by tomorrow and the NATO bombing would stop immediately. Then there will be boring, practical reconstruction stuff to tend to. They'll stop fighting and worry about how to get on the gravy train."

"From your lips to God's ear," says Susan.

Wakefield puts in his two cents' worth. "Why didn't the Communists make any lasting impression? Official atheism? Where the hell does this religious passion come from?"

"From hell, right you are. This religious-nationalist stuff apparently had an underground existence, suppressed, but when Communism ended, the old beliefs were revived intact. Maybe that's why it seems so primitive. They were frozen when the Communists took over after the Second World War, but thawed when the Commies lost control. Why do you think they called it the Cold War? It was intellectual refrigeration. The curious thing is that the Communists toppled themselves, they really did fall like the famous dominoes, but those same people are in power now, reincarnated as nationalists. They are the ones encouraging the fighting."

"But why?" Wakefield is sincerely baffled.

"Power," says Jackie. "What else? But also that indefinable quality called Stupidity, evidently stockpiled by the People the Commies held so dear. The belief that the stink of your own tribe is superior to the familial stink of the neighboring tribe, that your language is wittier and deeper; that the music you make when you wail about the muddy ravine where you were conceived is much, much more melodic than the wailing of your neighbors; that the smoke-darkened icons that hang on your wall are representations of the only gods worth praying to, and that the gods and prayers of the people over the hill are unspeakable offenses for which you must kill them."

"So you think that's what it's all about? Stupidity?" Wakefield is quite stunned, by Jackie's eloquence and the manifest truth she's revealed.

Susan doesn't say anything and Wakefield knows that she can't. It's too much to process.

"I'm sure Teleskou was stupidly killed by some very stupid people," Jackie continues. "These guys probably think that the fables he published in obscure literary magazines are coded descriptions of their conspiracies."

"And here we are having a nice time under the Freedom of Speech tower," sighs Wakefield.

"Ah, yes, freedom of the press," says Jackie. "A fragile concept. The paper I work for exercised that freedom with some honor when it defended Lincoln during the Civil War. Later in its history it became a mouthpiece for the publisher's protofascist leanings, campaigned against America's entry into World War Two, and was totally ready to dispense with freedom of the press."

"Didn't *his* family force him to retire?" Susan asks, refering to the fascist-leaning publisher.

Jackie nods, a master of the political history of her world.

Wakefield admires her authority and the ease of her command in the light of day. But there is always the night, and its ill-defined terrors.

SUSAN TAKES WAKEFIELD home to her apartment in a hip part of town, a former bohemian ghetto now gentrifying. A few years ago there was a thriving art scene in the neighborhood: small theaters, guerilla publishers, music studios, galleries, and coffeehouses, all because of the cheap rent. One day the neighborhood became fair game for real estate speculators attracted by the colorful improvements artists made to their lofts and apartments, and now there was war (another one!) going on between the original settlers and the profiteers.

"Some artists are putting up a fight, but mostly they are migrating in search of lower rents," Susan explains. She lives in a loft in a former dry-goods warehouse that a few years ago was a warren of studio apartments. Her neighbors are bankers, lawyers, and art administrators.

Wakefield knows that this process has happened in many cities; what's new is the speed of the displacement. Almost overnight, the artists who established the studios were cut out by heavily capitalized developers.

"The vanguard of real estate doesn't even have to be art at all, just a threat of art, a soupçon of style," Susan tells him, teacherlike. "Any hint of an emerging arts community, the speculators smell blood." There is a fundamental reason, Susan thinks, why living art communities should take precedence over profit, and she's got a point. Artists use the available materials of a place to fashion a city's identity, an identity that is an evolving collaboration between the past of the buildings they inhabit, the present of new technology, and the esthetic of the future. No urban planner or real estate developer, no matter how enlightened or forward-looking, can do the job as well.

"What they should do is protect cheap-rent areas from indiscriminate development," she concludes, unlocking the double-bolted door of the airy loft. Inside are two lemon trees in wooden barrels, one spidery-looking exercise machine on the floor, a futon bed surrounded by art books, and a striped cat named Maggie.

"Why did you name her Maggie?" Wakefield asks, scratching the cat behind her ears.

"Oh, you know. Tennessee Williams. Maggie the cat on a hot tin roof."

Jeez. Wakefield can't possibly make a move on a woman who has a cat with the same name as the last woman he slept with. Not possible, as the French say, though he suspects that Susan is truly in need of comfort after all that has happened in the past twenty-four hours. But watching her open a bottle of red wine, he doesn't feel any sexual attraction. She makes him nervous, and his unease grows when she puts on a CD of Spanish guitar, classically seductive music, and lights a scented candle.

The apartment is dim and cozy; beyond the large windows, street lights and swirling snow. If she asks, he'll say yes out of politeness, not desire. He can draw on the libidinal store of images that always arouse him: a girl (he'd picked her up hitchhiking) taking a bath in a motel tub, Marianna dancing in her panties to a pop tune on the radio. There are also some not-yet-tested arrangements in his storehouse, among them the entwined but blurry shapes of Milena and Tiffany, mostly Milena. He turns on the small television on top of the bookcase, and a CNN anchorwoman bursts into the room, dispelling the atmosphere of intimacy. There are images of streets filled with demonstrators. "Milosevic has abandoned the palace," exults the anchor, "and the protesters have occupied the former presidential suite. NATO bombing has ceased everywhere in the former Yugoslavia."

Susan leaps up and throws her arms around Wakefield's neck. "Jackie was right. The madness is over for now! Let the boredom begin!" She grabs her wineglass and waits for Wakefield to raise his. They toast. "To Mommy and Pop," Susan says.

"To you," adds Wakefield, relieved to see the (temporary) end of Susan's anguish and a nation's suffering. The end of the war will not be the end of her heartache, but for now she can celebrate along with the world, and Wakefield rejoices with her.

A high-level meeting on the New World Order has been called, and our Devil knows he can't afford to miss this one. He's one of the few old-timers left who is allowed, by virtue of seniority, to indulge in private whims such as the making of deals with individuals. Everyone else works full time on bigger and far more boring projects — problems involving hundreds of thousands, even millions of souls at a pop. Global work, no micromanaging. The bosses have sent out a rambling memo taking the workforce to task for various lax practices.

"You've got to take yourselves more seriously," the T-memo says, "at least as seriously as aliens who, hick reports notwithstanding, communicate not with individuals but with *species*. Contrary to popular belief, they do not extract kidneys and sperm, they *instruct* kidneys and sperm, with consequences for *all* humans. In the end, this whole human thing has to be deemphasized and we must research alternative biounits for heat and information storage. Many of you are attached to the old forms of demonic appearance for ontological reasons. Desist and imagine! You can look like anything you want. The upcoming conference concerns the New World Order. Not, of course, the one proposed by certain American politicians, but the *real* New World Order, ours. Attendance is absolutely required."

Our Devil shows up for the meeting on time because the meeting place, Mount Eumenides in Thrace, is just above his favorite cave. This place has been chosen because there is a natural amphitheater big enough to accommodate thousands of devils, and inside the hill itself are layered Celtic-Roman-Gothic-Greek-Avar-Bulgarian-Hungarian-Serbian-Croatian-Turkish-German-Austrian and Russian bones, the bones of Swedish, Tartar, French, Swiss, Mameluke, Syrian, and Persian warriors. In other words, the remains of every people in recorded history that has ever occupied the site.

His pride at arriving so promptly vanishes almost immediately: several hundred devils have already taken their places, and more keep coming, shoving from every side like hooligans at a soccer match. He catches snatches of their pretentious conversation, buzzwords like *telekinesis,* and *synergy.* These new corporate types make him gag, chasing every new fad, flicking their firm young tails and flashing their perfectly polished horns. And they are willing to work 24/7 for the greater glory of the company.

When the meeting is called to order, the Devil has already decided to speak up on behalf of liberty. No less than human beings, devils should not have to work any more than eight hours a day for the collective. The rest of the time they should be able to do what they please. Wasn't free time the issue that had gotten him hurled out of Heaven and into the prison of Time? God had assigned him some mindless task he has long forgotten, counting apples or angels or something, and he'd protested that he needed time off to think, read, and invent. The Lord thought that He had done all the inventing that ever needed to be done when he animated his clumpy clay dolls. So when Lucifer continued complaining, *blam!* the Pinkertons of Heaven all fired on him at once. And now here he is, reexperiencing an attempt on his liberty. No fucking way. Why does everything have to be so complex anyway? Can't a poor devil just enjoy a slice of stupidity strumming his lute or chewing a blade of grass with a thoughtless nymph gyrating on top of him?

The first point of order taken up by the demonic council is the problem of sexual reproduction. They declare it obsolete. Reasons: clumsiness, inefficiency, an excess of unproductive pleasure. That's it for him. The Devil rips off his name tag and, stepping on hooves and tails, makes his way out of the amphitheater and heads straight to his cave, where he seethes for an immeasurably long time. In the end he'll have no choice but to return to the damned meeting, but they'll have to drag him to it screaming and kicking. Which he knows how to do, believe you me.

PART FOUR

WEST

WAKEFIELD POINTS HIS rental car west out of the city, drives it through still-sleepy suburbs covered with snow and Christmas lights, past houses built of nothing more than fragile boards of pressed wood wrapped in twinkling light bulbs. The people in them sleep well, though they fell asleep watching war on TV, and Wakefield is grateful that these people, crammed together in shaky shelters by the freeway, are able to trust one another that much. They aren't afraid that their neighbors will kill them and burn down their houses. They probably don't even know their neighbors, because they rarely meet. And yet they trust one another enough to sleep, and their peaceful sleep is strong enough to wash over Wakefield as he drives past them.

What makes it possible for people who barely know each other, who live in straw houses, to sleep in America? It's amazing, he says to himself, amazing.

The Devil chuckles. Oh, Wakefield, you are a naïve soul! What about the billion-dollar home security industry? I get ten percent of the profits! What about the locks and bolts and floodlights and video surveillance and fireproof safes and gated communities and bomb shelters? What about the gigantic gun business that's been arming the populace since the founding of the republic? And what of the immense insurance racket that rakes in jillions from people's fear? Even the poorest of the poor sleep with revolvers under their pillows.

Nothing has profited the Devil so much as the fear of crime: he gets his cut from every gun sold, every insurance policy, every security system installed, every lock, every fence, and every pepper-spray cannister in every women's purse.

WAKEFIELD HAS THE luxury of time before his next gig for the art collector out West. When Wakefield was a young man he had made a generational right of passage: he drove to California a 1957 Oldsmobile called OhMy. It was 1966 and he was alone, like now, and sad. His girlfriend was supposed to go with him, but she changed her mind (another guy) at the last minute. He drove across the country with the Kinks, the Beatles, the Beach Boys, Iron Butterfly, the Mamas and the Papas, his father's well-thumbed road atlas, and worn paperbacks of *The Journals of Lewis and Clark, Leaves of Grass,* and of course *On the Road,* published, wow, in 1957, the same vintage as OhMy. His memories of that trip are mostly visual, though: the night sky in New Mexico, a starlit immensity that made him dizzy; a downpour outside Denver that turned the road into a river sweeping smaller cars down the mountainside but not bothering OhMy a bit; a gigantic cowboy hat on top of a gas station in Texas where he bought jerky and beer; the softening of the light in the early morning desert. And that hitchhiker, a dirty, brown girl who took a long bath in the motel and spent the night. He left her at the Second Mesa turnoff to Old Oraibi in Arizona, by a sign warning white people to venture no farther. She gave him a turquoise stone he's kept ever since.

Mostly he'd driven alone, and the people in diners and gas stations were not all that friendly, but reading his books late at night with his flashlight, he felt part of a tribe, traveling with like-minded explorers, hobos and bohos for whom the road was not simply a means to get from one place to another but a state of being, a symbolic way of viewing existence itself. The road had its own residents, drifters, wanderers, people made ill by suburbs. Born and raised in one himself, Wakefield saw the suburb as a metastasizing megamonster, the incarnation of nowhere, neither city nor country, a place that reduced people like his mother and father to appendages of their automobiles and the new interstates. In the days of Kerouac, when his Olds was new, the highways were slow and eccentric, and Wakefield found them: roads where gas stations with old-fashioned red pumps were powered by flying Pegasus, where motor courts had vibrating beds (fifteen minutes for a quarter), drive-in burger joints had flying saucers parked on top of them and peaches-and-cream cheerleaders on rollerskates flew with milkshakes between cars. He found rock shops with treasures in dusty trays untouched since the bearded, filthy prospectors had dropped them off; a museum built especially for "the largest snake in the world," entry fifty cents, where the snake was handled by the oldest woman with the hugest boobs in Oklahoma; enormous cowboys, lassos flying beside steak joints in Texas; jackrabbits with Christmas lights strung between their ears; tepees filled with mounds of arrowheads, fringed deerskin vests, Navajo blankets, and Hopi baskets in Arizona; lipstick-red motel neon in the California desert glowing in the lavender sunset.

Camped beside a rushing river in a canyon in northern New Mexico, he read the journals of Lewis and Clark and imagined everything they'd seen—the strange plants, the new animals, the wild rivers they charted, the bluffs and bays they named, the tribes they met or ran from, the strange things they ate—and he saw how they nearly died and made it anyway.

Wakefield had stopped along his way to walk over the ruts of wagon wheels, he ate fry-bread and jerky and barbecue, and everything was for him completely new and became part of him, which is why it's the desert that draws him now, where his heart had once filled and might fill again.

WAKEFIELD PUSHES ON over the superhighway, past exits that lead only to oases of pure pragmatism: Gas, Food, Lodging. There are two nervous systems that go by the name "road" in America: the neocortex-like network of interstates that sucks cars in at one end and spews them out another; the other hidden, vestigial, nostalgic, the roads of his youthful journey. Only a hundred years or so divide the epic-heroic endeavours of the first explorers of the West and the building of the interstate highways that now inscribe the face of North America. An even shorter time will elapse between the disappearance of these roads and the ascendence of the disembodied virtual highway. But the projections of dreamers and futurists blossom and fail in rapid succession, leaving behind a bizarre archeology.

Wakefield wants to find again the fragmented, narrative, homey roads he remembers. He drives all day and all the next night through Iowa, Missouri, a bit of Oklahoma, winter brown giving way to green, snow to rain, dark mud to hard, cracked soil, then the land becomes the desert. If he can succeed in finding again the hunger and curiosity of his youth, he might beat the Devil yet. Back then he didn't care about money or comfort or even company; he was moved by something awesome and divine. In the desert his whole being was lit by the knowledge of his connection with the universe. That is how the saints of the desert must have felt, tormented by the blazing sun, chilled almost to death at night, yet filled with the ecstasy of the holy spirit.

He's also stayed awake all night many times in the neon-lit insomnia of cities where the all-nighter is culturally certified and commercially mandated. But the all-nighter of the bohemian heroes was something else: it was spiritual work, the night shift; they stayed awake so the demons that haunt the world wouldn't get them in their sleep. Theirs was a celebratory song of a vibrant new night of jazz, sex, and vitality that defied Fifties America, a celebration conducted atop a trembling hill of youthful melancholy and fear. Kerouac's American night was a carnival and America herself was just waking up. His fraternity of the wee hours did not discriminate by age or economic status; nobody had any money and even bums were valued for their stories. Their booze was rotgut wine and whiskey, and their drugs were speed, pot, and the occasional morphine derivative. Hearts were broken, leaking love and sorrow, and were continually mended by rivers of talk and desperate sex.

WAKEFIELD IS A trembling hill of exhaustion when he pulls into the shiny, new truck stop and eats a microwaved burrito and a Snickers bar washed down by a large coffee. He consults with the teenager behind the cash register, who has no idea where the old highway is, but a Mexican truck driver sets him straight. He gives him directions to the Sirena Motel at the intersection of two old roads, one leading through the desert all the way to Arizona, the other through the mountains to Colorado. The Mexican repeats "la see-ren-aaa" and winks.

Wakefield finds the place and drifts off to the moaning of the wind rattling the windows, and the shrieks and moans of drunk girls and truckers who come and go all night, slamming doors and shaking beds.

In the morning brilliant white snow has blanketed the hills and everything is eerily quiet. Wakefield heads out on the old road toward Arizona. He passes a series of ancient Burma Shave signs that start just beyond the crossroad. They are faded but still legible:

THE POOREST GUY . . .

IN THE HUMAN RACE . . .

CAN HAVE A MILLION-DOLLAR FACE . . .

WITH BURMA SHAVE

These little billboards had exploited the narrative nature of the old roads, making their pitch in installments so that the traveler had to wait to find out what the next one said. Pretty soon another serial begins, the handlettered signs punctured by bullet holes. The first asks the question: AFTER LIFE WHAT? A grave question, which Wakefield cannot answer. Half a mile later, the next sign answers: THE JUDGE-MENT. That makes life a crime and death a trial. Wakefield doesn't like it: what kind of malevolent deity would conduct the trial? And why? Isn't each action rewarded instantly by a reaction, thus by an organic, instant judgment? "You can take your trial and shove it!" he shouts at the sign.

The sign pays no attention and he soon comes to the next one, asking another question: AFTER THE JUDGEMENT WHAT? This is something he'd like to know, but he doesn't expect to be enlightened by the answer. He drives on through the slush, hoping his tires don't sink in a snow-filled pothole, until he sees the answer: THE RESUR-RECTION. Well, that's better, but he still doesn't think it's fair to have to go through a trial to get there. After a few more uphill miles, near the top of the mesa, his irritation is piqued by the follow-up question: RESURRECTION FOR WHOM? Now he's sure that these signs are an evil trail of crumbs left by a wicked witch to lure Hansel and Gretel, and he vows not to stop for any old ladies selling gingerbread. A full five miles of snow-glazed high desert later, the answer is waiting for him: THE SAVED. Wakefield hums a scrap of a Grateful Dead melody to quell his growing anxiety as he scuttles on down the road.

There is no salvation, obviously, for anyone who's made a deal with the Devil. He will be unsaved and damned whether he wins or loses. If he loses, he'll be carried off in a cloudy wisp of darkness and guilt, one more of the Devil's triumphs. If he wins, he might live "authentically," but in the end he still won't be welcomed into the Light that animated his soul in his youth, a Light he still believes might exist. Wakefield is struck by a revelation. *What if I just go ahead and die? Not wait for the starter pistol, not look for any kind of life, not play the game at all? Just drive on until I find a good spot to die.* That would cheat the Devil out of his game and I'd end up where I'll eventually end up anyway. *Just drive until I die.* This seems like such an elegant solution to Wakefield, he nearly goes off the road.

Don't you dare! says the Devil, grabbing the steering wheel.

SOMEWHERE IN ARIZONA (at least he thinks it must be Arizona) Wakefield realizes he's getting younger. He has left behind snow and mountains and has received the benediction of the sun. The desert relieves him of his memory, and his past recedes. A saguaro forest stands guard on all sides as the road approaches an interstate overpass; a few wild pigs are under it, consuming the contents of a discarded Burger King bag. There are RVs on the road now, and smiling old folks driving big American cars.

At a rest area outside a national park, Wakefield sits at a picnic table and strikes up a conversation with the other travelers. One family—mom, dad, and five kids—is going to visit grandparents who've retired in the desert. A honeymooning couple is headed for a luxury lodge in a verdant canyon, a snazzy resort "with two golf courses." Two slender doctors' wives are bound for the Dream Ranch to ride horses, play tennis, and sweat in the sauna. A college boy on break is going to "party with some people I met at a party." Wakefield points at the spectacular saguaros rising from the desert floor with their arms in the air: "They look like they're either dancing or praying." The kid watches them for a long time, hoping to catch them at it, but the cactus forest just stares back. For the first time in a long time, Wakefield feels compassion for everyone, a nonspecific tenderness. The human thing, how strange.

The new bride asks Wakefield what he's doing out here. "I'm here for the light," he tells her, paraphrasing Saint Patroclus, an early fan of the desert. What was true for old Saint Patroclus is still true for these sun-worshippers and light-lovers, and it's true for him because (he startles himself) he is no different than everyone else.

Wakefield drives on, past the ramshackle houses of Mexican migrant workers, past RV parks and swanky retirement communities. He stops on the decaying main street of an old college town surrounded by desert mountains and decides to eat lunch in the hotel. A sign in the lobby announces a reunion for a Mexican family from both sides of the border: the American Hernandezes are hosting the Mexican Hernandezes, and most of them are already in the restaurant, shouting about NAFTA, shushing children, raising toasts, laughing loudly. Wakefield is ravenously hungry. He consumes a big plate of green chile, beans, rice, and a pile of corn tortillas, and washes it all down with a Dos Equis. He is thirsty, thirsty, drinks another cold beer and swabs the plate clean with one more tortilla. The din of Spanish and Spanglish mixes with the border music on the jukebox, and Wakefield feels pleasantly as though he's in a hot bath.

He picks up a copy of the local paper, *The Desert Star,* and reads the headline "Desert Development Ousting the Gila Monsters." The Gila monster, pictured full front, is a beady-eyed and beaded orange-and-black venomous lizard. He looks an awful lot like a gargoyle at Notre Dame, an old image of the Devil if there ever was one. The article says he makes burrows underground and is pretty invisible until you smash his house: then his "talon-shape teeth gnaw on the victim, pumping in venom." As usual in cases of man against monster, Wakefield is for the monster. He hopes a Gila will sink his talon-shape teeth into a developer before the Gilas are completely wiped out.

Outside of town he comes across a row of motorcycles parked on the roadside. He hears gunshots; the bikers must be out in the hills shooting Gilas, pigs, and possibly saguaros. He parks the car down the road from the bikes and follows a footpath into the scrub. As he walks he sees whirling, darting hummingbirds, and snakes and lizards and spiders. And there are more javelinas, plump, fifty-two-pound peccaries rooting about in the mud of an arroyo. He hears a coyote howl. The path ascends along a canyon wall crowded with prickly pear cactus; ocotillo, the "living fence"; purple brittlebush; and carpets of yellow desert marigolds, verbena, and sacred datura. A sage-and-creosote smell floats over everything. Hawks and turkey vultures float in the sky. Gunshots sound out at regular intervals, but nobody shoots him. I am not granted, Wakefield thinks almost sadly, the honor of dying with old nature.

My old nature, thinks Pan, is threatened by my own guns. Since when have I become so goddam universal? Why the hell is God sleeping? I'm going to wake him up, I swear. I can't do everything, moans Satan, *and* pay attention to the particulars. Maybe the bureaucracy is right: forget the individual cases, get to work on the species.

The hitchhiker is crouched by the side of the road, holding a cardboard sign: Will not Work for Money or Love. His prophet's white beard reaches to his waist and a smelly-looking green rucksack sits beside him. He approaches the car warily when Wakefield pulls over, says, "God bless the meek, for they have no automobiles," throws his odoriferous pack on the backseat and climbs into the front, emanating a stink of rotten bananas with a hint of something carnal.

"I'm called Never Stop. How do you do?"

"Wakefield," says Wakefield. "Driver."

"I'm an Imaginary Archeologist," Never Stop tells Wakefield. "I discovered Gatobilis, the city of cats, and now I'm going to Washington, D.C., to register it with the patent office."

Gatobilis, ca. 1200 BCE, was built by large cats—"pumas," surmises Never Stop—and it is mentioned by both Herodotus and the Old Testament. The city consists of intricately decorated hollows dug in the ancient sandstone, linked by ladders and toppled columns. Never Stop stumbled on it while looking for a place to starve to death, which had originally been his spiritual intention. Now he believes that the hidden city was put there to give him new life. He's spent three years studying the cat city, and has concluded that the Gatobilan dwellings were built for the purpose of lying down and stretching. Never Stop found a cache of scratching posts, combs, and musical instruments adapted to claw use, as well as hundreds of crystals that once decorated the city.

"There are cat cities," Never Stop raps on, "such as Rome and New Orleans, and dog cities like Prague and New York, but this burg was built totally by felines, man. In Gatobilis, cats built tombs for their cat poets, who are greatly honored in the religion. They fled two hundred years later and their descendants are the cats that live around the graves of poets all over the world. I found this verse." Never Stop pauses dramatically. Wakefield waits. "'Pet a cat and history ceases.'"

The desert is turning twilight magenta and mauve. A sickle moon follows the car. Mark Twain wrote that "cats are filled with music; when they die the fiddle-makers take out the music and make fiddles," something Wakefield has always remembered.

"My work will be done when I get my patent," Never Stop says modestly. "In the future, architects will study Gatobilis and give up pretending that humans are the measure of all things. This is not the case, as any pet owner knows, or like they say in Latin, *'In Gatobilis Arcadia est.'*"

"Amen," says Wakefield. "Only trouble is, I'm not going your way."

"What are you talking about, man? That's where I'm going. D.C. That's the patent office." Never Stop is pointing at a billboard for The Golden Eagle Casino, showing an eagle-feathered warrior holding cards in his hand and flanked by two sexy female representatives of the Asian and the Caucasian races. It's only a few miles down the road.

Never Stop reaches into one of his recesses and removes a dirty quartz crystal. "Thanks, man."

Wakefield puts it on the dash. The Devil might like something from Gatobilis.

"Blessed be, man."

Hours later, Wakefield brakes in the dust outside a roadhouse called The Dead Mule. There is only one other car in the lot, a beat-up Plymouth riddled with shotgun holes, and there's a well-kept old Harley parked by the door. Inside, the saloon is adorned with cracked saddles, a pair of longhorn horns, and frayed lassos; there are a couple of video poker machines and an unattended blackjack table with raked felt. Must be Nevada, Wakefield deduces. The bartender is watching basketball on a TV high above his head. He swivels around abruptly when Wakefield takes a seat a few stools away from a grizzled geezer planted halfway down the bar. He orders a bourbon and Coke.

"That would be Bourbon Libre, and tell you what, you ain't gonna see no Cuba Libre long as that Castro still smokes cigars."

"All his drinks come with homilies," the geezer pipes up, and begins to cough. He hacks for a minute and relights the butt of a cigar. "A bar is not a lecture hall!" he chides the bartender.

"Nobody ever lectured you on nothing that might stick, Alferez."

Alferez turns to look at Wakefield. "I've been here since they rid the desert of the Manson family. It's been a hell of a lot nicer since."

The bartender takes this personally. "I never cared for that sonofabitch, but there were a lot of interesting people around then. They discussed things. They did what they felt like. If a chick liked you, baboom, right up on the pool table. People didn't sit around worried about the stock market!"

It's the geezer's turn to take it personally. "If you'da bought that one stock when I told you, you'd be sittin' pretty in Palm Springs by now."

"Well, if you're so smart, why aren't you?"

"My teeth. Fifteen thousand dollars. Good as new."

"Anyway, who'd want to sit around fuckin' Palm Springs with all those goddam Republicans?"

Wakefield likes this bar. The purpose of a good bar, as far as he can see, is to provide a space for freedom of all kinds, and a great barroom can expand practically to infinity. It always amazes him to see a room full of people in the evening reduced to its true size in the morning. Empty, it's impossible to imagine how such a small space could have accommodated so many bodies and contained those bodies' dilatory bathos and need for attention. A body among other bodies in a grocery store or on a public conveyance tries to make itself small, to take as little room as possible. The opposite is true in a bar, where the aim is to achieve maximum presence in order to attract other bodies.

The conversation moves on to more pressing local matters. The bartender has an original take on the recent proposal to make a nearby mountain the repository of the nation's nuclear waste.

"With that stuff here, nobody'll be bothering us for a half-million years, and that's the way I like it. Look what the yuppies done to the rest of the West! Nothing but goddam mansions and water-suckin' lawns. Where does all that water come from? Colorado River, that's where. And what are they gonna do when it runs dry? Nothin', that's what."

After they debate prostitution (all in favor), gambling (we do what we please), and the water problem (again), they congratulate themselves for living where they do.

"Fifty people spread over three hundred square miles, not counting the whorehouse and commuter traffic," the geezer says. "That's what I call room. Try that in the East."

Enjoying his second Bourbon Libre, Wakefield joins the conversation.

"Don't you guys miss urban civilization?"

"There is nothing urban civilized," snorts the bartender. "Cities are jungles and the people are rats. We get your kind all the time in here. They run from some city, buy themselves a hundred acres and a bunch of sheep, and think they're gonna be happy."

"I did that. Chicago," the old man says, "never looked back. I shot a sonofabitch for playing bad music next door. If he'd a had some taste he'd be still alive."

The bartender takes a rifle from behind the bar. "Hey, you want to have some fun?" he says.

They all go outside and the bartender shoots a hole in the door of the Plymouth.

"Why did you do that?" the old man protests. "You're fucking crazy."

"Look at that thing," laughs the bartender. "Like one more's gonna make a difference."

Wakefield eats a couple of pickled eggs and a strip of rattlesnake jerky from behind the bar. Pretty soon more people trickle in: leathery cowboys with showy sombreros, tough middle-aged country gals in jeans so tight they look grown on, a few army personnel in civvies, and a fat man with a peroxide blonde. Johnny Cash, who owns half the jukebox, sings "Ring of Fire." Just as Wakefield thinks of taking stock of his condition, feeling a little too drunk to stay on his stool, a hand grips his shoulder. He turns his head to see who it is and sees a familiar face.

"Anton, what the hell?" Wakefield says as he literally falls off the stool.

Anton helps him up and sits him down again. It's too weird; this is the guy Wakefield used to call Marianna's SYL, her Sanctioned Young Lover. But his face is like a jowly mirror of his young, pretty mug, and a much heavier body carries the weary head.

Marianna and Wakefield met Anton at a yard sale; Wakefield had his eye on a small wooden box with a little window in the top through which could be seen a dollar bill, and Marianna wanted a baby doll with curly blond hair. It was rare that their interests converged in the same place and Wakefield was feeling pleased, until the box he was eyeing was picked up by a hand. The hand was attached to Anton, an innocent-looking young man with washed-out blue eyes and blond curly hair resembling uncannily but, as it turned out, significantly, the doll Marianna desired. Anton knew what the box was; he had seen one just like it at a magic show. The trick was to open the box, and he and Wakefield both tried unsuccessfully until Marianna, who had bought her baby doll, laughed, "Why don't we take it home, have a drink, and work on it there?"

Wakefield and Anton each pitched in five dollars for the ten-dollar object, and Anton followed them home in his vintage MG. They had lots of drinks, were frustrated late into the evening by the box, and by then Anton was too drunk to drive. He slept on their couch that night and for the next three nights. When Wakefield left on a travel assignment to Egypt, Anton stayed. In fact, he moved from the couch into their bed, and Marianna didn't hesitate to tell Wakefield about it when he called home. Strangely, Wakefield felt something like gratitude.

"Is he there now?" he asked.

"Don't you get ugly with him," Marianna said ominously.

"Not at all. I just want to ask him a question."

She put Anton on the phone. "Did you ever get that box open?" Wakefield asked.

"No, man. Either I'm stupid or it just can't be opened. I bit it with my teeth, I nearly took a hammer to it. But that would be cheating," he said mildly.

In further conversations from the staticky phones of Egypt, Wakefield reassured Marianna about her lover and invented the acronym

SYL as a code for their use. Then one evening on a hotel terrace in Cairo, Wakefield watched a magician perform the trick of the wooden box. He paid the magician to reveal the secret, and it was quite simple, really. It was opened by squeezing diagonally opposite corners simultaneously and then gently pushing the slightly sprung top.

When Wakefield returned from Egypt, he opened the trick box immediately, and Anton, humiliated, left that night. As far as he knew, Marianna never slept with Anton again.

Anton had been a student in those days, though it wasn't clear what he was studying. He'd been quite frank in describing himself as something of a gigolo, loved by gay men and straight women alike. At school, he told them, he had been passed like a toy from one woman to another, but none of the relationships lasted longer than three or four days.

After the affair with Marianna ended, Anton would call to talk about his life and problems, but his life and problems were boring and they couldn't wait to hang up. Then Anton had shared the good news that he had obtained a degree in something called creative writing. He was calling to see if Wakefield could help him find a job. As it happened, Wakefield had met an art dealer in Egypt who was looking for an attractive young man to learn the business and act as a buyer in Europe. The dealer was certainly gay, but he was sincerely looking for help. The job paid very well and it included an apartment in Paris. Wakefield set up a meeting; the dealer flew in and took Anton to an expensive restaurant. By the end of the evening they had agreed that Anton was perfect for the job, and he was enthusiastic about the idea (as he was about all things). Then a friend of his father's came through with an offer to work for an Internet newsletter in California. Choosing between Paris and San Francisco was a no-brainer for Anton, whose surfer good looks reminded everyone of the beach. He went West, and that was the last Wakefield heard of him.

The surfer-boy good looks are shot, but his enthusiasm is undaunted.

"Man, it's great to see you! What the hell are you doing here?"

"Running away." Wakefield is definitely drunk and wondering how the universe can get away with so much synchronicity. Perennial problem. Serious nonetheless.

"Let's catch up!" Anton drags him to a booth and proceeds to tell Wakefield the story of his life from the minute he went West. It's not a long story. The Internet newsletter paid well enough to live in an expensive apartment on Russian Hill. He also bought a new car, with big monthly payments. Three months after he'd settled in, he met the love of his life, a Las Vegas divorcée. She was living in Vegas at the time, but she flew in to see him every weekend. On the second weekend, she confessed that although she'd been married twice, Anton was the first man ever to give her an orgasm.

Here Wakefield permits himself a snort of disbelief.

"No, really," Anton affirms, with eternal earnestness, "I found her G-spot."

Now Wakefield laughs out loud. "I was wondering what happened to that damn G-spot. Never hear about it anymore. It must have fired its agent."

"No, seriously, man. Whatever. That's not the important part. Love, that's what I'm talking about."

They got married a month later, but she continued to commute because she said Anton's apartment made her uncomfortable. On their three-month anniversary she asked him for bigger breasts. Her breasts had always seemed more than adequate to Anton, but love is without price. He borrowed money to pay for the new breasts, and then the Internet company folded. He followed his wife to Vegas, where he found out that she was an exotic dancer, which was a good thing because he was broke, and she supported them both. After six months of vainly seeking employment, tired of living on the proceeds of his wife's work (in which he did have an investment), they split up and he moved to the desert. Now he sells real estate.

Wakefield's ex-wife's former SYL lays his hands on the table and his blue eyes quiver like water. "I can get you so much land for next to nothing, you'll thank me for the rest of your life!"

"What's next to nothing?"

"Four, five thousand. And you'll be literally next to nothing. Not another house in sight. Well defended, besides."

"Electric fence? Fortifications?"

Anton laughs. "Better than that. There's this one place next to a hardened missile silo. An intercontinental ballistic missile."

Wakefield has noticed the missile sites dotting the land, neat white fences enclosing what looked like the lid of a soup tureen. Hundreds of feet below ground were nuclear warheads.

"Hardly a defense, I would think. More like a target."

"Well," Anton says, "everybody likes attention, don't they?"

Wakefield is speechless: speechless before the vastness of the West, speechless before the vastness of the innocence between Anton's ears, speechlessly drunk.

"I gotta go piss," he says, and negotiates a path between dancing couples (the place is packed, a western-swing band has appeared, there's a dealer at the blackjack table), and is pointed to the john in an outbuilding across an alley. He inhales deeply the cold desert air that doesn't sober him up a bit, gazes at the star-studded sky (billions of pinholes of light, close enough to burn him), and pushes open the door labeled Hombres. There's a woman sitting on the lap of a man who's sitting on the toilet. The man is holding a mirror and a rolled-up dollar bill to her nose.

"Forgive me," Wakefield mumbles, staggering back, and he tries the other door, marked Chiquitas. There's another couple in there, a woman and a kneeling cowgirl with her head buried between the woman's legs. "Excuse me," mutters Wakefield, backing out once more. He waits a few minutes, during which his bladder is about to burst, and then he pees loudly on the side of the outbuilding. During this overdue exercise, both couples finally come out of the restrooms.

"Men are such pigs!" says the woman who'd just been snorting something in the men's room. The cowgirl and her lover just say, "Yuck."

Wakefield shoves his way back through the crowd at the bar, and tells the bartender, his new friend, "I understand that a great bar must have private places for a bit of furtive action, but do you know what people are doing back there?"

The bartender, his good buddy, turns mean. "I don't know where you come from, pal! But you're in the only goddam bar in this country that doesn't have cameras in the toilets!"

Several fierce libertarians put down their drinks and nod approvingly. One of them points to a sign above the cash register. Restrooms Out Back. Ten Minutes Maximum. No Cameras.

Soon Wakefield is leaning on Anton, who is leading him to an old MG convertible parked in the sand.

"It looks just like your old one," Wakefield observes blearily.

"Funny thing, after I sold the Mercedes and left the wife, I got my old car back. I'm more broke now than I was when I met you. Thing is I can never make a goddam sale." For the first time, there's a note of weariness in his voice, and Wakefield feels sorry for him. He wants Anton to be the way he always was. Somehow someplace somebody's got to stay the same, but no one ever does.

Anton lives in some kind of miner's shack, as far as Wakefield can make out by the light of the kerosene lantern. Anton points to a pile of burlap sacks in a corner and Wakefield, totally smashed, falls on them unconscious.

He wakes to a world of pain made absolute by a brilliant shadowless light that enters his head like knives. Anton is asleep in his clothes on an army cot. Wakefield takes a look at the puffy face, then stumbles into the desert to vomit.

It is almost noon when Anton stumbles out and finds Wakefield, a few yards from the cabin, staring fixedly at a bush where a rattlesnake is staring back at him. Anton's good nature has returned.

"Wakefield, my friend, back up really slowly, don't take your eyes off him, and we'll have us some breakfast."

The mention of breakfast nearly makes Wakefield sick again, but he follows the advice, backing on his haunches away from the rattler. Anton drives him to his car at the roadhouse, doing his salesman's spiel all the way, each word a stake through Wakefield's body.

WAKEFIELD DRIVES BLINDLY for a while, head splitting, reaching every few minutes for the gallon of water he had the foresight to put in the car. There isn't a cloud in the desert sky, but he sees a shape in it nonetheless. It's Marianna, spreading herself by occult means all over his horizon. What did I ever do to you? Wakefield admonishes the apparition. Nothing, she answers, but it's a vast nothing, skywide. He looks away but hears the snapping of her briefcase anyway. She's either letting out the orphans or shutting them back in. For a moment he regrets his lamentable lack of concern, but then he realizes: they are Marianna's orphans. If he as much as looked at them, he'd be Marianna's for eternity. He looks stubbornly instead at the dividing line in the road.

Wakefield is out of water, but he spots the eagle-feathered warrior holding playing cards and follows him to The Golden Eagle Casino. He's driven back a piece.

He pulls into the nearly full parking lot and squints in the direction of a domed white building. Two state troopers are dragging a man to a squad car. It's Never Stop, without his backpack. Wakefield would like to intervene, but his feet are leaden and he needs liquid.

The air inside the casino is thick with cigarette smoke. A group of old people in wheelchairs with oxygen tanks strapped to the handles are parked in front of a bank of slot machines. A couple of them are actually smoking, one through a hole in her neck. Loudspeakers announce slots winners and imminent drawings for prizes, and piped-in music blares from speakers clutched by giant eagles. The blackjack and craps tables are jammed, surrounded by people trying to place bets over each other's shoulders. The dealers are all Native Americans in dark vests stamped with golden eagles, standing boulderlike against the waves of sickly-looking gamblers. I have arrived in hell, Wakefield realizes, and he finds a seat at the bar and orders two Cokes from a broad-faced waitress. He is waiting for the Devil to show up. In case anybody asks.

After a few sips he feels anonymous and free. Smoke drifts about him, the shrieks and loud music wash over him. No one around here is in the market for redemption. The architecture of the place is intentionally hollow, a huge absence in the middle of what was once a native world. No one is alive here; he is surrounded by ghosts. Does it matter to anyone that eagles were once sacred? Or even that they once certified real value on gold dollars? Now they are plaster, money is dust, the Indians are smoke, and pain floats about touching maimed bodies, squeezing as hard as it can, without effect. People scream in pantomime, holding whiskey and pretending to drink, laying down fake money, shaking cups full of confetti; their corpses are carried out and more are brought in by tall, thin shadows.

Wakefield takes a room at the motel beside the gambling hall, a small, dark, windowless cubicle steeped in acrid smoke and bleached vomit. The threadbare blanket on the bed stinks of sweat. He can hear the chiming of the slot machines and the blare of loudspeakers all night in his sleep. Yet he is innured to annoyance, waiting to die.

When he wakes up, he feels less confident: he isn't strong enough to die, not all on his own. He lies another hour on top of the stinking blanket, looking mutely at the blank TV.

The Devil stares with him. He'd like to die, too, but he's immortal.

DAYS LATER, HE'S not sure how many, Wakefield is in a town perched on the edge of the Pacific, sitting on a bench, waiting for the diner to open. Along the street there's a health food store, a video rental place, an art gallery, a pottery shop, a dance school, and a surfing-gear rental place. He counts six joggers passing by at an even and optimistic pace. Five bicyclists glide by on sleek machines that complement the outfits molded to their perfect bodies. The sun gradually warms the cool sea-salty morning, and by the time the sleepy teenager inside flips the Closed sign to Open, Wakefield feels himself returning from the dead. The smell of coffee makes him want to cry for joy. When the girl starts frying bacon for his eggs, he is ecstatic. Diana Vreeland called the smell of bacon frying "the most optimistic scent in the world," and Wakefield agrees.

While Wakefield savors his bacon and eggs, his teenage cook sits at another table with her laptop open, researching homework with a friend via cell phone. Wakefield hasn't checked his e-mail for days; it's as if one of the cords binding him to the world has snapped. He feels no desire to reconnect.

"Rosa Parks. Yeah. The bus driver threw her off the bus when she refused to move to the back, right."

She sees that Wakefield is listening. "Black History Month." She shrugs. She reviews a few more salient facts with her friend, then gets up and refills his coffee.

"What's life like around here?" Wakefield asks.

"Boring." She smiles. "Are you a vampire?"

His lack of sleep must show. "Hardly. 'The key to the whole thing was boredom,'" Wakefield quotes someone, he can't remember who. He wonders if *l'ennui* can exist in this jewellike beach town sparkling gloriously on a sunny morning. Bored, bored, bored, ma petite. Be bored, sweet, it's a luxury.

Wakefield wishes he could offer her some wicked fun, but he's full of eggs and light. "Surely," he says, "there is something to do."

"My mom's having an olive pressing today. Tourists like it." These last words she pronounces ironically, dissociating herself from the tourists and from her mom. "She makes fancy olive oil."

He imagines hippies squeezing olives with hand-operated presses, or with their bodies. Doesn't sound like a symptom of ennui. He'll try it, why not. He still has time to spare before his next appointment in the City of Rain.

The teenager directs Wakefield to a stone house half-hidden among Spanish olive trees. He walks up a stone-paved path to the massive wooden door and finds himself inside a divinely scented and spotless factory. Mounds of Spanish olives on conveyor belts roll toward a device that pits them and passes them on to a big crusher. Other conveyors transport blood oranges to a different crusher, and another machine mixes the olive oil with brief spurts of oil from the orange peels. Three workers in white coats are supervising the process; one of them, a dark-haired beauty, waves to him and points to a sliding glass door, gesturing him to go through to where other visitors are sampling the finished product.

The olive oil glistens in miniature Japanese tubs next to fresh loaves of sourdough bread, and people are eating black caviar and pâté de foie gras, their wineglasses filled and refilled by a smiling waiter. Wakefield dips a piece of bread into the oil. Wide windows frame a view of rolling hills covered with grapevines and olive trees.

"Everything but the caviar is made in-house," a cheerful, cultivated voice is saying. "Olives, grapes, oranges, wine, goose livers." The voice belongs to a woman with gray-streaked chestnut hair gathered into a chignon. "What restaurant are you with?"

"The Beat," blurts Wakefield.

"Oh, you're not Argylle, are you?"

"No, unfortunately."

"Argylle is splendid, formerly of Chez Panisse. I'm Beth's mom, Sandina. She called to say she was sending you up here."

"Pleased to meet you." Wakefield shakes her hand. "Sandina?"

"Well, that's a story. I named myself after the Sandinistas. You know, Nicaraguan rebels. Youthful folly. I was in love with Ernesto Cardenal's poetry."

"And now?"

"Now I'm in love with olive oil. My partners, you saw them coming in, the people in the white coats. They are Portuguese. They bought the groves and vineyard from a bankrupt guru who had to flee the country after being indicted by the I.R.S. The Portuguese have a long history of oil, you know."

Sandina pauses for Wakefield to wipe a drop of oil from his chin.

"Our oil is some of the finest produced in this country." She gestures toward the other guests. "Buyers, chefs, some L.A. people. Are you buying?"

"Observing," admits Wakefield.

"My modest abode is nearby. I have a collection of ten thousand cookbooks. I also make wine, strictly for myself and my friends." Her tone becomes intimate. "Beth is not coming home after work today, and her sister is with their father in Switzerland. Would you like to taste my wine?"

This is as direct a proposition as Wakefield has ever heard. And as complete a biography as could be put in a few words. Clearly Sandina is a working member of the leisure class. After the tasting he follows Sandina's BMW convertible down the hill to town. She pulls up in front of a grocery store. "I need a couple of things," she explains, and Wakefield follows her inside. The store isn't what he expected; there are sacks of Colombian and Costa Rican coffee beans, wooden boxes of Peruvian amaranth, tin containers of Italian olive oil, and hard salamis hanging from the ceiling. An enormous wheel of parmesan covers a burled redwood table. A refrigerator case along the wall is stocked with mineral waters and imported sodas bearing colorful labels.

"Our modest grocery-cum-lunch place," explains Sandina, with a tinge of irony he finds quite attractive. Behind the deli counter, a chef wearing a tall white toque converses briefly with Sandina in German.

"He says you cannot leave without trying his duck."

Wakefield doesn't mind. Before he can even say thanks, he's handed a plate on which a roasted duck leg is nestled on a bed of lentils. Sandina takes one, too, and they sit at one of the burly tables, under the chef's watchful eyes. Wakefield takes a bite: the duck tastes slightly smoky.

"Slow-cooking," Sandina explains. "It cooks all night and he's very proud of it. Rescues his own ducks, too. And he has a bone to pick with me, haha."

When the store first opened, Sandina and her Swiss husband had grievously insulted the chef in some way that she has now forgotten. The chef, however, has not forgotten, and every time she comes in, he subjects her to his latest dish, then waits for her praise. It's been their little game for years now.

Wakefield takes a forkful of lentils, but they are bland, underseasoned for his taste. He walks to the counter and asks, in all innocence, for hot sauce.

At first the chef appears not to understand English. Then he turns away abruptly, and Wakefield could swear there are tears in his eyes.

"What did I do?" he asks Sandina, upset that the guy's upset.

"You've destroyed his ecology," she whispers.

"His what?"

"Seriously. You've stepped onto a battlefield. He came here to rescue Pacific cuisine from the Mexicans and the Chinese. It's like a holy war for him. You just asked for the enemy."

They leave in a hurry.

"There's more about the duck," laughs Sandina before they get in their cars. "It's wild duck, but it wasn't hunted. It was 'rescued' by volunteers after the oil spill. Beth and all her friends worked for a week without sleep, rubbing the oil off the ducks, but a lot of them died. Some local restaurants bought the ones that didn't make it. This rescued duck is the regular Friday special."

"Why did we go in there?"

Sandina laughs. She holds open her windbreaker for him to see. Peeking over the top of an inside pocket is a long package of ink-black squid noodles. "Part of the game. I always lift something. Anyway, I thought you would enjoy seeing the place."

As they drive, rising and dipping over the grapevined hills, Wakefield imagines lines of force over the landscape, connecting the people to the cosmos where the continent meets the restless ocean. People have always found, or made, utopias here, utopias of refugees and migrants, eccentric religions, infinite kindness, and silliness without end. The End of the World is often anticipated here, but the Garden of Eden just keeps growing.

Sandina's house is hidden inside a paradisical garden. Paths of seashells and smooth stones lead through it to a meditation gazebo and a windowless redwood building. Wakefield sits in the kitchen, surrounded by the ten thousand cookbooks, while Sandina rolls an enormous joint.

"My husband was a marijuana grower way back when. He perfected this strain of sensimilla. . . ." She licks the paper, completing her task. "Eventually he went into banking, like all good Swiss."

A young Asian girl comes through the kitchen door. "Will you need me today?" She smiles at Sandina, paying no attention to Wakefield. She's wearing a batik scarf over her hair.

"You could make a fire for the sauna," Sandina tells her, passing Wakefield the joint. "Use the balsam, okay?"

The girl nods and leaves noiselessly, trailing a scent of sage and leaf smoke behind her.

"She's with a Sufi-type group. They show up to do chores for people around here, but won't take any money for it. They won't even accept a glass of juice. They are required to do 'service': roof repairs, plumbing, gardening, anything. Some people don't like to have them around: they're so otherworldly, they seem almost weightless. I've even heard people say that their 'service' is some kind of ritual before they kill us all, but I don't think so. Do you?"

Wakefield doesn't want to think about it. He can get a little paranoid when he's stoned. He's heard of "skill gatherers" before, but he doesn't know why they prefer serving the rich rather than helping out the needy.

Sandina leads him to a wooden bench in the garden. He watches as she takes off her clothes, and he does the same. She's tan and toned, and unabashed by her nakedness. She takes his hand, examining his worm-white frame, and pulls him into the sauna, where they are enveloped in fragrant heat.

Sandina pours a dipper of water over the hot rocks and sits next to him, almost invisible in the aromatic steam. She hands him a cold glass; he grips it, lifts it to his lips, and takes a sip. It's champagne.

"Having fun yet?" Sandina asks.

Fun. What a concept. What a word.

"My husband never understood fun. In Switzerland they call it something that translates as 'cozy relaxation,' something you do with friends at the ski lodge. Fun is a little more hard-edged, I think," she says, taking hold of his edge, which grows hard under her touch.

"European fun is never close enough to surrender," she continues even as she gently plies his firmness. "It's more like a desperate pause between the wars, a release from immovable givens."

So this is American fun, West Coast style. He's lazing in a river of sensuality, his body a lute or guitar, champagne bubbles playing over his cartoon-figure head. Sandina's hand caresses, cajoles, and his hands cup her breasts. Did she straddle him as suddenly as he thinks?

Wakefield shudders, feels her grip, is within the moist darkness of woman, and he waits there, listening. He feels her interior rejoice, and she holds him there until Wakefield, who has never stayed in a sauna this long, begins to feel faint.

The air outside is cold. When he reaches for his clothes, she takes his hand and sprints toward the house, where she wraps him in a fluffy robe. She wraps herself in a short kimono, then disappears into the bathroom. He sits on the paisley futon and picks up the book lying there. It's called *The Art of Bathing*.

Reading it he realizes there is a lot to learn. The Japanese custom involves immersion in very hot water and steam while being laved by professionals trained in massage and music. Even the simple act of pouring a bucket of water on one's head is an art they've developed to poetic ecstasy. The Finnish subdue winter with a ritual of steam, snow, and hot springs. On leaving these womblike environments, they enjoy being birched with green saplings. The thrill of hot water followed by fresh stinging pain is also a favorite of Russians, who consider birching a form of purification. There's a photo of a plump, pink man emerging from a bath and a birching, glowing with physical and spiritual health. In Hungary the baths are like coffeehouses; men lounge about wrapped in towels, reading the newspapers and playing checkers.

Many serious bathing cultures use aromatic herbs to increase the headiness of the experience. The women's baths in Islamic countries, the hammam in Morocco, for example, are veritable herbariums that induce pleasant hallucinations through a subtle blending of aromas and perspiration. "You cannot imagine," the author of *The Art of Bathing* exclaims, "the arabesque interiors! The perfumes!" Wakefield cannot. He can barely read; his eyes keep shutting postorgasmically, his mind subdued by pleasure. Sandina finds him nodding off and pushes him gently down on the futon, where he sleeps.

• • •

"Aw, Sandina, he's just a tourist!"

Wakefield opens his eyes. He's lying on the futon, covered by something angelically soft. He must be dead. He runs his hands over the material and it makes him want to sleep again. Sitar music is playing in the clouds. But then he hears Sandina say, "Don't be such a square, Beth."

Through the bedroom door he can see Beth sitting on the butcher-block counter in the kitchen, bringing an Inca Cola to her lips.

"I'm not square! I thought we had a rule! No tourists or monks!"

"He's not a tourist, Beth. He's here for a reason."

"To you, Sandina, everybody's here for a reason."

Time to intervene. Wakefield rises and looks around for his clothes. He finds them draped over a trunk at the foot of his nest. His nakedness covered, he approaches the kitchen and coughs.

Both women turn toward him.

"I don't know what to say. I should know what to say, but I don't." He realizes that he's still stoned, a little drunk, and his body tells him that he's just had an extraordinary sexual experience. Of course he doesn't know what to say.

"Say thanks," grimaces Beth, "and then leave before my dad gets back tomorrow."

Sandina smiles enigmatically. "She's probably right. But I should be the one to say thanks. Thank you for letting me use you, mister."

"Oh, freakin' jeez, you're disgusting, Sandina." Beth leaps off the counter and heads for the kitchen door. "I'm never giving directions again to anyone. I'm going to Ella's to study."

"Black History Month. Good luck," Wakefield calls after her.

Paradise, it turns out, is only temporary. Sandina hands him a bar of soap wrapped in a banana leaf, tied with red silk. "Finely milled eucalyptus-oatmeal soap, handmade by my very best friend."

Wakefield kisses her hand, slips the soap in his pocket. Oh, you lucky Devil.

THE ROAD THAT Wakefield takes out of Eden climbs and curves and doubles back on itself, refusing to conform to any traditional narrative structure. He drives all night up the coast, startled occasionally by lights flashing in the dark ocean, deer running across the road. Near dawn he stops to rest for an hour in the car, his sleep accompanied by the pounding of the surf six hundred feet below.

He arrives late the next afternoon in the northwestern city where it always rains and where he is expected by the mysterious art collector. They've put him up in a classy joint; two valets rush to park his car. Moments later he's sipping his customary cocktail and studying the fauna in the opulent lobby. This is the best, he muses: best hotel, best fauna, best time in America. The cigar smoke is Cuban, the money is high tech, the languages are multi. Women in splendid evening gowns and men in tuxedos float up to the mezzanine, and couples in expensive jeans and Italian leather lounge in the bar. Everyone looks as though they train in gyms, climb mountains, tan by lakes, and rub themselves with expensive lotions. The women glow like security lights outside of million-dollar homes; the men walk erect, chin forward, like rising stock.

Still, this is not Typical, where the new lies clearly on the snowy fields like the outline of a crime victim on a quiet street. The brash, impatient new wealth of the West is struggling with the past, a past that's not so old either. Here and there the old rich sprawl in armchairs, wondering where the young rich came from. There's a fleshy gentleman sitting with his mistress, an ex-stewardess he's kept for seventeen years. Her mouth is turned down, her eyes red rimmed from years of waiting by the phone. He is doughy, gone to seed, his money is still in industrials, his kids don't speak to him. Wakefield can see this, and more. The two have a reservation at the Georgian Room for the forty-eight-dollar steak and the fifty-eight-dollar macadamia-crusted rack of lamb, and they will get roaring drunk on champagne, after which his credit card will be rejected and he'll have to wire his

Bahamian bank for cash. Then they will climb into the turned-down bed with the fine linen sheets and have perfunctory sex. In the morning she'll be gone, and the note she will leave by his balding head will read "Enough is enough." When the old fellow sees it he'll take a long bath, put on the heavy cotton robe provided by the hotel, take out his shiny Beretta, and blow out his brains. Good-bye, whispers Wakefield, turning away from the vision.

Drifting in on an effluvium of French perfume, two dizzying fifteen-year-olds examine the oyster of the world they are about to consume with cruel glee. Then the famous host of a TV game show waddles in wearing his signature tennis shoes. A camera crew is not far behind, fronted by a reporter shaved as smooth as a dental mirror. A group of Russians holding grande double mocha cappuccinos from Maxdrip bubble over with joie de money. They have arrived. Ah, dream city of the Eternal Chip!

Wakefield has been in a lot of great hotels over the years, but he's never seen anything quite like this finely restored grand dame, home to a new generation of gold rushers. He can literally smell the money. There isn't enough stuff in the world to spend it on.

After rising next morning from the angel cloud of a heavenly baldachin bed, Wakefield opens the glass door to the balcony of his magnificent room overlooking the bay. A Japanese fishing boat is idling in the blue; sky and water are touched by the rising sun; a mountain peak topped with snow looks like Mount Fuji. Dense forests climb to the snow line. Here and there a plume of smoke hangs like a question mark over the trees.

On another balcony, a big-bellied man wearing blue shorts with red anchors on them is struggling with a fishing rod. His equally rotund wife comes to his aid in shorts and white brassiere. She wraps her hands around his and pulls. The line is taut; something in the water is putting up a big fight. Wakefield sees the slick white skin and gills of a small shark twisting at the end of the line. Inch by inch, they bring the creature halfway up to the balcony. The man's belly strains against the railing like a hairy balloon about to burst. The wife groans, their four hands gripping hard, and then the line snaps, whipping up through the air inches from Wakefield's head, and the shark plunges back into the sea.

Only a few years back this grand hotel had hit rock bottom and was known only for providing guests with fishing reels and bait so they could fish out of their windows; many guests left fish behind to rot, so the management now discourages the practice, but some of the old-timers, the ones who can afford the place, still fish anyway.

Downstairs the concierge tells Wakefield that he is very lucky to see the sun. "It's been raining for ninety-nine days," he quips, "twice as long as it took to break Noah." Taking advantage of the fine weather, Wakefield strolls along the waterfront.

Before the new economic boom this had been a place with rough characters about, dim bars, working girls, anarchist bookstores. None of that remains: no flophouses, no indigents, no winos, no whores, no sailors—pretty boring. Bright eateries crowd the water's edge serving "fusion" cuisine: Asian simplicity, fresh herbs, poached not fried, fine wines, French desserts. When Wakefield was young and poor his friends, who like himself were poor, despised luxury. He should feel sad about the loss of idealism, but he doesn't. These days he enjoys good food and other expensive pleasures.

In the restaurants on the waterfront young waiters recite the poetry of the menus, the structure of ingredients in each dish growing ever more vertical, each layer complementing the next with perfect esthetic restraint, each special on display like an Amsterdam whore ready to be pointed at with ivory chopsticks. Maybe a clue to the authentic life Wakefield has pledged to find, his *real* life, lies in his youth when, aroused by concealment, everything was bigger than himself. Hiding, he had made himself even smaller, leaving more room for everything that was bigger, more room in the overcrowded human universe. That the world is full of hiding places was an invitation to withdraw from the overinflated ambition of human expansion. It was also a refuge from the malignancy that he felt was pursuing everyone he knew. He was like the acolyte of a monastic order that called its adherents into hiding from the moment they were born. Perhaps this hidden order that he had always imagined was not imaginary at all. He was a bona fide member.

He returns to his freshly made-up suite and resolves to face the e-mail he's been avoiding since he drove away from Wintry City. Amid the abundant spam he spots a message from Maggie. "Thank you for this wonderful warm feeling that hasn't left my body," she begins. "Everybody at The Company is giving me funny looks. The House of the Future hasn't yet returned my shoes. I think it's because you took that glass. PS: maybe we should have used a condom . . ."

No, please, not that. Wakefield flashes forward years hence: he's standing in front of another audience, having a public debate with Maggie about *their* child. No, he can't imagine it. He replies anxiously: "Are you late?"

It's funny how quickly well-being can dissolve when the universe singles you out. Suddenly everybody and everything is late and the only thing that will right the world and keep it spinning is resumption of Maggie's menstrual flow. If Maggie gets her period, the earth will correct its erroneous orbit and head away from the meteor, disaster averted. But what if—and here Wakefield has a truly frightening thought—one determined, wayward sperm was actually the shot he's been waiting for? One shot from the Devil's pistol could start a new life for him, for Maggie, for the poor child they may have created. "You better not, Your Scabrous Majesty, or the deal's off, totally off!" Wakefield shouts out loud. He doesn't know exactly what he means by this threat; maybe he's offering to die rather than force another life into being. Wakefield stares at his computer screen, whispering, almost praying, "Please, please, no." Then Maggie responds by instant message: "Strange," writes she, "I *was* late, at least six days, but my period started at the exact moment I got your message. Had to run and take care of the sudden flood. Are you happy? Were you scared?"

Immensely relieved, Wakefield pumps his fist victoriously into the air. "Scared," he writes back. "Weren't you?"

Thank God or the Devil, he's been given another chance, released by Maggie's flood like Noah from the chores of earthbound husbandry.

The demonic conference on the New World Order on Mount Eumenides is still dragging on when the Devil decides to return. By the looks of it, he hasn't missed much, just a bunch of boring lectures about new technologies of reproduction and the streamlining of data collection. But he's interested in the workshop on the psychology of humans. The consensus of opinion, as far as he can tell, is that demons need no longer be concerned with human doubts and misgivings. The primitive moral skeleton left by God inside his toys has become an annoyance that gets in the way of the vast transformations ahead. The demon leading the workshop, dressed in a doctor's white coat and with a stethoscope around his neck, puts forth the proposition that "humans themselves are eliminating their need for guilt and redemption through the invention of drugs that make all such concerns and all the talk about them unnecessary. Our job is to ensure their success by opening our vast stores of knowledge to the best researchers."

By way of demonstration, the doctor produces the image of a perfectly formed human female, magnified a hundred times, with glowing numbers all over her body. Using a laser pointer, the speaker identifies each physical feature: "Breasts, artificial. Face, reconstructed. Feet, hips, buttocks, hands, surgically renovated." He turns his attention to the brain: "Guilt feelings reduced to zero by class P drugs. Memory centers reprogrammed by class M drugs to recall only pleasurable experiences. Connectivity and sociability controlled by electroneural processors. Sex drive disconnected from the need to procreate, the result of multiple biochanges. Transcendent religious yearnings replaced by simulated ecstasy available through a wide variety of psychotropic medicines. Moral skeleton atrophied almost completely, but still showing traces of biological and even social concern. If we sever the production of these traces we completely eliminate species solidarity, leaving a creature propelled only by self-interest, that is to say, *our* interest. In that ideal condition, human units will be extremely efficient and, perhaps, worth preserving. Oh, and one more thing: the will to continue living can be engineered by the placement of *complete belief* in superstitious divinatory systems. This is already occuring without our intervention. Most people are at least partly guided by numerology and other oracular mechanics, from tarot cards to coffee-grounds readings."

The Devil cringes. Where is the fun in that? What's the challenge if people don't have feelings anymore? Maybe he is ontologically attached to humans, but it's not a superficial attachment. He likes their murky interiors, that weird blend of baseness and divinity, that struggling conscience. The sleeping God did make humans in his own image—He looked a lot like a monkey back then—and reengineering them goes against the grain of the Original Creation, an act of cosmic impertinence that even the Demonic Order cannot challenge. It goes against some kind of Primal Directive.

The Devil leaps to his hooves and shoves the doctor aside. The female form vanishes. And then he does something unprecedented in the annals of deviltry: he takes up the Defense of God.

"We are making a grand mistake here, the greatest we have ever made, possibly eliminating our own raison d'être. Without guilt or the need for redemption, they aren't human anymore, they are *us*. If we generalize human beings to the point where they are reduced solely to their cosmic function of information gathering, such as we believe it is, we are making obsolete one of the oldest and truest truisms of our kind: *the Devil is in the details*. Without detail, we will have no place to live. Functional abstraction is not our home; the flesh is. Furthermore, what the good doctor, and many of you, think is waste, such as an excess of pleasure, is in fact the composition of our own beings. We are made of inefficiency, waste, moral quandaries, uncertainty, doubt, guilt, absurd architecture, seemingly useless art, gratuitous gestures, spontaneous contradiction, and humor. This is both what makes us and what keeps us going. I'm sorry to have to tell you this, but only the most conflicted and absurd humans are capable of generating those treasures for us."

There is a huge moment of awesome demonic silence, resembling the great silence preceding the distribution of communion. The assembled demons wait for the other shoe to drop. Lowering his voice to a whisper, the Devil drops it: "We cannot make any such decisions without the presence of God. Therefore, I have found it necessary to awaken Him."

Pandemonium ensues. Our Devil retreats to his cave. Let them freak for a while. Anyway, some humans are perfectly aware of what the devils have in store for them, and are taking preventive measures. Some, like his pet project, Wakefield, know how to hide. Others are already fully arrived in the realm of the imagination where everything is possible, including the nonexistence of deviltry itself.

THE RAIN RETURNS that night, and Wakefield sails in the ship of his great soft bed. He rises after . . . how many hours? and pulls aside the drapes, opens the balcony doors. The sky is dark and water falls in steady sheets, wind rattling over the black hole of the agitated bay.

On television, stock analysts are weighing the impact of the president's penis. Is it good or bad for the market? It's good, they decide. The more it stays in the news, the higher the market will soar.

Wakefield soaks in the bath, listening to the steady beat of the downpour, savoring his sweet aloneness.

He must have dozed off, because he wakes with a start and the smoke detector is shrieking in the ceiling and now the sprinklers begin to spray. In the street below he can hear a crowd yelling and in the air the roar of helicopters. He jumps from the tub, pulls on his pants and shirt, and runs downstairs barefooted.

The lobby looks like a field hospital: there are people lying on the floor gashed and bruised, medics running back and forth. Stinging white smoke pours through the lobby doors every time another wounded person staggers in.

"What happened?" he asks a woman dressed all in black who's holding the broken head of an Uncle Sam puppet like a baby.

"The police went crazy when the protest reached the hotel where the delegates are staying."

"What delegates?"

"What planet are you from, man? World Business Group delegates!"

A troop of riot-geared policemen marches into the lobby. One of them speaks through a bullhorn: "All wounded anarchists will be escorted to a hospital!"

There is a chorus of protest.

"We can guarantee your safety," the bullhorn says.

Nobody moves. After some negotiations, it is agreed that two of the most seriously hurt will go in the ambulance waiting outside. The policemen retreat, flanking the two stretchers. As soon as they're gone, everyone starts shouting at once. "They just attacked. Tear gas grenades, nightsticks. It's criminal!"

One of the medics shakes her head. "What do you expect? You people broke the windows at Maxdrip, the largest coffeehouse chain the world."

"Precisely," laughs a boy with a bandage over one eye. "Maxdrip is putting coffee in the water supply."

The wide-screen TV in the lobby is blaring live reports from the street riots against the World Business Group. In addition to expected peaceful protests against global trade treaties, thousands of young anarchists have come from all over the world, surprising the unprepared city. When the outnumbered police reacted violently, groups of black-clad youth had smashed the windows at Maxdrips throughout downtown and had rushed the delegates' hotel to stop them from attending their meetings. People surges! Tear gas! Reporters fall all over themselves on the scene and some of them are on the wrong end of nightsticks. The spokesman for a peaceful French group explains its goals: "We are here to stop the disappearance of Camembert!"

Unbelievably, Wakefield recognizes the guy. His shop, the finest fromagerie in Paris, was smashed up by protesters in 1968. When Wakefield wandered into the place a few years later, there were bars on the windows. Is this the revenge of Camembert? The radicals of 1968 are Camembert junkies now, and new young protesters are defending it as a national product against imported cheese from America, but window smashing remains the eternal constant of protest. No plateglass window anywhere is safe from the wrath of an angry mob, and with the world becoming more and more transparent as borders vanish, products flow, local cultures dissolve, air and water refuse to be owned . . . , the world is becoming glass! Maxdrip has outposts around the globe, producing rivers of caffeine consumed by the bourgeoisie of the planet. No wonder our nerves are shattered. Tanked on coffee, with a little Ecstasy on the side, the kids are smashing the windows of the Mother Ship! But something about this protest doesn't quite make sense to Wakefield. Is American prosperity from coffee to cheese really the source of all global misery?

On television chanting butterflies and turtles face a line of helmeted police. They're all wet; rain keeps falling and there are odd reflections from the street puddles and drops of water on the camera lens. A butterfly waves a banner with the images of a Coke can and a computer crossed out. A gang of vampires and ghouls with blood dripping from fangs and eye sockets, representing American global corporations, is singing "Singing in the Rain." Where have these turtles, butterflies, and vampires come from? From peaceful suburbs with a TV and a computer in every room, Wakefield imagines. Lovely places where their parents eat Camembert and croissants on redwood decks. They are the offspring of the Home of the Future. Egad! The cheesemonger is on camera again. This time he's complaining about Mickey Mouse.

The number of refugees in the lobby steadily decreases. There is only one Red Cross medic left after a while, and five or six pale, bandaged kids watching the news. They come to life whenever they see themselves or their friends on the screen. The tear gas is subsiding and the TV says that the situation is under control. Four hundred protesters have been arrested. The delegates are attending their meetings. Then comes the news that five hundred local sex workers have gone on a partial strike. The reporter is standing in front of The Orchid, the city's premier strip club, interviewing the spokeswoman for the Sex Workers' Union. "The club will be closed to delegates," she tells him, "but we will let protesters in for free." The rain streaking the camera lens makes it look like she's speaking through tears.

"I'm trying to understand," Wakefield tells the boy with the bandaged eye. "How did you all know to come here?"

"That's funny. How come everyone thinks we came from outer space? We connected on the Internet, man. We trained for nonviolent resistance since last summer. The multinationals are destroying the planet, but nobody seems to know that, either. It's amazing how much people don't know. Ever hear of genetically engineered corn?"

The boy has an age-appropriate sneer, and smells sweetly of sleeping bags, no showers, and youth.

"Genetically engineered corn bad?" Wakefield baits him.

The boy turns away, exasperated.

"Sorry," Wakefield insists, "but what exactly is cultural imperialism?"

The boy turns his good eye to Wakefield. "That's when Indian kids play with Mickey Mouse instead of kachinas. Kachinas mean something to their people. The mouse means nothing."

"He must mean something," Wakefield says.

"Yeah, he means money. A kachina tells the story of the earth, of the people, of dances, rituals, how to make rain. . . . Talk to the fucking mouse and see what he tells you."

"Well, good luck to you," says Wakefield, walking back to the elevator, hoping the fire sprinklers haven't destroyed his room.

"Stay busy bein' born, not busy dyin', man!" the kid shouts after him.

Certainly. He has a deal to that effect.

What is culture? And what culture is being imperiled? Beyond his balcony the bay is a gray cypher, the mountains invisible. Should he feel sad because the French are unable to resist Big Mac? Since his experience with the hate-filled micronations in the Wintry City, he just can't feel sentimental about this antiprogress, this defense of the past. He enjoys (intellectually) Baroque mittel-Europa for its hint of decadence, its illuminism and Mozart, but would he defend overpriced hot chocolate and a putti-filled Viennese café against McDonald's? Not a chance. Where are you more likely to find somebody like the neo-Nazi Heider of Austria or another Milosevic? At Café Mozart or at the McDonald's down the street from it? Whatever idea of European "culture" is hiding in Heider's chocolate, they can keep it.

Still, there is something disappearing from the world, something composed of many instances of tradition and skill, or maybe not disappearing, but translating. Maybe culture, like physical matter, doesn't disappear, but is subject to infinite play, and the world is a vast workshop for making and remaking everything, including people, and the engine of this play is desire. . . . Enough, Wakefield warns himself, you'll end up dematerializing.

THE ORCHID, A so-called gentleman's club, is just a few blocks from his hotel, so Wakefield walks there, bareheaded in the rain, to see how the strippers' strike is going. A squarely built bouncer with black-dyed bangs and tattoos on her pecs guards the door.

"Delegate or protester?"

"Heads or tails?" Wakefield answers, then sees himself through her eyes. A middle-aged swaggerer with a long face, sad eyes, smooth shaven, no tattoos. More delegate than protester. "Really," says Wakefield, "can one declare oneself so readily?" He glances behind her into the bar and sees the kid with the bandaged eye standing by a vending machine, looking uncertain. The kid looks up and Wakefield waves to him. The bouncer turns around and sees the kid waving back.

"Okay," she says, "you know the wounded. Go on in."

Wakefield heads straight for the boy, who is still pondering the vending machine. "It's unreal," he says, "there isn't one thing in this fucking machine that's not manufactured by a multinational."

"Aw, go ahead and have a Coke."

"I guess you think that's funny."

The bar is occupied by all kinds of people, some of them watching the strippers, others deep in conversation. The stage with its shiny brass pole is bathed in red light; a bored Black girl with small breasts is pulling on her G-string, doing her routine. The tables directly in front of the stage are empty except for two enthusiastic women, fans or friends of the stripper on stage, waving dollar bills and wolf-whistling.

The place has a blue-collar feeling, perhaps because some of the nonprotester-looking folks at the bar are heavy-duty lesbians wearing lumberjack shirts.

The one-eyed boy has settled on some kind of peanut bar and sits on the stool next to Wakefield. "Sad, don't you think?"

"What's sad?" Wakefield orders two longnecks from the bartender, who looks familiar. "Do I know you?"

"Sure, if you watch television. I did a Maxdrip commercial last year."

That's it. Wakefield gives his young friend one of the beers.

"What's *sad* is the trade in human flesh. We exploit everything, animal, mineral, and human." The kid takes a swig, nearly missing his mouth because of his bad eye.

"Try not to be so programmatic," Wakefield suggests paternally. "People do what they want. They've been doing it forever. What makes you think it's exploitation? They have a union."

"Yeah," adds the bartender, "and most of them are artists. Caddy, the girl dancing now, is a filmmaker. There was a big art show by the sex workers last year."

Caddy finishes her dance and drifts over to the bar. "Tip for the dance?"

Wakefield hands her a five. The kid looks away.

"What do these lumberjacks do in real life?"

"Drive trucks, cut down trees, drink. They really do! It's kind of boring here without the delegates. Hey, kid, wanna tip me?"

"He doesn't approve," says Wakefield.

Caddy puts her arms around the kid's skinny shoulders and rubs her bare breasts on his back. "You're bony, boy. Tell Auntie C what's the matter."

"I don't know," the kid says, afraid to move. "I came here to protest the ripoff of the planet by multinational corporations, and now I'm in a strip bar."

Caddy laughs heartily. "Titty bar, honey. Hey, I'm editing my new film, wanna know what it's about?"

"Sure," says the kid, hoping she won't stop pressing against him.

"It's about my friends' rededication ceremony. Know what that is?"

He doesn't. Neither does Wakefield. He buys Caddy a champagne cocktail and she enlightens them.

"Every year they rededicate themselves as a couple in an S and M ceremony. You know what that is?"

"What, 'couple' or 'S and M'?" says Wakefield.

"Don't get cute, mister, I'm asking the kid."

The kid nods yes, barely moving his head.

"Sadomasochism is a very popular subculture here. So anyway, the film opens with all our friends at Teresa and Lu's loft, everybody dressed in leather, high-laced boots, leather teddies, whips, chains, all that, beautiful women. We haven't seen each other in a while so there is all this chat, Girl, you got a new clit ring, Honey, let me see your new tongue stud, and so on, girl talk. Then the maids of honor, haha, that's an inside joke, set up the gear, the hooks in the ceiling, the silk ropes, the whips. Excuse me, honey, can I have another drink?"

"My pleasure. What you gonna do with that boy?" asks Wakefield.

Caddy's still got her arms around the baby anarchist. "Make him protest till he comes." She moves her hips and squeezes. "Anyway, then the girls get in a circle and undress the two sweethearts very slowly, making sure to kiss them a little and stroke them here and there. . . . So then you see them being lifted up and suspended from the ropes that have these velvet cuffs. Now they are both about two feet off the floor and the girls tie their ankles. The lovebirds are facing each other about three feet apart, looking into each other's eyes. Now comes the fun part. Okay, there is soundtrack, too, this gorgeous piece of music performed by the Three S&M Graces—they just put out a CD. We all make a toast, and then the maids of honor stand behind each lady with a cat-o'-nine-tails, and they bring them down over their naked butts, sending the honeybees swinging toward each other. They get just close enough so their tits touch, and then swing apart and back toward each other, and they never break eye contact.

There is just enough slack for their nips to kiss, but nothing else, except for eye contact. The music crescendoes at this point and the maids are really whipping them now and there are tears in their eyes, great closeup here, but they never break eye contact. They are rededicating, see. They can take the pain for each other, it's an offering, they suffer because they love each other. There is a great shot of the welts on their asses and backs, you can see them swelling, there's no broken skin, no blood or anything. The maids are pros, if they break skin the blood cools off the pain, and pain is the point. Then just when they look like they are going to pass out, the girls let them down and lay them out on this bed all covered with flowers and everybody rubs healing ointment on them and they get kissed and toasted and fooled with. Isn't it beautiful?"

Wakefield hasn't touched his drink since Caddy started describing her film, and he's gazing at her affectionately. The kid has simply frozen. A fat tear hangs from his eye. Caddy takes her arms from around him and laughs. The kid's shirt is soaked, he's sweating so hard.

"How about another drink?"

"As many as you like."

"Okay, boys. Don't forget, filmmaking is not for wussies. I gotta dance. Have some ones?" She takes Wakefield's money and puts it in the jukebox. Soon she's back on stage, swinging her hips to Waylon Jennings, and another man at the bar leans over to Wakefield.

"Her film is going to Sundance. She's first-rate. The first showing will be at my gallery, that's where we had the sex workers show. Name is Palmer."

Gallery-owner Palmer and Wakefield shake hands. "Kid, this is Palmer, shake his hand. The kid is a protester."

They shake. Palmer says, "You wouldn't believe how much artistic talent there is in this room. It's the greatest art community in the whole country. There's this Jamaican singer, Claudette, she's one of the Three S&M Graces, she's headed for a Grammy."

"Community," sighs the kid. "That's what it's all about. You can't stop a united community."

"United?" Palmer laughs. "They are unionized, but you can't imagine how catty they can get, and jealous, too, just like artists anywhere. You know who chartered their union? The Teamsters, that's who. Hard to believe, but it's true. This community has some major muscle behind it. Where is your community, kid? I don't see any of your pals here. Were they all arrested?"

"I don't really know any of them," the kid bursts out with unexpected candor. He turns to Wakefield. "We all met on the Internet, like I told you."

Caddy is followed on stage by a bosomy mom with stretch marks who spanks herself energetically, and then by Claudette, the Jamaican chanteuse, looking like Josephine Baker, who moves to her own hypnotic, slow singing that makes the whole room fall silent. Magic, thinks Wakefield, appreciating the satisfying anonymity that a room full of strangers (it helps that they are naked) can bring about. Peace, born on the fringes, swamp flower of urban *mal*.

Caddy brings Claudette over to meet them after her set, and orders more champagne cocktails.

"*Enchanté,*" says Claudette, who used to be Claude.

"I'm putting her in all my films," gushes Caddy.

"Me, too," says the kid, with third-beer courage.

"Darling!" Claudette kisses him on the lips.

A pink feather boa like a free-floating spider web settles over the kid, wrapping him in sweaty heat and perfume. He's a goner. The girls will eat him for breakfast. The songs on the jukebox get sadder and melancholy sweeps the room, a ripple at first, then a wave. It's whiskey-golden, existential. Wakefield can't see the shore; he's happy again. Palmer offers to walk back with him to the hotel, and Wakefield tells him about the party he's being paid to attend the next evening. Palmer claps his hands in wonder.

"You're going to be at the Redbones' party!"

Wakefield thinks so.

"Phenomenal!" cries Palmer. "You know the party's a benefit, don't you?"

Wakefield doesn't know much. He's only been told that it's a party and he's been hired to listen . . . to something.

"You must be shittin' me, man. It's a benefit for the next sex workers' show. The Redbones are raising money for film, studio time, equipment, art supplies, you name it. They're gonna get the moneybags around here to write checks for a million dollars each. All the girls have applied for grants. I'll be there, my friend."

Wakefield is not all that surprised. This is the West, after all, where good-time girls have always represented civilization, from the first whaling camp to the end of the gold rush. It makes sense that they should continue to uphold culture with their art. But he still doesn't understand what his own role is. Be cool, he thinks, you're being paid to do what you always do: plunge into the unknown. Still, it might be nice to know how he's supposed to go about it. He checks the desk in the lobby and is given a message in an embossed envelope. It's from his mysterious employer. A car will be sent to fetch him the next evening.

THE REDBONES' MARBLE villa stands in a forest of first-growth sequoia on a bluff overlooking both the bay and the wide river flowing into it. The driver whistles admiringly as they follow the mile-long driveway to the house. A valet dressed like an escapee from seventies night at a gay disco rushes to open the limo door.

By contrast, Wakefield is ushered into the house by a doorman as solemn (and as ornate) as Kaiser Wilhelm. There are already a few dozen guests in the vaulted great hall, sipping champagne served by a liveried waiter, but their costumes (it is, apparently, a costume party) pale beside the collection of modern masterpieces that occupy the large space. Wakefield's attention is drawn to the visual anxiety of a gigantic Rothko monochrome, but a playful Dubuffet sculpture beneath ameliorates the effect immediately. Flanking the Rothko are glass cabinets crammed with Greek antiquities. This tension is repeated between a Roy Lichtenstein cartoon and a kore from the sixth century B.C. On another wall an early Picasso nude and a small Giacometti sculpture on a pedestal keep company with a medieval tapestry and a large Attic amphora. A roaring blaze in the immense fireplace casts a red glow over the endless Aubusson rug that covers the marble floor.

A female voice interrupts Wakefield's self-guided tour. "Mr. Redbone collects Greek antiquities, while my passion is modern art. My first husband collected mistresses. I'm Aphrodite Redbone. Mr. Wakefield?"

Wakefield is unaccountably glad to grasp her languid hand.

Mrs. Redbone herself appears to be a triumph of cosmetic surgery. Tonight she is in flapper dress and mood. "What did you think of our riots?" Mrs. Redbone inquires.

"I don't understand global," mutters Wakefield.

"Don't worry, honey," she reassures him, laying her skeletal, gorgeously beringed fingers on his arm. "None of the fortunes here are global. Mr. Redbone is in lumber. Western lumber. His father was in lumber. His grandfather was in lumber. Doesn't own Indonesian hardwoods, I made sure of that!"

Arriving guests begin to fill the room, without obscuring the art.

The theme of the event is Art Sluts, which explains the parking valet in hot pants and the hors d'oeuvres in modified genital shapes. A fat gangster in a white suit, perched on a tall Beuys chair, remarks to Wakefield, apropos the skinny Giacometti: "Looks like he needs to eat some pussy."

Palmer arrives, wearing a tuxedo jacket over his boxer shorts; his long, white legs end in a pair of Arabian slippers.

"There he is, the bad boy!" calls Mrs. Redbone.

The actual "art sluts" begin arriving, dressed quite tamely in contrast to the interpretations the moneyed patrons have given the theme. Caddy, gripping her video camera, looks like a schoolteacher at the prom. Claudette has on a low-cut sequined white gown. Western fortunes and their spouses ride in on an effluvia of Belle Époque frills and Moulin Rouge ruffles. The Three S&M Graces, clad in professional-looking leather, set up their instruments near the glowing hearth.

"This is all quite amusing," Palmer confides to him. "The wives are all their third or fourth; some of them even worked at The Orchid. You can't really tell the old money from the new, not that there is much old money in the West. It's mainly a difference between hard goods and the new economy."

An equestrian "art slut" in jodhpurs and jeweled brassiere vibrates on the arm of an old man wearing a top hat and silk scarf, Montmartre ca. 1910. Wakefield tries to suppress a giggle.

"Don't knock it, baby," says Palmer, "that man has a hardware empire. He could plier out your teeth one by one."

Wakefield is feeling a touch of anxiety. Why is he here? The mysterious lumber baron still hasn't made an appearance. The other guests, Wakefield notes, have finished with polite champagne and are bellying up to the bar for stronger liquor.

Mrs. Redbone latches on to Wakefield's arm again, and introduces him to a tanned art administrator without a wrinkle anywhere. Wakefield is familiar with these body-laundered bureaucrats, the pressing and ironing that goes beyond clothes.

"The director of our art museum."

Wakefield isn't sure if "our" refers to the Redbones' private collection or some public institution. The value of the holdings is probably equal.

"Isn't this marvelous? Very much your idea, taking the museum out of the building. . . . I can't think more 'out' than this," says Mrs. Redbone.

The director is not entirely comfortable with Mrs. Redbone's interpretation of his rather more abstract idea. "We must also have gravitas; that is what constitutes the Museum's essence," he answers crisply.

"Oh, you're so droll," Mrs. Redbone dismisses him, and leads Wakefield toward a smaller salon, where Claudette is surrounded by admirers. Standing apart from them, studying a small Hans Arp painting, is a thin reed of a woman whose mushroom-pale shoulders are almost hidden under an extraordinary hat. She peers out from under the vast brim at Wakefield with violet Elizabeth Taylor eyes.

"Persephone," cries Mrs. Redbone, "I've been looking for you. This is our special guest, Mr. Wakefield."

"Where is Redbone, by the way?"

That's what Wakefield wants to know.

"You know him, he'll be up when he's good and ready. You've been here a month now, darling. The longest visit since we were at Gable."

"The tragedy," sighs Persephone, "of the provinces!"

"Come, come now, princess. You love it here and you know it."

"You look like . . . art!" Wakefield blurts.

"Let me tell you about art. That idiot drooling over that lovely whore over there owns more art than anybody west of Philadelphia. I was married to him and his art for eight years. We had to live in a hotel for two years while Philip Johnson built us a nasty cube in Houston, but it was better than the damned cube. The windows leaked, the air-conditioning didn't work, nothing stayed level, and there weren't any closets. After a week, I checked myself into a psych hospital in New Orleans."

"Ah, your Citizen Kane past!" Mrs. Redbone consoles her. "That man also owns more newspapers than Hearst, but I agree with Perse. He's a boor."

The boor turns from Claudette and catches sight of his ex. He heads over and peers under her hat, without acknowledging either his hostess or Wakefield.

"They still get to me, those eyes."

"Fuck you," intones Persephone.

The party moves into a huge dining room, where the seating arrangement has been strictly organized, despite the bohemian theme of the evening. While they wait to be seated, Palmer identifies a sympathetic city councilwoman ("I think she used to strip in San Francisco"), an undecided shipping heiress ("undecided about whether to join a cult or give her money to us"), the most-powerful-defense-attorney-in-the-West, the curator-boyfriends of various collectors, board members ("of every board I can think of"), the curator-girlfriends of board members ("you'd need a flow chart to keep *that* straight"), and assorted nouveau-riches with Philanthropy Angst, all well on their way to being four sheets to the wind. Seated at last, between Mrs. Redbone and Persephone, Wakefield toys with the lemony soup of the first course and sinks into the bath of voices and music. Still no sign of Mr. Redbone, but he has a good view of a Max Ernst Loplop painting, hung over an omphalos with a skyward erection, ca. 1200 BC.

Palmer, as the stripper-artists' representative, is the master of ceremonies. He taps his knife on a wineglass and addresses the patrons of art:

"The Greeks, ancient and contemporary, thank you. The agora and Athens thank you! The vestals, the temple whores, the butterflies of Pigalle, and Madame Coit's girls, all thank you. And the Sex Workers' Union is exceedingly grateful!" Palmer is still recounting the history of hookers through the ages when a basso voice interrupts.

"Get to the point, Palmer. Tell them to pull out their checkbooks!"

Mr. Redbone is as solid and square as a gold brick, his eyes overhung by enormous black eyebrows. He's no "art slut," appearing as he does, beneath Loplop next to omphalos, in an elegant black suit. An unlit cigar juts from his lips, perpendicular to the phallus of the omphalos.

Palmer laughs nervously and cuts his spiel short.

So, this is the man, his phantom patron. Wakefield stands up to shake his hand, but Redbone pushes him back down in his chair.

"Eat, eat! I don't want a hungry audience," he says to Wakefield. Wakefield usually feels the same way, though he himself never eats before a speech.

Tunicked waiters are circling the tables, filling glasses with wine.

"How do you like the avgolemono?" Mrs. Redbone asks Wakefield. "They say it was first served at the table of Aristophanes after he wrote a play about the meeting of a chicken and a lemon."

"That's lovely," interjects Persephone. "I thought it was first served at the Greek diner on Twenty-third Street where I first had it."

Avgolemono is a lovely soup, light, pale as the crest of a wave, filled with sun, the rice like grains of sand on the beach at Kios. I must be getting soft, thinks Wakefield: I'm making soup metaphors. I've got to toughen up. He searches his psyche but can't find "tough." He's even appreciating Persephone's alien wit.

"What is it you do, Mr. Wakefield?" she asks, but doesn't wait for an answer. "I hear you're a paid guest. Me, too, except I'm the one who pays. Every three or four parties I am so depleted I have to have surgical repair."

"Her surgeon is a regular architect," Mrs. Redbone intervenes. "Are you interested in architecture, Mr. Wakefield?"

"Yes, the architecture of adolescence."

"Ah, you're a chicken queen," Persephone sighs.

"The lamb!" announces the chef, and a whole roasted lamb is carried in on a silver platter. The golden brown body lies on a bed of white rice; the head, with its poached black eyes and budding horns, nestles against a golden bowl of steamed and seasoned brains.

After dinner, Wakefield follows Mr. Redbone to the oak-paneled library, where they stand before a bookcase full of volumes bound in reddish Moroccan leather.

Mr. Redbone growls, "So you went to a good school, make a bunch of money spewing BS to a bunch of geeks, you have employment and shelter, then you go on to badmouth everything because . . . it's too fast. You slay me, Wakefield!"

Wakefield isn't sure exactly what Redbone is referring too, but it is most decidedly aimed at him or, at the very least, at his opinions.

"I've been reading your stuff, even have some transcripts of your, what do you call them, speeches? The 'material world is disappearing,' huh? You must be out of your mind."

He doesn't know what to say. Wakefield may be out of his mind, but he's still wondering what the man is getting at. "I'm here to listen, as you asked," he shrugs, "but I hope it's a conversation, not an indictment."

"Conversation, my ass. I'm going to show you some things, then you tell *me* what's disappearing. Let me tell you something, Wakefield. When my great-great-grandpa came out here from Philadelphia, this town didn't exist. He had to start from scratch, in a log cabin he built with his own hands. That cabin, by the way, still stands. There is no shopping mall there. Anybody doesn't want their precious home bulldozed better feel strong about it. Can't anybody take it from him. The right to property is sacred, but it's gotta be defended. We agree on this?"

Quite. Wakefield owns only an apartment, but he'd certainly defend it if anyone tried to take it from him.

Redbone leans against the bookcase and it swivels out of the way, revealing a heavy wooden door. He pushes this open, too, and suddenly they are outside. The rain has stopped, the starry night is lit by a full moon, and Wakefield can smell the redwoods and the ocean. Redbone leads him through a formal garden dotted with marble statues to a neoclassical temple guarded by two naked Aphrodites. Redbone touches one of the marble breasts and the statue swivels off its pedestal; beneath is a narrow marble staircase. Wakefield is reminded of his trick box long ago, so simple and yet so difficult. The stairs are bathed in white light. Redbone leads the way and Wakefield follows, down hundreds of steps that end in a vaulted room. Four corridors with veined marble walls lead away into the darkness. "Down through there"—Redbone points to one corridor— "and you're under the bay. That's the defense area. I've got everything there, a nice submarine, a seaplane, smoked salmon, ham, and enough cans to feed Troy for five hundred years. Through there"—he points down another corridor—"is Ali Baba's treasure. I've got everything but the Elgin marbles in there. Plus some cannon and acoustic grenades. This other way are living quarters for fifty good-looking guests interested in spending eternity in comfort. The baths alone make you want to stay forever."

"How about the fourth? What's down there?"

"That's the command-and-control center for our commonsense vision. It's being brought on-line now. We can continue to function even if they shoot down our satellite, which I hope to God they don't. Can't go in there now, people are working."

"What kind of people work down here?"

"Good people, Wakefield. You're going to be one of them."

Wakefield hopes he didn't hear that right. Redbone grins.

"Let's go see Ali Baba. You're an art guy, you'll appreciate it." Redbone is nothing if not literal. Ali Baba's cave is a series of round rooms festooned with treasure like a pirate's lair: half-open trunks spilling jewels, paintings propped against the walls, sculpture, Greek and Roman pottery, strongboxes full of gold coins. Everything seems at least two thousand years old. Redbone gestures to a set of carved chairs and sits in one himself. He offers Wakefield a cigar and lights it for him. He pours brandy from a Roman glass decanter.

"Why?" asks Wakefield, not knowing what else to ask in the face of this excess.

"It's a big country," Redbone says, "but it ain't getting any bigger. From now on it's just got to get deeper. You know what I'm saying, friend?"

Wakefield does not. Redbone presses a button on a handheld remote control, and a holographic map of the United States a good eight feet across and five feet tall appears.

"What do you see, Wakefield?"

"A map of the United States?"

"Yes, indeed. The American Homeland."

Wakefield feels even more distressed than he felt the moment they descended into Redbone's labyrinth.

"What do you mean, homeland? That's such an odd word." Creepy, actually. In his mind, "homeland," along with "fatherland" and "motherland," is associated with the warlike rhetoric of Slobodan Petrovich and his ilk. In countries so small that land is actually an issue, it's possible, perhaps, to feel paranoid about the homeland, but here, in the country of free trade, globalization, virtuality, what's the point? But he's being paid to listen, so he bites his tongue.

Redbone runs his finger along the West Coast.

"What do you see?"

"The West Coast, the Pacific Ocean?"

"That's what you and your liberal globalist weenie friends see. What do you think the Japs saw during World War Two?"

"North America?" tries Wakefield.

"That's right, my friend. The United States. Los Angeles, San Francisco, Portland, Seattle, all the in-between. Your pal What'shisname, with the empire in cyberspace, he doesn't see this coast. Well, guess what I see?" He doesn't wait for an answer. "I see a threatened border. I see how they see us. A big fat sheep with no sheepdog, no shepherd. I see the Pacific, too, but it's our ocean, not theirs. We lose that

to some cockamamie idea of a borderless world and we're fish food."
Redbone outlines the East Coast to the Mexican border. "Everything
inside here is the American Homeland. Outside, it's sharks and
wolves massing for the kill. We are fat, we are asleep, we are lambs.
You know what we look like to them? Like that thing on Mrs. Redbone's table. And you know what we are doing about it? Nothing, my
friend. Think about that. The Russians were pussies compared with
what's out there now."

Wakefield's feeling a little sick. America is unassailable, isn't it?
Who'd dare come up against a country, a continent, armed with intercontinental ballistic missiles, nuclear submarines, armies, navies,
air forces? I must be crazy, he thinks, to be down in a bunker with a
paranoid gazillionaire.

"Mr. Redbone, are you sure our enemies are external?" Wakefield
ventures to ask, almost hoping to hear the familiar litany against Jews,
bankers, globalists, and professors—the stock characters of the right-
wing, fundamentalist operetta.

"Not to the extent you might imagine. I'm not a kook, Wakefield.
Why do you think you're here? The battle within is being fought on
intellectual ground. Sure, there are plenty of paranoids and crazies
crawling around in the mountains waiting for the ATF to get them,
but those are not my people. I don't deny having pragmatic relations
with a number of patriots, but they are not pragmatic people, for the
most part. I am not paranoid."

"I didn't say you were. But your fears sound out of date to me. The
Cold War is over; we have a finely tuned military defense. Who wants
to come after us? America is just an idea now, a very good idea that
can lead the world into a future where land is just a link in a production chain or a right-of-way to somewhere else. And if it's picturesque
land, then a place to vacation. Whatever you want to call this place,
we're not going to be invaded. Borders don't mean anything in the
new economy."

"That's the bunk stock-market visionaries want us to believe, pal. The same thing that makes the borders vanish makes them permeable. If there are no frontiers, it means we're vulnerable. What's to stop people from using our technology against us?"

Redbone makes the map vanish. Wakefield's mind is racing.

"There was a controversy after Germany surrendered, Mr. Redbone, about what to do with Hitler's bunker, make it into a museum or pave it over. They paved it over. Good move. To my mind, hiding in a bunker is inimical to everything the American people believe in."

"What do you *believe* in, Wakefield?"

"I believe in . . . the tent, nomadism. The bunker is the opposite of the tent, it's the antimobile home. I realize that the bunker is an idea as old as the tent, a pair of opposites dancing across the human sky . . ." Wakefield stops himself. He doesn't want to sound crazier than Redbone. "Granted, it's possible for some lunatics to exploit our openness," he starts again, more reasonably, "but why do you, at this point in history, reject the benefits? Instead of fortifying ourselves in compounds, we should build housing for everyone in the world, that's what I think. Forgive me, Mr. Redbone, but you are stuck in a religious tradition . . . waiting for doomsday and surviving it, one of the chosen . . . like you are expecting the Second Coming."

"Don't insult me, Wakefield. Look around. Do you see any Christian paraphernalia? All this stuff's older than Christianity, older than the first coming, for God's sake!"

"Sorry. I just thought . . ."

"Okay, I'll tell you what's really American. The fort was our first structure. It's going to be our last. Now, my purpose in bringing you here is not just to listen to me yammer. I want to offer you a place in our community, because my wife thinks that you are one of the most original thinkers of our time, a conclusion based on rather thin evidence in my opinion, but I looked into it myself and she may be right, if you can see the light. We need smart people for our broadcast studio. It will be the only one left functioning after the war, and your face could be the face of hope for anybody left out there."

Wakefield doesn't know if he should be flattered or run as fast as he can. He'd like to laugh, but he can't do that either. He's just been offered a comfortable afterlife, a hell of a lot better deal than the one he has with the Devil. But for some reason, he trusts his own Devil a lot more.

"You don't have to give me an answer right away, Mr. Wakefield," Redbone says, reading him like a newspaper, "but give it some thought. Here's something to help you ponder." Redbone holds out a gold coin. "Here, take it. It's Greek, fifth century B.C., the golden age of Pericles. It's a bonus. Your fee has already been deposited in your bank account." He takes Wakefield's hand, puts the coin in his palm, closes Wakefield's fingers over it. "And I appreciate your keeping all this confidential."

"Sure thing," he promises, wondering what will happen to him if he doesn't. He drops the coin in his pocket.

BACK AT THE PARTY everyone is dancing to the very danceable sounds of the Three S&M Graces.

"Where you been?" shouts Palmer. "We've raised a shitload of money! These girls are going to turn the art world upside down!"

"And Art will dig it, that's for sure," says Wakefield.

While the party parties on, Wakefield keeps up a mental conversation with Redbone, thinking of things he should have said. Redbone himself has disappeared again and Wakefield resists, graciously, he hopes, the assaults of Persephone, Mrs. Redbone, and his new stripper friends, who all try to get him to dance. Redbone, his fantasy conversation continues, you're suffering from a mental illness. A very American illness, I must say. Going it alone, making it in the wild, surviving a hostile environment, that's us. The fort was our model and necessity until, let's face it, the genocide of the Native Americans was complete. But even then, the fort mentality and the terror of the outside didn't leave us for long. In the fifties people had backyard bomb shelters, and they expected to be nuked any minute. And after the nukes, what? Eating Spam in the dark for years? Wakefield tries to imagine himself underground after the nuclear war, seated eternally between Mrs. Redbone and Persephone, taking lit cigars from a solicitous Mr. Redbone. He'd rather die in a plane crash. The only good thing about bomb shelters was that they gave teenagers a place to lose their virginity. The best efforts of this country were not spent on bunkers. During the Depression and the Second World War, Americans pulled together and built highways, dams, and bridges. Why then, in the wide-open age of the Internet, do you want to hide, Mr. Redbone? And not just hide, but hoard the wealth of several small nations? A future architectural psychologist will look at your doomsday structure and will find in you a perfect example of millennial psychosis. America has served the world as a place of escape from fortified homelands for three hundred years; why turn the place into an armed camp *now*?

Wakefield wishes he'd made these arguments to Redbone, but somehow he can't even convince himself. Why does Redbone's vision of the threatened "Homeland" disturb him so? He believes, or thought he did, that humanity lives in an uprooted, deracinated, global, nomadic, and permanently exiled state now that we've traded the territorial idea of "homeland" for the freedom of living peacefully nowhere. In cyberspace, or hyperspace. But Redbone has put a major dent in his recently acquired feelings of well-being, joy, and spiritual satisfaction. Damn.

PART FIVE

HOME

*Z*AMYATIN IS WAITING for him outside baggage claim, leaning against his taxi like a bearded bush. There is no sign of the Devil.

"Back just in time for the Library Convention, my friend. Fifty thousand librarians with bodies on fire under their boring librarian clothes for a whole week! Can you imagine?"

Wakefield throws his bags in the backseat. He's home; the air is as thick as soup, saturated with humidity.

"When I was a kid I got under tables in the cafeteria and looked up ladies' skirts. When they chased me away, I went to the library. Ah, Soviet librarians! Severe creatures filled with horniness!"

"I brought you something, Zamyat." Wakefield fishes the tiny salt spoon out of his pocket. "I stole it from the salt bowl at a Polish restaurant where I dined on cabbage with three beauties. Jealous?"

"Salt! You collected the beauties' salt right at the table? There is a library in St. Petersburg made of salt, it blinds you when you see it on a sunny day. It's the Borges library, it's infinite. Or maybe that's the *bibliothèque* on Captain Nemo's submarine. There is a salty, red-haired beauty standing by each shelf, reading over the top of her glasses."

Wakefield indulges Zamyatin's excessive verbal fantasy; it's how the Russian expresses his happiness. Wakefield loves libraries, and has forever inscribed in his memory a schoolgirl masturbating quietly in government documents.

"The library is the eminent symbol for opposing barbarity," Zamyatin goes on, as he does (Wakefield calls him Volga sometimes for his speech-*fleuve*), "it is synonymous with civilization. Great libraries are the secular equivalent of the great cathedrals. Public libraries are sanctuaries for the homeless. Think about it, the librarians are like nuns, I bet they can't wait to get to work in the morning, to wash and feed the crazies. . . ."

Wakefield has his doubts. "You'll have to ask the librarians, but take me home first so I can shower. I feel like the grunge of the nation is on me. Anyway, I don't think that Andrew Carnegie had the homeless in mind when he endowed public libraries."

"It makes no difference what imperialists like Carnegie think. We are going to have a drink at the window, then you can retake possession of your cave. There are a lot of things that we should discuss, and not a single one of them is important. Actually, nothing big has happened while you were gone."

That's how Wakefield likes it. Home should be immutable, unchanged. Let the big things happen elsewhere, not in my fun-loving town. Zamyatin actually has an apartment Wakefield has never been to, but he knows it's in one of those buildings next to the freeway, halfway to the airport, where people who are never at home live.

"Do you ever take the 'bartenderess' to your place, Ivan?"

"Are you joking? I take her everywhere. In the taxi, behind the bar, once at the library. I take her any place. Right where you are I have taken her."

Wakefield fidgets. Didn't need to know that.

"You know what this taxi is? This taxi is a library, my friend, the greatest library in the city! Whole books come in here. I had a church guy the other day who tells me he fell in love with a Ukrainian girl at a mission in Kiev. He divorced his wife, brought the Ukrainian beauty to America, she runs away from him, and he follows. Now he chases her everywhere. She is a high-class prostitute, I know her. She takes my cab. The whole time this guy is telling me the story, I'm thinking, I know her, small world. It's like a book, for sure."

"Maybe I should drive a taxi, too. I think I'm done flying!"

"That would be great, Wakefield. You could be the only native-born taxi driver in the whole city. Join the Russians, Pakistanis, Haitians, Palestinians, and Mexicans. You could be an ethnic group of one, you could read your fares instead of books, and the stuff you'd hear! I'm like a priest and this is the church."

Wakefield can't believe how happy he feels to be back in Ivan's company.

"On the other hand," Zamyatin laughs, "foreigners are loud, freaky loud. When three Russians are together the noise is impossible. Five Russians, you can't even hear a police siren. You stay away from fellow cabbies, you'll be fine in taxi-library, Comrade."

These are the days of full employment in America. The huddled masses drive yellow taxis. The taxis are libraries. Their drivers are poets.

"This is great country!" the Russian exults. "In other countries every man has to have his own books, he only goes to the library for the librarians, not the books. One day, I drive a Mexican couple from Oaxaca. The man says he lives in a house of books, because he has to own every book he needs for research, he can't get books outside Mexico City, no interlibrary loan, no computers. His wife, very beautiful woman with eyes like black diamonds and black, black hair, says to me, Zamyatin, you love books, move in with us in Oaxaca, we have thousands of books and many pets, and sexy sculptures made by our artist friends. They live in mysterious mountains, the home of Mayan gods, and she smiles all the time. The husband laughs, and they are both like seventy years old. And then you know what she says?"

"I'm sure you'll tell me." Wakefield is envious. Sounds like heaven; he'd move in with the Mexican couple himself.

"She says, the thing you will like is we have all the Russian poets in the Russian language in our house and we read them all the time because they are like Mexican painting, close to majesty of death. If you live with us, you can read Russian poets to us in your language and we listen and die happy! Can you believe it?"

Not really, but there is no telling. Wakefield doesn't like to think about death, which is why he keeps away from Russian poetry, though all poetry does tread close to death, either in slippers or in boots. What he fears is that death will not be comforting like poetry, but painful and hissy like a steam vent, agonizing and slow like a wire tightening around his neck. No, he would rather be an old man, forgotten by death—pursuant to the successful conclusion of his pact with the Devil—working on the top floor of an old library, in an office with a window that looks out on a melancholy, autumnal square. He knows the place: in the square there's a statue of George Washington holding a scroll. From the bottom of the hill, the scroll looks comically like an erect penis, and fathers bring their sons there and say proudly, "See? This is why they call him the Father of our Country!" The square is covered with fallen leaves, and pigeons sit on George Washington's scroll. He will look out the window of his corner office at the square, watching the leaves swirl. He will read. Seasons will pass. There is no hurry.

Zamyatin is still talking. "Computers are dangerous to the imagination. The blinking screen will never replace the book, no matter how much memory your machine has. Books are erotic, they mix public and private, expand both inner and outer life. You know those lions at the Public Library in New York? I met a girl there once, like in all the movies. We go inside, my cock is up to here." He takes his hand off the wheel to make a gesture halfway up his chest. "Think about it! This convention is filled with the daughters and mothers of all the books! I can't stand it. I'm biblio-aroused!"

Librarians! His daughter, Margot, finished her degree in library science last year. She's probably here with the rest of them. He feels guilty, but he doesn't really want to see Margot right now, or rather, he doesn't want to *hear* Margot. He would like to see her face, though, see if she's happy. Before graduate school, she smoked like an existentialist, danced like a demon, and looked like a hippie. She paused only now and then to yell into her cell phone at her absent father. Wakefield had a hard time with her in those days, and started calling her a Digital Hippie, a generation-gap insult.

Ivan parks the cab in front of the bar. Wakefield relaxes. The bartendress is not at her post; the Irish boy who tends bar before her is still on his shift, and he likes Wakefield.

"Hey, Mr. Wakefield. Welcome home. An Irish coffee? I know what *you* want, taxi man. She won't be in for an hour."

There are only a few customers, so the boy pours himself a Guinness and sits down with them. Wakefield feels cozy.

"It's good to be home," he admits.

The barman laughs. "I haven't been home in six years. I miss good old Belfast."

"Home is weird, though. I mean, I live in a place where most people are tourists walking around with guidebooks, and they never seem to know where they are," Wakefield says truthfully.

"Yeah, but you know where you are, right?"

"Maybe." He's been thinking about writing an imaginary guidebook to the city. He'd make up restaurants, hotels, cafés, history, and the tourists would never know they weren't real. He feels like he's just been a tourist himself, roaming around with an imaginary guidebook. Then he remembers Maggie and Susan, Sandina and Redbone. He hasn't been on vacation, exactly.

"It must be great to travel," the Irish boy says. "I'm stuck behind the bar. One of these days I have to go home to see my mum."

Zamyatin is watching baseball, the Tigers are mauling the Twins on TV. He loves baseball.

"Even after all this time, you still think baseball is American democracy and the other way around, don't you?" Wakefield winks at the Irish boy.

"Baseball relaxes me," Ivan explains, never taking his eyes off the pitcher. "It's pleasure, not politics. You should say a prayer of thanks that the crowd calls only for hits, not blood. That is the difference between crowd and mob. Any crowd can become mob, but this game of baseball stands between, not letting it happen. Look at soccer, crowds go mob all the time, and kill each other, make riots."

The only traveling Zamyatin does anymore is to ballparks; old, intimate ones like Wrigley Field, and newer ones like the Astrodome in Houston, and he always comes back happy. Stadiums define cities, he often claims, more than the teams do: "Baseball players are traded and sold and have no problem playing for their old enemies, and that's great. The stadium is a community, the people eat hot dogs and drink beer and love their team no matter where the pitcher is from."

"What's your favorite stadium, Comrade Zamyatin?" the bartender asks.

"Don't have a favorite," says Ivan, "but I hate the one in Chile where Pinochet executed people."

Wakefield basks in this familiarity. His friend has a sense of belonging and of time quite unlike his own fractured one. He's painfully aware that he has more moods than the weather.

. . .

HIS SLAVE-QUARTER APARTMENT smells dusty and warm, an evocative aroma, like that of an old lover, or rather, of all his old lovers. His bed, behind its velvet curtains, sighs with pleasure at his return. He opens the shutters and lets in the light; it filters through the branches of the old magnolia. A branch has bent over his chaise longue on the balcony, which is covered with leaves. A spider has made a magnificent web over one of the bookcases.

The profound silence of late afternoon in the old quarter is deeper than he remembers. There's only the gurgling sound of the angel in the courtyard fountain, holding the fish spout. He puts a Bach compilation in the CD player and unpacks slowly, laying out the trophies of his journey on the mantelpiece: the whiskey glass from the Home of the Future, the gargoyle's ear from the Tribune Tower, the dirty quartz from Gatobilis, the finely milled eucalyptus-oatmeal soap from paradise, a gold coin from the age of Pericles. He shakes out his kilims and drapes them over the balcony railing to air, sweeps the floors, dusts the bookcases, changes the sheets, then lies down on the freshly made bed and drifts off to sleep to a Baroque melody.

He dreams he's in a seventeenth-century casino. Elaborately coiffed ladies and gentlemen are frozen around the gaming tables, and everything is as still as a painting. Wakefield wanders among the figures—he touches one—they are made of wax. A voice says, "They are waiting for you to make a speech." There's a sound like a judge's gavel falling on a wooden desk and the figures become animated.

Wakefield awakens at the sound of the gavel, but it keeps pounding. Slowly, it dawns on him: this must be the Devil's starter pistol! He looks around the room, but there's no one there. The hammering continues, joined a few minutes later by a strange scraping sound. Wakefield sits upright in bed and looks at the clock. The digital face is blank; it must have come unplugged. The hammering and scraping become more and more frantic; Wakefield goes into the bathroom and opens the small window that looks onto the courtyard next door.

His neighbor, whom he has seen but never met, is standing on a ladder, hammering on the brick wall his courtyard shares with Wakefield's bedroom. Several workmen are milling about, scraping mortar from loose bricks and stacking them in a huge pile.

Wakefield calls out and asks his neighbor what's going on.

"Restoration!" the man shouts back.

"Well, bully for you, but the noise is unbearable!"

"I have permits!" the man shouts, and keeps hammering.

We'll see about that, thinks Wakefield, closing the window.

The hammering stops at dusk and recommences at dawn. Wakefield makes inquiries; the man has indeed been certified by the city to restore the old building next door. The townhouse was the birthplace of a famous jazz musician in the nineteenth century, but over generations it has been carved into a warren of cheap apartments, housing winos, whores, bohemians, and sailors on leave. Now the real estate is extremely valuable, and his neighbor plans to restore the house brick by brick to the original splendor into which the bawling baby musician was born. The powerful city agency charged with preserving historical authenticity has given him the permit. No one can tell him how long the project will take.

When he sees Zamyatin and complains about the noise, his pragmatic friend is not sympathetic.

"The economy is booming, there's construction and renovation everywhere. It's progress, comrade! Why should this optimistic noise stop because you want some peace and quiet?"

It is true, the sound of pneumatic drills and hammers is as ubiquitous in America as the crowds lined up in front of new restaurants on Friday nights. But Wakefield has a feeling that the project next door is of another order. It is neither construction nor renovation: it is something called restoration. He's not even sure what that means, but it sounds ominous, like the guy wants to reestablish a monarchy or something. Maybe Wakefield is being punished. The high tide of prosperity has lifted all boats, including his, and now he feels seasick and sad.

"It's not a crack in your head, it's a flaw in the universe," Ivan says, mocking his queasiness. "Let's see, what have you done to deserve this? You seduce anxious rich people and cause them to take their anxieties to tropical islands and exotic cities, driving up real estate values and increasing my business, and I thank you! You are like a pimp," he adds, ordering another vodka on Wakefield's tab. "You can't be a pimp and suddenly hate prostitution."

Every day, all day long, the hammering continues. The guy next door seems possessed by demonic, maniacal energy, and Wakefield spends more and more time away from his apartment to escape the noise.

ONE AFTERNOON, WHILE he's reading *Crime and Punishment* in the bar and Zamyatin is chatting up some sexy librarians, a young, smiling woman appears at the window. "It's me, Dad, Margot. I thought I might find you here."

Wakefield hugs his daughter, profoundly ashamed for his neglect. "You look great, honey! You know, I just got back. . . . How did you find my hangout?"

"I have my sources."

She sits down with him and orders a beer.

"My life's a mess. My shrink says we need to talk."

"Sure, sweetheart," Wakefield says, trying to quell his anxiety, "what do you want to talk about?"

"My shrink says that I have a problem with men because of you. I really don't know you, you know? Marianna says nobody can know you. She says you're a cipher."

So it's judgment day, just as he feared. Wakefield is aware that he's been, at the very least, a complete jerk.

"What can I say? I could tell you everything that's ever happened to me, but it won't help much, I promise. Psychiatrists are full of shit, you know."

Margot seems to have expected this resistance, and she's come prepared to breach her father's defenses. She begins reciting a poem by Lawrence Ferlinghetti. It's a sad poem about a guy driving around in a car with changes of clothes for all his different lives. The last line of the poem is about his children: "they've dropped out into the Jungian nothingness / with parents their own age."

The pathos gets to both of them, actually, and Margot ends up sniffling. Wakefield puts an arm around her and smooths her brown hair with a caress.

"Maybe we just need some time together," she says, wiping her eyes.

Wakefield feels like the most abject bastard on earth. "I never had much time, honey, but you're right. We should be together while you're here." He thinks for a moment. "Maybe we could go to a movie."

He's struck gold; Margot's eyes light up. "I *love* the movies. *The Moviegoer* is my favorite book. I'll skip the cataloguing workshop."

For the next three days, Wakefield and his daughter go to the cinema, something Wakefield wouldn't ordinarily do. He's always disliked the feeling he gets on reentering reality when the film is over, and being with Margot makes it even stranger. He feels her presence in the dark, his spawn, his flesh and blood, as they say, but she's an alien presence. In some ways, though, Margot is very much him, with her own specific questions. On the one hand, she has questions about herself, her mother, and him that seem to Wakefield a different order of inquiry from his own; they are female concerns, they deal with the dimensions of the intimate circle, and he fears intimacy. On the other hand, her mind moves quickly from the particular to the general. Whether because she is well read or because she is a librarian whose profession demands that she answer questions ranging from the triv-

ial to the cosmic, Margot has sudden insights that startle Wakefield as
if they had come from his own mind.

They go to matinees when it's still light outside and come out after dark, and everything seems changed. Reality is so tawdry compared to the screen; melancholy and sadness rule the wet sidewalks,
the dirty walls, the stupid faces. He feels disoriented, cast out of the
light into this solid weirdness. And he's not used to walking with
someone who sometimes takes his arm and leans close to him, puts
her head on his shoulder.

Part of the problem with the movies, he thinks, is that a film can
tell a whole life story in two hours, whereas real life takes years and
years, and though you can talk about your life—as Wakefield does
with Margot, in short installments—you can never tell how the story
ends. The moral of the movies is that everyone's life can have a plot,
but life is really more like the parking lot outside, mysterious and un-
scripted. You can drive off it and get killed, but it wouldn't make any
sense. Margot, however, is excited and animated after each film.
Sometimes she calls Marianna from the bar (where they go for a drink
after the movies) and tells her the plot, as if the film has somehow advanced her to a new level of understanding.

Every night he walks Margot back to her hotel, usually pretty
drunk by then, and they laugh about Zamyatin's increasingly desperate come-ons. He sees Margot as his ideal librarian with perfect
muse potential, and he knows she's perfectly unattainable since she's
Wakefield's daughter. Every night Wakefield returns to his apartment
and lies awake, worried about the racket he knows will start promptly
at seven A.M. His brief, violent dreams are like movies without a
script, and every morning he wakes up as cranky as a kid at the first
thud of the hammer.

The day before Margot's scheduled departure Wakefield experiences an unfamiliar feeling. He's going to miss her when she's gone.
Walking through the dark streets after their last movie, he tells her

about the night manager of the bookstore where he'd worked, the saddest person he ever knew. Every afternoon this man would go to a movie, and when the shift was over at midnight, he saw another one. In those days disaster movies were fashionable. People liked to watch people die or be saved from towering infernos and man-eating aquatic creatures. He would stay in the theater until dawn, then go home to sleep until the next matinee. This man was happy only when he was at the movies. Reality, of which the bookstore clerks were such a substantial portion, disgusted him.

"I suppose when you're gone," Wakefield concludes, "I'll just have to keep going to the movies."

"Maybe you can take a date to the movies now, someone who's not your daughter, so there will be no incest taboo." She lays her head on his shoulder.

When Wakefield was about twelve he had taken his first date to the movies, but he was too shy to put his arm around her, so he held her watchband for two solid hours. The movie was a Western. He can still remember thundering herds of cattle and the smell of her cheap cologne. When they left the theater he felt worn out, like the grass trampled under the hooves of the movie herd. Maybe only adolescents can take the movies, thinks Wakefield, which is why most movies are made for them. They use the dark theater to project their own films of stickiness and desire; the feature film is only background to the more intense drama in the seats.

"I read somewhere that movies are actually alien entities," Margot tells him. "They're beings made out of light who slowly remake our lives in the shapes of the stories they tell. Don't you love that? Isn't it scary?" She says this as if she doesn't think it's scary at all.

Wakefield thinks it's very scary, but he doesn't let on. He kisses Margot good-bye on the lips and feels for a moment the hidden body that Zamyatin had no doubt intuited correctly. He's glad that whatever Margot's narrative expectations of a dad had been, they were briefly met. He silently wishes her many, many more movies, better and better endings.

WITH MARGOT GONE, and the infernal hammering showing no signs of abating, Wakefield starts to fantasize about living in a tent somewhere in a vacant lot or, even better, in a swamp or a national park. He reads books about portable houses and nomadic furniture. Anything you can't fold up and take away with you is a blight on the environment and an insult to liberty, one nomad author claims. Wakefield makes a note on a cocktail napkin: *I believe in the tent, the foldup table, and the trailer.* He reads the stats on contemporary nomadism: lots of people, driven mad by instant suburbs, renovation, restoration, and condoification, are leaving everything behind and taking to the road. For every housing development carving up the land, a flock of houses on wheels and pontoons is taking off somewhere. The mobile home, the floating boat house, the tent—these are the abodes of the future! Even newly constructed houses are impermanent. A house in the suburbs is not portable but is certainly interchangeable with any other house in any other suburb, while the suburbs themselves evaporate rapidly and without a trace. America is on the move. Redbone can keep his bunker!

"Personally, I like a place with some history," Zamyatin says as he and Wakefield nurse their drinks, "but too much history can be bad for your mental health." He has a theory that poets should live in one place just long enough to acquire nostalgia for it. When that putative Eden is destroyed by History (and History inevitably destroys everything), poetic invention begins. "In your trailer parks," he says, rather gravely for Zamyatin, "paradise has already been compromised, perhaps by the sins of immigrant parents. I think the presence of wheels under one's consciousness permeates the body with unsteady vibrations that are not conducive to creation."

"The guy next door probably grew up in a trailer on the edge of a swamp subject to tidal instability, and that's why he's obsessed with bricks," Wakefield agrees.

Zamyatin closes his eyes oracularly. "His body vibrates and it is only when he touches bricks that he becomes momentarily calm. Maybe he is a poet, like me."

It is always a confusing pleasure to listen to the Russian, especially after a few drinks.

"I've seen many American cities," Zamyatin expounds. "Nearly every building in them has been demolished so that no one can revisit their past except in memory, and people's memories now must accommodate a great many things because of what they see on television. Maybe when they think of their old house, they substitute for it a Venetian palazzo, a Mongol yurt, or a Buddhist temple from a travel documentary. It must be exhausting to squat in someone else's memories."

THE RESTORATIONIST NEXT DOOR continues his maddening work, treating every historic brick as if it were a sacred object. His workmen carefully deconstruct each wall, scraping the slave-made bricks clean with historically correct tools, and then they mortar them back in place, but often the restorationist is not completely satisfied with the results, and the wall comes down again in an endless, demented cycle of noise and dust.

On every side of the historic house are the bedrooms and studios of other neighbors inconvenienced by the work. Some of them have complained about the hammering, chiseling, and scraping; one even called the police, but the restorationist is authorized by his permit to work from seven in the morning until seven o'clock at night. Like Wakefield, some made calls to the city agency that issued the permit, but their complaints went unanswered; their calls were not returned. Soon they simply stopped hearing the racket, and Wakefield reflects that in this they are like many Americans: hear no evil, see no evil, speak no evil. Their lives go on quite normally, but Wakefield's does not.

"Oh, my poor *casa*," he laments every day as the banging begins. He doesn't use the English word *house* because it doesn't adequately describe his cozy nest. An American house is not a French *maison* or a Spanish *casa*; his apartment is shuttered against the heat of noon and his balcony is shadowed by a magnolia tree with deep green leaves, and the courtyard walls are covered by flowering vines. Beyond them could be the Mediterranean, the lights of Morocco dimly visible across the water. Not only has his peace been shattered, his sweet illusion of elsewhere is also dimming.

Under other circumstances, Wakefield might have shared his neighbor's passion for preservation, but the more he thinks about what's happening, the angrier he becomes. The interior partitions have been removed from the old house and what was once a dozen apartments is now an empty, hollow space. Its accumulated history has been erased, its secret places dismantled, and its ghosts, if they remain, now share the attic with new central air-conditioning ductwork. The soul of an old city is the aggregation of human souls over time, and such aggregations are rare in America. The old quarter where Wakefield lives is one of the few, and it should be preserved, but the restorationist is eliminating the secrets of the house and killing the ghosts that have lodged in it over time. And in the process, he's killing Wakefield.

At about the time of the second rebuilding, Wakefield opens the small window between his bathroom and the neighboring courtyard and screams, "Stop! Just stop that infernal noise!" The workmen look up from their bricks, and the restorationist appears on the scaffolding.

"Don't swear at my men!" he shouts back. "They are master bricklayers!

Master bricklayers! Perhaps Italian Renaissance craftsmen just arrived by packetboat from Carrara!

"This is my home!" yells Wakefield, sounding slightly hysterical. "I must have quiet!"

"Get a job!" screams the madman, and just then a brick, which all the banging has dislodged from Wakefield's side of the wall, falls on his bed with a thump. Wakefield slams the window shut. Smoldering, he fits the fallen brick back into the hole it came from, trying to process what has happened. The man is obviously insane, and that crack about getting a job, it's a declaration of war!

That afternoon the madman fires his "master bricklayers": Wakefield hears him screaming like mad King Ludwig, except King Ludwig eventually finished his castle after bankrupting the kingdom. He calls his crew dreadful names when they refuse to take down a wall for the umpteenth time. After the master bricklayers have gone, the madman starts going it alone.

Now Wakefield is certain that the first hammerstroke that shattered his peace was the Devil's opening salvo. The continuing racket is just some kind of torture. Normally a starter pistol fires just one shot, he fumes. But it occurs to Wakefield that there was no clause in the contract as to the *duration* of that shot. In fact, there was no written contract at all. I should have known! The Devil is a lawyer, it's in every book, and I've been tricked!

El Diablo, are you out there? I get the message, but I'm not going anywhere, you bastard! Fuck authenticity! I'm home and I'm staying!

Wakefield waits for the Devil's angry reply, but it's as if El Sataniko has gone on a long vacation. When he gets no answer, Wakefield begins to worry. Is the Old Goat okay?

THERE IS NO WAY to explain to a person living in a quiet neighborhood, by a placid lake perhaps, what the unending racket has done to Wakefield's psyche. He begins to feel that the insane man with the hammer has always been there, that the torture will never stop, that his entire life has been a dream, now a nightmare, punctuated by the Hammer. He resolves to resist, to fight, and he begins to plan. He studies his neighbor, observes his movements, and in a little notebook makes a chart of his comings and goings.

ONE AFTERNOON HE calls Zelda. She's hurt by his not calling sooner, but they agree to meet at the café in the square where they went when they were dating. Wakefield wonders if the weather will hold, and buys an umbrella just in case.

In the days before the restorer, all he had to do was walk out of his *casa* and head for the square, where amusing and spontaneous spectacles always restored him, tonic for the soul. As he walks now he merely notes the familiar buildings on his street; he knows exactly which façade hides a hideous suburban-style renovation and where the attic and the new kitchen join, leaving a dark hollow perfect for a small acrobat. He can tell from the slant of a roof where a forgotten chamber is hidden by the latest partition.

After his review of the street, he occupies the corner table at the café, but today the square doesn't amuse him. He sees only the broken paving stones and the panhandlers. Once called the Place d'Armes, it was the site for public whippings and the occasional hanging. Today he thinks he can see the outline of an ancient gallows. Actually it's a bit of scaffolding erected on the façade of the old cathedral, but still the tourists gathered there look to him like spectators to an execution. Their fat bellies and stupid T-shirts seem particularly sinister. Many times he's heard people from Japan or France remark how "European" the city is. Now he sees that the source of their delight is the smoke of a murderous history that fills their minds when they inhale.

Wakefield orders an amaretto and an espresso and waits for Zelda to turn up. Someone has put an old phone book in the wire trash container and he retrieves it, reading it randomly to pass the time. There are eighteen pages of "occult businesses," including Zelda's own Crossroads Travel, along with palmists, aura readers, past-life therapists, exorcists, shamans, telepaths, channelers, and musical magicians. He looks up attorneys, whose listings take up at least as many pages—he thinks he might need one to stop the restorationist, or even to draw up the terms of his deal with the Devil. Then he looks up plastic surgeons; if he looked like someone else, he could go to a psychotherapist to *feel* like someone else. This Someone Else would be tolerant and philosophical about the madman, and he would bear the sound of the hammer as lightly as a feather. Then his lawyer would see to it that silence was restored.

Across from the café is a small museum. A mysterious object was displayed in its forecourt for years: an iron blimp, a Surrealist dumpling, thought to be the world's first submarine. It had been fished from the bottom of a lake, and no one knew how it got there. The thing had made Wakefield happy because it had a childlike absurdity, but now he notices it's gone, removed while he was away. A larger-than-life-size fiberglass figure of Marilyn Monroe, standing over the subway grate holding on to her skirt, has taken its place. The absence of the submarine is a blow to Wakefield. What does it mean? And where is Zelda?

An angel-girl wearing a short white skirt, golden sandals, and big white wings crosses the square and leans casually against Marilyn. Wakefield hasn't seen her around before; she's not one of the regular "statues" who make their living standing still while tourists challenge them to blink. She looks directly at Wakefield, an ice-blue gaze. He wouldn't be surprised if the new angel doubled as a hooker, yet the gaze is not mercenary. He beckons her over, and for a second it seems as if he's insulted her, but then she smiles faintly, flaps her wings, and sits down at his table.

"What's the matter, Wakefield? Don't you recognize an angel when you see one?" Zelda asks, kissing him on the cheek.

She's dressed for a costume party for the Jungian Therapist Convention in town this week and she's determined to take Wakefield with her. He balks, but the angel Zelda is very persuasive and so is the nearly imperceptible jiggling of her heavenly breasts, and he finally succumbs to her charms.

As Wakefield helps Zelda wiggle into the driver's seat of her car, one of her wings catches in the door and he gently frees it. The wings look so natural, he touches the place where they join her shoulders. It really does feel as if they've grown there, and Wakefield is tempted to believe that they have. After all, he didn't doubt the reality of the Devil. And where the devil is that devil, anyway?

The party is being staged on somebody's fancy houseboat on the lake. As they drive Wakefield tells Zelda the saga of the madman, the restoration, and his own pathetic desire to live in a tent.

Zelda is frowning. He knows that frown; it will translate itself in a minute into a flood of advice. "The trouble with you, Wakefield, is that you don't take care of your karma. The guy next door is obviously a demon you let in yourself. What we should do is work on the healing angle. There will be some people at this party you could talk to."

"Can't I just kill him?" Wakefield says, thinking this will shock Zelda.

"Sure, but the next demon will be worse."

They drive on in silence.

Wind is blowing at the lakefront; the water is choppy and the swaying houseboat looks like a sunburned egg with smoky windows. The Jungian therapists are crowded inside, and the crowd and the quaking make Wakefield feel slightly queasy. He loses Zelda pretty quickly in the mob and wanders among the Jungians, all costumed as archetypes of one sort or another, including Liberace and Elvis. There are lots of other angels, and a number of devils and demons, and everyone is shouting at the same time, amazed, he presumes, by the myriad synchronicities that attend their Jungian lives every second. After accepting a pink drink dipped from a silver punch bowl by an aging Elvis, Wakefield finds Zelda seated on a couch with one of the other angels, a Black one.

"Wakefield, meet Reverend Telluride. I was just telling her about your problem. The Reverend is a voodoo priestess. Actually, I'm her student. She's willing to take you on as a client."

Wakefield would like to say no thanks, but the Reverend's eyes are looking through him, orbs of cloudy onyx, and Wakefield realizes she's blind.

An hour later Zelda is driving the three of them to the Reverend's place, a narrow shotgun house shaded by thick hedges of ligustrum. The houses on the block lean against one another as if for support, their meager backyards separated by improvised sheds and rusting appliances.

The front room is lit by two sputtering black candles. Wakefield makes out various items displayed on what look like discarded magazine racks: herbs, oils, incense, candles, salts, and jewelry. There are some large African statues in the corners and some smaller ones on a black desk. Behind the desk is an old-fashioned photo booth with a ratty velvet curtain.

"I'm only here to observe," says Zelda. "I'll be very, very quiet."

That would be a first, thinks Wakefield, who has no idea why he's here, but then, that's his m.o., isn't it?

Reverend Telluride takes off her wings. "Do you mind?" she asks, deftly stepping out of her feathers. She hangs them inside an armoire and Wakefield glimpses a row of wings in a rainbow of colors. Then she sits down behind the desk and takes a deck of well-worn cards from a drawer.

"It's a Braille tarot, if you're wondering. Now tell me what it is you want to know."

Zelda busies herself lighting a stick of sage incense.

"I'll be frank with you," Wakefield begins. "There is a man next door who is hammering on my wall. I want him stopped."

"I don't do black magic," the Reverend frowns, and Wakefield sees by the soft furrow between her eyes that she's younger than he thought. "But tell me what it's all about anyway," she says, the furrow disappearing. "Why is he hammering?"

Why indeed?

"He's hammering because he's jealous," interjects Zelda. "Oops, I said I'd be quiet."

"Over a woman? I might be able to do something about that. Did you steal his girlfriend? I have prayers and potions for any love situation."

"There's no woman," Wakefield says firmly. "The man has embarked on an endless restoration project. Actually there is a woman there sometimes, maybe she's his wife, but she never seems to stay long. Probably can't stand the hammering."

"Some women like hammering. Some women like to get hammered." Both angels laugh. "So why is he jealous?"

"I didn't say he was jealous, but I don't know, maybe he is. He's making it impossible for me to work. Maybe he hates me because I'm sort of famous. But to tell you the truth," Wakefield says, suddenly weary, "I think he's the signal that I should try to find my 'true life,' whatever that is." He's decided it would be too complicated to explain the whole thing with the Devil.

"Well then, that's another matter. Why don't you help him, so he can finish faster?"

"I don't think so." Wakefield would rather kill himself than help his enemy.

"There is no woman?" she asks again, and Zelda laughs.

"Why does there always have to be a woman?"

"Okay. How long have you lived with the hammering?"

Wakefield doesn't like this game. "Since birth," he answers sarcastically, "but with this particular hammering, about two months."

The Reverend puts the tarot deck back in the drawer. "I'm going to read your feet," she says. "Zelda will learn something new."

"All right!" the ever enthusiastic body practitioner exclaims.

Wakefield is confused. "Read what?"

"Your feet."

Wakefield thinks about his feet. They are sturdy. They have walked the earth. Why not? "What do you call this? Foot reading?"

"Piedaterrology." The finest hint of a smile, like a floating feather, passes over her face. "Take off your shoes and lie on the sofa."

Wakefield obeys. He can feel Zelda watching as he takes off his socks and shoes. At least they're clean. The Reverend pulls up an ottoman and takes his naked right foot between her hands; he's startled by her light, warm touch. The foot is calloused; it's climbed in the mountains, pounded city pavements, survived thorns, ant bites, and tropical crud, and now it's held in an angel's soft black hands like a sensitive instrument.

"You're a traveler," the Reverend says, tracing a line from the ball of his foot to the heel. "There's a long line, strong, it keeps straightening itself out."

It tickles. Wakefield tries to keep from laughing, but when he looks at Zelda's studious face he giggles.

"That's the past." The Reverend smiles. "Now let's see about the future." She takes hold of his other foot and traces other lines with a warm finger. "You are going to stay home awhile," she says, pressing down hard with her thumb on a spot apparently connected to his entire body. Wakefield shudders.

"She's doing some reflexology in addition to reading," says Zelda. "It will probably cost you extra."

Reverend Telluride chuckles. Wakefield doesn't care; it feels good. Maybe he has been barking up the wrong tree, so to speak. Maybe his body is the only home he's ever had, and he should stop thrashing around like a fish out of water.

"This point connects to the spinal cord." Her fingers dig into the arch, putting pressure on the maze of lines there. "The arch, it's your destiny," she tells Wakefield.

Wow, the arch, of course. His foot *is* architecture! His brain tries to keep up. "I'm an architect, sort of, an arch fancier, I guess," he stammers, his whole body relaxing.

"Well, that's what architecture is," she says. "The arch of the foot, the work of the hand. The foot and the tool, the arch and the grasp. The whole human story. Your story. There." She brings his feet together and cradles them, gripping his toes hard. Eyes closed, he considers getting up but feels that he can't.

"You've got me by the balls . . . of my feet."

"Redress. Think of Chinese women. Their feet bound, they had to think on their backs. They wrote poetry." Holding his feet, Reverend Telluride recites: "'My lover will not walk to me tonight, I cannot walk to him. Wind, carry our love.' Tien Li, third century."

"That was our story," says Zelda. "The weather, every time."

Wakefield would like to get back to earth. "The hammering guy, what do my feet say about him?"

"He's really you," the angel says softly, concentrating. "You walk his walk, but you have both lost your way."

She speaks like a fortune cookie. And she's wrong, he thinks. Not only is the madman not him, he's going to squash him under his foot like a bug. *Crunch.*

"*How* is he me?" Wakefield is losing patience with this poetry.

"Restoration, renovation, it's *your* need. You need to be restored, rededicated, start fresh. He doing it to a house, you need to do it for yourself."

Wakefield recognizes this as gobbledygook, but it's true-sounding gobbledygook. Of course he needs to work on himself, but first he has to get rid of the madman. One project at a time. Besides, it doesn't do to mix reality with metaphors. The madman is real; spiritual "restoration" is just a metaphor, and a silly one at that. People are not "restored," they become ruins and then they die. Cryogeny and transplants are not in his future.

"What did you call this, piedorology?"

"No, piedaterrology, as in pied-à-terre, a home base, a place to be for a while. I read where you've been, where you'll be." He feels a slow, tentacular languor, like a vine climbing lazily from his foot, up his ankle, into his hips. He pulls his feet away from her hands and fumbles for his socks and shoes. "I've heard enough, thank you."

"Okay," the Reverend says, "I have to go to work anyway."

"To work?" Suddenly Wakefield is sorry he ended the reading so soon; he misses her touch, he wants her to tell him the names of places he's been, places he'll go, hidden places he'll discover. He wants this angel, this voodoo queen, this pieda *terror*ologist to tell him what to do next. He looks to Zelda for reassurance, but her eyes are closed, her knees to her chin, her arms around them, her wings folded.

Reverend Telluride is already changing from sandals to athletic shoes. "I've got appointments to keep. I just squeezed you in for my girl here."

Wakefield thanks her, pays her the twenty dollars she asks for, no extra charge for the reflexology.

Back in the car, Zelda gives him some background on Reverend Telluride: she was adopted by a Jewish couple in New Jersey, but when she was eighteen she traveled to Haiti, where she was initiated in voodoo by a babalao called Audevie and learned divination by means of cards, shells, coins, coffee grounds, tea leaves, hands, feet, and foreheads. Then she lived for a year in Telluride, Colorado, where she found her name. Now, in addition to moonlighting as an angel, she ministers to a voodoo congregation plagued by angry ghosts.

"What's with the ghosts?"

"Well, there seem to be more than ever," Zelda explains, turning onto his street. "The Reverend just exorcised three ghosts from a house where three wives of one man had committed suicide. There are so many ghosts in this town, even the bars are haunted."

"Whoa. She's some powerful chick. The stuff she did to my feet . . ."

"Your feet are your primal hands, that's why it's important to read them."

"Come on, Zelda. Primal hands?"

"Feet are to your hands what the body is to the mind. They are not the tool users, they carry the whole toolbox around. If you want to know where you're going . . ."

She stops in front of his building. As usual, a ghost tour is clustered next to the hotel across the street. Zelda waves to the vampire guide.

"You know him?"

"I own him, so to speak. Crossroads Travel is doing city tours now. Do my multiple personalities bother you, Wakefield?"

"It is a little hard to keep up. Where's your girlfriend, by the way?"

"Oh, she met this Peruvian guy and went straight. I'm practicing abstinence now. It feels good. You should try it, Wake."

"Do you want to come up?" Wakefield asks, ignoring her suggestion. He glances at his watch. It's six o'clock. "One hour of terror to go, you can hear it for yourself."

"Some other time, honey. I have to get out of my wings and check in with the office. Don't forget what Telluride said, it's all about self-restoration. And don't worry, I don't kill my old selves, I'm everybody I ever was, but I'm only one person at a time. When I'm that person, the others have to keep quiet and watch me work until their turn comes. They wait in the wings as ghosts, afterimages, spectators. Then after a while, they get a chance to act and then the one I just was becomes a specter. Everybody I am was a ghost once and will be a ghost again. The angel will be a piedaterrologist and then a travel agent and then a—"

"Zelda, I have no freakin' idea what you're talking about!"

She kisses his cheek. "Never mind. The working self. It's not easy for actors to wait patiently for their moment, it takes discipline, staying in character, getting along . . . that kind of stuff. It takes readings, rehearsals, steady nerves, soothing words, massage, confessions, confidence . . . I call all that the restoration of the working self. It's a never ending job."

Zelda's litany is actually scaring him. Do lots of people believe in this business of multiple personalities? Is it a cult? In the sixties he knew spiritual seekers who made long and convoluted journeys to "find" themselves, but most of them gave up when they discovered that the cosmos didn't give a crap about them personally. Wakefield assumed that the wave of seekers had left behind only a flotsam of tarot readers, holistic body workers, and people like Zelda. But Reverend Telluride . . . she's something else, a blind woman with a closet full of wings, the queen of feet.

ONE NIGHT, IN addition to the dust and bits of mortar that are chronically knocked from his bricks by the madman, Wakefield notices a viscous substance oozing through the wall by his bed. He decides to sleep on the couch, afraid that the wall will collapse and kill him.

Influenced by his contact with the Jungians, he's been reading a book on Greek myths, but he never gets through more than a few pages before he dozes off. This night when he opens the book he finds the story of the Labyrinth at Minos, and it electrifies him.

The Labyrinth was built as a prison for the Minotaur, a sad, hoofed creature whose only sin was that he was freaky. Wakefield realizes in an instant that the story concerns him. The Labyrinth was infinite, built by the father of architecture himself, Daedalus, on orders from the king. For Daedalus the meaning of the prison was in its construction; he didn't care about the sad Minotaur trapped there in the dark with nothing but his own thoughts of revenge, forced to survive on the flesh of the assassins the king would regularly send to kill him. The maniac next door is building a Labyrinth, Wakefield realizes, and the creature trapped at its center is me.

All night he lays awake thinking about the sad Cretan beast. Maybe all architecture denies nature, and so requires blood sacrifice. He remembers the wrenching story Mrs. Petrovich told, of the mason who built his daughter into the wall so that the mosque might stand. Perhaps any shelter that is not a cave transgresses the natural order and offends the gods, who must then be placated. Wakefield imagines an unending labor of construction; the night becomes filled with the hammering of architecture and the howls of its sacrificial victims.

Clearly the insane man next door is the slave of Neurotic Architecture, he concludes, and I am the sacrifice. He has an archetypal hereditary disease that afflicts the descendants of Daedalus. It takes all kinds of forms. Like the heiress to the Winchester rifle fortune, who so feared the spirits of Indians killed by her dead husband's guns that she consulted a psychic, who instructed her to build an endless house full of hidden rooms and corridors. She hid there from the angry ghosts, her carpenters working twenty-four hours a day until her death.

Somehow he must have managed to fall asleep, because when Wakefield opens his eyes it is morning. He hears the hammering, then a woman's voice. She's pleading, "Please . . . no . . . don't . . ." Wakefield stumbles to the bathroom window. There's the maniac standing on the scaffolding, holding a hammer. He is alone. Wakefield no longer hears the woman's voice, but he's convinced he wasn't dreaming. The madman has made a blood sacrifice, he's sure! It's absurd, but he calls the police anyway and a couple of officers come and investigate. The restorationist's wife is just fine, they report, and they obviously think Wakefield is nuts.

WAKEFIELD HAS NO choice but to move to the hotel across the street, taking with him only what he would carry if he were traveling out of town for a lecture gig.

The woman at the reception desk knows his face, and greets him quizzically. "Don't you live across the street?" Wakefield just hands her his credit card and she assumes her usual mask of discretion. She's been in the hotel business a long time. He could tell her that his apartment, a place of refuge and solitude, has been destroyed by a yuppie with a bank loan and she wouldn't bat an eye. But Wakefield isn't interested in fraternizing. He has a plan.

He takes a suite twice as big as his apartment and well placed for his purposes. Behind louvered shutters, the window overlooks the front of both buildings, his and the madman's. The suite has its own patio and a tiny oval swimming pool. The furnishings are comfortable, even luxurious, especially the pharaonic-size bed. The suite is impersonal in a naughty way: the air shimmers with the afterglow of quick trysts and improvised parties; salesmen, conventioneers, and honeymooners have done unmentionable things there, leaving behind a psychic substance both human and forgivable. No amount of cleaning can remove it, it has accrued over time, it adheres to all new guests, filling them with giddy but functional stupidity. Wakefield breathes it in; it comforts him. Maybe I am still human, he sighs.

When darkness falls, Wakefield sits at his window watching the entrances of the buildings across the street. People come and go from his building, carrying in groceries, going out for the evening. No one goes into or out of the madman's house. Wakefield's sleep is wonderfully untroubled for the first time since he returned.

In the morning he takes a swim in the oval pool, showers, then peeks between the louvers. The madman's truck is parked outside; he must be in there hammering. Wakefield has breakfast in his suite: coldish scrambled eggs and bacon with burned toast, four cups of coffee. Then he dons a baseball cap and sunglasses, stuffs a hotel towel into a gym bag, and heads for the City Club, the health club where, he's discovered, the restorationist works out. He walks through the square; it's empty, too early for the fortune-tellers and the living statues. Marilyn doesn't look too bad, holding on to her skirt, though he still misses the iron blimp, his personal monument to the absurd.

THE CITY CLUB has a long and sometimes scandalous history. It has stood for a century in the middle of what was once a notorious red-light district, and husbands of a certain era were said to be "at the Club" if anyone asked. When an overzealous mayor shut down the district after World War One, the club remained, and some of the district's sexual services moved discreetly inside in the form of an ever changing crew of masseurs and masseuses skilled at soothing both flesh and spirit.

Wakefield feigns interest in becoming a member and is admitted on a three-month guest pass. Once inside, he puts himself into the hands of an old masseur, under whose ministrations he learns, for a tip, that the Historical Preservation Commissioner has been known to issue permits in exchange for favors, while cruelly persecuting anyone who runs afoul of the strict preservation regulations in the old quarter.

After the massage, Wakefield helps himself to a bottle of fancy water in the dark-paneled bar and reading room. The bookcases hold bound volumes of the club's weekly magazine, written by members for members. In an issue from 1891, a judge writes candidly that he will be happy to help club members who might find themselves in his court accused of anything short of murder, for which charge he advises "a prolonged sojourn in the Orient." However, "alienation of the affections of a mistress" was an unthinkable offense and one to be resolved with pistols. Dueling is mentioned in the journal often, sometimes offhand, sometimes cryptically. "Dr. LB will be greatly missed. We have commissioned a medal made from the bullets that killed him and will bestow it on Mr. KD, the most likely among us to end the same way." Racist jokes and choice crudities about the female sex abound in short poems and cartoons. The content of the current newsletter is slightly more self-conscious, but the candor of the members is still evident. In the first issue of the current year Wakefield finds a satirical comment by the Historical Preservation Commissioner about the purchase of the historic townhouse next door to Wakefield. "Our good friend, P., has acquired a former bordello in the illustrious old quarter. He has sworn to me that he will restore it to perfection, sparing no expense. I hope that he means this in both form and content. Sex is such a trifle these days, one misses the 'sporting life' enjoyed by our forebears. I have wagered him an original Blue Book if he succeeds."

The Blue Book was published monthly in the heyday of the red-light district, listing all the fancy brothels, including portraits of the prettiest girls, and their prices. An original Blue Book is a sizable wager, worth quite a lot on the rare book market, and gambling is one thing that the members of the club have taken seriously since its founding. The members have regular card games, too, and large sums are won and lost.

Wakefield lingers in the deep chair, soaking in the masculine atmosphere of the room. Rows of trophies line the shelves, and the faded photographs of men in trunks and boxing gloves, men lifting weights, holding tennis rackets, bending over the green felt of a billiard table, or hefting a glass, generate an aura that envelops Wakefield, as does the lingering aroma of Cuban cigars and Irish whiskey. It is the lair of his enemy, Wakefield thinks. I'm here to hunt him down, maybe catch him in some illegality that will put an end to the restoration. He decides to continue his investigation in the steam room.

With a towel draped over his head and one wrapped around his bottom, he lounges in the fog with a liquor distributor and a city court judge. They are discussing a liquor license for a new bar, talking right over his head as if he isn't there, and maybe he isn't. In the dim, steamy room he is truly invisible, his lifelong urge to disappear gratified. Wakefield returns to the club every day on his free introductory pass, picking up interesting information, becoming more and more inconspicuous now that he's a regular.

One day he overhears a bit of intriguing news. In a few weeks the city will conduct its annual termite fumigation, a foggy and poisonous affair. For three nights in the tropical spring the termites swarm; hordes of insects funnel out of the buildings and swirl around the streetlamps. Walking through the bugs is an ordeal, and most citizens stay indoors while city trucks pass through the streets releasing dense clouds of pesticide. The unfortunates caught on the streets get the dying insects under their eyeglasses, in their ears, and on their skin, transparent wings glued by sweat to their every pore.

The termites have been bad news for the city for decades, a century, but now, Wakefield hears a termite specialist explain to his companion in the steam room, Formosan termites, a new species, have arrived. The foreign bugs have a voracious appetite, fifty times more destructive than the native variety. They can consume an entire wooden building in less than a month, and killing them is almost impossible: houses have to be enclosed inside a plastic tent for ten days until poison gas penetrates every crevice. The specialist is not optimistic. The insects collected so far are being studied at the city's Termite Bureau. The peculiar distinction of this termite is that it is not detectable on the surface of the wood; it eats it from within until the beam or plank becomes sheer gossamer, or as the specialist puts it, "lace." When someone steps on, let's say, a stair tread that looks for all practical purposes sturdy, his foot goes right through the board. "Just five of those bastards could gut a floor joist in twenty minutes," the entomologist confides in his friend. Wakefield files this information away in his Catalogue of Horrors, which is housed in his memory opposite his Libidinal Store and has no connection to it, at least none he's aware of.

Weeks pass before Wakefield gets the information he's really after. The Commissioner of Historical Preservation and the mad restorationist stroll into the steam room one morning, wrapped in identical black towels. The commissioner is portly and jowly, the restorationist muscular and hard. They sit on the bench opposite Wakefield, involved in a conversation that must have begun on the treadmill.

"Dogs," says the commissioner. "You train 'em to sniff for genuine period. If something's fake, the dog sits down just like a drug dog. Add dogs to plainclothes looking for illegal additions and we got them."

The maniac approves: "Dogs! Damn! Walking up to doorknobs. Sniff, sniff. It's fake! Not 1823 by a long shot. They could smell acrylic paint, fiberboard, all kinds of synthetics . . ."

Amused, the two friends try to outdo each other thinking up means to detect inauthentic restoration: an elaborate system of mirrors that can catch people cheating on paving stones in courtyards; video surveillance to bust them replacing genuine Victorian fountain angels with cement replicas; piercing alarms that go off when someone repairs an old wall with new bricks.

At the mention of bricks, Wakefield listens even more closely.

"Bricks are a big problem, Chief," the restorationist confides. "Antebellum bricks are selling for five dollars each. I'm being bled dry by my supplier."

"I might be able to help you with that," the commissioner says, lowering his voice.

Wakefield hopes he really is invisible, and pulls his towel over his face.

The black market source for old bricks—Wakefield strains to hear now, they are whispering—is somebody called the Grave, or Gravier, who gets them from historic cemeteries, for which the city is famous. Wakefield gathers that this Gravier dismantles old tombs under cover of darkness, replacing the old bricks with new, and he sells the stolen bricks at a fraction of the legitimate market price.

"The guy is great with faux finishes, covers over the new stuff with cracked, stained plaster," snickers the commissioner. "The parvenus never notice the difference."

Wakefield can hardly breathe. The two conspirators go on discussing the nasty business of grave robbing. "Can't let them sniffer dogs anywhere near the cemeteries," laughs the madman. "Not 1823 by a long shot."

Wakefield is a mass of sweat-stung wrinkles and he feels as if he is about to faint. When the steam-room door opens and a fat man with loud flipflops comes in, Wakefield slips out, unobserved.

A few days later he's watching from behind the louvers of his hotel room as a truckful of old bricks is unloaded across the street. He fancies he can even smell the dankness of the graves they came from. He can't quite believe the brazenness of the scheme, even though he heard it from the mouths of the conspirators, men charged with a public trust, looting the city's true historical past for the purpose of "restoration."

More and more, Wakefield feels enveloped in invisibility: people in the street don't seem to notice him. Acquintances pass him by without a glance; even Ivan acts as if he isn't there, and he's blasé when Wakefield tells him about the cemetery thefts.

"Big fucking deal, that's how business is done everywhere, my friend. You want that the dead should have the best houses? Look, this whole detective thing is stupid. You should just take a vacation," he says, but Wakefield continues his surveillance.

One afternoon the courtyard gate is left open and Wakefield trains a pair of opera glasses on the construction site. The project looks in a sorry state, more unfinished than ever; there is scaffolding in the middle of the courtyard, on top of which is a wooden chair where the madman sits surveying the chaos. He's a long way from getting that Blue Book, Wakefield concludes.

The hotel where Wakefield has taken refuge was built on the site of a Civil War hospital, and every evening he listens to the ghost stories of the tour guides as they pass under his windows. Then one night he actually sees a spectral soldier with blood-soaked bandages and a comely nurse hovering in midair over his bed. "Why are you here?" he asks telepathically, and they dissolve into a plume of white smoke. When he falls asleep he dreams that flames are licking the walls and soon he is lying in a sea of fire, but he's not afraid. The fire is on its way somewhere else, only coincidentally going through him. He wakes up feeling cleansed somehow, and that's when the solution to his problem comes to him.

The night guard at the hotel is a bored ex-con, a guy trying to keep his probation but on the lookout for any scam. Wakefield has seen him hustling hookers to guests, paying bookies, selling dope. The guard smiles and smooths down his khaki pants when Wakefield approaches. Wakefield gets right to the point.

"How would you like to make, let's say, a couple of thousand dollars?"

"You kiddin', man? I'd hang myself for that much fucking money."

"Then you couldn't enjoy it."

"You got a point. What would I have to do, brother?"

"Steal some bugs."

The guy laughs. Then he listens.

And where, one might ask, has our Devil been all this time? It's not an easy story to tell, not even for the Devil, who is a master at telling his own story. He is, in fact, doing just that, but not to us: he's telling it to a psychiatrist, of sorts. Not just any psychiatrist, of course, but a supernatural mental health professional charged with the rectification of wayward demons. In short, after the Devil made his revolutionary speech at the demonic conference and then stormed back to his cave, the Dark Powers-That-Be had a closed-door meeting. The Devil, the Dark Powers concluded, is suffering from depression. The inevitable transitions ahead have upset him because he is overly attached to the beings it is his job to torment. Instead of just doing his job and collecting what is objectively his due, he's allowed his clients to identify with him and they have become prideful, believing in their own demonic divinity. Now he's allowed one of his clients to flaunt the terms of the Deal! Hubris in humans, as everyone knows, screws up the universe, which is supposed to be coldly efficient in every circumstance. The Ancient One has gummed up the works and he has compounded the situation by threatening to awaken the sleeping God, a prospect so terrible to every right-thinking citizen of Hell that it can hardly be imagined. To wit, this Devil is out of control. An intervention, followed by therapy, is called for and approved.

Our Devil looks inside each of his colleagues and sees nothing but his own reflection. Perhaps he has existed entirely too long, and exhausted himself in the effort, admittedly futile, of prolonging the Romantic era into the postmechanical age. His malignant minders authorize a raid on his quarters, sealing him in his cave with the aforementioned "psychiatrist." The Devil is reminded of times when he was in similar predicaments: chained to the bottom of a well, imprisoned inside a labyrinth, tied to a rock with vultures pecking his liver, paralyzed by John of Patmos, hurled into an abyss by Milton. But during all those ordeals he had been alone. He's never before had someone to talk to while he contemplates his singularity, certainly not some kind of demon head doctor. But that's progress, he sighs, and begins to talk.

He does admit that awakening the sleeping God could have unforeseen consequences; God is asleep and dreaming the universe and

His anger at being awakened will be incalculable. If His dream is lost, so are all things. He asserts that his own attachment to humans, including Wakefield, is a whim, with no great echoes. If humans can choose their mates and companions, why can't he, a loner and a bachelor, whose infinite solitude could use a bit of solace? In addition, the Devil sees no reason whatsoever why waste, corruption, and confusion should be eliminated for the sake of efficiency! Humanity has for all its existence done what the universe has asked of it: it has multiplied, it has recorded, it has abstracted, it has slaved. They've earned their R and R, by Jove. Now let them play.

The Devil argues and berates the representative of the Dark Powers-That-Be. He would rather be actively participating in the long stretches of Wakefield's story he's been left out of, but he's currently a prisoner of his own kind. Of all things!

It's the usual evening hour for Wakefield to go to the bar, but he walks past it and no one hails him from the window. He can hear foghorns on the river; the quarter is blanketed in haze. There is a little café in an alley behind the cathedral, a mysterious place with a few tables outside and a dark, inviting interior. Two women are sitting at the bar chatting in French with the bartender. He's explaining that they should stay indoors tonight because this is the night of the swarming termites and the poisonous gas. Indeed, the moon is already obscured by clouds of flying insects.

"We must then stay in here all night!" one of the women says, in English.

"Another Corbu?" The bartender pours brandy, Coca-Cola, and milk over ice in a slender, tall glass.

The woman's voice sounds familiar to Wakefield. He sits down at the bar and asks for "whatever it is that the ladies are drinking."

"We make it up," the woman says, her accented English a lot like Marianna's once was.

"It is because we are architects we make up drinks named for other architects. The Corbu is after le Corbusier," her companion adds.

Wakefield still suffers occasionally from an auditory hallucination that began with Marianna. After living with her for a year or so, he was on a city bus with a group of Hispanic high-school girls. They all sounded to him like Marianna speaking English. Only, the girls were speaking Spanish. Even after he realized the words were Spanish, the illusion persisted; he even imagined he could understand what they were saying, though his knowledge of Spanish was zilch. He got pretty rattled and got off at a coffeehouse to calm down, but the woman at the counter also spoke with Marianna's voice, though her accent was German. All accented speech thenceforth was uttered by his ex-wife, and there was no dispelling the disturbance with the aid of reason. The hallucination dissipated on its own after a while. Wakefield suspects that there was something primal about the timbre or pitch of Marianna's voice, like an urvoice that unsettled the language root in his brain.

Wakefield drinks his Corbu and orders another, and more for the French women, who introduce themselves as Françoise and Cybelle.

"You know," the bartender says, pouring more brandy than cola into the glasses, "I'm an architecture student, and I didn't even know there was an architects' convention in town."

"Figure the odds," Wakefield mutters.

"This city reminds me of France," Cybelle tells him. Wakefield has heard that before; it's no hallucination. "Françoise and I get our best ideas in cafés talking with our friends. You don't have that in most of America."

The bartender raises a hand. "Listen. The trucks are coming." He comes out from behind the bar and closes all the doors and windows. Then he turns off the lights and sets three candles on the bar: "So we can watch the show." The cloud of insects and poison swirling in the air outside *is* eerie, but they feel safe enough inside.

"Since this is a café and you are architects," Wakefield suggests, "perhaps you would design an ideal home for me, to pass the time."

The women take up the challenge with typical Parisian aplomb.

"You must tell us what is your dream house," Françoise urges him.

"Yes, leave nothing out!" naughtily, in Marianna's voice from Cybelle's lips.

Wakefield looks thoughtful. "I want a house that's mobile but stationary, situated in a safe place without borders, where the people are peace-loving." Redbone glares at him from a dark corner.

"I want one of those, too," says the bartender.

"Hmm. You would like to live in a paradox," Cybelle observes. "Are you going to live by yourself in this house, or do you picture in it a beautiful woman?"

"Women understand well paradox," Françoise adds, a little smugly.

The two women begin to draw on napkins, questioning Wakefield on his preferences as they draw.

"Two rooms only, library and bedroom, and kitchen and bathroom, of course," Wakefield answers when the problem of partition comes up. Soon, a blueprint of home emerges, looking a bit like a Gypsy wagon. Cybelle adds some solar panels, Françoise designs a bed and adjustable bookshelves.

"It's wonderful," Wakefield says, "but if there is a woman . . ."

"What if there are *two* women?" Cybelle suggests.

"What about me?" protests the bartender.

"Oh," Françoise slaps her forehead, "I forgot the café!" She adds a collapsible awning on one side of the wagon, and draws in a little round table and folding chairs. "Now it's perfect, very French, no?"

Wakefield couldn't be more pleased. Emboldened, he invites everyone for a swim at his hotel. Cybelle and Françoise debate for a moment. "What about the bugs, the poison? Is it safe?"

The bartender is already putting a bottle of brandy and the other ingredients for Corbu in a plastic bag. "It should be by now. I see people walking around again."

The four of them leave the café linking arms, strutting through still-floating wisps of poison fog. The sidewalks are carpeted with the silvery corpses of millions of termites, and the little group begins to dance along, inventing steps as they go through the square, past the cathedral, and down the silent streets. As they go, Wakefield tells them the story of the insane man with the hammer, and how he was forced to leave his apartment.

"Tomorrow," he tells them, "I will have my beautiful revenge." They ask for details, but Wakefield is mum. "You'll see," he promises. "It will be very amusing."

The foursome are frosted with termite wings by the time they arrive at the locked gate of the hotel. The night guard is waiting expectantly with a grin on his face.

"I'll be back in a minute," Wakefield whispers to him.

He leads his guests to the suite, shows them where the ice and towels are, and returns to the gate to talk to his man.

"I got them," the guard says, pulling a stoppered vial from his pocket. Five silvery-winged insects flutter around inside.

"Now comes part two," Wakefield instructs him. He points out the house across the street, and describes what is to be done there.

"Shouldn't I get half the money now?" The thug makes a tough face.

"You'll get it all tomorrow, when the job's done."

The guard shrugs. Tomorrow Wakefield will place a call to Termite Control and tell them exactly where the stolen Formosan bugs can be retrieved. He prays that they've been sterilized and won't be laying any eggs. He doesn't want to destroy the city. A nonnative species, like the mongoose in Martinique or the nutria in Louisiana, is like an arsonist in the forest, or a single lunatic with a homemade bomb; destruction is all too easy. Low tech. No tech.

Françoise, Cybelle, and the bartender are already paddling naked in the pool when he returns to the suite, their snifters of Corbu on the glass table with the towels. Wakefield strips down and joins them. The water is bathtub warm, vibrating with the energy of their bodies.

"Water," says Cybelle, swimming up to him, "is such a perfect medium. It's the origin of our bodies."

After some playful foolishness—the women become water-spouting sprites, the men sea monsters—they pad back into the suite wrapped in hotel towels. The night passes in lovemaking, their bodies fluid, familiar; aural, visual, and tactile senses joined. In the dark, Wakefield is no longer invisible.

Dawn slips tentatively through the fog, and there is a soft knock on the door. The guard is back from his errand.

"It's done."

Wakefield finds his pants and rummages through his pockets, taking out the Greek coin Redbone gave him in the bunker and pressing it into the guard's palm. "Look it up on eBay, it's not a fake."

"You sure about that?" he asks, examining the little disc of gold.

"Believe me. It's authentic."

When it's fully light outside Wakefield gathers his friends at the window overlooking the madman's house.

"In a few minutes, that door will open," he tells them, "and a man who is Daedalus will come out through it." Wakefield readies his opera glasses.

The monster appears before he can finish speaking.

"*C'est lui?*" whispers Cybelle.

"*Le monstre, le minotaure, l'hypocrite lecteur!*" says Françoise.

"Mr. Termite, we're ready for your closeup!" commands Wakefield.

The madman opens the courtyard gate, and they watch him studying the brick wall adjoining Wakefield's bedroom. Wakefield can feel his dissatisfaction with the wall, his neurotic compulsion, and knows that he intends to take it down again. So strong is their psychic connection, Wakefield wonders if the madman can feel him watching. His enemy climbs to the top of the scaffolding and, as usual, sits down on his chair to survey his work.

The chair buckles under him like cardboard. They watch him fall in slow motion and hit the flagstones near a pile of bricks.

"Mon dieu," Françoise cries, "he's dead."

Cybelle is very pale but calm. "What have you done, Wakefield?"

His horrified paramours rush from the window, pulling on their clothes as fast as they can. Wakefield doesn't move, and he does not go with them when they all burst out the door.

Wakefield remains motionless at the window for a long time. Then he gathers his belongings methodically, packs his toothbrush, toothpaste, shaving cream, and razor in his travel case, and returns to his empty apartment.

The room is quiet; there is no more hammering, no sound at all. "I have killed the monster," he says aloud, and he stretches out contentedly on his curtained bed. He hears sirens in the street, then voices in the courtyard next door, and promptly falls asleep.

He wakes in the afternoon to silence. He takes a long shower, then goes to the bar. Ivan Zamyatin is not in his seat at the window. A stranger is sitting in his place, drinking vodka on the rocks. Wakefield sits next to him and the bartendress brings his usual whiskey without a word.

"I enjoyed the way you handled the situation next door, but it wasn't really necessary," the Devil says. "I hope you didn't do it for my sake."

Wakefield turns to the stranger, an old man wearing a ski cap and smelling to high heaven. "Self-defense. I just reacted. And what do you mean 'it wasn't really necessary'? When I heard that hammer, I went for my bugs. It was a shootout."

"The hammer wasn't the starter pistol, you know," the Devil says.

Wakefield is calm. "Really? Then I still have some time before my quest begins?" But he has a sinking feeling, made worse by the Devil's grudging approval. You'd think His Holy Hoof would approve murder as a proper conclusion, or at least a deal sweetener.

"I don't honestly know," the Devil says, only slightly amused. "They keep changing the agenda on me. Your case has been shelved, for the time being. There's a big deal brewing and I've been called up. Don't know when we'll talk again." But he doesn't want to hurt Wakefield's feelings, so he adds, "I did enjoy our travels, I really did."

"What's that 'we,' white man? I didn't see you around."

The Devil chuckles. "You saw me all right, but you were too busy paying attention to 'important' things, haha. Remember the geezer at the desert roadhouse? 'I shot a sonofabitch for playing bad music next door.'"

"That was you?"

"How about that beefy bodyguard stage left in Wintry City?"

"That creep was you, too?"

"Sunglasses, gun, and bulk, my favorite getup. I was also a projectionist and a few other folks you either ignored or forgot. Don't feel bad about it. I'm all about amnesia."

Wakefield is speechless. He had felt so free, so at liberty.

"Ah, well, all good things must come to an end. At least you get to keep mucking around until we activate your file again. *Adios, amigo. Adiablo* is over for now." The stranger extends his hand, and Wakefield holds it for a moment, palming the old man a twenty.

"Thanks, man," the old guy whispers.

Wakefield doesn't even finish his drink. He heads home, to read. What else could a silence-loving man do in a hammer-wielding world?